THE LOST DREAM OF DON QUIXOTE:

A ROMANCE OF CHIVALRY

# THE LOST DREAM

# OF

# DON QUIXOTE

## A ROMANCE OF CHIVALRY

Janet Rigg

**TENTH STREET PRESS**

# THIS EDITION

© Copyright 2000, 2011 Janet Rigg

Published by Tenth Street Press 2014

Edited by Eleanor Taylor

Cover design by Tenth Street Press

ISBN-10: 0-9923861-9-5
ISBN-13: 978-0-9923861-9-1

PRINTED IN THE U.S.A.

TENTH STREET PRESS Ltd.
MELBOURNE LONDON
www.tenthstreetpress.com
Email: contact@tenthstreetpress.com

I would like to dedicate this book to Gabriel Garcia Marquez

.

# CONTENTS

# Chapter One

The historians of the Cuban Revolution tell us that the leader of the Wars of Independence, José Martí, awoke from death on August 13, 1923. His spirit was shrouded in dense white fog and mist, a sleepwalker in a trance, not really present but not entirely absent either, as if still very much between two worlds. Transformed by the crucible of death from a man into a ghost, he floated through the captivating mists of the enormous pine forests of the Sierra Maestra. He passed great prehistoric ceiba trees with orchids weaving in and out of their branches under the canopy. Once the phantom stopped to touch and smell the flores de mariposa under the speckled sunlight.

Awakening from death dumbfounded him. He hadn't anticipated the possibility of such a thing when mortal. He thought by now he would have gone on to a better place. His present circumstance was a great mystery to him during those first few hours when walking the forest floor. A thick green carpet of vegetation surrounded him with big plants of malanga. He saw the faces of his comrades in the Wars of Independence dispossessed of a former lifetime. They were also floating through the fog and mists of these same mountains where they had fought as guerrillas against the Spanish. The phantom had to fight to stay awake. The pull of death being such that he might have succumbed at any moment to sleep and forgetfulness. He kept floating through the fogs and mists until he came to an enormous hillside of gigantic ferns that gave way to a powerful waterfall with a crystal clear pool. He stared at his image in the pool waters and discovered he was dressed in a tight velveteen black suit and matching bow tie. His appearance was exactly the same as when he was mortal. He had thick black hair, a prominent forehead and a perfectly shaped moustache. Up in the sky dozens of colibri and a tocororo were chirping in the distance. The morning was bright and as he came out of the ever-darkening forest of the Sierra Maestra into the clearing, he could see the whole of Oriente Province spread out below him like a bright blanket of green strewn out upon the clear aquamarine Caribbean Sea.

Dazed with a strong desire to fall by the wayside instead of continuing down the mountain, he made a great effort to keep on going. He soon discovered that the more he moved the less stiff he felt. He followed the paths of the mountain people or Guajiros down the mountain's side. As he passed through their villages and saw them again, he felt more and more energetic and alive. Suddenly he was full of life as he felt his old enthusiasm returned full force. He was always vigorous and full of energy. He walked with more briskness and intention in his stride. He felt confident that he had passed from one lifetime to the next. In his descent from the highlands to the lowlands over the course of several weeks the ghost felt more and more life in him. Although he still felt stiff and his bones ached, the more he kept up a brisk walk, the more aware he became of his surroundings.

As he continued to make his way down the Sierra Maestra, he enjoyed tremendously the rich endowments of Mother Nature. Despite the fact that he was invisible, to his surprise he discovered that his five senses were more acute than when he was alive. In fact the sight of the mountains mixed with sun and sea were even more striking and dramatic than when he was mortal. This pleased the ghost no end. The sight and sound of birds and the feel of the soft mists which enveloped him made him recall that he had come this way before. As he continued down the Sierra Maestra, his senses awakened even more. The sight and sound of birds and the feel of the soft mist enveloping him enchanted him. The phantom remembered having coming this way before during the wars on horseback with a small band of guerrillas to rout the Spanish troops. Suddenly he realized that this was the very spot where he was ambushed and killed by a Spanish regiment. The phantom almost succumbed to death right then and there. He had to keep walking as fast as he could in order to stave off yet another bout with death.

When he reached the hills and valleys of Oriente Province in the lowlands, bands of campesinos on their way to cut sugarcane wielded their machetes right through him. The phantom recoiled for a moment then let go. His memories of the lush green tropical landscape, alive with the sounds of tropical birds, were sights and sounds that seemed sweeter to him than ever. His memories were surpassed by the portrait of nature's perfection before him. The warmth of the tropical sun and the sounds of the nearby waves crashing on the beach made him feel that much more human. Blown east by the winds of history, José Martí soon found himself on the outskirts of Santiago de Cuba. Still somewhat unconscious in his present state, he keep on going attracted by some superior force that he was neither capable of understanding nor controlling. He continued his journey toward Santiago, and after a while, he finally reached his destination. He definitely needed a rest. He felt absolutely exhausted from so much walking. He made his way through the streets of Santiago, bumping into crowds of people returning from work at the end of the day. Suddenly he came to a small plaza. In the middle of the plaza was a statue of him along with a Cuban flag. The phantom was astounded to see his image right in the middle of Santiago. It was indeed a strange feeling to look at his portrait when he was now a mere phantom. The Cuban flag waving in the wind showed him that Cuba no longer belonged to the Spanish, but instead was now a republic.

José Martí continued to walk the streets of Santiago until sunset looking for a place to rest. He stopped short in front of a small pension situated on a side street. He opened the door and went inside hoping to find the owner. She appeared, looking like she needed more guests. He tried to start a conversation with the woman but soon realized it was futile. The old woman ignored him when he reached out and touched her hand. It was as if he weren't there at all. Again he tried to establish a dialogue with her asking her about the price of a room. But again she neither listened to nor recognized him. With great reluctance, José Martí accepted the fact that that he was invisible and for all practical purposes non-existent to the living.

He walked through a roomful of diners and headed straight to the kitchen for a glass of water. It seemed that in passing from one lifetime to another he had accumulated a great deal of thirst. He drank down the glass of water then helped himself to another glass and another before he felt his thirst subside. He turned around and headed through the dining room. He was very disappointed he was not to be visible to at least some of the guests in the room. Again the thought of being separate from people forever proved devastating to the phantom. How could he, José Martí, consummate orator and poet ever accept such a fate?

Shocked and overcome with grief, the ghost wished to be alone to gather his thoughts. He climbed a set of stairs to the left of the entrance, which led to a series of bedrooms. He then proceeded to explore each one. They

12

all had boarders in them and there was only one vacant room at the end of the hall. He entered the one empty room looking for a refuge, a quiet place where he might lay down and rest. Overcome by a deep sense of hopelessness and desolation, the phantom remained awake all night grieving the fact that he was no longer mortal. The phantom slept off and on. Sometime in the early morning, despondency and sorrow turned to regret. He continued to contemplate his newfound state, feeling that all this might be only a dream from which he would awaken at any moment. He spent several nights in the pension up in the empty room wishing he were alive. Resigned to becoming a ghost, he got up from bed and left the pension each morning to walk the streets of Santiago. He continued to hope against hope that someone would recognize him. However, his wish was futile.

He was frustrated with his diminished state yet he realized that death, the great seducer, was not yet ready to let go of him. The phantom had to keep on moving about the streets of Santiago just to remain conscious and awake. As he moved about, he saw women with children in their arms begging for food and money. The working poor were coming home clothed very badly, while the rich were dressed with great pomp and circumstance. Nothing had changed in Cuban society since his untimely death. He felt a terrible pain in his heart and for a moment thought that he would succumb to death once more. The sadness at not having achieved social justice in Cuba through the War of Independence overwhelmed him. He knew he would in fact disappear if he didn't move on. He got up the very next morning early and abandoned the pension. He needed to find his compass and get his bearings. Something told him to head for the province of Holguin.

As he reached the outskirts of Santiago once more, he heard the load voice of a newspaper vendor trying to sell papers. "Buy the Diario de la Marina." "Uprising in Cienfuegos by Civil War Veterans over Pensions." The ghost walked toward the vendor and looked over his shoulder to see the date. It was August 22, 1923. He read the headlines in big black letters: Strong Public Protest of Veterans Due To Lack of Pensions.

Again a tremendous sense of sadness and remorse overcame the ghost as he confronted the terrible truth that he could no longer participate in historical events. He would somehow have to adjust to a second lifetime as an exile without the ability to communicate his thoughts to mortals. During his first lifetime, above all else he was an orator and a poet. To remain mute went against everything in his nature. For a while it was touch and go. The authors of this history were not at all sure that José Martí would not succumb to death again if he could not participate in and influence the lives of mortals. He started to move forward without being in control of where he was going. Suddenly his head was swimming with all kinds of images, thoughts and doubts, which continued to torment him as he went along.

He asked himself what was happening to him? What had caused his death? Looking at the poverty stricken peasants working the fields by the side of the road, he concluded that even when the war made Cuba a republic, the island was still a colony of the Yankees. All his dreams for Cuba and social justice were just that, only dreams. He asked himself what had been the destiny of his closest comrades, the other generals in the War like Máximo Gómez, Antonio Maceo, Calixto García and the other comrades belonging to the Mambise army. He could answer none of these questions, which frustrated him enormously. But in the end, after all these questions and ruminations, he simply came to the conclusion that an inscrutable event had taken place for which there was no logical explanation.

He spent the following week walking from pueblito en pueblito, staying in inns along the way. He slept in empty beds without leaving a trace of having slept there. Getting used to his new existence was becoming more difficult as time went on. At one inn he saw a table of veterans complaining about never getting a pension as they sipped their coffee and smoked their cigars. Struggling to find his footing in the afterlife, he kept moving with the faith that he was going somewhere rather than nowhere. He could float in the wind or stand still in the sun and let the warmth penetrate him. In the course of his wanderings, even during those first few weeks of renewed life, he would soon come to know some of the benefits as well as the many limitations in having become a phantom.

As he wandered the Oriente countryside, taking in the breathtaking beauty of the island, his senses were becoming even more acute than when he was making his way down the Sierra Maestra. The green and fertile valleys of Oriente province seemed even more vibrant and alive than when he was mortal. What a strange contradiction he thought. Could this be a dream from which he would awaken at any moment? As the phantom made his way toward Holguin, he looked at the large latifundios on either side of the road. He saw the Haitians working under the burning hot sun. Nothing had changed since his death in terms of social justice. Cuba was still feudal and colonial. This fact was confirmed when he passed through the gigantic latifundio of the United Fruit Company. Large portions of land were still in foreign hands. He and his comrades who led the Wars of Independence had failed in carrying out their mission to end human suffering and poverty in Cuba. The large black smokestacks of the United Fruit Company's sugar mills were testimony to the fact that the island had still not found independence.

As he moved from pension to pension the thought that he had not completed his mission of freeing Cuba depressed the ghost no end. Having to wander the earth with a life left unfinished was a terrible burden for any phantom to have to bear. According to the authors of this history, about that time he started looking for a place to get his footing. He needed a refuge where he could become accustomed to being a phantom, if such a thing were possible. The ghost wandered on down the dusty country roads of Oriente day after day in search of asylum. Up to now he had moved from pension to pension without really feeling as if he had reached the end of his journey. Thinking about the past and curious about the future, the ghost continued making his way towards Holguin. He walked down a hill until he came to another dirt road. He followed it for a while until he came to the top of a knoll where he could make out another beautiful green valley before him. In the middle of the valley he saw a perfect circle of sugarcane. He had never seen such a sight before either in his past life or this lifetime. He walked toward the perfect circle of sugarcane blowing in the winds of history. He saw a fork in the road and followed a sign marked 'Biran' that indicated the entrance to a small town. Walking on a bit further, he came to a large tract of land surrounded by a fence with a sign 'Hacienda of the Spirits.'"He stopped short in front of the sign in disbelief. The ghost immediately felt as if he belonged here and that at last he had come to the end of his journey.

He hurriedly opened the gate and walked down a small road. He saw a large barn, a blacksmith shop along with a general store. There was also a telephone and telegraph office. A band of campesinos headed out the fields passed right through him. He followed them with his view and he could see an entirely valley full of sugar cane plantations. The blanket of green together with gigantic palm trees blowing in the wind surpassed his memories and made him swoon. His curiosity about this hacienda grew when he saw a yellow and blue wooden house with doors and windows painted white. The house represented a strange construction and diverged from the typical haciendas in Oriente Province. It rested above the ground on enormous concrete piles. There was a place for cows and sheep underneath. Placed as it was on these concrete piles, there was a vertical staircase which led up to the back door. The house seemed suspended in midair and was reminiscent of the houses built on the hillsides of Galicia in northern Spain. José Martí had to wonder whether the owner of this large estate were Galician or Spanish. For a moment he thought how ironic it was that he had landed on the hacienda of a Spaniard.

The yellow and blue house on stilts was not the only house on the hacienda, but it was the biggest. The house itself had a large extension of land directly adjacent to it, where the people who lived there had planted an enormous garden. As he approached, the structure seemed to loom out at him from a long way off and it was then he concluded it must be a mirage caused by the heat or some failure in perception due to the fact that he had yet to accept the afterlife as fact not fiction. José Martí hesitated a while. He didn't know if he should go in because he did not want to disturb the people living there. On the other hand, he thought he might as well take advantage of his new condition. If there were people in the house, they could not see him anyway. Therefore, he would not be interrupting their privacy. So he headed up the large wooden staircase painted white and opened the door. He found he was standing in a large kitchen with a wood-burning stove and a large round wooden table with several wicker chairs. He walked through the kitchen to a parlor that also had a set of wicker furniture. There was a large wicker divan and several wicker chairs.

He then continued to explore the rest of the house and found several bedrooms with beds perfectly made up with sheets and blankets. He walked down a long hall with more bedrooms on each side. He looked inside each one but they appeared empty. At this point, he had to wonder where the occupants of the house were at the moment. The house looked lived in and one room had a cradle so he assumed there were children. At the end of the hall, he found a room with a medicine chest and mirror. While he was examining the medications in the chest, he smelled the aroma of rich Cuban coffee which made the phantom swoon. He quickly shut the door to the medicine room and made his way back down the hall to the kitchen. He looked to his right and again saw the parlor. Someone had opened the windows. He looked out and saw a consummate picture of the Haitians working in the rich green fields. Again the smell of coffee got the better of him and he turned to his left and headed into the kitchen. He saw a hot pot of coffee on top of the wood-burning stove and then a mug on the round wooden table. He grabbed the mug and poured a cup of rich dark Cuban coffee. He felt the warm coffee trickle down his throat and the taste pleased him no end.

This mysterious and deserted hacienda, with no signs of life apparent to the naked eye, made him feel the weight on his shoulder of these many weeks subside. His wanderings were over for the moment. As he looked around, he felt that he had finally found a resting place. Hacienda of the Spirits was a place where he might spend some time to catch his breath and find his bearings. José Martí stood there staring at the kitchen, feeling as if he already belonged there. He felt certain now that he was passing through that blankness full of meaning that separates one lifetime from another.

The phantom continued wandering around the house and in and out of rooms. Then he headed back to the kitchen for another cup of coffee. He stayed there for a while, looking around the kitchen, typical of this kind of home in the Cuban countryside. Everything was made of local woods, including the walls, the counters and the drawers. Right behind the windows giving out on the Sierra Crystal, his eyes fell once more on the wood-burning stove. The stove made the ghost think about real Cuban food, always cooked on wood that gave it that special delicious flavor, something that he really loved when he was alive. He walked straight there and luck would have it that there was still a pot with some hot coffee on the stove. Obviously someone was there just a few minutes ago because on the counter next to the stove there were things used to make coffee.

The ghost helped himself to another cup of delicious Cuban coffee. He sat down on one of the wicker chairs at the round wooden table in the middle of the kitchen. Looking out the back door, a beautiful view of that perfect circle of sugarcane appeared once more before him. He continued to enjoy that rich taste of the black coffee and stare outside. The scene made him feel a lot nostalgia and sadness because it reminded him of war and his compatriots. After an hour or so, the phantom walked out the back door to survey the perfect circle of sugarcane blowing in the winds of history. The place was still deserted. Suddenly, he noticed with great surprise and joy two of the greatest veterans in Cuban history seated in chairs on either side of the back door. To his left was Manuel de Cespedes, the man who had started the first War of Independence, and on the right was Ignancio Agramonte, another great hero of the first War of Independence. Each of these ghosts was transparent. They just sat there blowing perfectly round rings of white smoke into the cold crisp morning air. When he tried to speak to them neither moved an inch. Soon it became obvious to José Martí that these two old soldiers were living in another dimension far removed from him. Again, his eyes found their way to that perfect circle of sugarcane.

The phantom thought the owner of this hacienda must have a vivid imagination. He wandered again inside hoping someone would appear. But no one did that first evening. He found a liquor cabinet in the living room and reached for a bottle of delicious Cuban rum. Then he went out on the porch which circles around the entire house to this day and gave thanks to God for having brought him to this place. He sensed that great things awaited him on this hacienda. When the sun went down, he found a room with empty beds and lay down until the next morning.

# Chapter Two

José Martí awoke the next morning feeling refreshed and ready for a new start. He walked over to the stove and reached for the pot of newly brewed coffee keeping warm on the stove. Then he ventured out the back door and out onto the porch where he surveyed the picturesque surroundings including that perfectly sculpted circle of sugarcane. The circle was a source of fascination to him. Again it made him wonder about the owner of this hacienda who was nowhere in sight. Martí went back to the kitchen for a second cup of coffee. Then he grabbed the newspaper, el Diario de la Marina, off the table. He sat there reading a good long time. Afterwards, he proceeded outside and took a turn around the buildings nearby. Eventually the ghost felt tired and returned to the kitchen to take a load off his feet. He went looking for an empty room to take a rest. He found a bedroom with three empty single beds. The phantom sat down on the corner of one of the beds. To relax his neck he moved his head from side to side. Suddenly he felt the bed moving as if someone else occupied it. He turned his head very carefully to the right and was surprised to see one of his former comrades lying there asleep. It was Antonio Maceo, one of the great generals of the War. More amazed than not, he left the bedroom for a short while. He remained in the corridor considering whether or not he should go back. Finally he did return to the bedroom, but the bed with Antonio Maceo was now empty. Martí decided he must have been having visions of his comrades out of sheer loneliness.

He slept for an hour until a frightening noise awakened him. There standing over him was Calixto García, another great general in the Wars of Independence and a trusted comrade. As soon as not the vision had disappeared. Again the phantom concluded that he was hallucinating out of feelings of solitude. He thought he might be dreaming. He rubbed his eyes to make sure he was really awake. Then he heard a noise and looked at another bed only to see his old comrade Máximo Gómez fast asleep snoring. The scene was too much so he left the bedroom and headed straight for the kitchen to grab another cup of coffee. Then he saw a picturesque nature outside spread out before him. The diversity of nature and the perennial greens of the hillside made him suddenly feel extremely lonely. As if by magic a circle of his old comrades had appeared around the kitchen table. He blinked his eyes momentarily and when he looked again, could no longer see these old soldiers. He had probably been imagining it he thought himself, and moments later they had appeared once more. He saw that his comrades had aged and he wondered whether they were a figment of an imagination fed by solitude.

Calixto García had a large chest and he appeared to be a warrior. He had the same black moustache, short curly hair and chocolate brown skin. Antonio Maceo was regarded as one of the bravest of all the soldiers of the Mambise army. Máximo Gómez was sitting right beside him, with his penetrating eyes, as serious as he remembered. He was a great general and leader in the War of Independence and the person who signed with him el Manifesto de Montecristi. This was the document which outlined the political program of the War in 1895. He was the person who together with him and the other comrades who prepared the War of Independence. They had a strong desire to fight for the freedom and independence of Cuba in order to see the noble dream come to fruition.

As José Martí sat there looking at his beloved comrades, he knew the dream of real independence was lost. For an instant he experienced the same feeling that he had felt once before, when all of them were gathered together in a meeting preparing for the war, deciding what would be the strategy to follow. At this meeting, Martí was elected the supreme leader of the revolution when it came to non-military events. All these comrades, with the exception of José Martí, wore their old white uniforms of the Mambise army. They each wore white pants and shirt with a leather belt from which hung their swords. They all wore big black boots.

Outside, seated in the chair next to the screen door in the right side was Carlos Manuel de Céspedes, blowing rings of smoke into the cold crisp morning air. On the left side in balance, Ignacio Agramonte, the main hero of the first war against the Spanish in 1898. For Martí it was a very emotional moment because unlike as with the others, he had not yet met these two men personally. They were both doing the same thing, as if they had all the time in the world to enjoy the taste of rich Cuban tobacco. José Martí pointed out these old heroes to his counterparts and they all shed a tear when they realized that both Céspedes and Agramonte were permanently senile. He was ecstatic once he realized he was no longer alone. Once awake they all recognized each other and embraced each other after these many years of separation through death. All were leaders of the revolutionary guerrilla forces, which had set out to end Spanish rule and to keep the Yankees from invading the island.

In the course of the conversation their memories improved, so that soon they were talking about the last time they had seen each other, along with real battles. Martí noticed sometimes their memories were confused when it came to some events which had transpired. He attributed their memory problems to the struggle of passing from one lifetime to the next. These conversations went on for some time. After a while, the phantoms started to fade away and disappear except for José Martí. Then they would return and continue their conversations about the Wars. José Martí realized that to keep them from succumbing to death, he had to keep them interested. His tactic worked because the more dynamic the conversation became, the more present the old generals were around the round wooden table.

General Máximo Gómez had lived the longest of all the phantoms. So he began to fill in the blanks for the rest of the group, going into great detail about the progress and outcome of the War. Everyone wanted to ask him questions at the same time. So as usual, José Martí took matters into his own hands and suggested that they talk about events in chronological order and that each phantom ask Gómez one question at a time.

Máximo Gómez, filled in the Apostle, as these old veterans liked to call him, on the progress and outcome of the War. All the phantoms, including José Martí, were fearful that this afterlife or second lifetime would come to a sudden end. This made them talk all the faster, as they thought they might not have another opportunity beyond the present moment. José Martí tried to calm them down and assure them that if they made every effort to remain conscious and awake, chances were that they would be around the hacienda awhile.

Everyone except the Apostle asked all kinds of disorganized questions at the same time. Gómez's answers were also disorganized, and again José Martí asked for calm. Then he wanted to know who died after he did. Maceo was the second victim of the Spanish army. It was he who recounted the part of the history from the Apostle's death to his own demise. José Martí had died on May 19, 1895 in the Battle of Dos Rios. He learned that he had perished at the hands of the Spaniards during his first time in the field of battle. Then Antonio Maceo started to talk. "After your tragic death, many other things happened in the course of the battle for independence." He continued to recount anecdotes about battles, victories and losses. He went as far as his memory would take him. Then Máximo Gómez and Calixto García contributed to the conversation with their own anecdotes. José Martí had not felt as good since awakening from death as he did at that moment. Sharing stories about the war brought him alive and he was feeling like his old self again. The comrades then got involved in a long polemic that was to last the entire afternoon about strategies and tactics which had failed in the war. The talked about certain mistakes that had they been avoided, could have changed Cuban history forever.

Máximo Gómez continued his tale saying that in January of 1898 things seemed to be going better for the rebels. However that same month, the Yankees sent a ship, the USS Maine, to Havana harbor with the objective of protecting North American interests. Two weeks later the ship exploded in the port of Havana. There were many victims and the Yankees accused Spain of carrying out a terrorist act against the ship. This represented the beginning of the so-called Spanish American war. The War continued and their troops won all the battles.

"We were sure that we would win the War, and Cuba would finally be free. Our dream of national independence would come true. Then much to our surprise, the Spanish and the Americans resolved among themselves without any input from us the terms of the end of the war.

They discussed in our absence the future of the island. This caused us tremendous frustration. It also accounted for all the repulsion we felt towards the Yankees. The First of January 1899, Spain passed its power over Cuba to the United States. The Yankees then established a provisional military government on the island, supposedly to protect their interests."José Martí and Antonio Maceo had not heard this part of the history before, and they suffered greatly upon learning the outcome of their efforts. They could not believe the course of events, but neither did they wish to interrupt Gómez who then continued his tale.

"In February 1901, a new Cuban constitution was adopted and some months later, a Cuban constitutional convention accepted the so call Platt Amendment. This was one of the saddest episodes of this era. It has had a devastating effect on our freedom and independence as well as the economy, even when the Republic of Cuba was recognized by the United States in May 1902. The Platt Amendment calls for the United States to intervene militarily in Cuba any time the Yankees deem it necessary. The Amendment also establishes strong limitations on our economic activities. We can reluctantly only trade with the Yankees and the terms of trade are very favorable to them."

Antonio Maceo looked at his comrades with a mournful look on his face. By way of conclusion, he said that not only does the Platt Amendment allow them to intervene militarily; it also allows them to maintain military bases on the island. It prohibited Cuba from trading with other countries. In a word companeros, this Amendment is a way of establishing the politics of imperialism on the island.

"The God Dammed Yankees!" José Martí exclaimed furiously. "That explosion of the Maine was their doing in order to take control of the island!"

All the veterans had a mournful look on their countenance. Collectively, they felt the loss of the dream of independence much more poignantly than any one of them could alone. They had all played great roles in history, but at this moment all the great generals could do was weep quietly at the round wooden table. Their collective despondency was overwhelming and without words. They all looked terribly depressed as if they might disappear momentarily from this belated history.

José Martí and the group eventually overcame their sadness and frustration and directed themselves toward the door. There they found Céspedes and Agramonte in their usual spot blowing tiny white rings of smoke into the crisp morning air. They tried to talk to them but to no avail. The two heroes of the first War of Independence had no idea of what was going on around them since they were totally senile. The other veterans went back inside the house while José Martí stayed with the two old senile veterans for a while hoping they might somehow magically sense his presence. When he turned and went back into the house, none of his comrades were there. This seemed very strange, so he began to look for them throughout the house. He was looking in all corners and in all the rooms but he did not manage to see any of them.

It was as if the wind had swallowed them up. Then suddenly he saw one of his comrades pass him by in the hall, but the image passed by so fast he couldn't discern which veteran actually was there. Then he saw his comrades floating through the house like leaves being blown by the winds of history. They disappeared each time he ran after them. He saw them walk through walls. Such a thing never occurred to the Apostle, but he tried it, and it worked. So for some hours, the reader of this veracious history would see Gómez, Maceo, García and the Apostle walking through walls or floating up to the ceiling. They seemed to have lost all consciousness in the wake of the long conversation about the War. José Martí firmly planted his feet in the kitchen and wondered if the tragic outcome of their collective dreams could make them succumb to death once more. His heart ached at the thought of being left alone again. He sat at the round kitchen table contemplating an afterlife alone when suddenly nightfall came. The sun disappeared behind the mountains of the Sierra Crystal creating a combination of colors from the softest yellow to the strongest orange. Together with the green of the palm trees and other trees of the mountainside along with the kikirikear of the cocks outside, he thought he had never seen such a beautiful picture in either his former life or his life as a phantom. The inexorable beauty of nature in Oriente had a calming effect on his spirit. He was now more hopeful that his comrades would return around the round wooden table in the kitchen. As surely as not, one by one Antonio Maceo, Calixto García, and Máximo Gómez returned to the table looking much more content than when they disappeared from sight.

Rapidly the Apostle spoke the first words and asked the rest of his comrades "Have you stopped to think about the reason we are here united together once more in a second lifetime? None of us has had a retirement before so why not take advantage of this second lifetime as phantoms?" Calixto García agreed with Máximo Gómez. They felt their common dream of independence was lost forever. Antonio Maceo and José Martí on the other hand disagreed. They hated the idea of giving up. They also resisted the idea that as phantoms they could no longer influence historical events. There simply had to be a way and thus they were committed to finding a solution for the relationship between their mortality and their ghostly state.

They could not go along with the resignation of their comrades. He told them that there had to be a purpose to this second lifetime. If they were there all together, there had to be a reason which he, José Martí, thought would reveal itself in due course. What they needed was both faith and patience. If they were all lucky enough to awaken from death in the first place and catch up on current events, they had to make an effort to not succumb to sleep. He told them that for now they would have to lead a moment by moment existence. It was not enough to assume that this was the end of their journey or they were retiring to a veteran's home. Rather they should assume that they were embarking on a new beginning. This was to be a different kind of life, with great limitations but also many unknown possibilities, which would become evident in due course.

He explained to them that any transcendent experience worth its salt involved both discipline and faith. They were involved in a life and death struggle for transcendence. They should feel very gratified to have appeared together in order to help each other battle for an afterlife worth living. The phantom went on to stipulate that beginnings were always hard and coming back to life was no exception. He told them they were here for a reason and that the afterlife had to have a higher purpose. Although that purpose for the moment might elude them, it would reveal itself in due course. They had to keep their faith and confidence.

All the while Martí was talking to them, the veterans remained mute. But he went on at great length anyway, trying to make them understand his logic in living each moment to the fullest. The Apostle then suggested that they accept their present state provisionally at least and live with the unknown. Finally the phantom ended his philosophical speculations by assuring them that the afterlife would have its compensations. After he finished all the veterans rose and thanked the Apostle for his speculations. They were all tired so they decided to retire to the bedroom with the three beds. José Martí stayed in the kitchen feeling that he had gotten somewhere with his comrades when it came to justifying the afterlife. He sipped another cup of rich Cuban coffee and thought some more about what he had just told his comrades.

José Martí then went to another bedroom with a child's cradle next to a large double bed. There was a large oval mirror in the corner and the Apostle took a good look before turning in. At dawn, he went to the kitchen where he found all his comrades seated around the large round wooden table drinking their first cup of coffee. But this time, the veterans were not alone. Seated beside them at the table was a man whom they did not recognize, assuming he was the owner of the hacienda. He was a tall man with lots of thick black hair and black eyebrows. He had very white skin and a large nose. The rest of the veterans continued talking among themselves drinking coffee. They did not pay much attention to the presence of this man. But José Martí was more curious than his comrades. He wondered if the man were mortal or just another ghost like themselves. Suddenly José Martí looked at the wood burning stove and saw a small dark haired woman with dark brown eyes. She was wearing an apron. The veterans interrupted their conversation to admire her looks. She was very attractive despite her small size. The small woman with dark brown eyes directed her conversation to the unknown man at the table. She asked him "Do you want some breakfast Angel?" He answered her in the affirmative with a Galician accent. "I have already had a cup of coffee thanks. Now I am trying to catch up on the news so that I can then go out to work on my perfect circle of sugarcane. By the way, I couldn't find my cup this morning. Do you have any idea where it is?"

"No darling, I haven't the slightest idea of where it might be!" the small woman replied. "Here is another. Would you like a second cup?"

"Yes darling thank you. There must be phantoms in the house drinking our coffee.""Oh Angel Castro, don't be ridiculous." She laughed.

"No! I swear to you darling that for the last couple of days my coffee cup has just disappeared." Castro insisted. The veterans were amazed at the owner of this marvelous hacienda and his wife. The bonds of affection between them were obvious. Angel Castro soon finished reading the newspaper and quickly went out the door to undertake his work on his perfect circle of sugarcane. Doña Lina Castro stayed in the kitchen and helped herself to a cup of coffee. She was in the middle of making a guayaba cake. The veterans were speechless and sat there admiring her every move. José Martí got up from his chair and approached this beautiful mortal while she cut the guayabas in strips to make marmalade which would serve as a filling for the cake. The Apostle could not resist and with a great deal of tenderness reached over and touched her face. She, of course, had no idea what was happening around her. She was a woman with a very sweet look, which inspired good feelings among the ghosts.

Her hair was dark and curly. Her lips red by nature and very tender. Her eyes were dark brown, and she had very fine eyebrows unlike her husband. While she was making the cake, she looked out the window to admire her husband who was working on that perfect circle of sugarcane alongside the Haitians. All the veterans were charmed by that sweet woman. They spoke of her beauty as well as how delicate she was, but José Martí was the most taken by her of all his comrades. The veterans followed her around the house while she made the beds, watching her every move. They watched her pick colorful flowers from her garden and place them in a vase on the kitchen table. The flowers smelled fresh and sweet. Then they followed her under the house on piles and watched her milk the cows. She then took the fresh milk back to the kitchen. José Martí thought that she was the sweetest thing he had encountered in passing from one lifetime to another.

That afternoon the veterans found a pack of cards in the parlor and decided to play on the round wooden table in the kitchen. They also found Angel Castro's liquor cabinet. About three o'clock, after several games of cards, they all helped themselves to some rich golden Cuban rum. José Martí was always bored by these games in his first lifetime so he did not participate. Meanwhile the veterans passed the days away playing cards and drinking rum. Both seemed like a waste of time to the Apostle. He had better things to do, so he retired to the parlor with Angel Castro's newspapers to keep abreast of current events. The veterans couldn't be less interested. Each day that passed at Hacienda of the Spirits, the veterans become more and more used to the card games and drink. At the same time they remained enchanted by the small woman with dark eyes as she went about her routine. José Martí was particularly taken with Doña Lina Castro. In fact he felt a profound love for her growing inside him. The way she walked, her smile, the way her hair undulated in the winds outside, her red lips, all conspired to make him feel more alive and alert. He also loved the way she treated her husband.

The Apostle tried to get interested in the card games for a while, but ended up being bored. These were superficial pastimes which he strove to avoid. Rather, he wished to contemplate the larger purposes of the afterlife. He tried to get his comrades interested in philosophical speculations about the meaning of the afterlife. They all but ignored him, preferring instead to place their attention on card games and drink. Their attitude frustrated the Apostle no end and he wished they would show a little more interest in finding meaning and purpose to their second existence.

As the weeks passed, even the veterans started to get bored with cards and drink. They all fell into a profound depression. Soon they were wandering around the house randomly in a somnambulistic state. They had lost all sense of time. José Martí saw them again walking through walls without direction or floating up to the ceiling. Apparently their idyllic view of retirement had left something to be desired. The Apostle called each of them by their individual names. They ignored him and seemed to fade away in the process. Again José Martí found himself alone. A terrible feeling of solitude came over him once more as it had when they previously disappeared from this veracious history. Meanwhile that night, Lina Castro started to light the fire under the large cast iron stove before she put a pot of rice and beans on to boil for hours. She let the rice and beans, or Moors and Christians as they are called in Cuba, boil until there was practically no more water left in the pot. She had to go out and pull the bucket up from the well before Angel Castro came in from the fields for dinner.

Suddenly the veterans appeared around the round wooden table. The Apostle was delighted to see his comrades return to the kitchen. He was afraid that he might have lost their companionship forever. They all followed the aroma of rice and beans and thought they couldn't stand the wait a second longer. Lina Castro set a plush plate of rice and beans down in front of them. Angel Castro finally came in from the fields and picked up the newspaper and started reading. Every day there were stories about the boom and bust economy of Cuba. No one was more familiar with the boom and bust cycles of the Cuban economy than Angel Castro and the other sugar growers in Oriente Province. Some years he sent off his perfect circle of sugarcane to the mills of United Fruit and made a decent amount of money. But most years as of late proved to be difficult, and he was lucky to make just enough money to keep his livestock and put food on the table for Lina and their two children, Angelita and Ramon. That night he continued reading the newspaper before dining with his wife. Lina started spooning rice and beans onto the plates of Angel Castro and his two children.

The smell of rice and beans and the pork, really brought these old veterans to their senses and without saying a word, they all suddenly came alive inside. Calixto García took a big spoonful of Moors along with a few Christians underneath and wolfed them down in a single mouthful. Máximo Gómez found a loin of pork. For his part, Antonio Maceo was content to eat Moors and Christians alike and had no yearning for other delicacies. José Martí was licking his chops in anticipation of his first plate of rice and beans in the afterlife. Their heads bowed in prayer, these phantoms gave thanks to God Almighty for their first plate of rice and beans in two decades. The veterans reached for their end of the bargain, and soon the nostalgia for rice and beans brought on by the long wait at the dinner table disappeared into thin air. Angel Castro his wife and his children in the company of the most distinguished veterans of the Wars of Independence wolfed down one plate of Moors and Christians after the next until Moor and Christian alike disappeared, leaving behind only a memory of their distinct fragrance.

The ghosts had felt such nostalgia for their sweet smelling fragrance for so long now. Each night they crowded around the one pot of rice and beans about to come to a boil on the stove as if it were the greatest mystery the afterlife had offered up thus far. Doña Lina, who by all accounts was always an extremely devote woman, somehow sensed the presence of the ghosts gathered around her dinner table. Suddenly she stopped short of the dinner table and bowed her head with that pot of rice and beans swinging back and forth on the handle in her hands. She looked at her husband and children and then gave thanks to her Maker for such a wonderful life on Hacienda of the Spirits.

In the weeks that followed, José Martí and the veterans tried to adjust to living the lazy life on the plantation. The veterans were content to sleep away the afternoons feeling full of themselves. They would often stand out on the porch at sunset staring at the perfect circle of sugarcane, sipping Don Angel Castro's best rum before sitting down to a game of cards that would last all night. José Martí could not be content with what he considered a false sense of well being, as tempting as it might be. The Apostle wondered how men who had exhibited such courage against the Spanish regiments during the war could now fall prey to such lethargy. He wondered whether or not the fact that all the veterans had led such harrowing lives contributed to their ongoing trips to the liquor cabinet. The phantom concluded that having their mission interrupted before Cuba was free from the Gigante del Norte accounted for their lack of direction and purpose as well as their ongoing sense that on Hacienda of the Spirits they had found eternal retirement.

For the next several weeks, José Martí spent his time observing the owner of the hacienda and his offspring. He would follow Lina Castro around the kitchen, enjoying long cups of hot coffee as well as the smell of freshly baked bread every morning. He wandered around the hacienda and out into the perfect circle of sugarcane to watch the Haitians cut cane under the morning sun. He made his way down to the Bay of Nipes and looked out upon the aquamarine Caribbean Sea. He purposely skirted the lands belonging to the foreign investors, and most particularly the lands belonging to the United Fruit Company where Angel Castro and the other sugarcane producers had to send their harvest for refining. He would also occasionally wander up to the Sierra Crystal and also down to the banks of the Biran River. Watching it flow by, he would dwell for hours on the more numinous aspects of the afterlife.

After a few weeks however, José Martí discovered a spiral staircase leading up to the attic of the house. He walked up the staircase and discovered a beautiful hand carved mahogany door. He walked through the door and into the attic which seemed to welcome him at first glance. The attic was a large rectangular space with a huge picture window looking out on the Sierra Crystal. There was a large overstuffed easy chair next to the window. Next to the chair was a small table with an oil lamp that was lit. There was a long wicker divan like the one in the living room on the far side of the rectangular room. There were several more chairs strewn about and a large antique desk and chair in the middle. It seemed to the Apostle that this space was reserved for him and him alone. The ghost sank down in the overstuffed easy chair his authors had provided him and immediately fell prey to a deep depression. He stared out at the gigantic mountains in the distance. For a moment he wished to return from whence he had come. Right then and there he decided the suffering of ghosts far outweighed the suffering of mortals. He then fell to wondering again why he had come back from the dead as well as what the future might have in store.

As night came on he pinched out the flame of the oil lamp and fell asleep dreaming of his former life. Upon awakening, all the frustration of not having achieved his mission hit the ghost full force. He was deeply despondent over the present state of affairs in Cuba and thought that things had not really changed much at all since his death. He felt an enormous frustration over the fact that apparently he could no longer change the outcome of historical events or have an effect on the lives of mortals.

The phantom was given over to resolving the enigma of an otherwise wholly enigmatic existence whose possibilities still eluded him. The moon rose over Oriente. Under the light of the moon, suddenly there appeared bookshelves full of books lining the walls of the attic. "How could it be?" wondered the Apostle. The attic appeared like a library invented just to satisfy his lust for learning. Wandering over to the shelves, he ran his fingers across the books looking for some comfort. He came upon some old books whose bindings had come loose. He recognized some of his favorite writers from the Spanish renaissance. He picked up Calderon's Life Is a Dream. The phantom thought once more that all he had experienced thus far since leaving the Sierra Maestra might well be a dream from which he would awaken momentarily. He then found another familiar book of poetry by the great Spanish renaissance poet, Francisco de Quevedo. He flipped through the poems until he reached one with which he was already familiar and read the famous lines, 'I looked at the defenses of my native land: empty silos, bombs and rockets melted down'. The poem reminded him of his beloved Cuba and the present colonial situation so far from his dream of independence. José Martí again grew despondent and returned to the overstuffed easy chair next to the window. Staring out on the Sierra Crystal in the moonlight, he held the thought that at least he had this magical library during the night where he could contemplate the more mystical aspects of life after death.

The Apostle, as the veterans around the poker table below called him now out of respect for his leadership role in the wars, suddenly turned his attention back to his books. As he turned back towards the room his eyes landed on the antique desk in the middle of the attic. There, lying on the top of the desk was a thick book bound in deep green leather with lettering in gold. The book seemed to beckon him from across the room as if waiting for him to pick it up. The ghost walked over and took the enormous history in his hands. He read the title and immediately a broad smile came across his face, for he realized that he was now holding his favorite book of all time; and one which had inspired him perhaps more than any other to rise up against the evils of colonial rule. The Ingenious Gentleman, Don Quixote de la Mancha, was the book the Apostle was so delighted to have found.

Standing there in the moonlight, the ghost gleefully flipped through the history of the knight looking at all the beautiful illustrations of his adventures by some of the most famous artists across the centuries. The great etchings by Dore were the first to catch his fancy. The ghost looked at the portrait of Don Quixote in his library reading novels of chivalry. Then the etching of Don Quixote being tossed over the plains of the Mancha by windmills the knight mistook for giants. Thumbing through the book and reading some of his favorite passages with great enthusiasm, he couldn't help but admire the artistry of Don Quixote's famous Arab historian, Cide Hamete Benengeli who could turn a phrase and invent a conceit in ways unparalleled by any other author in the Spanish language before or since.

The Apostle took Don Quixote in his hands and walked over to the overstuffed easy chair where he proceeded to sit down and read as much as possible before the sun came up. As he flipped through the book in search of some of his favorite adventures, the moment shrank to nothing and a sense of absolute timelessness permeated the library. Once again he read about the knight going mad from reading too many wild adventure tales of the great knights of Christendom from Amadis de Gaul to Tirant lo Blanc. He went on to read how the knight got it into his head to leave his hacienda and go in search of adventure like the great knights of old in order to bring chivalry alive in the modern world.

As the ghost poured over the adventures in the first part of the tale, he saw how the knight mistook giants for windmills, how he turned inns into castles and common kitchen maids into high born princesses. He continued on and observed how Don Quixote had himself dubbed a knight by a local innkeeper. He read about all the interesting shepherds and shepherdesses he met up in the mountains while carrying out his penance in imitation of the great knight Amadis. He paused to look at the famous illustrations of the adventures of Mambrino's helmet and the adventure of the galley slaves. Then he saw Dore's incredible etchings of the adventures where Don Quixote flays at wineskins and imaginary armies from the past. He read on with sadness how the curate and the barber from his local village tricked the knight into giving up his life of adventure.

As the sun came up in the east, the ghost waited for Don Quixote to disappear along with all the other tomes on the shelves. Low and behold, the history of the knight stayed put between his two hands while all the other books evaporated into thin air. The Apostle was shocked but delighted with this new turn of events. Up to now the ghost still believed that the library in the moonlight was just a figment of his imagination or perhaps even a dream to offset his solitude. He again wondered why this book stayed put in the light of day out of all the other books that appeared on the shelves. He concluded that it was due to the fact that he had such admiration and love for the knight.

The phantom did not go downstairs to breakfast that morning like he did most mornings. He was too engrossed in Don Quixote to give a damn about the time of day or his morning toilette. Rather, as the sun came up over the Sierra Crystal, he went right on reading. His powers of concentration nowhere served him better than while poring over each and every one of those unprecedented exploits. His understanding of the knight and his ideals was that much more poignant than when he was alive. All the evil giants who were Don Quixote's enemies now raised their ugly heads. As the moon came up over the Sierra Crystal under the light of the oil lamp for the second night in a row, all the evil magicians who placed enchantments on the knight came back to life in the undaunted imagination of the ghost, along with all the damsels in distress, all the wrongs righted, and all the grievances grieved. All these things came back to life again in his mind's eye in ways not possible when he was mortal.

As the Apostle read on, each adventure seemed more real and true to life than the previous one, and it did not seem to matter in which order he choose to follow Don Quixote's exploits. Going back and forth remembering key exploits, the phantom found the adventure of the windmills, then passed straight through the adventure of the galley slaves, back to Mambrino's helmet for a moment, before skipping on to the adventure of the enchanted bark and then back to the library of Don Quixote where the ghost once more rested his glace on the magical etching by Dore. The picture presented by his historians of the knight turning inns into castles intensified and became more vivid and colorful given the sensibilities of the ghost. When the knight was almost bludgeoned to death by one of another of his enemies the events seemed even more spectacular and extraordinary than when he read then as a mortal.

While his reading abilities in the afterlife had already proven themselves to be beyond those of mortals, it seemed that these abilities and skills were nowhere more rigorously applied than to the reading of this, his favorite book. All of Don Quixote's adventures seemed more vivid and dramatic each time he read them. He stopped to wring all the meaning he could out of each adventure. The author's descriptions seemed so convincing, so mimetic and true to life that the ghost started to confuse the library he was seated in at the time with the library he had just found in the book he was holding in his hands. The line of demarcation between literature and life, history and fiction, for a moment was unintentionally blurred in his mind.

# Chapter Three

For the next week the ghost sat still in the easy chair looking out over the Sierra Crystal and meticulously poured through the exploits of the knight. José Martí came to appreciate the power of the word of Cide Hamete Benengeli, the famous Moorish historian who faithfully recorded all Don Quixote's exploits. He read and reread the history of the knight, unraveling the plot and winding it up again like a ball of yarn in his imagination to understand the warp and woof of the fiction. By this time, the ghost had reached the second part of the tale and had learned that the first part of Don Quixote was already in circulation throughout Europe. He followed the curious adventure of the Knight of the Mirrors and the bachelor Samson Carrasco who assumed a series of disguises in order to demoralize and disillusion the knight. The ghost witnessed how Don Quixote hacked all Maestro Pedro's puppets to bits, mistaking the battle on stage for a real battle. José Martí practically came undone at the seams as he fought off laughter. Finally he took great care to record in his mind all the adventures or misadventures that the famous ducal pair, the Duke and the Duchess, trumped up for Don Quixote to keep him from bringing back the era of chivalry. José Martí was struck by the theatrics these members of the ruling class resorted to in order to keep him from achieving his mission.. Finally all the exploits in the first and second part of the history conspired to become one impenetrable image in the mind of the ghost.

He concluded as he read and reread the book that to get at the deeper meanings of these famous adventures he would have to concentrate even more than he had previously. As he read along, the ghost was convinced that the spirit of Don Quixote would always triumph and provide an example of courage equally satisfying to mortal or ghost. He could not recall when he was mortal having so many insights about the knight and the theatrics and carnivalesque trickery invented by his enemies to keep him from reviving the era of chivalry. Thus, after being completely engrossed by the tale, the Apostle came to understand the only true history of the knight in ways we, the idling readers of this history, never could or would, even if suddenly we were to turn into phantoms for this very purpose. The ghost quickly observed that more than any other knight in Christendom, Don Quixote acted as a magnet when it came to the enemies of chivalry. No knight had been the victim of so many enchantments, evil spells, and other kinds of entrapments invented by the ruling classes of his era.

After such a profound series of readings about the adventures of the knight, the ghost concluded that Don Quixote was not so mad after all in terms of his wanting to bring the values of the chivalry alive in the modern era. Without those enemies who manufactured a set of misadventures to frustrate the knight's mission and throw him off course, he certainly would have succeeded in achieving his dreams and fulfilling his destiny. José Martí concluded right there and then that if it hadn't been for the curate and the barber, Samson Carrasco and the like, the knight certainly would have made his impossible dreams come true.

Then it occurred to the Apostle of the first Cuban Revolution that the plight of the Mambises who had tried to liberate Cuba was like the plight of Don Quixote. Their mission was interrupted by the theatrical tricks of the ruling classes. Succoring the weak and needy, fighting for social justice for all, the heartfelt belief in brotherhood, all these things were as important to the Mambise warriors seated around the kitchen table as they were to Don Quixote. He could not recall when he was mortal having so many insights about the knight and his enemies. The ghost went about proving that phantoms understand more than mortals when it comes to deciphering the subtle nuances of any literary text.

The exploits and adventures of Don Quixote of the Mancha seemed to have enhanced his powers of concentration. He became so engrossed by the text that he lost the ability to distinguish fact from fiction. The scenes portraying Don Quixote lifting his sword to defeat the enemies of chivalry were more true to life than the attic he was seated in at the moment. Soon he was finished with the text and back reading the preface once again. The unique lucidity befitting his intelligence seemed to lift the print right off the page. Before he knew it, the phantom who had planned the Cuban War of Independence had spent another week reading and rereading Don Quixote. The Apostle was determined not to rest until he had pulled the last drop of meaning out of the text.

After several readings of both parts of the history over the course of a week, José Martí always grew sad when he reached the end of the tale. He witnessed Don Quixote on his deathbed 'giving up the ghost', surrounded by his niece and his housekeeper. José Martí grew more and more despondent about the fact that so many of the knight's dreams were frustrated by the literal minded, cynical enemies of chivalry. The image of the Knight of the Mournful Countenance on his deathbed grew increasingly more poignant and tragic each time he reached the end of the book.

The Apostle also noted something very strange after he read through the entire text several times. Immediately preceding Don Quixote's death, there was a phantom chapter of blank pages, as if the author had intended to insert them but changed his mind at the last minute. The ghost found this most curious and despite his best efforts, was not to resolve the enigma of the phantom chapter until many years later in this belated history.

Meanwhile, the strangest most magical of all possible events started to happen in José Martí's lonely sojourn up in the attic in the library of his own making. Each time he reached the death bed scene where Cide Hamete tells us that the knight 'gave up the ghost,' José Martí looked up and saw the Knight of the Mournful Countenance in his nightshirt stretched out on the divan in the attic with a pained and contorted look upon his countenance. His face was so gaunt that his large brown eyes stood out, as well as his crooked nose and thin beard. José Martí immediately dismissed this first vision of Don Quixote in the afterlife as the result of the great esteem and affection with which he had always held the knight. However, the Knight of the Mournful Countenance, or the vision of the knight, vanquished by his enemies as the saddest of all moments, continued to reappear to the Apostle. This time the ghost dismissed the vision as some kind of delusion or trick his mind was playing on him, as a consequence of the tedium and boredom of an afterlife spent in the company of highly unimaginative veterans below playing cards in the kitchen.

The vision of Don Quixote with a mournful look upon his countenance appeared again and again to José Martí over the course of the next few days. Each time the knight appeared to be grieving his own death. His pain and suffering seemed so intense that José Martí felt the knight was not prepared to commit to a second lifetime. These visions of the Knight of the Mournful Countenance lying on the divan across from him seemed so real that the ghost tried to reach out and touch him, but whenever he did the vision disappeared. The phantom felt he must be hallucinating again. Don Quixote seemed so authentic; the ghost had to wonder whether or not his authors were exercising their craft from beyond the grave. José Martí felt great empathy for Don Quixote because he too had failed to achieve his dreams. He too had enemies who had used deceit and trickery to keep him from resurrecting chivalry.

Then just as unexpectedly as this first vision, there appeared a second vision of Don Quixote in his suit of sixteenth-century armor with his makeshift cardboard visor covering his face. His legs were crossed and he was leaning with one arm on his sword and the other poised against the bookshelf where an entire set of Books of Chivalry in Spanish and Portuguese appeared behind him. Don Quixote appeared transparent so that the Books of Chivalry were shown through his armor. A third vision that tormented the ghost was when he came up to the library to find Don Quixote sitting in a chair in a corner of the attic in front of all thirty-one volumes of Amadis de Gaula. José Martí walked over to touch the vision to see if it were real and the picture of the knight evaporated along with the books of chivalry.

Once, when the Apostle was reading about a character in Don Quixote's history, the Renaissance gentleman Don Diego de Miranda, Don Quixote appeared in front of him dressed in dark green stockings and a velvet waistcoat of the same color, embroidered with gold threads. He was wearing black boots to the knees and a broad-brimmed green hat made of felt with a tan ostrich plume sticking out to one side. As he came towards him, Don Quixote seemed cut from a bolt of cloth out of the Renaissance. The ghost blinked and blinked again thinking that he was going quite mad. The work had so captivated his imagination that he could no longer distinguish between literature and life. These visions continued to appear before him in the library as he read the book from cover to cover over and over again.

Finally convinced that the history had gotten a hold of him in ways he had never anticipated, he slammed Don Quixote shut one morning and preceded down the spiral staircase to the kitchen. There he saw the veterans with swords drawn arguing about who had completed the greatest exploit during the Wars of Independence. José Martí was horrified at the scene before him. When they saw the Apostle, these old soldiers stopped their fighting and sat down at the table. For the next few days the Apostle steered clear of his precious library above and remained on the first floor. He spent his time as usual, walking out in the morning to greet the Haitians on their way to the perfect circle of sugarcane. His usual walk down to the Bay of Nipes and then on to the Biran River proved most invigorating. His head started to clear up, and he felt refreshed as he made his way back to the hacienda, where to his great surprise Don Quixote was standing on the back porch with a glass of rum in his hand staring at Angel Castro's perfect circle of sugarcane. Now the ghost really started to get worried. He no longer could dismiss the knight as a vision born out of his loneliness and sense of frustration with the afterlife. When Don Quixote came down the back steps and walked right through him, José Martí remained shaken for hours, lost in his own incredulity.

Whether he chose to believe it or not, José Martí continued to see Don

Quixote in a series of strange poses throughout the first floor of the house. The Knight of the Mournful Countenance appeared on the divan in the living room looking sad and remorseful. He was found in the kitchen dressed in his rusted sixteenth-century armor struggling to lift his makeshift cardboard visor. When he finally did get it off, he peered into the pot of rice and beans on the stove as if he couldn't wait to try them. Then a few minutes later, the Apostle saw Don Quixote seated at the kitchen table trying to get a spoonful of rice and beans through his makeshift visor. Apparently the knight was quite hungry because he kept trying to wolf down all the rice and beans on the plate before him as if he had not had a square meal in centuries. The Apostle could not believe what was transpiring before him.

Next José Martí saw the knight out near the barn in the pig pen covered in mud, and then running around the barnyard trying to catch a chicken. He then saw the knight behind Angel Castro one night peering over his shoulder trying to read the newspaper. Then once again down on the kitchen floor playing with the children. Later he saw him down in the room beneath the house on stilts where Angel Castro keep his accounts, and then at night seated in front of the kitchen stove trying to keep warm. All these images of Don Quixote remained invisible to the veterans who failed to notice the knight the morning he sat down next to them at the kitchen table to break bread. Martí wondered why the knight was invisible to his comrades, but then remembered that they had not had the pleasure of reading the history of his exploits as recently as he had. If so, thought the Apostle, surely the knight would seem as real to them as he did to him.

Not being able to forget the knight and seeing that seemingly he was not to disappear for the moment at least, José Martí returned to the library of his own invention. He sat down in the overstuffed easy chair and picked up the knight's history. Again José Martí mourned the fact that he and his comrades had not achieved their dreams. Like Don Quixote, the Apostle and the veterans had to fight against a powerful enemy who invented all kinds of trickery and deceits to gain the upper hand to defeat the values of brotherhood and social justice.

Don Quixote appeared again in front of all thirty-one volumes of the history of his favorite knight, Amadis de Gaula. Each volume was bound in dark red leather with gold lettering. Don Quixote could hardly contain his enthusiasm. José Martí just sat there staring at the image of the knight convinced that he must be happier than he was when coming out of the pen of his historians. Literally he had nothing to do except read books of chivalry to his heart's content. The Apostle figured that this was the perfect afterlife for the knight and that probably he was a fixture here to stay in the library. Don Quixote could not have planned his own afterlife better if he were reborn for that very purpose thought the Apostle. He was free from all obligations like the veterans around the poker table. Now he would be able to reread all thirty-one volumes of Amadis and the thirty-two volumes dedicated to his son Esplandian, to say nothing of the Palmarin series. Don Quixote it seemed had enhanced reading powers just like the veterans. The Apostle noted this fact because the knight seemed able to read a book of chivalry out loud and make the appropriate comments on the various exploits he encountered along the way in the space of an afternoon or evening.

# Chapter Four

After another lengthy absence up in the attic, the veterans at the poker table in the kitchen started to wonder what had happened to their Apostle. Máximo Gómez put down his cards late one night and addressed Calixto García and Antonio Maceo about their leader's absence. The three of them then went in search of their mentor, looking out on the perfect circle of sugarcane from the back porch. The Apostle was nowhere in sight. Then they all wandered down to the barn and passed by the smithy's before wandering down to the Bay of Nipes where they all rested awhile before going on to the Biran River. The Apostle was nowhere to be found so they returned to the hacienda and sat down in the kitchen for a cup of coffee before searching the house.

Finding the spiral staircase for the first time, the three veterans climbed up to the door of the attic. Máximo Gómez pushed the big wooden door open only to find the Apostle slumped over in the big overstuffed easy chair fast asleep with a book in his lap. The veterans now looked to see the source of José Martí's anguish and pleasure. Each veteran stood in line and waited their turn to get a look at the book that had held the Apostle spellbound for two weeks running. The history held such fascination for the Apostle that he was quite content to give up the most sacred privilege awarded to those who reach the afterlife, the privilege of eating and sleeping.

Each veteran scanned the History of Don Quixote looking for their favorite adventure while José Martí slept on, dreaming of the exploits he had just read about in the book. Then, as the veterans struggled with each other to see who would get to read the book first, José Martí woke up. Surprised to see his comrades in the attic, he was not surprised about their passion for Don Quixote. All Cubans, but most especially the Mambises who had carried out the first Cuban Revolution against the Spanish, were undying fans of the knight. There were so many parallels between the life of the knight and the struggle of the veterans to free Cuba. Both the knight and the Mambise warriors of the first Cuban Revolution tried to lift up the values of brotherhood and social justice in the face of a much more powerful enemy. Both were robbed of their dreams.

Looking at them staring at the etchings of Don Quixote, it occurred to the Apostle that the veterans were like a holy brotherhood of knights defending the values of chivalry as a means of ending colonial rule in Cuba. As all the veterans crowded around the Apostle, he suggested that they sit down on the floor and form a reading circle. As they did so, José Martí sat down once again in the overstuffed easy chair and started to read the History of Don Quixote out loud to them. The moment shrank to nothing and a deep silence permeated the attic as the ghost read on. He read about how Don Quixote went mad from reading too many books of chivalry, and how he left his hacienda to go in search of adventure in imitation of great knights like Amadis. All the veterans were mesmerized by the book each of them had cherished so when alive. As with the Apostle, the adventures of the knight seemed even more fantastic and true to life to the veterans than when they had read them as mortals. The book had impressed them as perhaps the greatest history ever written in the Spanish tongue while they were still living. In death Don Quixote's adventures proved even more captivating and awe inspiring to the veterans.

Simultaneous to hearing the adventures of Don Quixote read out loud by the Apostle, all the veterans were impressed by the attic and the bookshelves. Over the course of the past several weeks, more and more books had appeared on the shelves under the light of the moon and would remain after sun up. The Apostle did not fail to take note of the fact that the library was no longer an illusion visible only under the light of the moon. After the appearance of Don Quixote the books seemed destined to stay put. The library was destined to become the most important room in the house for José Martí if not the rest of the veterans.

The reading circle up in the library continued for several weeks, as reading aloud took more time and left more time for commentary by the ghosts. The Apostle found that the phantoms of the first Cuban Revolution could not tear themselves away. They were so engrossed by the book that they too José Martí left off eating and sleeping for a couple of weeks just to hear the adventures of Don Quixote. These exploits proved even more enticing and fantastic in the afterlife than they ever could have imagined when mortal. José Martí read the book several times over and each time, the veterans would ask him to repeat their favorite adventure. Antonio Maceo loved the adventure of the galley slaves, while Calixto García was fascinated by the adventure of the windmills, while for his part Máximo Gómez liked to hear about the disenchantment of Dulcinea.

Then again the strangest thing started to happen. Whenever the Apostle came to the last episode describing Don Quixote on his death bed, a vision of the Knight of the Mournful Countenance started to appear again on the divan across from them. His face was contorted and he was writhing with pain. It was as if the knight was struggling to come back to life but the disillusionment of his former lifetime was just too great to overcome.

The circle of centenarians could not believe their eyes. José Martí was quick to interject that these visions were a function of their affection for the knight. Nonetheless the vision of the knight on the divan seemed so real that the veterans half believed that the knight was returning from the dead. Yet Máximo Gómez was quick to ask the question how a literary character could have an afterlife? José Martí pondered the question for a moment then decided not to be so cynical. After all, Don Quixote had experienced enough cynicism in his first life, so why not believe in him at least for the moment. The veterans weren't so sure.

As José Martí continued to read out loud to the veterans several hours a day and sometimes way into the night, the knight would appear in other poses throughout the library. Don Quixote appeared looking larger than life in front of the bookshelves containing books of chivalry. He was dressed in a full suit of sixteenth-century armor, leaning on his sword with his old makeshift visor fashioned out of cardboard. The knight creaked whenever he moved. His old set of armor was so rusty that it literally was about to fall in pieces on the floor. Then again the knight appeared, looking much younger, dressed in dark green leggings and a waistcoat of the same color embroidered with fine threads of gold. He had black boots to the knees and a broad brimmed dark green felt hat with a tan ostrich plume sticking out to one side. The veterans marveled at this fantastic image of the knight that they never recalled seeing before, but which nonetheless seemed perfectly plausible and in keeping with his character. Máximo Gómez concluded that Don Quixote looked more real than ever in the afterlife.

As José Martí continued to read the adventures of the knight out loud, the ghost noticed that many of the chapters were missing, the print having disappeared from the page. He could see that with some exploits such as the trick adventures invented by the Duke and Duchess, the print had disappeared altogether leaving the pages blank. The print of some of the other adventures, such as Maestro Pedro's puppet show and the Knight of the Lions seemed to be in the process of fading so that soon there was nothing left. José Martí continued to be mystified by the phenomena. Earlier when the Apostle was reading the book, the print faded and came back. But this time, the print seemed gone for good. Why was the print disappearing and why was it happening so fast now? Finally the ghost put together the fact that the more Don Quixote appeared around the hacienda and up in the library, the more text went blank. Finally there was almost nothing left except a book of pristine white pages. It was as if the knight's history had never been recorded by Cide Hamete Benengeli in the first place. When José Martí put the large green leather history with gold lettering down on the antique desk, there was no writing left but rather nothing more than a book of blank white pages.

Finally, after the print disappeared from the text and there was nothing left about the exploits of Don Quixote, the veterans tired of the library and the reading circle. They went back to a life of sleep, cards and drink on the hacienda they now called home. Spending most of their time in the kitchen gambling and carrying on, José Martí again grew desperate at the thought of having to spend another lifetime trying to motivate them to become involved in something other than eternal retirement. As chance would have it, the veterans would not return to the library very often. They preferred instead to sleep away the afternoons, playing poker and drinking rum way into the night.

The Apostle's afterlife was to take a different turn from the veterans. He spent most of his time now in the attic reading the great classical works of the Renaissance as well as other periods. He was thrilled at the prospect of now having a real library rather than one which simply came forth in the moonlight. More and more books appeared each day. They seemed to become visible in chronological order starting with the classics and ending with modern times. He also discovered that whenever he went looking for a particular book and it was not the shelves, magically, the very book he wanted appeared on the shelf where it belonged. This delighted the ghost no end, thinking that simply by recalling a book he would soon have it in hand. Then the Divine Comedy appeared on the book shelf and he pulled it off and read it from beginning to end.

As the Apostle embarked on his reading of the great classics and more and more books stayed put on the bookshelves, Don Quixote seemed to disappear into the background. But just as soon as the Apostle and his comrades below had forgotten about him entirely, Don Quixote started to reappear all over the house. In the parlor, the veterans could be found discussing who carried out the greatest exploits during the War of Independence. Don Quixote would inevitably appear in his nightshirt sprawled out on the divan with a terrible pained look on his countenance. Again it seemed that the knight was trying to come back to life, but the disillusionment of his former lifetime prevented him from doing so. This time the image came alive in the minds of the veterans. The Knight of the Mournful Countenance started to wave his arms in the air and flay about.

The veterans couldn't believe their eyes. Although they wanted to believe in the return of the knight, they kept in mind all the beatings he had taken by his enemies. They could not forget all the enchantments of the curate, the barber, the student, Samson Carrasco, and the Duke and Duchess which had in the end lead to his demise. Antonio Maceo found it doubtful that the knight could come back to life. Due to the suffering he had endured, it would be impossible for him to commit to a second lifetime. Calixto García regretfully agreed thinking that Don Quixote would rather stay put in his tomb. The veterans then entered into a discussion about the difficulties of being an idealist. Then they started to note the many qualities they shared with Don Quixote, including courage, honor, and a love of beauty justice and truth.

The weeks passed and José Martí stayed put up in the library reading all kinds of books to his heart's content. He thought how privileged he was to have all this spare time. He was putting his enhanced reading powers to good use by continuing to read the great writers across the centuries. As he read his favorite novelists and poets, Don Quixote would regularly appear most often now seated in a chair in front the novels of chivalry on the bookshelves. The Apostle would look up at him from time to time but the knight would always disappear of his own volition. José Martí was pleased and taken aback at seeing his own works published on the book shelves.

Meanwhile the veterans kept to their established routine of sleeping until noon. They finally discovered the importance of exercise and moving around instead of remaining sedentary around the kitchen table playing cards. After waking up, they had several cups of coffee conveniently left in the pot on the stove by Lina Castro. Then these centenarians would wander up to the Sierra Crystal and walk among the mountain people or

Guajiros, visiting their villages and observing their ways. They would also visit the huts of the Haitians who worked on the perfect circle of sugarcane. From time to time, they would disappear from Hacienda of the Spirits only to reappear on a neighboring hacienda. These tired old veterans often commiserated with each other about the fact that Cuba was still a colony, if not of Spain any longer, then certainly a colony of the Gigante del Norte. The social injustice they had tried to eliminate in their former lives still prevailed wherever they went. This lead to an ongoing disillusionment and sense of hopelessness on the part of the veterans which José Martí noticed was getting worse rather than better. He worried greatly about his comrades but was at his wits end in terms of knowing how to get them to take a more positive outlook.

Over time, José Martí did succeed in getting these centenarians interested in reading again. All of them to one degree or another had been avid readers in their former lives. So that once he got them up to the library and showed them all the books now lining the shelves, Antonio Maceo, Calixto García , and Máximo Gómez did find great pleasure in reading. In order to encourage them José Martí would interrupt their poker game and lead them up to the library where once again they would have a reading. Their Apostle and leader would read passages from many of his favorite books. He read El Cid Campeador, La Aruacana and Cecilia Valdez.

In the circle the veterans would lend their undying attention to their mentor and hang on his every word when he commented on the books he read them. Often the figure of Don Quixote would appear between two veterans in the reading circle. The knight would put his hand behind his ear in an effort to hear better. He seemed to very much want to become part of the group. However whenever the veterans reached out to touch him, the knight disappeared with a coy smile on his countenance.

More and more Don Quixote appeared in the library and throughout the hacienda. Whenever José Martí and the veterans were up in the attic reading, Don Quixote would inevitably appear in the corner reading novels of chivalry out loud. The knight would make all kinds of strange commentaries about the feats of individual knights. His favorite knight it seemed was Amadis de Gaula. As was the case in his former lifetime, the knight would read the adventures of Amadis for hours on end. He was completely oblivious to his surroundings. In fact, the vision became so prevalent that the Apostle started to speculate that Don Quixote was here to stay, as implausible as that might sound. When alone up in the attic at night looking at Don Quixote across from him, the Apostle wondered about the words of the veterans. They constantly cited the fact that the knight was after all a literary character. Even though he had a highly imaginative author, it seemed improbable according the Apostle at least that Don Quixote could actually appear here in this history.

As the weeks passed into months, and José Martí and the veterans kept to their appointed routines, Don Quixote would inevitably appear in the library reading novels of chivalry. He would, however, often join the ghosts at Angel Castro's dinner table. Each veteran was willing to give up his appointed seat at the table so the knight would have a place assured him. The existence of Don Quixote remained a mystery to the phantoms around the poker table. As for José Martí, his faith in the impossible dreams of ghosts had increased in the afterlife. If anything his ideals were more intact now than ever. He thought of Don Quixote and how the image of the knight had inspired Cubans across the centuries.

Slowly the Apostle's reservations about the real nature of the knight started to subside and even disappear at times. In the afterlife, Don Quixote's deeds seemed more and more convincing and true to life.

Don Quixote at this point in the history became a regular fixture around the Hacienda of the Spirits. Forever mindful of having returned from the depths of eternal life, he was not unduly distracted by the event. The knight was overjoyed by the simple fact that he was actually walking the earth with his boots on his feet on a hacienda not unlike the hacienda he had left behind to go in search of adventure. He would explore the hacienda, often wandering out into the perfect circle of sugarcane which fascinated the knight. Then he made his way up the Sierra Crystal and down to the Bay of Nipes where he marveled at the color of the Caribbean Sea. The knight also discovered the Biran River and would stare for hours at a time, mesmerized by the waters passing him by.

Less concerned now with his ghostly counterparts and whether nor not they believed he was real, Don Quixote spent a considerable amount of time getting to know the living members of the Castro household. The knight was quick to observe how Angel Castro was unlike the hacienda owners in Spain who had an inborn prejudice against working their own land. Angel Castro, was awake each morning at dawn along with his wife. He would work along side the Haitians all day long on the perfect circle of sugarcane. Often in the evening when Angel Castro would return from the fields, he would put his poker through Don Quixote on his way to stoke the flames in the wood burning stove.

During that cold winter in Oriente Province, the reader of this veracious history would see the same scene repeated again and again. Each night Angel Castro continued to stir up the fires of his enormous stove, as he and his wife and children continued to share their household with some of the most famous phantoms of all time. As winter drew to a close, Don Quixote became a part of the local landscape. As in his first lifetime, the knight would spend most of his time in the library reading books of chivalry. Of course he would usually join the veterans and the Castros for dinner. However, he still preferred to spend most of his time engrossed in the fantastic adventures of Amadis de Gaula. Often when José Martí was reading up in the library, the knight would carry on for hours at a time, making all kinds of outlandish comments about the exemplary life of knights errant.

One day between a quick read of Amadis de Gaula and Tirant lo Blanc, Don Quixote came upon a book he had never laid eyes on before which he took to be a book of chivalry. He thought he had found a book of chivalry about some famous knight whose existence had escaped him. However when he opened the book and started reading, he discovered something quite different. From the very moment that the knight discovered The History of New Spain by Bernal Diaz Castillo, he was smitten with the descriptions of the New World. The ghost read with such rapidity that he seemed to transcend the normal constraints of time. José Martí took heart in the fact that Don Quixote was now reading other things besides books of chivalry. He thought that the knight's mind might be open to conversation. José Martí decided to take advantage of the situation. "Tell me Sir Knight, why is it that you have chosen this particular moment to walk among us." Don Quixote stood there looking at his interrogator for an indeterminate amount of time before answering the question. "Your Grace I cannot tell you the precise reason that the heavens have granted me this boon, putting me before you at this moment. I can tell you however, that our meeting is not the work of fate or chance. Indeed there is a reason for my appearance. Also, Your Grace, although I am in ignorance about what that reason might be, I can say with confidence that the answer will be revealed in due course."

The Apostle was so taken aback by the sophistication and intelligence of the knight that he just stood there frozen like a painting staring at him. He was amazed by his wisdom and comportment which seemed very much in character. He still had some lingering doubts about the existence of the knight relative to his comrades, but from the moment he first exchanged words with him, these doubts started to subside. As hard as he tried during the next several weeks, the Apostle could no longer in good conscience deny the existence of Don Quixote. Nor could he deny the fact that for some reason unknown for the present but surely to be revealed in the future, the knight had appeared on Hacienda of the Spirits to improve the lot of the veterans. As the weeks passed, José Martí felt more deeply identified with Don Quixote than ever. The ghost relished the thought that he would be spending more and more time with him. He wondered how the other veterans would react when Don Quixote would speak to them. He delighted in the thought that Don Quixote de la Mancha might take up permanent residence on the hacienda of Angel Castro's dreams.

The veterans for their part continued with their daily routine somewhat oblivious to the presence of the knight. Máximo Gómez still believed that the visions of Don Quixote were a figment of his imagination. He told his comrades that they were so closely identified with the knight and that they wished to see him so much, that they actually saw him. Antonio Maceo had not decided whether or not the knight was real or an illusion. He questioned his ontological status telling his comrades that a literary character can hardly claim to have participated in historical events. It would seem unlikely that a literary character could become a ghost since a second existence as a phantom must be predicated on having shaped history. Therefore, he found it implausible if not wholly improbable, then highly unlikely. Calixto García for his part was willing to accept the knight as an equal at least for the moment until history proved otherwise.

Don Quixote reveled in the opportunity to read novels of chivalry to his heart's content. As winter turned into spring, one morning the knight looked up from the overstuffed easy chair and his gaze followed the view out the large picture window. The green and verdant valley below with Angel Castro's perfect circle of sugarcane captivated his imagination. Never before had nature exerted such a powerful influence on him. Don Quixote found he was unable to resist the drama of the tropics played out by sun, earth and sea, a drama unique to Oriente Province. Beyond the valley and the mountains in the distance, the knight saw the dance of powder blue and emerald green on the surface of the Caribbean Sea. Although he still resisted on some level, its feminine loveliness reached in and touched the depths of his soul in a way the Mediterranean never really had. Right there and then the knight understood that before this moment, he had never comprehended the beauty and splendor of the New World. The island before him reminded him of the descriptions of the enchanted islands described in his beloved books of chivalry. Cuba was just as Christopher Columbus described in his diaries which Don Quixote had come across during his first lifetime.

Suddenly Don Quixote threw aside the book of chivalry he was reading at the moment. He got up from the overstuffed easy chair and descended the spiral staircase. Heading out into the morning sun, he spied the splendid figure of Don Angel Castro returning from the fields on his prized black Arabian stallion. Don Quixote stood breathless staring at both the man and the animal as if they were one. The man who was soon to become Fidel Castro's father portrayed such an incredible image that the knight concluded the gentleman was the reincarnation of some great chivalric hero. From that morning forward, whenever he saw Angel Castro on the Arabian stallion, the knight climbed up directly behind Angel Castro, where, although invisible to the Idle Reader, he still cut a better figure than when he was astride his old nag, Rocinante. José Martí and the veterans stared on in amazement from the back porch while Angel Castro and Don Quixote made their way through the well manicured fields of the perfect circle of sugarcane undulating in the winds of history. Angel Castro now fell under the timeless scrutiny of the knight seated behind him. As they rode along the perfect circle of sugarcane, Don Quixote was particularly taken by the gentle ways this gentle Galician had with the peasants who worked his fields. Don Quixote concluded that the owner of Hacienda of the Spirits was clearly an aristocrat, if not by birthright, then surely through his sense of decency and honor. The knight concluded that any knight of old would be delighted to join with him in battle.

Angel Castro was unlike his neighbors who received their lands through inheritance and lived in Santiago or Havana in grand homes. They would most often leave their haciendas to overseers who customarily mistreated the Haitians who worked in the fields. Don Angel Castro was radically different. He had come out of dire poverty in Galicia to build his own fortune with years of sweat, blood and toil. He therefore had an instinctive repugnance for the ostentatious life style of the nuevos ricos surrounding his property. He isolated his family from these snobbish individuals who had no understanding of the value and the rigors of physical labor.

The veterans continued to see Don Quixote seated behind Angel Castro on his stallion. The two of them would often ride through the hills and valleys belonging to Angel Castro. The knight determined that this hacienda was not unlike his own fiefdom. His own lands were not as extensive, and the responsibilities for maintaining them were significantly less. He saw the peasants cutting cane and couldn't help but remember the peasants who worked his lands and all the time required to keep the fields productive. He remembered all the days of his youth had been dedicated to taking care of the land. That was before he lost all tract of time as a result of reading those infamous books of chivalry.

# Chapter Five

Just as the veterans had returned from the dead to take up permanent residence on the hacienda of Angel Castro's dreams, so it seemed that Don Quixote was also becoming a permanent resident. As the days passed, the knight became more and more visible to the veterans. He was up at dawn with the Castros and had a first cup of coffee with Angel Castro. The knight often peered over his shoulder to get a glance at the morning paper. One thing which struck the veterans from the outset was the knight's apparent interest in current events. Whenever he left off reading books of chivalry, he would often delve into the newspapers though he as yet had no historical context in which to put events described in the papers. One night when he had finished the flan his wife had prepared him and the ghosts, Angel Castro started to read the paper and was outraged by the fluctuation in sugar prices as well as the fact that he had to take his harvest from the perfect circle of sugarcane to a foreign mill each year. The situation in early 1926 was very bad for the farmers in Cuba. The Yankees were controlling the prices on the world sugar market and Angel Castro and the other hacienda sugar growers on the island could do nothing about it.

Martí could see that the ghost was feeling uncomfortable and he was quick to remedy the situation. The Apostle patiently explained in terms that Don Quixote could understand the problem of colonialism and foreign domination. He told the knight that Cuba was like an island in those famous novels of chivalry which were dominated and exploited by evil giants. He said that he and the veterans had lead the struggle for independence from an evil Gigante del Norte.

Don Quixote thought awhile without uttering a word. Then he turned to all the veterans as well as Angel Castro and announced that what Cuba needed was a great knight errant to liberate the island from the Gigante del Norte. The veterans couldn't help laughing at the knight's comments. For his part, José Martí marveled at Don Quixote's sophistication as well as his apparent ability to see the analogy between the struggle to liberate Cuba from foreign rule and the battles of the great knights of old. As was his habit and custom, Don Quixote held forth on the topic of chivalry and the great knights errant. José Martí lost all sense of time, which is particularly problematic for phantoms and especially phantoms with a sense of history like the Apostle's. The knight, on the other hand, didn't care how much time it took him to get all his thoughts out of his mouth. José Martí remained in a trance for hours listening to tales of chivalry and the greatest exploits of all the famous knights errant who had saved islands from evil giants. The veterans soon were part of Don Quixote's audience. All phantoms present experienced a heightened sense of pleasure at hearing about tales of chivalry coming from Don Quixote.

Then came the time that the knight would disappear for days at a time. Presumably he was somewhere else on the island, perhaps up in the Sierra or down by the sea. These disappearing acts bothered the veterans enormously for they had become used to his presence. There was a real vacuum now when the knight was absent. One morning José Martí became obsessed with finding the knight. He searched all the rooms on the first floor, including the parlor, the bedrooms and the medicine room. He even went downstairs under the house to the small room where Angel Castro kept his accounts. Then the ghost returned to the main floor and found the veterans lined up in front of the medicine room waiting to do their morning toilette. They were putting on their white trousers over their dirty underwear and tucking in their shirts. By the time the Apostle finished searching the house and barn he was exhausted. He then somehow made his way down to the Bay of Nipes where he half expected to see the knight peering out on the Caribbean Sea. Don Quixote was nowhere to be found. He then returned to the house and immediately went to the library where lo and behold there was the knight in the overstuffed easy chair reading a book called The Mirror and Flower of Chivalry as if absolutely nothing out of the ordinary had happened. The knight was making such strange commentary out loud that the Apostle was unhappily forced to the conclusion that his brain was even more addled in this particular respect than when he was alive. Death had only served to increase his madness when it came to recreating the adventures of the famous knights. Then Don Quixote went back to reading in silence. José Martí was much relieved for he feared the knight might just disappear from this veracious history as magically as he appeared in the first place. Then these thoughts left his mind and turning on his heels, the Apostle left the library and left Don Quixote to his own devices

Later that night José Martí returned to the library to check on the knight, fully expecting him to be reading in his chair as usual, but he was not there. The Apostle started to search all the rooms on the first floor thinking that he had surely grown tired of reading and gone to bed. He went downstairs and started to search the bedrooms on the first floor. He then peeked into Angel Castro's boudoir. The room was buried in darkness. The ghost could hear the steady breathing of husband and wife asleep in their bed. The only thing visible in the room was a candle next to a large oval mirror. In the candlelight, José Martí could see Don Quixote staring at his own image in the mirror. He was rearranging the various pieces of rusty old armor as if he had put it on moments ago rather than centuries earlier. José Martí stared on in amazement as the knight continued to finger his breastplate with his left hand. Then he reached out with his good right arm to touch his own image. Then as if to prove it was every bit as real as he was, the image in the mirror reached back towards him. José Martí thought the image in the mirror looked every bit as real as the knight. Apparently the knight was quite pleased with the figure he cut in the mirror, because he walked around in back of the mirror half expecting someone to be there. Then Don Quixote concluded that he was dreaming some impossible dream and that he would awaken momentarily, or even better, perhaps this was the beginning of some great adventure or even a spell or an enchantment.

José Martí decided to leave well enough alone and turning on his heels, the ghost closed the door behind him. He went to sleep for the night. In the morning when he awakened, the Apostle found the veterans had finished dressing and were lined up outside the bathroom each waiting for the chance to trim his moustache in front of a small mirror. In the wake of everything that transpired, the Apostle decided to skip his toilette that morning. Instead he returned to the kitchen where he found Lina Castro pouring Angel Castro a cup of coffee from the perennial tin pot on the stove. Angel Castro was reading about the fall of sugar prices in the paper and had a mournful look on his countenance reminiscent of Don Quixote. The Apostle concluded that he was going quite mad and returned to the library. Don Quixote was nowhere to be found, and the Apostle was relieved. The ghost had a sudden desire for solitude. He sat down in the overstuffed easy chair and stared out on the Sierra Crystal.

The light of the half moon was visible in the early night sky. He loved staring mindlessly into the distance to leave his troubles behind. For the moment he preferred not to think about the veterans around the poker table or his past life.

As night came on, his mind fell to wondering about the larger purposes of the afterlife, the more mystical aspects of a second existence. Without thinking the ghost grabbed a copy of Plato off the shelves and turned to his theory of ideas. The ghost put the book back on the shelf for he was already well familiar with the ideas of the classical philosophers. He thought for a moment about the power of ideas in the afterlife. He wondered whether or not ideas were more potent for those who were dead than those who were alive. He then picked up a copy of Aristotle. Thumbing through the work, he happened upon Aristotle's theory of fiction and his thoughts on the plausible and possible in art and literature. The ghost asked if his theory of plausibility and probability applied to art in the afterlife. All these ideas espoused by the philosophers seemed to affect him differently now just as the books he read. Then the phantom returned to his old favorite Hegel. He wondered if the dialectics of history applied at all to life in the afterlife and to what end a sense of history served a ghost.

As dawn raised her head in the Oriente sky, the light came through the enormous picture window. José Martí slowly made his way down the spiral staircase of the house Angel Castro built to fit his best recollections of a childhood spent in Galicia. Whether or not the spiral staircase and the attic with the picture window was an afterthought remained a mystery to the ghost. He walked down the long hall on the first floor and peered into the nursery where Ramon Castro was fast asleep. Lina Castro was rocking the child back and forth in the cradle. The Apostle closed the door behind him and proceeded to the kitchen. After a few fleeting thoughts about the whereabouts of Don Quixote, he had a cup of coffee from the tin pot on top of the wood burning stove. The Apostle saw the veterans slumped over the kitchen table fast asleep from staying up all night drinking Angel Castro's best rum and playing poker.

José Martí stood there looking at them waiting for his coffee to cool. Taking a sip he thought what a waste of time poker was in the afterlife. The ghost felt the coffee burn as it trickled down his throat. For a change the ghost floated across the kitchen floor without anyone seeing him and landed outside with his two feet on the back porch. There was Carlos Manuel de Céspedes where he always found him, dressed in the same faded white uniform he wore at his funeral. Céspedes was considered the father of the homeland. Totally senile now, the old centenarian sat there blowing rings of white smoke into the cold crisp air from his perennial cigar. Then he turned and went through the screen door and put down his first cup of coffee. The veterans were starting to wake up and as they did so, Don Quixote appeared in the doorway dressed in his nightshirt. The knight looked around at the veterans, all of whom were coming out of the fog of drunkenness. They were staring at him so incredulously that the knight quickly disappeared only to return moments later highly embarrassed in his suit of sixteenth century armor. He entered the room and went directly towards the woodburning stove. The knight warmed his hands and looking around him, greeted the phantoms. The veterans responded with a "Buenos Dias" of their own and the knight was delighted.

72

After reading about the great exploits and feats of the knights of old, Don Quixote was not in the mood to listen to the pointless arguments of the veterans around the poker table. He instead turned his attention to the living members of the household. There before him in the kitchen taking a loaf of hot fresh bread out of the oven was Doña Lina Castro. Having read novels of chivalry all night his mind was filled to the brim with images of damsels in distress. For a moment the knight got confused and held the thought in his mind that the little woman with large brown eyes putting the bread on the kitchen table was none other than a lady in waiting or perhaps the consort of some high born prince. Once again the knight confused literature and life.

As the morning wore on, Lina Castro left the kitchen for the laundry where she gathered the washing to hang out to dry. Don Quixote continued to follow her wherever she went and walked outside to the clothesline beside her. As the knight stared at her still and radiant face, he was completely in the dark about the role destiny was about to assign him. Nor did he have any idea that his fate in the afterlife would be so tightly intertwined with the fate of the woman with the big brown eyes and tightly drawn bun. She now looked in his direction for absolutely no reason. She had a face that was so angelic Don Quixote was tempted to reach out and touch her, but he exercised all the self control he could muster. At the moment she stared right through him, penetrating him with her glance. Suddenly the knight had a vivid memory from his former life. He saw his neighbor Alonza Lorenzo winnowing wheat. Then the memory disappeared. Later that afternoon, the knight followed Lina Castro under the house where she fed the animals. The knight again remembered Alonza Lorenzo feeding the cows, sheep and pigs. The veterans grew concerned for the knight because he seemed wedded to the little woman with dark brown eyes. The knight seemed obsessed as it were by her presence.

The veteran's assumption was correct; Lina Castro held a magical fascination for the knight that seemed to get more and more intense. She reminded him of someone significant in his first lifetime, but for the life of him, the knight could not recall who that might be. He was too absorbed in his own thoughts and the woman before him to concentrate on anything the veterans might have said about history, politics or war. Then he again turned his attention on Lina Castro as if she were the most beautiful woman he had seen in passing from one lifetime to the next. He was like a lovesick child. To the knight she had skin of porcelain, cheeks of rubies, eyes of emeralds, and hair spun of gold. She was as real to him as any high born princess described by those ancient books of chivalry. Right then it occurred to the knight that his own Lina Castro was not like the veterans. She was not a phantom. Rather she was very much alive. At the moment the knight realized that Lina Castro was flesh and blood and not the invention of some author. He quickly concluded that she along with her family were more plausible than the ghosts scattered about Hacienda of the Spirits.

The weeks passed into months and all the residents of Hacienda of the Spirits, be they mortal or ghost, were pretty much settled into a habitual routine. Don Quixote and José Martí were always up at dawn with Angel and Lina Castro. Both knight and ghost were present when Lina Castro set the fire under the stove. Often Don Quixote would watch Angel Castro shave in front of the mirror in the bathroom. The owner of the hacienda was not in the habit of wearing a beard. Then Lina Castro served Angel Castro breakfast. He would of course read the paper and again complain about the fluctuation in sugar prices. As soon as Angel Castro left for the fields of his perfect circle of sugarcane, Don Quixote was right behind Lina Castro. He observed her every move. He did not miss the fact that the wife of Angel Castro never failed to leave a fresh pot of coffee on the stove for the veterans. Nor did she ever forget to take the bread out of the oven in plenty of time for them to enjoy it with their coffee for breakfast.

Most of the veterans slept until noon. Don Quixote remained fixated on the short dark little woman with large brown eyes that seemed to penetrate the thoughts of the ghosts. The knight again felt that she was familiar to him and that perhaps he had come across her or someone like her in his former lifetime. Finally the knight joined José Martí up in the library in the early afternoon to commence his favorite activity thus far in the afterlife. The thought that he could go on reading books of chivalry forever and that he would never run out of them pleased him no end. Each day more and more histories of the knights of old were appearing on the bookshelves of the attic. The magical appearance of new books of chivalry on the bookshelves greatly pleased the knight. He stared at the Apostle engrossed in reading the great philosophers. That night, Don Quixote read about the lady Oriana in Amadis de Gaula. She was the lady to whom the great knight of old dedicated all his exploits. The peerless lady Oriana caused the knight to suffer so much and carry out a terrible penance up in the mountains alone with nothing to eat but herbs and grasses. Don Quixote sat back and thought a moment and then remembered his own peerless Dulcinea del Tuboso. She had porcelain cheeks of roses, eyes of emeralds and hair spun of gold. The knight felt a sudden pang of guilt that sent him flying. All the wind had been taken out of his sails. Right there and then he wished he were dead and buried in his tomb. The knight realized that he had done a terrible thing and betrayed his whole former existence. Without meaning to do so, he had broken his vow of chastity to the peerless Dulcinea. In passing from one lifetime to another, he had forgotten the sacraments of knights errant, that of always remaining faithful to the mistress of his dreams.

José Martí and the veterans noticed how upset Don Quixote had suddenly become. He immediately questioned the knight as to the reasons. Tears were rolling down the face of the Knight of the Mournful Countenance. All the veterans got up and surrounded the knight. They put their hands on his shoulders to help him bear his unnamed burden. Then Don Quixote turned and whispered something into the Apostle's ear. Now he understood the knight's dilemma and the source of his guilt and remorse. José Martí took Don Quixote aside and explained the situation. He pointed out to the knight that he had not betrayed his beloved Dulcinea and that he had remained chaste. He could do no less as a phantom. He had no choice in the matter and could only admire women from afar in a platonic sense. The word platonic rang true enough for the knight. However, he was still visibly upset. He was convinced that he had betrayed one of the primary values of chivalry. He decided that a knight couldn't live without the value of remaining faithful.

José Martí once again pointed out to the knight that he was faithful to the idea of love. He said "perhaps there was a higher principle of order which is operative and beyond our comprehension. Neither you nor I can glean why this event happened to you at this time in the history. If we cannot understand events now, let us be patient and wait for the future to unfold." Don Quixote felt somewhat consoled for now. Little did he know that this was one of many experiences he would have during his second lifetime where he would come upon a familiar scene only to discover the scene connected to his former history.

There was nothing José Martí or any of the other veterans could do to console Don Quixote. The majority of the time he just sat alone in the kitchen or in the corner of the library lost in a deep depression. This lasted for some weeks. One morning the knight came down for his customary cup of rich black Cuban coffee to wake up. He looked at Lina Castro standing next to the stove. Suddenly Don Quixote noticed her belly was protruding slightly. For the moment the knight decided not to say anything to the veterans. But he thought his observation to be momentous. In his mind, Lina Castro was a lady in waiting who was now pregnant.

A month passed and Lina Castro's belly continued to extend into the room. Don Quixote forgot all about his guilt and remorse towards the peerless Dulcinea. Instead he focused all his attention on the little woman with dark brown eyes. He noticed that it was hard for her to bend over to take bread out of the oven. When she milked the cows in the early morning, the knight by her side felt the effort she had to make to squeeze the udder. Her belly was now so noticeable that José Martí and the veterans were quick to comment to each other about Lina Castro's state. One afternoon, there was an entire discussion as to the affect another child would have on the household. The ghosts had a tremendous amount of sympathy for both Angel Castro and his wife. They thought she already worked way too hard. A new child would only add to the burden. Meanwhile Don Quixote wouldn't hear of such talk. He was ecstatic at the prospect of another child. He never let Lina Castro out of his sight from the moment he realized that she was destined to give birth. As the weeks turned into months, the veterans observed that Don Quixote felt a special connection to the child in her womb. The knight sensed the spirit about to be born was similar to his own spirit. However, he couldn't be sure whether or not the spirit was from the past or the future. Nonetheless the knight continued his routine for the next several months. He was awake at dawn with Lina Castro lighting the fire in the woodburning stove and fixing the pot of coffee for her husband and the ghosts. The knight was as dedicated as ever to her and in love, despite his best efforts not to be. He remembered the words of the Apostle that perhaps there was a reason for his deep felt attachment to this woman from Pinar del Rio which he could not understand at present. Nonetheless, having more faith than the average knight errant, Don Quixote rested easy with the words of the Apostle uppermost in his mind. He was happy-go-lucky for the most part and really seemed to be enjoying all that the hacienda of Angel Castro's dreams had to offer. By now the knight fit in perfectly and certainly would be missed by the veterans and particularly José Martí found his company absolutely delightful. José Martí also noted Don Quixote's attachment to Lina Castro as an example of the mystery between the living and the dead. Somehow he intuited that the knight had passed through that dumb blankness full of meaning that separates the life and death to exert an effect on Lina Castro as well as the child in her womb.

As the child grew, so did Don Quixote's fascination with her belly. It was downright embarrassing the way he followed her around now openly rubbing his hand over her stomach whenever she stood still. José Martí and the veterans seemed to shortly follow suit. They made it a habit to surround her in the afternoons when she was hanging the wash out to dry. When least expected, the phantoms gently rubbed her belly as if to impart some magical and mystical influence on the newborn in her womb. By now it was the fifth month and the ghosts could feel the child moving around and flaying about. Lina Castro by this time was enormous. The child inside her was larger than life.

By the seventh month Lina Castro was bigger than normal. The child seemed determined to come forth into the world earlier than he should. Everyone, including Angel Castro, thought that she was to give birth to him during the seventh or eighth month. The veterans and José Martí thought he would be born any minute.

If the child wished to come out of the womb earlier than he should, he didn't get his way. Instead he remained flaying about in her womb for the whole nine months. Don Quixote thought that he was witnessing the first great battle of a child, who like Amadis, was destined to become a great leader like the knights of old. Don Quixote thought this child must be extraordinary. He had limitless energy. Given how much he moved about, he certainly was destined to play a great role in history. Don Quixote now called him the Child of the Sea. José Martí and the veterans laughed at the thoughts of the knight but Don Quixote remained convinced that Lina Castro was about to give birth to another Amadis or Esplandian. He then ran off at the mouth about all the famous exploits reserved for this novice knight for some time while the veterans stood there, amused if not amazed.

The ghosts watched the child grow inside the womb of Lina Castro. Don Quixote went back to reading books of chivalry. However, this time the knight decided to bring several volumes about the birth of knights errant to the attention of the veterans. By this time, Don Quixote had lived on the hacienda long enough to conclude that Cuba was like an island described in books of chivalry that was under the domination of an evil giant. There was a long struggle on the part of the people to resist the Giante del Norte. Tragically, those efforts for the moment at least seemed futile. Don Quixote meanwhile concluded that he was about to embark on a second lifetime and that many adventures and exploits awaited him. He concluded that he was here for a reason, and that the reason was linked to the magical child in the womb as well as the plight of the island.

One late night the veterans were playing cards in the kitchen and José Martí and Don Quixote were in the library. The knight was reading about the birth of Tirant lo Blanc. Suddenly he heard a frightening scream coming from the bedroom of Angel Castro. It was the morning of August 13, 1926. Lina Castro was starting to give birth. The screams continued from the bedroom and all the veterans and Don Quixote immediately rushed to her side. There was a Haitian midwife helping Lina Castro breathe and two other Haitian women present to assist in whatever manner possible. Angel Castro was extremely worried and had his doubts about whether his wife would survive the birth in one piece. The Haitian midwife told Lina Castro to push down hard but it wasn't enough and the child remained flaying about uncontrollably in her womb. Lina Castro was having a real time of it now as she desperately tried to give birth to the monster within her.

Don Quixote stepped in and bore down at exactly the right moment and when most needed, so that the child would pass through the birth canal and leave the womb. Fidel Castro came out in one piece looking healthy and sounding very much alive at exactly two o'clock in the morning. Don Quixote noticed his enormous head on its way out of the womb followed by and equally large torso. The infant entered this life waving its arms and legs in the air. The child's screams were louder than his mother's, who was now holding the newborn in her arms wrapped in a blanket. Fidel Castro continued to let out some enormous yelps which pierced the silence of the ghosts. Everyone in the family heaved a sign of relief. Fidelito continued to scream until Lina Castro gave him her breast to start nursing.

José Martí and the veterans couldn't believe their eyes. Never had they witnessed such a traumatic birth at close hand. They all crowded around trying to get a look at the child's face. As they did so, Fidelito looked up at José Martí. His large deep brown eyes penetrated the Apostle and he was taken aback for a moment thinking that the child had seen him. The ghost wanted to believe it possible but soon thought better of it. Meanwhile, Fidelito was content to suckle on Lina Castro's breast and finally fell asleep. Angel Castro took the child and placed him in a cradle he fashioned out of local pinewood. He sat down in a rocking chair next to the cradle and moved it back and forth as the child slept on into the wee hours of the morning. Máximo Gómez was the first to notice the enormous size of the infant now asleep in the cradle. Using his inordinate talent for public discourse, the ghost proclaimed the child the "biggest little son of a bitch born around these parts in centuries." Antonio Maceo and Calixto García were also taken aback by the child's enormous size. They whispered something to each other about how he looked like he had what it took to make it as a prize fighter in the ring. As for Don Quixote and the Apostle, they preferred to stare down into the child's face. They were both transfixed by the infant's deep, mysterious, large brown eyes. They also noted that he had a good amount of hair on his head. The rare combination of beauty and strength radiating upwards from this child's face left the old poet and orator and Don Quixote absolutely speechless.

Over the course of the next few weeks all the veterans stayed close to the child. They gave up their game of poker and put the cork back into the bottle of rum. These tired old sentimental centenarians dedicated themselves to seeing about the wellbeing of the newborn. Fidel Castro in his first few weeks of life exerted a tremendous influence on the household. He had such charisma that word of his birth reached beyond the Hacienda of the Spirits. Neighbors came from far and wide to see Angel Castro's newest son. Don Quixote marked his time and usually spent the days up in the library reading about the birth of each and every one of those famous knights of old. He would often sneak out of the library in the middle of the night and go downstairs to Angel Castro's boudoir. He would find Fidel Castro was normally asleep in the cradle. Don Quixote caught a glimpse of his portrait in the large oval mirror where he first saw his own image in the afterlife. Leaning back in the rocking chair, his heart seemed to grow larger and his breathing grew easier. He sensed the spirit of the newborn in the cradle. Memories of times past and his recollections of childhood made the knight sitting there in the dark better able to comprehend just why he had come to live on this particular hacienda. He found his mind wandering back to the hacienda where he was born on La Mancha. It was a large hacienda in northern Spain not unlike Hacienda of the Spirits. There it was colder, the people more austere, and the land more barren. His family was less cheerful and more reserved than Angel Castro's. Staring down at Fidel Castro in the cradle, all the knight could remember now about his childhood was a terrible feeling of solitude. Overcome with sadness, he wished for something very different for the child asleep in the cradle.

Now the knight, in the presence of the child, could see all the unfulfilled dreams of his early childhood. As he gazed down at the child's face, the knight recalled that no one in his youth had paid any heed to his dreams and aspirations.

Even though it was now the middle of the night and all was silent, the raucous sounds of laughter from the merriment of the children in the house during daytime filled his ears. His senses were awakened as the cool breeze of early autumn rustled in the trees directly below the window. Don Quixote thought he detected the scent of ancient orange blossoms transplanted from the gardens of Seville centuries earlier mingled with the poignant scent of honeysuckle on the vine. The knight rocked back and forth in the chair thinking how fortunate he was to have ended up on this hacienda. He looked out the window and saw a crescent moon hanging in the sky. The sounds of the Caribbean Sea weaved in and out of the stillness of the night broken only by a lone Bird of Paradise calling for its mate.

Don Quixote was poignantly aware of how much more present he felt next to the child. Whenever he started to loose touch with his surroundings from reading about the exploits the knights of old, he went down to the bedroom and sat in the rocking chair next to Fidel Castro. The mere presence of the newborn rekindled his oldest hopes and dreams. He once thought these dreams were lost forever. Every day the knight became more and more convinced that the reason he had appeared here on Hacienda of the Spirits was linked to the birth of Fidel Castro. He believed that his future as a ghost was dependent on the relationship he would build with this child.

José Martí noticed the fact that Fidel Castro was exceptional from the beginning. Surrounded by the veterans and Don Quixote, the child had experienced a miraculous birth. His first few months of life also proved incomparable as he continued to be the object of affection of some of the most magnanimous phantoms ever to reach the afterlife.

Whenever he sat in the rocking chair next to Fidel Castro's cradle, Don Quixote felt his spirits sour to new heights. All his old ideals returned to him full force. He now believed that he had a future. A future informed by his past life was that much more appealing. Don Quixote felt something deep within him stirring. He couldn't put his finger on it. The knight came alive in ways never anticipated by the illustrious authors of this history. As the tropical night engulfed and reinvigorated the knight, he listened ever so carefully to the breathing of the child. The whole of eternity rushed towards him filling the moment with endless possibilities. Confident now that Fidel Castro was sleeping soundly and dreaming the dreams he intended for him to dream, the old knight fell into a deep slumber from which he did not awaken for hours. He dreamt that he was still alive, sleeping under an old twisted oak on a knoll beneath the August moon back on La Mancha. Fidel Castro awakened now and then for a moment and stared at the knight sensing his presence in the room. Then he would return to a sound sleep. These conditions remained the same for Fidel Castro's first year of life. The ghosts rarely left the side of the newborn. Don Quixote above all others stood vigil over the child. José Martí and the other veterans gave Fidel Castro lots of love and attention. However, it was Don Quixote de la Mancha that became his alter ego. Nothing the child did went unnoticed by the knight. The knight realized that to have participated in such a direct manner in Fidel Castro's birth was to change his life forever. As much as he might wish it otherwise, he knew he could not go back to just reading novels of chivalry. His former existence was now at an end. It was as if his very existence in the afterlife depended on his connection to the newborn infant. José Martí was the first to notice the ties between the knight and the child. He took notes in his journal about how the child's destiny seemed magically connected to the destiny of Don Quixote.

Fidel Castro was a very precocious child from the start and blossomed early in all respects. The range of his voice was obvious from his first screams and yelps. Also his parents and the ghosts noticed that he was enormously willful. He let Lina Castro know in no uncertain terms just when he wished to suckle. He never wasted any time in letting his parents know when his diapers needed changing. Everyone on the hacienda was aware of Fidel Castro from the beginning since his voice reached out beyond the house whenever he screamed. The child had a certain charisma which attracted everyone's attention. It was as if from the beginning Fidel Castro had everyone in the Castro household under a spell. All the Haitian workers lined up on the first Sunday after his birth to get a look at Fidelito. They couldn't help but notice his enormous head and torso as well as a full head of pitch black hair and enormous magical large brown eyes.

Due to Fidelito's demands, Lina Castro continued to nurse him for an interminable amount of time. The child loved to suckle for long periods of time, and Lina Castro would run out of milk. A local Haitian woman who had just given birth came to help feed the infant. When he started to eat solid foods at six months he also continued to suckle. Fidelito loved to sit up in his highchair at the kitchen table with the ghosts and throw his food at them. Lina Castro was continually clearing up the mess as the child proceeded to develop all kinds of games with his food, putting some in his mouth while throwing the rest at the ghosts. Lina Castro could not control him because he was so strong and willful. His arms and legs were always flaying about. Don Quixote was sure that Fidel Castro's historians would record these events in a way that was true to life. When at nine months he began to crawl about the house, Lina Castro, followed by the ghosts, had to chase after him all day long because the child never stopped moving about. He was also quick to discover the crayons that Angel Castro bought him in Santiago. Fidelito would sit on the floor of the kitchen for hours drawing circles in different colors of the rainbow. He seemed enchanted with his own pictures and proudly showed them off to his parents. The child was into all the drawers in the pantry and even opened the oven door. He quickly learned to pull himself up by grabbing on to the side of the chairs around the table. Then he would fall down on his bottom again as all the veterans and the knight stood by bemused and amused. As the veterans and Don Quixote continued to lavish their attention on Fidelito, the child soon came to feel that he was both different and exceptional.

At this time, Don Quixote could be found wandering around the house with a copy of Ramon Lull's Recipes for the Perfect Knight Errant. He kept drawing parallels between the life of Fidelito and the childhood of the great knights of old. He was quick to inform the veterans that the birthplace of Fidelito qualified him to become a knight errant. All knights were born by a river flowing into the sea. The most famous and successful knights of old at birth were called 'Child of the Sea'. Hence, Don Quixote proceeded to call Fidelito the 'Child of the Sea'. He read about the qualifications of knights to the veterans. All knights must be endowed with great physical beauty and strength as well as intellectual prowess. In this respect the Fidelito fit the bill. He was an enormous child with boundless energy. He could focus early on specific tasks like drawing, trying to talk, trying to walk, and throwing his food in the direction of the ghosts. Often the ghosts got the sense that Fidelito actually could see them because the child inexplicably could follow their movements with his enormous brown eyes. Then Fidelito passed through the stage where he wanted to put everything in his mouth. He somehow got a hold of a book Angel Castro had on a table in the parlor. He grabbed it and started chewing on it when Lina Castro whisked the book away.

The veterans and Don Quixote noticed how curious the child was from the start. His eyes seemed to focus early on the objects around him. He would often point at something and try to say a word. One morning while the veterans were all seated around the kitchen table watching him, he threw a piece of bread in Lina Castro's direction and said "mama". The veterans were beside themselves with joy over the first word of the infant. Don Quixote immediately registered the time and place so that the historians could record the event accurately. Later that evening, the infant looked at Angel Castro and said "papa".

Then something strange happened which the historians have to note. Fidelito stopped eating solid foods and again reached for Lina Castro's breast. The ghosts could not figure out this strange behavior but were not very concerned. Don Quixote was extremely upset seeing Fidel Castro nursing again. He was frustrated by the fact that he could find no precedent in Ramon Lull's Recipes for the Perfect Knight Errant. Lina Castro was trying to get Fidelito back on solid foods again. However, the child was extremely willful and determined to continue nursing to his hearts content. Angel Castro thought that they should let the child do what he wished. Then, as quickly as he had demanded to be nursed, Fidelito went back to solid food. He again took great delight in throwing food at his brother and sister as well as the veterans. Fidelito continued drawing on the floor of the kitchen but this time he drew human figures with white uniforms with a leather belt holding a sword reminiscent of the Mambises.

The veterans and José Martí were absolutely dumbfounded as was Don Quixote at Fidelito's incredible imagination as well as his powers of concentration and apprehension. José Martí now wondered if Fidelito saw the ghosts. This miraculous child endowed with so many attributes impressed all the residents of Hacienda of the Spirits. At one year old he was pointing and saying words and trying to construct complete sentences, often ordering Lina Castro to attend to his every need. The ghosts, and particularly Don Quixote, were again struck by the force of will of Fidelito. He seemed to be able to communicate his needs and desires better than most children. He loved his brother and sister from the time he first recognized them playing on the floor alongside him. Fidelito continued to draw in ways that impressed his elders. He often drew pictures of Ramon and Angelita.

Once Fidelito was in Angel and Lina Castro's boudoir. The historians tell us that he was no more than a year and a half old. Fidelito found the large oval mirror in the corner and crawled towards it. He saw his own image for the first time in much the same manner Don Quixote had first viewed his image in the mirror. He stood up by grabbing onto the side of the mirror and looked at his image. Just as Fidelito was touching his portrait in the mirror Don Quixote came up behind him. The child suddenly fell back on his backside. Don Quixote couldn't help but laugh.

The child sat there on the floor staring up at him as if he saw him. José Martí walked into the boudoir at that moment. He was struck again by the special connection between the knight and Fidelito. Their connection seemed much more complex and intimate than that between most ghosts and mortals he had observed. José Martí also noted that the child seemed to have preternatural powers of discernment which allowed him perhaps not to see the phantoms populating the hacienda, but at least to sense their presence.

The veterans continued to sleep late and play cards well into the night with an ample amount of the best Cuban coffee supplied by Lina Castro. Don Quixote found their behavior disappointing. What he knew of the veterans and their former lives did not compute with their present behavior and lack of motivation.

José Martí and Don Quixote continued with their own routine of getting up early along with Lina and Angel Castro. To the surprise of all the veterans Don Quixote left the side of the hijo prodigo. He started to follow Lina Castro around the hacienda as he had before the birth of the future Comandante en Jefe. Then the knight turned his attention away from the veterans and the Castros and back to his beloved books of chivalry. He decided to embark on yet another reading of Amadis de Gaula, his favorite knight. His adventures had provided him with a road map in his former life. This time, the knight chose to do his reading on the wicker divan in the parlor. He started one early afternoon and was about halfway through the knight's adolescence when he heard a terrible row from the kitchen. He got up and walked into the kitchen where he saw the veterans on their feet with their swords drawn shouting insults at each other about why the wars had ended so badly. Don Quixote was aghast at the scene before him. Like José Martí before him, he wondered why these great warriors of the past had sunk so low in the afterlife. He quickly took the situation in hand. His mere presence stopped the heated arguments of Antonio Macao, Maxim Gómez, and Calixto García. He slowly managed to get them to follow him into the parlor. Fidelito followed the veterans and sat down on the floor with them in front of Don Quixote. Then the knight opened the first tome of Amadis de Gaula and started reading in the presence of Fidelito. José Martí then joined the group. He wondered why the child sat so still next to the veterans when he usually was flaying about. The veterans were deeply touched hearing books of chivalry read out loud by Don Quixote de la Mancha in the afterlife. These old veterans were on a hacienda not unlike the hacienda Don Quixote once called home. The veterans, in the company of Fidelito, passed the afternoon listening to all the famous exploits of Amadis. They took particular delight in all the magical spells and enchantments which were placed on the knight. Once he was frozen in time in a cave. Once he had to dive into a bubbling black lake only to find a crystal castle at the bottom. As the afternoon wore on to evening, the veterans asked Don Quixote for a short break. They were quick to let the knight know they were enjoying the reading enormously. They went to get some glasses and Cuban rum from Angel Castro's liquor cabinet. Then Don Quixote and the veterans stood out on the back porch watching the yellow and orange sun set on the perfect circle of sugarcane.

Soon the veterans and José Martí were back under the spell of Don Quixote reading the adventures of Amadis out loud to his hearts content. Don Quixote was ecstatic because he had never had any company before when reading tales of chivalry in his library. He was always isolated and alone when following the adventures of the famous knights of old. But now here in the parlor of Angel Castro with Fidelito by his side, the knight was able to share his enthusiasm for the fantastic exploits of Amadis, Esplandian and Tirant lo Blanc. The knight often stopped to make commentaries and observations about specific exploits which were as amusing as the exploits themselves. Don Quixote was a virtual encyclopedia when it came to the adventures of knights, but no one had appreciated his love of the knights' exploits back on La Mancha. Don Quixote was able to provide enough entertainment to the veterans to leave off their poker game in favor of books of chivalry. The knight got through all thirty-one chapters of Amadis in less than a fortnight. The veterans hung onto his every word and were amazed at how much the knight knew about the exploits of all the famous knights of old. He would stop to compare knights and went on at great length about the best and the worst exploits of knights like Amadis, Esplandian, Palmerin de Inglaterra, and Tirant lo Blanc. José Martí never ceased to be amazed by the depth of knowledge and memory of Don Quixote when it came to deciphering the meaning and significance of these adventures and exploits.

The veterans wanted to continue discussing the exploits of the great knights in the reading circle. José Martí was delighted by the fact that his comrades were interested in something beyond poker and rum. Eventually Don Quixote moved them back up to the library. He sat in the overstuffed easy chair just as José Martí had earlier. The knight read to the veterans all afternoon and into the evening as he had before in the parlor. According to the authors of this history, one afternoon when he had learned to crawl about the house, the precocious and energetic Fidel Castro crawled up the circular staircase leading to the library of José Martí's invention. The child pushed open the door and crawled into the library for the first time. Don Quixote and veterans couldn't believe their eyes. They looked at each other in amazement and then back at the child. However, it was perfectly plausible that the child had made his way to the attic because he was so active, energetic and curious beyond his years. Fidelito proceeded to make his way across the room on all fours until he reached the middle of the circle of centenarians listening to books of chivalry. Then he sat still as if he were waiting for Don Quixote to continue reading out loud. The knight took his cue from the child and started to read again while the veterans and José Martí stared at Fidelito incredulous at his precocious manner. For a moment Fidelito not only seemed to hear the knight but also see him. When Máximo Gómez commented to the effect that the child was aware of their presence, José Martí warned against such assumptions, telling his comrades that there was no known evidence to suggest such a thing. The veterans were a bit surprised at the Apostle's rather guarded attitude. Don Quixote had his own opinions on the topic of the relations between mortal and ghost. He believed that there was no proof that there was communication. Neither was there proof against communication between mortals and phantoms. The veterans, José Martí and Don Quixote left off reading books of chivalry for the moment. They embarked on a long conversation about the possible influences that phantoms might have on this magical child

José Martí did believe that some people were more open to ghosts than others. He cited as living proof the fact that they had received such a warm welcome on the hacienda of Angel Castro's dreams. The Apostle thought that Angel and Lina Castro were not typical hacienda owners. They were hardworking people who lived close to the earth, worked in the fields alongside the Haitians, and had a healthy respect for their ancestors. The fact that they had made the phantoms feel so welcome and at home from the start warmed their hearts. The coffee pot was always full on the store waiting for the ghosts. The plentiful leftovers each night after dinner were ready and available for the taking.

The future Comandante en Jefe of the Revolucion exhibited preternatural powers of discernment from an early age. All these things and more made José Martí feel that there was a grand plan afoot to change the destiny of the island which included Fidelito, Don Quixote and the ghosts. As the reading circle of centenarians continued up in the library, each afternoon Fidelito would join his ghostly counterparts as if he were actually hearing about the exploits of ancient knights. The great battles, the fantastic enchantments and magical spells, the bubbling black lakes, the castles made of glass, the damsels in distress, the great armies going up against each other, all these things filled the imagination of the veterans. According to Cide Hamete Benengeli, in his second History of Don Quixote, all these magical happenings in the lives of the knights of old filled the imagination of the future Comandante en Jefe of the Revolution. Neither the veterans nor Angel and Lina Castro knew it at the time.

Fidelito continued to make it a habit to go up to the attic when Don Quixote was reading books of chivalry out loud to the ghosts. The veterans noticed that he would often grab onto the leg of a chair and try and stand up. Every afternoon for a month, the child made an attempt to walk but was unsuccessful. Then one afternoon, the historians think it was in early August, not even a year since his birth, Fidelito stood up in the presence of the ghosts.

Don Quixote was beside himself with joy and threw the adventures of Amadis to one side. He could do nothing but focus his attention on

Fidelito's attempt to take his first steps. The child took several steps before falling down. But then he would find a chair and stand right back up again. Once Fidelito took his first steps up in the attic with the veterans nothing could stop him. He was tremendously willful. It took him almost a month, but finally the child walked from the reading circle to the door of the attic and pushed it open. He fell down again and crawled down the stairs to the first floor. Don Quixote was right behind the child and the veterans and José Martí right behind Don Quixote. Fidelito got to his feet by grabbing onto a wall in the hallway and walked as far as the door to Angel and Lina Castro's bedroom. There the child fell down and started to scream. Lina Castro came rushing in from the kitchen wondering what was wrong with the infant. Fidelito continued to cry in her arms as if the events of the last hour had finally overwhelmed him. He was ready for a nap so Lina Castro put him in the crib next to her bed and left him to sleep. Don Quixote and the veterans did not miss any of this interchange and stayed by the infant for some time. They too were exhausted from all the activity around Fidel Castro's first steps.

In the weeks that followed Fidelito was up on his feet most of the time. By now he had explored both the first floor of the house and the library of José Martí's invention. Soon he was out on the back porch climbing into the lap of Carlos Manuel de Céspedes. The old veteran just continued to blow rings of white smoke into the distance as if nothing unusual had happened.

The veterans started to chase the child around the porch which encircled the house. Soon Fidelito was running circles around the house screaming to his heart's content with the veterans in hot pursuit and Don Quixote not far behind. Fidelito was delighted that he had involved so many people in his amusing and frivolous pranks. Lina Castro had no idea that the phantoms populating her homestead were also chasing her child around the porch, which to this day is wrapped around the house built on stilts to the best specifications of Angel Castro's childhood memories of Galicia.

By the time he had reached the age of two, Fidelito had indeed distinguished himself to his parents, his siblings and the ghosts. His charisma continued to mesmerize all who came in contact with him. Don Quixote had no doubts that Fidelito was indeed a magical and extraordinary child. He talked and walked at an early age. Soon, according to the knight, he would be having all kinds of fantastic adventures that could compete with the best of them.

The historians tell us that it was Christmas time when Angel and Lina Castro would bring gifts to the Haitians in their huts. Fidelito followed his parents and was given a warm welcome by the Haitians. They immediately took note of this exceptional child. The Haitian women would give Fidelito fresh corn from the husks which were cooked on the fire. Fidelito put the corn in his mouth and was delighted with the taste. The phantoms thought this was extremely funny and laughed for hours at the hijo prodigo.

Fidelito never forgot after that Christmas how to reach the huts of the Haitians who worked the land. Often Lina Castro would grow desperate at not being able to find him. He was always going off now somewhere on the hacienda. More often than not Lina Castro had no idea where he went. Don Quixote would follow Fidelito to the huts of the Haitians and watch him eat the corn along with the other Haitian children. Soon Fidelito, Ramon and Angelita were playing with the Haitian children regularly. Lina Castro seemed somewhat upset by the fact that her children, and most especially Fidelito, were always in the huts and gardens of the Haitians. She had no class prejudice as such but was concerned about the health of her children. The living conditions of the Haitians were substandard and often unclean. Lina Castro would worry about Fidelito eating the corn. However, there was not much she could do to control the situation. Angel Castro dismissed her worries and told her that all the workers were trustworthy and reliable.

By the time he turned three, Fidelito had distinguished himself as a highly imaginative, intelligent child. He often walked up the spiral staircase to the library and pulled some old books off the shelves as if he were ready to read them. Don Quixote was amazed at how perceptive the child seemed about the books around him. He took a special liking to the library. He felt very much at home up there, so much so in fact that Lina Castro would often have to sweep him off his feet and carry him downstairs for dinner. Whenever he wasn't in sight, his mother would always look up in the library. More often than not, she would find him pouring through books looking at the illustrations and the words and sentences as if he understood them. The child read Robin Hood, The Three Musketeers and José Martí's La Edad de Oro along with other adventure stories.

Don Quixote noticed that the child had great powers of concentration at an early age, and that he could follow the words and sentences across the pages of the books. José Martí concluded then and there that this child was destined to become an avid reader, not only because of his innate curiosity, but also because of his ability to focus his attention on words. José Martí would sit by the child as Fidelito would look at the words in a book. The phantom would pronounce the words out loud even through the child could not hear him, hoping against hope that something would reach his ears. The child seemed affected by the presence of the Apostle, because he sat up straighter and concentrated even more on the sentences at hand. Soon he was pronouncing out loud several sentences at a time. The ghosts were so aware of Fidelito's enormous talents and skills. They felt a great frustration at not being able to communicate their thoughts on this magical child to Angel and Lina Castro as well as the Comandante en Jefe's historians. This frustration would only prove to get worse in the course of this veracious history. The distance between phantom and mortal inevitably became a point of contention among the historians and all those who wished to get to the truth of the matter.

By age four, Fidelito divided his time between the Haitians and the house built on stilts and the rest of the hacienda which he was getting to know. Usually accompanied by Don Quixote, the child now walked around wherever he wanted without an adult to guide him. Lina Castro was usually so busy keeping up with the housework that she pretty much left her prodigious son to his own devices. The child would wander down to the smithy to see the horses get new shoes. Then he wandered over to the bakery and asked for a bun. After that he went on to the local tavern and looked up at the workers having a drink at sunset.

Accompanied by the veterans, Fidelito walked out into the middle of the perfect circle of sugarcane and looked at all the Haitians working the land. There he saw nothing but miles and miles of sugarcane blowing in the winds of history. He would often see Angel Castro working beside the workers out in the fields. He and Don Quixote watched the harvest with great interest. They witnessed how the Haitians would load enormous piles of cane on their backs to load onto the oxcarts to take to the sugar mills owned by United Fruit. Each year the phantoms, and especially the Apostle, would lower their heads and fall prey to a deep depression at the thought of the island being still under the domination of the Yankees.

By age four, Fidelito was taller than Ramon who was two years older. He was taller and more filled out than the children of the Haitian workers. Don Quixote and José Martí did not fail to note how Fidelito was a natural-born leader from the very beginning of his life. The charisma he held as an infant continued to grow. At four, Fidelito was already organizing the children on the hacienda into children's games as well as trips to the Biran River. Don Quixote and the veterans enjoyed seeing how the hijo prodigo organized his brother and sister along with the Haitian children into small bands which would play hide and seek for hours on end. Then Fidelito would lead a band of children, including Ramon and Angelita, down to the Biran River. There they would strip down to their underwear and jump gleefully into the river and swim for hours on end. At sunset Fidelito would bring his brother and sister along with the Haitian children back to Hacienda of the Spirits.

Often Lina Castro would have a plate of freshly baked buns and a jar of milk waiting for them. All the children came running into the kitchen. The children stepped on the chairs where Máximo Gómez, Antonio Maceo and Calixto García were seated, and grabbed for the hot buns on the plate. The veterans were all amused and amazed at the energy of the children and how infectious it was for them. They too started to grab for the hot buns and enjoyed the snack along with Fidelito, Ramon, Angelita, and the Haitians. By the time he was four, Fidel Castro was familiar with all aspects of life on the Hacienda of the Spirits. He often visited the Lecheria, the telegraph and telephone office, and the general store where he saw the Haitians buy goods for their families.

Fidel Castro had constant contact with children who lived in very squalid circumstances. According to the phantoms, he developed a social conscience at a very early age. As he entered the huts of his Haitian friends, he would see the fact that they all slept in one room on a dirt floor. They rarely ate meat and were lucky to have rice and beans rather than just plain corn. The children were scantily dressed compared to Fidelito, Angelita and Ramon who always had freshly ironed clothes. Fidel Castro had a deep feeling for these people and they had an eternal place in his heart. The child also appreciated his own circumstances which were far better by comparison. The Castros had a good diet of rice and beans along with fruits and vegetables which were plentiful all year round.

At age five, Fidelito had become a natural born leader and inventor of tiny exploits. Now in addition to organizing the children on the hacienda into games in the barnyard, he would take them on hikes up to the Sierra Crystal. Don Quixote was convinced that these were the first adventures of a famous Caballero Andante. The knight thought that they would be recorded in the history books when the knight was already famous. Fidelito would always plan the exploit and lead the pack. He seemed to know exactly where he was headed. He would stop to look at all the gorgeous tropical vegetation along the way. Fidelito would create as interesting an adventure for his comrades as his prodigious imagination would allow. Often the children brought along slingshots and with stones shot at the birds and tiny animals of the magical jungles of the Sierra.

Sometimes these outings would last all day. Don Angel Castro and Lina Castro would be beside themselves with worry. Then Fidelito would appear walking across the perfect circle of sugarcane followed by a long line of well disciplined children. When Angel Castro would ask his son where he spent the day, Fidelito would be full of tales of roaming around the forests of the Sierra and encountering the Guajiros or mountain people who lived in huts like the Haitians. These adventures outside the hacienda organized by Fidel Castro caught the attention of the phantoms. One morning Don Quixote, José Martí and the veterans packed a canteen of water, and followed the children up the Sierra Crystal with Fidelito in the forefront of the group. They walked for miles over creek beds and thick vegetation. Tropical blooms were all around, and the birds were singing loudly. The phantoms were having a hard time keeping up with the children as the youngsters had so much more energy and stamina. Don Quixote, José Martí and the veterans stopped to drink at a stream. Don Quixote remembered the Sierra Morena and his adventures with the shepherds and shepherdesses of the mountains in his former lifetime. He looked around him halfway expecting them to appear. He then remembered that he had carried out a penance in imitation of Amadis de Gaula and foregone both food and drink for over a month, living on herbs and grasses in the mountains

The veterans were amazed by the organizational skills of Fidelito. As they proceeded up the mountain, all of the Haitian children stayed in line and did exactly what the small Comandante en Jefe told them. He shouted out all kinds of orders about which direction to go and when to stop and take a rest. The children delighted in his leadership and so did the veterans. The sojourn up the mountain and over streams and through the thick green jungle vegetation thrilled José Martí and his comrades.

The adventure reminded them of their guerrilla warfare against the Spanish regiments up in the Sierra Maestra.

The hijo prodigo led the band of children and ghosts up to a Guajiro village high in the Sierra where people from the valley rarely came. The Guajiros were amazed to see this organized band of children and their leader greet them. Then Fidelito saw a young Guajira his age and ran after her. The girl was so quick that she disappeared and obviously Fidelito was disappointed. He wanted to talk to the young Guajira but she had escaped him. Finally Fidelito led the band of his comrades including his brother, Ramon, down the mountain side then across the valley and along the Biran River where they stopped for a swim and a drink of water. Then the adventurers arrived at the edge of Hacienda of the Spirits.

It seemed that Angel and Lina Castro were frantic for hours searching all around them for the children. When they saw the band of children they were overjoyed and rushed up and hugged Fidelito before scolding him. Angel Castro was very angry and asked him why he had not told him where he was going. Fidelito as usual remained silent and uncommunicative in answering Angel Castro's questions. Angel Castro gave up and lead them all back to the house on stilts where Lina Castro bid the Haitian children goodbye and insisted that both Ramon and Fidelito take a bath and go to bed.

Many were these inventive exploits led by the future Comandante en Jefe of the Revolution. Fidelito got to know the mountain people and the mountains in which they lived. He and his band of followers roamed the valleys belonging to Hacienda of the Spirits. They continued to explore the Biran River and follow its path to the sea. Fidel Castro was exposed early on to the freedom that came from living in the tropical paradise that was Oriente Province at that time.

As he grew older Fidelito discovered that at times he needed solitude. Often he would walk up the spiral staircase at night. He would take a book which José Martí had imagined for him and sit down and read it. Due to his great intelligence and precocious development, Fidelito learned intuitively on his own to recognize many words. He still lacked vocabulary but was able to put sentences together and read entire paragraphs. This child's love of words was obvious to the phantoms who shared his space up in the library of José Martí's imagination. Often José Martí would convince the veterans to come up to the attic to the reading circle to read out loud. José Martí asked the veterans to choose a book and read some of their favorite passages to the rest of the group. Máximo Gómez loved the challenge. He perused the bookshelves looking for a familiar tome, and his love of books returned to him full force. He put his hands on one of his most cherished tomes that he read many times over as a mortal. The book was "The Brothers Karamazov". He started to read some passages comparing the lives of the three brothers which he remembered in passing from this life to the next. José Martí compared the brothers Karamazov to his three comrades. The conversation went on for hours, often turning into a heated argument about who among the veterans seemed most like Ivan, Alyosha, and Dimitri. The veterans were enthralled. Fidel Castro seemed to be aware of the reading circle as well as the words being read aloud. José Martí hoped this magical child could hear these words but he could not be sure. Still, he couldn't help but conclude that the ambience created by the phantoms was of significant influence on the child. He thought that the ghosts were having a formative effect on the five-year-old Fidelito.

The child seemed to need to be alone with the books surrounding him. Many times he would pick up a book. However often he didn't really concentrate and he let his imagination soar into flights of fancy. But then he would come down again and hit the ground with a thud, very aware of the circumstances surrounding him. He was aware now that he was born on a hacienda and that he was privileged because his father was the owner. He was increasingly aware of the situation of the Haitians and the social injustices that prevailed on the hacienda. Often the child would need to escape. By the time he was five, he would make his way all the way to the Bay of Nipes on his own volition. There he would run on the white sand beach and stare at the emerald green Caribbean Sea. He had learned to swim in the Biran River. Now he was ready to take on the sea. Fidelito jumped gleefully into the warm clear waters and dove deep where he saw schools of colorful fish swimming by him.

A grand fish with an artfully colored face started straight at him. Fidelito stared back, mesmerized and excited by the colorful face of the fish. He never saw anything so lovely as the magical fish. After looking straight into Fidelito's eyes the fish seemed to swim right through him. Fidelito came to the surface and swam back to shore and lay down on the white sands next to the waves lapping at him. Then he fell asleep and dreamt of the perfect fiefdom where all the workers were well-clothed, well-fed, well-housed and well-educated. There were knights dressed in colorful armor riding through the fields protecting the campesinos from harm and making sure they were well cared for as was their duty and privilege. Fidelito awoke from his dream and remembered the perfect fiefdom so reminiscent of those books of chivalry. But the historians of this veracious history are quick to point out to the reader that this was a pivotal event in the life of the Comandante en Jefe. As far as Cide

Hamete Benengeli was concerned the dream was proof of the fact that the ghosts were having their influence on him

As time wore on, Fidelito continued to lead the carefree life of a privileged child born to relative wealth. He was conscious of his surroundings and even aware of the dire economic and political realties of the island. As Fidel Castro grew, so did his enormous intellect, his prodigious imagination, and his social awareness. He was conscious from the start that he was special and privileged among his Haitian friends. Finally the day came when Lina Castro took Fidelito by the hand at age five and led him off to local school #15 in the village of Biran. Fidelito entered the one-room classroom and recognized his fellow students as the children of the Haitian workers with whom he played. The teacher tried to teach all the children the A, B, Cs. But she was destined to fail from the start as far as the Haitian children were concerned. They simply lacked the exposure to spoken Spanish to be able to comprehend words and sentences. These children came to school hungry and unable to concentrate on the lesson while Fidelito came well dressed and well fed. Once again Fidelito noticed the difference between his own circumstances and the circumstances of his classmates.

Don Quixote, José Martí, and the veterans in those days were always found in the back of the classroom looking on as the Haitian children struggled to learn and Fidel Castro excelled at his A, B, Cs. Fidel Castro, from the first time that he entered School House #15, exhibited powers of concentration and apprehension which dumbfounded both the teacher and the other students as well as the ghosts. He learned to read more rapidly with more comprehension than any other student she had ever taught before or since. Whatever she gave him to read, Fidelito quickly digested it and was on to his next book. Each day more and more of the Haitians children dropped out of first grade and went to work in the fields to support their families. Finally the only child left in the local school was the child seated in the front of the class. He was reciting the lesson at will with a row of ghosts in the rear witnessing the event. Fidelito did nothing but talk back to the teacher and give her a very hard time. The veterans immediately noticed his rebellious behavior. The teacher complained to Lina and Angel Castro but there was really nothing to be done.

One afternoon when Lina Castro was leading Fidelito by the hand home from school, the child tripped and fell. There was a nail on the road which pierced his tongue. The pain was unbearable. Lina Castro pulled him along until she reached home. In the kitchen, she tried to clean the wound but the child kept on screaming. Finally exasperated and at her wits end, Lina Castro told Fidelito that the reason the nail pierced his tongue was because he talked back to the teacher.

The veterans and the knight were left speechless and sympathized with the child. After all he did nothing but learn his A, B, Cs backwards and forwards. Don Quixote and José Martí were horrified at the education of Fidelito. The teacher would send him to the corner and punish him for speaking out and sassing back. Both the Knight of the Mournful Countenance and the Apostle were depressed about the limited educational and intellectual advantages afforded Fidelito. They were now convinced that with their help and guidance, Fidelito would come to play a great role in the future of Cuba. Each day Don Quixote would lecture the veterans on the need to believe in the influence between mortals and ghosts. José Martí would listen politely, as would his fellow veterans.

Out of respect for the knight and his ideas, they remained silent on the relationship between mortal and ghost.

The circumstances which surrounded him as a child were to have a lasting effect on Fidel Castro. He no longer took anything for granted. He appreciated regular meals and all the learning he was able to achieve at local school #15. Within the first 6 months of being there, Fidel Castro learned to read anything the teacher gave him. He excelled early on and read way beyond the third grade level by Christmas. During these times, Fidelito would spend lots of time up in the library pouring through the books on the shelves. José Martí noticed that Angel and Lina Castro had scant reading material available for their children. José Martí would wish for a particular children's tale which he thought appropriate for the child. The next day it would inevitably appear on the bookshelf next to Fidelito. One such book was a tome José Martí had written for children called La Edad de Oro. The future Comandante en Jefe would devour these stories with great enthusiasm and José Martí could not keep up with the child when it came to wishing for appropriate children's stories. The amount of joy the child took in reading was stupendous. He did so with little guidance and help excepting the influence of the phantoms. He had already consumed more books than anyone in the house. Angel and Lina Castro were both practically illiterate and had taught themselves to read and write only recently. So the intellectual stimulus in the Castro household was provided by the ghosts.

While he was attending Local School #15, the Apostle and Don Quixote started putting books out on the desk and the table next to the overstuffed easy chair where Fidelito would pick up a book to read. They started giving the child books which were meant for adults. His skill as a reader had reached the capacity of the ghosts.

When Don Quixote went back to reading books of chivalry out loud to the veterans, the future Comandante en Jefe immediately joined in. The Apostle felt strongly that it was the child's destiny to participate in some manner in the life of the ghosts now. José Martí felt badly that the child had no mentors or guide beside the hostile school teacher with a bad temper and limited intellect. Don Quixote was also obsessed with the education of the knight. Reading Recipes for the Perfect Knight Errant, Don Quixote told José Martí and the veterans that all knights had mentors or tutors. Most commonly, these guides would see them through all the exploits they needed to carry out in order to become full fledged knights. In this case, however, the Knight of the Mournful Countenance said firmly to his comrades that they had to believe in the mystery between man and ghost. In his view, they were definitely having an influence on Fidelito. Again José Martí went along with the knight.

Given his knowledge of chivalry, Don Quixote was very concerned with the proper education of the future knight. He was convinced now that he had a great historical role awaiting him. Both the veterans and Don Quixote believed that his future life would be linked to the liberation of the island. The ghosts would also participate in this second war of independence in some way. Since he had as yet to solve the riddle between man and ghost, the Apostle could not stipulate with any degree of accuracy just what the role of the ghosts in the pending liberation of Cuba might be. But the Apostle was certain in his heart that he and his comrades were also destined to play a role in history. Whether direct or indirect, explicit or implicit, there would be room for the comrades around the kitchen table to affect change through this magical child.

# *Chapter Six*

Playing with his Haitian friends on the hacienda, swimming in the Biran River, running down to the Bay of Nipes and jumping into the sea or climbing up the Sierra Crystal to visit the mountain people, reading to his hearts content in the presence of the ghosts. All these things that conspired to create the bucolic and idyllic life of the Caballero Nino, as the ghosts liked to call him, were about to come to an abrupt end. One night, the padrino, as he was called, both a politician and friend of Angel Castro's arrived at the hacienda. He and Angel Castro had a long talk about the education of the Castro children. The padrino could not emphasize enough that there was nothing more to be had from the local school. He suggested that Angel Castro board Fidel and Angelita at the home of the teacher of School House #15. From there they could attend La Salle Christian Brothers School. Fidelito did not wish to go anywhere. He was perfectly content on the hacienda and his time with the ghosts up in the library of José Martí's invention. He couldn't imagine life away from the Oriente countryside, the Sierra Crystal, the Biran River or the Caribbean Sea.

So imagine his horror when one morning Angel Castro loaded up the family wagon with suitcases. He took Fidelito and Angelita and put them inside the wagon beside Lina Castro. The Castros retraced the steps of the Apostle and the veterans along the dirt roads that led from the hacienda to Santiago. Arriving at Santiago at sunset after a long day's ride, Fidelito saw the tall buildings and paved streets for the first time. The buildings made a tremendous impression on him as did the wide open sea extending beyond the bay. The wagon slowly made its way from the center of Santiago up a long hill to the edge of town. Sitting on the hillside was the wooden shack belonging to Miss Hibbert. The teacher of School House #15 had moved back to Santiago out of disillusionment with her profession.

Immediately Fidelito felt out of place. He longed for the hacienda and his Haitian friends. The house was dark and dank. Water was dripping from the roof. In a small living room Fidelito noticed a large piano which took up most of the space. There were two small bedrooms and one bath. There was a tiny kitchen with an adjoining dinning room. Fidelito and Angelita both immediately took a disliking to the place. However, as compensation, the Caballero Nino thought about the new school he was to attend.

In his discussion with the padrino, Angel Castro talked specifically about Catholic schools and how they would instill discipline in the child. Angel Castro had liked what he heard. He was concerned about how wild, willful and uncontrollable Fidelito had become without any guidance or structure to his life. Angel Castro recognized all the advantages to the bucolic and idyllic life on the hacienda. He realized that his children were basically happy and content children. Angel Castro debated hard and long about sending them away from such a privileged, if not almost sacred, existence.

Fully expecting to be enrolled the following week, Fidelito was not too concerned about the sparse lifestyle of the pretentious Miss Hibbert and her sister. He was horrified that he was put into a tiny room with Angelita with no desk or any space for books. He wondered how and where he would study. Most of all during that first week, he felt this house to be a prison from which he had to escape. As the weeks passed, slowly Fidelito accepted the dreary routine of the household with all its limitations. His illusions of going to school slowly evaporated in the face of these meager circumstances. Slowly he came to realize that there would be no school and there would be no books or classmates. The child was disheartened and filled with a feeling of solitude that he had never known before. His sister Angelita seemed oblivious to the situation and satisfied for the most part with doing nothing. But it was a tragic circumstance for the bright precocious child who since birth had fascinated the ghosts.

Back on Hacienda of the Spirits, indeed the atmosphere had changed in the absence of Fidelito. His enthusiasm and boundless energy was contagious. It filled the hearts of the veterans and motivated José Martí and Don Quixote to look to greater things. Don Quixote was the first to feel that anything was wrong. He was up in the library reading books of chivalry out loud to José Martí and the veterans when suddenly the knight stopped in his tracks. A terribly pained look came across his countenance and he looked at his comrades. The knight then declared that they must leave the hacienda of Angel Castro's dreams and go to the Caballero Nino. The knight said that the child was in grave danger and that this history was in danger of being lost forever. José Martí looked at the knight and immediately agreed. He too felt the absence of the child poignantly. He also felt the child was somehow being kept from fulfilling his destiny. José Martí always had a deep premonition about the future. His comrades often thought him to be a kind of seer. He told the group that they must leave immediately for Santiago in order to help the Caballero Nino in his present circumstance.

Hence the ghosts set out on foot from Biran and retraced their steps to Santiago. They arrived at the outskirts of town at sunset. It took them some time to get oriented and to find the run-down home of Miss Hibbert. As it would happen, according to Cide Hamete Benengeli in his second history of the knight, the ghosts arrived at dinner time. Immediately they were struck by the squalid and meager circumstances of the two teachers. One look at Fidelito's room showed them that the child had no chance of furthering his education. Then Don Quixote and the veterans saw Fidelito and Angelita at dinner time. There was a small piece of dried fish and a tiny portion of rice and beans on their plates. Don Quixote could not believe his eyes. The situation was worse than he had imagined. José Martí concurred that this was indeed a blow to the Caballero Nino. Don Quixote remembered the importance of education for knights errant. He fell into a deep depression from which he would not emerge for sometime.

José Martí, the veterans and Don Quixote were all in agreement that they could not desert the child under these circumstances. They were at a loss, but Don Quixote reminded them that it was imperative to believe that they could have some influence on Fidelito. These tragic circumstances would impose a limit on his development. Although José Martí still had his doubts about his ability to impact the lives of mortals,. at this point in the history he was willing to suspend disbelief and try and find some kind of solution for the child. The Apostle told the knight and the veterans that they would have to develop some kind of routine that would support Fidelito and allow him to stay sane. Knowing this magical child as they did, they knew that his spirit would be broken if he did not have books and outside stimuli. Unlike Hacienda of the Spirits, where he was free to run wild, now Fidelito rarely went outside. If he did, it was only in the afternoons when the neighborhood children were out of school. There in the streets, he would see the other children buy candy. The children would tease him because he had no coins with which to buy sweets.

José Martí and the veterans turned the house upside down looking for books and other things to occupy the mind of Fidelito. It was the Caballero Nino who found a tablet with the arithmetic tables printed on the inside cover. From then on, Fidelito would practice adding, subtracting, multiplying and dividing in his mind. He also practiced writing the words he remembered from the books he had read up in the library of José Martí's invention. He practiced his penmanship. He wrote his name over and over along with passages from books he could remember. His heart ached for books to read. He felt like someone had cut off a limb he missed his books so. The ghosts would form a circle around Fidelito. The child would remember the lessons from the school in Biran and revert back to practicing his A,B,Cs. This really concerned José Martí because he felt like the child was being forced by his circumstances to regress rather than grow to his full potential.

Don Quixote and José Martí were beside themselves. José Martí blamed Angel and Lina Castro for not monitoring the treatment of their children. It was obvious that they were being abused. They were half starved to death, but also due to the lack of stimuli to the senses and the intellect. It was starvation on all levels. In the afternoon and into the night, the ghosts would surround the Caballero Nino wherever he might be in a circle of protection. They would feel the terrible pain of abandonment felt by the Caballero Nino. During the dreary rainy afternoons, the water dripped in from the leaky roof. José Martí would gather his comrades in a circle to discuss the present political situation of the country under the dictator Machado.

Don Quixote, on the other hand, was quick to focus on all the books of chivalry he had read out loud to the veterans. He began to evoke the exploits of the great knights of old like Amadis and Tirant lo Blanc. The ghost hoped against hope that the Caballero Nino would be reached by the mental stimulation of the phantoms. The child had absolutely no other source of encouragement. Cide Hamete Benengeli, that famous Moorish historian who wrote down all of Don Quixote's exploits, was now beginning a second history of the knight. The old Moor was of the opinion that the efforts of the phantoms were paying off. Somehow, miraculously in some fantastic fashion, the suffering and disillusionment of the Caballero Nino was alleviated somewhat by the mysterious appearance of the phantoms in Santiago.

So it went for the next two years. The veterans and Don Quixote kept doing all within their power to stimulate and encourage Fidelito in the face of the obvious neglect of his keepers. Although the ghosts made a tremendous effort to motivate the child, the tragic circumstances in which he was placed by his parents inevitably had their effect. From near starvation Fidelito grew thin and gaunt, looking very unhealthy to the ghosts. Don Quixote tried to look at the positive side, and consulting his book by Ramon Lull Recipes for the Perfect Caballero Andante, he decided that this was an exploit planned by his Maker to test his strength. Caballero Andantes often had to perform a penance and abstain from sustenance for months at a time. The knight felt that the child would learn to withstand hunger. More often than not, Fidelito would confuse hunger with an appetite. When he was hungry at night, the child assumed that he just had a large capacity for food. The ghosts knew better and continued to commiserate with Fidelito.

Then unexpectedly one afternoon Ramon showed up with some coins in his pocket. Fidelito was delighted because now he had money to buy sweets at the corner store. He was elated because he had not eaten anything to speak of in such a long time. Fidelito did everything he could to get Ramon to stay with him in Santiago, so Ramon now became a boarder at the home of the disillusioned teacher. However, things only got worse instead of better since there was now one more mouth to feed. This fact was not lost on the ghosts, who at this point were openly angry with Angel and Lina Castro for abandoning their children.

Several months passed and the abuse of the children continued on as usual in the dilapidated household of the disillusioned teachers. These ladies, despite their poverty, were full of aristocratic pretensions coming from France. There were all kinds of rules about how to hold knife and fork at the dinner table and where to place the napkin. Fidelito hated all these rules and regulations. It would only be a matter of time before he rebelled. Don Quixote concluded after awhile that this house was like the house of picaros. Seeing the meager meals provided to the children reminded him of a picaresque novel where people starved to death while maintaining their good manners.

More time passed and the only thing available to Fidelito was the table of arithmetic and the scribbling pad where he could practice his penmanship. José Martí and Don Quixote both witnessed over a two year period the effect of deprivation on the Caballero Nino. He was sad most of the time and his attempts at playing war games in his mind could not disguise his utter frustration. All the ghosts noted how these tragic circumstances had disheartened and disillusioned Fidelito. He was not the same child. He had in a very dramatic way lost his innocence. The ghosts felt a terrible frustration at not being about to ameliorate the situation. They were ever more painfully aware of the distance between man and ghost. Finally one afternoon, Lina Castro showed up unexpectedly to the dilapidated house on the hill. She took one look at Fidelito and gasped in horror. She immediately took the three children for ice cream and they all demanded several portions before they were through. Lina Castro was convinced now that her children were being starved. She gathered them all up immediately and returned with them to Hacienda of the Spirits.

Fidelito was never as blissful and exuberant as when he returned to the hacienda. He immediately went to the huts of the Haitians to see all his friends. They all embraced and were delighted with the appearance of Angel and Lina Castro's third son. So the games began. Soon the future Commandant en Jefe and his followers were riding on horseback, swimming in the Biran River, and hiking up the Sierra Crystal to see the Guajiros. They ran all the way down to the Bay of Nipes to dive into the Caribbean Sea. The Caballero Nino looked for the beautiful magical fish he saw as a child, but the fish remained invisible.

As much as he enjoyed all these things, Fidelito could not wait to get up to the library of José Martí's invention. There he recognized the many books he had read before made available to him by José Martí and the ghosts. At first it was hard for him to read because he had experienced the absence of any reading material for going on two years. However, as the weeks passed, the Caballero Nino soon regained his reading powers so that once again they mirrored the reading powers of the ghosts. He ripped through all the books he had read before and was soon on to more adult reading. José Martí was delighted at this turn of events because he was very concerned that in the absence of any real reading material, the child would lose his aptitude. The Caballero Nino to his amazement proved him wrong. At this point, Don Quixote could not resist and made sure that a copy of Amadis de Gaula was sitting on the table next to the overstuffed easy chair. As chance would have it, Fidelito came up to the library one afternoon and found the first volume of the history of this great knight. Fascinated by the illustrations of magical spells and enchantments, bubbling black lakes and crystal castles, the child started to read and did not stop until he had finished the first volume. As he read way into the night, Fidelito was more and more taken with the grandiose adventures and exploits of the famous knight.

The historians of this history, along with Cide Hamete Benengeli, tell us that Fidelito read all thirty-one volumes of Amadis in a fortnight. Nothing could tear him away from his reading. Now he was reading with the rapidity of the phantoms, comprehending and remembering everything he read with incredible powers of retention. The ghosts often sat in a circle surrounding the Caballero Nino as he read books of chivalry that summer. He divided his time between the library and his adventures to the river, mountains and sea with his brothers and the Haitians.

In the fall, much to his surprise and shock, Fidelito was whisked back to Santiago where he was again placed squarely in the middle of the same misery he had known before. Along with Angelita he was returned to the home of the disillusioned professor. This time however, he was allowed to enroll in the La Salle Christian Brothers School in first semester of first grade. He went to school each morning but was forced to return at noon for a meager lunch and then had to bear the lonely nights. Although he was much happier than he was before when he was a prisoner of the house, this time he could not stand living under the strict French norms of the household. One afternoon he exploded and insulted the teachers out loud shouting all kinds of profanities at them. The women were horrified and threatened Fidelito with making him a boarder a La Salle. They expelled the child from the house immediately.

So it was that Fidel Castro enacted in his first real great rebellion against unjust adults. Don Quixote and the ghosts were sure that this would be recorded by the historians as one of the most important exploits of his life. Standing up to the Hibberts gave him the confidence to stand up to injustice. All the ghosts saw Fidelito's rebellion as a sign of great inner strength and fortitude. According to Don Quixote, he would need plenty of strength as he went forth to meet his destiny as a full fledged Caballero Andante.

There were thirty boarders in La Salle and two hundred external students. Don Quixote concluded that Fidelito finally had the kind of education appropriate for the future knight. Still Don Quixote was always suspicious of priests. In his former life, he was victimized over and over again by various members of the church. Hence his suspicions were well founded. Fidelito was a good student but never followed the prescribed norms of his teachers. Often bored by the priests, when he would attend class he would never listen to the lecture. Then he would spend all night reading the textbook before his examination. He had a prodigious photographic memory. The ghosts took great delight in how he could memorize entire pages from his assignments and write them down verbatim on the exam paper. The priests were duly impressed by Fidelito's reading skills which they noted were well beyond his years. History was his favorite course. The child marveled at the tales about the great heroes of the Wars of Independence in his textbooks. Don Quixote was quick to recognize that like Amadis and Tirant lo Blanc, Fidelito had developed great intellectual and critical powers at an early age. The knight felt that Fidelito was striking the right balance between being active and contemplative, one of the prime requirements of any knight.

He was quick to excel in sports including basketball, baseball and soccer. The La Salle school had many programs to make sure the students could develop their physical skills and attributes. In addition to sports, there were weekly outings to the foothills of the Sierra Maestra. There, due to his experience climbing the Sierra Crystal, the Caballero Nino out climbed all his classmates and always arrived first to the top of the Sierra. Fidelito quickly gave the ghosts the impression that he had to excel in everything. Despite the abuses of the ignorant teachers and the priests he had developed a keen sense of competition. Don Quixote noted that like all great Caballero Andantes, this novice knight was both active and contemplative just as the Recipe for the Perfect Caballero Andante stipulated.

In the third grade Fidelito, now eight years old, was joined by his brothers Ramon, now ten, and Raúl, now four. The three of them together made quite a reputation for themselves as troublemakers. Often they were the recipients of corporal punishment. Fidelito grew to hate many of the priests who hit the children. One evening after an outing away from the school, Fidelito got into a fight with a classmate who was a pet of the priest leading the group. When he went to chapel later than evening, the Caballero Nino was greeted by the priest who asked why he had gotten into a fight. Without giving him a chance to respond, the priest whacked Fidelito across the cheek causing tremendous humiliation in front of all the other students. Then he hit the child across the other cheek.

Fidelito was in a complete daze and did not recover for several hours. Later that semester, Fidelito was arguing over first position in the lineup to pitch in baseball. This same priest came along and hit Fidelito on the head just because he wanted to be first in line. As the ghosts and all his classmates looked on, the eight year old child instinctually had the courage to hit the priest back with his fists. Don Quixote, José Martí and the veterans were quick to note the decisive nature of the event. Of course the knight characterized it as a formative event in the life of the novice knight. They were right. Cide Hamete recorded the event exactly as it happened. The old Moor stipulated that it was one of the most important exploits of the Caballero Nino's childhood in terms of standing up to injustice. Fidelito, despite his instinctive rebelliousness, also had a sense of order in his studies. Despite the reports that he and his brothers were the biggest bullies to ever grace La Salle, the child did well in his courses. He had He had prodigious reading skills which were recognized by the priests and put to good use in all his classes.

All during the school year, despite his interest in his classes, classmates, and sports, Fidel Castro longed for the life on Hacienda of the Spirits. So did the ghosts. Although the veterans and Don Quixote accompanied Fidelito throughout the school months, they too longed for the idyllic life on the hacienda of Angel Castro's dreams. So ghost and child were thrilled to be returning home. Angel and Lina Castro piled all the belongings of the three children into the wagon and drove all the way to Biran following the dirt roads back to the hacienda.

Within the first week of his arrival home, Fidelito had explored all corners of the hacienda. He stopped by the bakery for his usual bun. Then he grabbed his favorite horse and rode through the perfect circle of sugarcane watching the Haitians cut cane. According to Don Quixote, who accompanied him everywhere, the Caballero Nino organized all his Haitian friends along with Ramon and Raúl into all kinds of novice exploits. The knight witnessed the children walk in single file to the Biran River and up into the Sierra Crystal with the tiny Comandante en Jefe leading the pack. He was absolutely certain that these adventures were crucial to his development as a famous knight. The child's interest and love of nature and especially his love of climbing mountains would hold him in good stead in the future. As he passed the summer, there was talk at home about not sending the Castro brothers back to La Salle. Fidelito was horrified. As much as he abhorred some of the practices of the priests, he recognized the value of an education.

Fidelito was determined not to give in to Angel Castro's whim. The child felt that he and his brothers were treated unfairly at La Salle. So did the phantoms. José Martí felt tremendously frustrated at not being able to talk to Angel Castro about the education of his son. Máximo Gómez, Calixto García and Antonio Maceo felt the same frustration. Ramon did not care because he preferred to spend his time on the hacienda working alongside Angel Castro on the perfect circle of sugarcane. The question of whether or not he would return to school was up in the air for most of the summer. Fidelito was uneasy but prepared to battle to the bitter end for the right to continue his education. Don Quixote was enormously pleased because he recognized education as the right of knights.

Meanwhile as in previous summers, Fidelito carried out all kinds of exploits with his Haitian friends to the amazement of Don Quixote and the ghosts. He also read to his heart's content all kinds of books in the magical library up in the attic. He would disappear for days reading all the books which José Martí provided him. Meanwhile, Don Quixote continued to make available all the books of chivalry ever published in Spanish and Portuguese. While he liked other kinds of books, Fidelito was developing a real taste for those books of chivalry. In emulation of Don Quixote, the child would pore through the thirty or so volumes dedicated to the exploits of this or that knight without batting an eyelash. He was hooked on all the fantastical and magical spells and enchantments, as well as all the proves or challenges which had to be met by each knight.

Finally, after several weeks up in the library with no explanation, Angel Castro fetched his son away from his books and took him down to the room below the house on stilts where he kept accounts. There he tried to instill in the child the need to learn how to keep the books. Fidelito couldn't have been less interested. He feigned as if he understood and cared about his father's explanations but all the while he was thinking about the magical exploits he had just read about up in Amadis.

Up to now Angel Castro had put up with his son but had fought relentlessly to instill a sense of hard Galician discipline. But Fidelito grew tall well beyond his years. He filled out early so that at age nine, he looked as if he were approaching his teens. Angel Castro had more and more trouble controlling his behavior. While he admired him there was a certain battle of wills between the two which came to a head at the end of the summer. Fidelito was determined to continue his education. All the ghosts were in agreement, and especially José Martí who now saw the child as potentially a great liberator of men. Although he had no idea what the future might bring this child, he hoped that it would have something to do with the independence of Cuba. The Apostle was quick to tell the veterans that it was really too early to tell whether or not Fidelito would become a great leader. However the Apostle was hopeful.

In time Angel Castro dug in his heels and declared that Fidelito would not go back to La Salle. The Caballero Nino took matters in his own hands by convincing Lina Castro that he would burn down the house if he was not allowed to go back to La Salle. Angel Castro was at his wits end. Lina Castro encouraged him to let the child go. Angel Castro held out for several weeks. Then his old and trusted political friend appeared one evening at dinner. The father of the future Comandante en Jefe was evidently very frustrated by the willful nature of his son. He was sufficiently frightened to believe the child capable of actually burning down the house. The padrino suggested that Fidelito needed discipline. The kind of discipline he was talking about could only be incurred by sending him to study with the Jesuits at the school for the rich called Colegio Dolores. So right then and there it was settled to the ghost's delight. Don Quixote again signaled the historians that this was a significant event in Fidelito's life and one which was certainly going to be recorded as an event that would shape his future.

Not unlike his first experience in Santiago, Fidelito was enrolled as a day student in Colegio Dolores. He lived with a merchant not far from the school, which was located in the center of town next to the port. Fidelito was not used to the high academic standards and discipline of the Jesuits.

He admired these Spanish Jesuits for knowing how to inculcate a deep sense of personal honor. Don Quixote was of the opinion that they would shape Fidelito's character in ways consistent with becoming a knight.

The curriculum of the Jesuits was deeply humanistic and included the sciences as well as the humanities. Fidelito immediately showed his skills in reading and writing. He also stuck out from the other students in terms of his prodigious photographic memory. As in La Salle, throughout his time at Colegio Dolores, he was autodidactic. Although he attended classes regularly, he passively listened to the lectures of the priests. Often he would daydream and think of his adventures back on Hacienda of the Spirits. The priests were always afraid that Fidelito would not pass his exams at the end of the semester. The child always proved them wrong by doing very well. Soon he grabbed the attention of his classmates as he excelled in sports like basketball, baseball and boxing. He was the hero of the school due to his tremendous athletic prowess and abilities. Fidel Castro now took all his inner anger and frustration and put it into sports. He learned great discipline from the Spanish Jesuits, whose rigorous and Spartan approach to life reminded Fidelito of Angel Castro. However, just like his experience living with the abusive teachers when he was at La Salle, Fidelito was left with the family of a local merchant who lived near the school. Each afternoon when Fidelito came home and wanted to go out to play with the rest of the children in the neighborhood, the merchant would lock him up in his room and force him to finish his studies.

Fidel hated this household as much as he hated the Hibbert's house. He would spend the afternoons and evenings shut up in his room dreaming of great battles and remembering all the adventures and exploits he had read about in books of chivalry. He had a prodigious memory. Whether or not he actually had these books in hand did not matter. He was able to distinguish and recall each and every exploit of Amadis and compare them with the exploits of his son, Esplandian. And so the Caballero Nino spent the first semester at Colegio Dolores thinking about the exploits and proves of the great knights.

One afternoon Fidel Castro had another great rebellion and told the merchant to go to the devil. The same afternoon he was enrolled as a boarder at Dolores. Here Fidelito in the company of his fellow classmates thrived on learning and sports. He became better acquainted with the priests. One morning he met a priest who had come from Guernica Spain and survived the Civil War which was still in progress. The rest of the priests simply called him El Padre Jesuita. He appeared to be very old and walked with a cane. His weather-beaten face was full of wrinkles, and he was very thin. He lived in a small cell which looked more like a cave. The Padre Jesuita immediately took a liking to Fidelito and asked him to come and see his private library. He had brought all the great classical writers from Spain and was well versed in both Greek and Latin literature which he read in the original. Fidelito was absolutely enchanted with his new friend. Often his classmates made fun of him because they were from Santiago's aristocracy and thought Fidelito was a country bumpkin. This would not be the first time that Fidelito would be subjected to such class prejudice. Therefore, being taken under the wing of this distinguished priest made up for whatever suffering Fidelito had to endure at the hands of his classmates.

Soon after they met, Fidelito learned to his great delight that the Padre Jesuita was a great fan of books of chivalry and also well versed in the exploits of all the great knights of old. The two of them passed many evenings discussing and debating the merits of one Caballero Andante compared with another. Both agreed that Amadis de Gaula was a far superior knight compared to his son and that Tirant lo Blanc was much more realistic a tale than were any of the Spanish and Portuguese books of chivalry. And so, priest and child would pass many an evening in the priest's cell pouring over books and discussing ideas.

José Martí, Don Quixote and the veterans who were always around Colegio Dolores in those times. They were ecstatic about the new relationship between Fidelito and the Padre Jesuita. Don Quixote declared that finally the Caballero Nino had found a legitimate tutor. The knight was convinced that he was on his way to becoming a full-fledged knight, because they all had tutors when they were growing up. These guides would provide them with the intellectual powers needed to carry out grandiose exploits. José Martí was also satisfied about the new arrangement because he recognized the fact that the Padre Jesuita was well versed in Greek and Latin. He thought it would be a great advantage to the child to be exposed to the ideas of the classics.

Fidel read everything the Padre Jesuita gave him to read. The child had great powers of comprehension and retention, Fidelito could keep up with his regular studies and do lots of additional reading on the side. The relationships between priest and child grew deeper and more intimate. Each one enjoyed the other's company enormously. Fidelito would often sit in his geometry class thinking about all the conversations he had had with the Padre Jesuita as of late. Often they would speak of the power of ideas. The old padre would talk about great battles of old like the noble Spartans who had died holding back the Persians at Thermopylae. The two became inseparable as they never tired of discussing books. Don Quixote and José Martí were delighted as they followed the Padre Jesuita and his effect on the child. He was privileged to have such a mentor at such a young age.

Fidelito was also blessed with superior intelligence and imagination. It seemed no book now was beyond his grasp except certain books of philosophy which were way too theoretical. The Padre Jesuita was always pushing the limits of the child's intellect and imagination by providing him with books beyond his years. Fidelito especially liked the literature of the Spanish Civil War. Fidelito loved the poetry of García Lorca and Antonio Machado. He did not understand it all, but he understood enough to enjoy this wonderful poetry. He always asked about the words and ideas he didn't comprehend. The Caballero Nino had a fascination with words and language from the earliest of times. One evening when the Caballero Nino visited el Padre Jesuita in his cell, he caught the old priest holding a large book with a green leather cover. The Padre Jesuita opened the book and started to read the preface. The preface told of an elderly man obsessed with reading books of chivalry. The scene was described by the author, one talented ancient Spanish Moor. He wrote down each and every adventure about the old hidalgo who wanted to resurrect the age of chivalry. The name of the old hidalgo was Don Quixote de la Mancha.

The Padre Jesuita opened the tattered old tome and started reading out loud to the Caballero Nino. He read the episode of how the old knight, well past his prime, spent his days and nights locked up in his library reading those ancient books of chivalry. It seemed that he needed neither sleep nor sustenance. His life was nothing if not feeding on those ancient books of old. Finally he took leave of his hacienda and went in search of adventure. By the time the Padre Jesuita found the old caballero andante asking a local innkeeper to dub him a knight, Don Quixote was convinced that he was about to embark on a series of exploits which would bring back chivalry.

As those ancient knights tried to bring back the era of chivalry, they all failed one after another. Cide Hamete Benengeli, the knight's author, believed whole heartedly that his hero would succeed where others had failed or die in the trying. Never in all his years had el Padre Jesuita seen a person take to a book like Fidel Castro took to the History of Don Quixote. Soon he was reading the large tome over and over. The Padre Jesuita witnessed how the Caballero Nino now carried the large green tome with him wherever he went. In his classes he read about Don Quixote mistaking windmills for giants and other such entertaining episodes where the knight confused fact and fiction. He laughed at how the knight took common kitchen maids for high born princesses and common innkeepers for high born princes. By the time the Caballero Nino reached the middle of the book, he could plainly see that Don Quixote believed beyond a doubt that he was well on his way to bringing back the age of chivalry.

The Padre Jesuita saw how much the Caballero Nino identified with Don Quixote. The old priest saw how much Fidelito hoped that one day he would proved worthy enough to carry out the knight's dream of returning chivalry to the world. The Padre Jesuita saw that in many respects they were a carbon copy of each other. Never had he seen such rapport between mortal and ghost. The old priest was quite disturbed at just how much time the Caballero Nino spent reading and rereading all the adventures. In no time he had memorized the entire collection of exploits recorded by that famous Moorish historian, Cide Hamete Benengeli.

Soon Fidelito was ignoring the lessons provided by the priests in class and secretly fingering his way through Don Quixote's adventures. Why, the child forgot all his lessons in the interest of memorizing the adventures of the knight. The Padre finally took the History of Don Quixote away from the Caballero Nino. Fidelito was forced to return to the books assigned him by his teachers and pay attention in class. However as that truthful Moorish historian has noted, all the Caballero Nino did in class was to daydream about Don Quixote along with those other knights of old whose adventures were already engraved in his memory. Meanwhile, while all those events occurred concerning Fidel Castro's introduction to the History of Don Quixote, the phantom could not believe how much the Caballero Nino was enthralled in this book. Never, neither alive nor dead, did the ghost think a child could take such a strong liking to Don Quixote.

Don Quixote felt more alive than ever when the old Padre Jesuita and the Caballero Nino read all the knight's adventures out loud until the wee hours of the morning. José Martí and the other veterans from the Wars of Independence were amazed but delighted to see the love affair between the Caballero Nino and Don Quixote. José Martí then told the ghosts, including the ghost of Don Quixote, that the old knight and the child were locked at the hip.

José Martí, Don Quixote and the veterans felt that the child was now in good hands and well on his way to fulfilling his potential. José Martí had more and more hope for Fidelito as time passed by. The ghosts were delighted when he studied the great heroes of the Wars of Independence.

Fidelito seemed well familiar with the character of the veterans and enjoyed studying their writings. He studied their strategies in battle as well as the great battles themselves. He was intrigued by guerrilla warfare and read as much as he could on the topic, taking books out of the school library.

The priests at Colegio Dolores did not fail to note the tremendous intellectual curiosity and discipline Fidelito brought to all his studies. Equally disciplined in terms of his physical prowess, Fidelito was to excel in the outings to the foothills of the Sierra Maestra where he climbed El Cobre and El Gran Piedra. He was named Head of the Explorers which was a great honor because the group was comprised of the most athletic members of the school, all of whom followed Fidel Castro up into the foothills of the Sierra Maestra. These sojourns would stand him in good stead in later life.

José Martí remembered passing down through these same foothills shortly after awakening from death, where the Explorers crossed swollen rivers and streams and made their way through the jungle just as Fidel Castro would do many years later up in the Sierra Maestra. Of course Don Quixote was convinced that these trips up to El Cobre and El Gran Piedra, as well as to the foothills of the Sierra Maestra, were adventures which held great significance for the future knight. He was forced to endure physical challenges to test both his mental and physical endurance. He excelled in both ways. The priests accompanying the Explorers were all proud of the strength of character of Fidel Castro. Once he had set a goal, he never wavered and would follow through to the end. The priests noted that Fidelito had a great personal sense of honor. He would take responsibility for the wellbeing of his small comrades on these outings.

Often the veterans and Don Quixote would go on an outing with Fidelito and the Explorers. They would take the bus from school to the base camp where there were tents set up to sleep in. The future Comandante en Jefe would organize the boys into small work groups and assign them various tasks such as collecting wood for the fire, setting up tents and cooking dinner. At first light, Fidelito was up and calling all his classmates to attention. In single file they left for the foothills of the Sierra Maestra where they were followed by the phantoms.

Fidelito seemed to know all the paths to follow. He knew how to forge swollen rivers and to make his way through dense jungle. Often the boys, in single file with the Caballero Nino at the head, would pass through the same Guajiro villages that José Martí passed through on his way to Santiago shortly after awakening from death. These same jungles were also familiar to the veterans because here they had engaged in guerilla warfare against the Spanish Regiments. Now el Caballero Nino was organizing his friends into little armies that would do battle with each other in the jungle. Their only weapons were their slingshots. The veterans were fascinated because obviously Fidelito's reading about guerilla warfare had paid off. The children were involved in hiding from each other and in looking to see when they could take a shot at a classmate.

José Martí was delirious as he observed these children's games which after a while did not appear to be games but the real thing. The ghosts and the Explorers were dressed in their Mambise uniforms or their military fatigues. As they made their way down the Sierra, the veterans grew sad. For a while it seemed as if they were back on the battlefield and living through the many battles of their former lives. The exploit proved so exhilarating to the phantoms who had participated in the guerrilla war games of Fidelito. They often wished for a repeat performance by the tiny Comandante en Jefe. Now at the end of his fifth year of school he was feeling for the first time that he was in control of his destiny. He was no longer at the mercy of adults who through cruelty or ignorance could have a negative influence on his life.

Back on Hacienda of the Spirits after his fifth year of school, the jungles of the Sierra Crystal looked exactly like those enchanted lands described in books of chivalry. As far as Fidelito was concerned, he and his small comrades where undertaking some great exploit that would certainly be recorded in the history books. They trekked through the jungles and across rivers and streams to the villages of the Guajiros. Fidelito also thought of the exploits in Amadis and Tirant lo Blanc through similar jungles. Fidelito would tell tales of the knights of old to his Haitian comrades. They would all sit on the ground in a circle listening intently to his every word. The ghosts would join the circle and Don Quixote would sit next to the Comandante en Jefe and correct him as he described the most famous exploits of the knights of old. The Haitian children remained mesmerized by these magical tales of adventure and couldn't wait for the tiny leader of children to continue with his stories.

So these oral tales of chivalry were also spread among the mountain children as they too often joined the circle. José Martí was absolutely amazed how the child was able to translate what he had read in what were after all adult books of chivalry into oral tales that children without any formal education could understand. It was there and then that summer that José Martí and the veterans noticed that Fidelito would make a marvelous teacher. He was so patient in explaining all the battles of old to the children up in those magical green and verdant mountains, surrounded by jungle noises and the sounds of the Guajiros. Whenever there was a question, the future Comandante en Jefe would patiently explain the answer in terms these uneducated children could understand. He had a real knack for connecting with humble poor people of the countryside, a fact that was not lost to the ghosts.

As the tiny Comandante en Jefe recreated the most famous exploits of the great knights, he thought about the social injustices on the hacienda. The poor living conditions of his comrades disturbed him more and more as he grew older. He developed a full blown social consciousness by age nine. Don Quixote and the veterans were amazed at how vividly and dramatically Fidelito portrayed the magical adventures of the knights of old. With his unique turn of phrase he could render them in the greatest detail imaginable. The knight could not believe his ears sometimes and even suspected that Fidelito was changing around events just to make them more interesting.

José Martí already noticed the makings of a great artist. One afternoon, the Caballero Nino called all the Haitian children up to the library. There he had them sit in a circle like the ghosts had always done. Then the future Comandante en Jefe started to read the true History of Don Quixote to the Haitian children. He would always stop to explain any adventure the children could not understand without his help. Within a week the Caballero had finished the book and already began reading the book for a second time. Before the summer ended, Fidel Castro had read Don Quixote's history to the Haitian children, and the ghosts who were always present at these readings were thankful to have the chance to get to know their favorite knight even better. The Caballero Nino always was sad when he reached the end of the book which found Don Quixote on his death bed. All the ghosts and especially Don Quixote mourned the loss of their hero. They felt extremely disappointed that he did not achieve his mission of bringing back the age of chivalry. According to Cide Hamate Benengeli, the knight had too many enemies in the form of giants and other unsightly beasts waiting to do him in. Their sole purpose in life was to destroy any hope that he might have of bringing back chivalry to the world. Fidel Castro in reading the tale out loud to the small Haitian children realized just how far the enemies of chivalry would go to defame and malign Don Quixote.

Fidel Castro continued that summer between fifth and sixth grades at Colegio Dolores both out in nature conducting his first exploits and the library in the attic. He was reading all kinds of books that summer. The historians tell us that he was capable of reading almost anything the ghosts put into his hands. He spent so much time up in the library that Angel Castro had to come up and drag him downstairs to work on the accounts. Fidel Castro hated these times with Angel Castro and developed a hatred of his authority in the household. He was growing fast and filling out and was almost as tall as Angel Castro.

During that summer, Lina Castro took on a cook for the household. After one meal the ghosts fell into a deep depression. The meals were terrible. Fidelito would often go off to the huts of the Haitians to eat corn cooked on the open fires. Lina Castro was glad to have someone to keep the coffee coming and keep the pot of rice and beans, or Moors and Christians, boiling.

It was the summer of 1938 and Angel Castro received several newspapers from as far as Havana in the mail. Each day the old Spanish cook would go to the post office to retrieve the papers. Then, knowing about Fidelito's reading powers at age ten and how advanced he was for his age, he would ask the child to read articles from El Mundo, El Pais, and Diario de la Marina. Fidelito would read all about the great battles of the war in Spain that summer. Every week the papers would arrive and the child would dutifully read all the articles requested by the Spanish cook. The ghosts listened in, especially Don Quixote as it was his beloved Spain that was being torn apart by a bloody civil war. The old Spanish cook was very grateful to Fidelito and tried to make the future Comandante en Jefe and his comrades some sweets. They all turned out so badly that the children could not eat them and escaped to the porch outside.

Fidelito climbed up on Carlos Manuel de Cespedes and interrupted his cigar smoking. And so the summer past, Fidelito was up in the library reading books of chivalry to his heart's content. Angel Castro was fuming at not being able to control his son's behavior. No matter, as Fidel Castro was on his way to becoming an authentic true-to-life knight according to Don Quixote. The knight never ceased consulting Ramon Lull's The Perfect Knight Errant just to make sure Fidelito was on the right track.

Fidelito returned to Colegio Dolores for his sixth year. Immediately he went to the cell of the Padre Jesuita. Student and mentor embraced for a very long time. They spoke of all the books of chivalry which the Caballero Nino had read during the summer. Fidelito continued to be self-taught, doing his assignments but never on time and leaving everything for the last minute. Then he would bring his prodigious memory to bear on learning the lessons. The future Comandante en Jefe continued to seek out the company of the Padre Jesuita who proceeded to tell the child more about the Spanish Civil War. The old priest was a Republican, as was the old Spanish cook back on the hacienda. The freedom seeking anarchists were most often the topic of conversation. Together they started to reread the History of Don Quixote which the Padre Jesuita had gifted the hijo prodigo. The Padre Jesuita was amazed at how at each reading the child understood the tale as if he were an adult. Nowhere was it more clear than in these joint readings of the manuscript by that ancient Moor. By this time Fidel Castro had almost memorized the entire book, reciting adventures and exploits recorded by the ancient historian.

Fidelito also continued to go on outings with the Explorers. He always lead his comrades on challenging and exhilarating hikes up the Sierra Maestra just as he would do many years later with the revolutionary guerrilla forces. These many trips to the mountains throughout the school year proved to be a great preparation for the challenges that Fidelito would have to meet in later life. Don Quixote and the veterans were also convinced that these hikes up the Sierra Maestra were training missions for the grandiose exploits Fidelito would undertake to bring social justice and national independence to Cuba. The ghosts would always go with Fidelito and his comrades and would enjoy the guerilla war games played by the children. These games seemed so real to the ghosts that José Martí took them to be fact, not fiction. He was sure, as was Don Quixote, that the historians would record all these events faithfully and accurately.

Fidelito was particularly serious in his studies during his sixth year. He was a thoughtful student of catechism and faithfully read both the old and new testaments. His interest in the bible was more historical than theological. He liked the legends of wars and battles such as Joshua's destruction of the walls of Jericho or Samson's bringing down the temple with his bare hands. He would often discuss the bible with the Padre Jesuita. Another reason why the Padre Jesuita and Fidelito were such close friends is that Colegio Dolores, like Colegio La Salle, was populated by children of the local aristocracy. They looked at Fidelito as socially inferior. However, Fidelito more than made up for whatever faults his classmates may have wished to find in him through his tremendous intellectual prowess and incredible physical abilities. No one could challenge him when it came to reading and writing. One afternoon in study hall Fidelito wrote President Roosevelt of the United States. He told him he was an admirer and asked the President to send him a ten dollar bill. When he got a response, all the priests were surprised. The letter from the President thanked Fidelito for his sentiments but told him that sadly it was not possible to send the ten dollars. Fidelito was very disappointed.

Fidel Castro was physically mature beyond his years and always had an imposing and charismatic presence. If not liked, then he certainly earned the respect of all his comrades at Dolores. By this time the Padre Jesuita, like the ghosts, believed that Fidelito had a specific destiny related to the liberation of Cuba. The future Comandante often discussed the national political situation with the old priest who had vast experience in this area. His opinions were respected by all the other priests who often came to him for guidance. Don Quixote and José Martí were of the opinion that the Padre Jesuita was a kind of link between ghost and mortal. The knight was convinced that the old priest knew of the presence of the phantoms and in fact would be coming their way soon. Colegio Dolores was close to the port of Santiago. Often Fidelito would walk down to the bay and talk to the local fishermen. He was enchanted by their stories of fighting fish on the open seas. Fidel Castro's love and trust of the sea would follow him throughout his lifetime.

When he was fifteen, Fidel Castro completed his studies at the Colegio Dolores. He returned as usual jubilant about the fact that he had an entire summer to spend reading up in the library of José Martí's invention. He also looked forward equally to organizing exploits for his Haitian friends and Ramon and Raúl. Again all the small comrades headed out to river, mountains, and sea. Fidelito also had a need for solitude. Usually he would go up to the library and read. But often he would go down to the Bay of Nipes and walk on the beach, drawing circles with his toes in the sand. Then the boy would dive into the Caribbean Sea with José Martí, Don Quixote and the veterans following close behind.

Fidelito loved all the beautiful colored fish in the sea. One day he saw a school of sharks swim by and they ignored him completely. He then swam back to the beach and lay down on the soft white sand. There he dreamed of Hacienda of the Spirits. He dreamed that all the Haitians had their own piece of land to work, along with good housing and plenty of food. There was a large school where all the children attended and finished their studies. All the peasants were healthy and content. The great knights of old were protecting the perfect circle of sugarcane while the Haitians were working. Fidelito woke up and remembered his dream

As he walked back to Hacienda of the Spirits, he saw the sad social realities that surrounded him since birth. There were peasants working all day in order to buy food at the company store. Each day these workers went more and more into debt. This was the feudal system that Fidel Castro was born into and which he abhorred since early childhood. Some Haitian children ran towards him and embraced the future Comandante en Jefe. Always ripe for an adventure, Fidelito and his gang all ran down to the Biran River and jumped in for a swim. The ghosts followed the children as always, and all the veterans took off their uniforms and bathed in the river. José Martí and Don Quixote looked on a bit surprised. They appeared to be more modest than the other phantoms.

Fidelito was growing tall and although he was thin, he was very strong and always eager to show his physical prowess. After reading about the exploits of Amadis and his son Esplandian in strange enchanted lands, Fidelito would often take his horse and ride way up into the jungles of the Sierra Crystal. There he would always look for the Guajira whom he fancied, but she always outsmarted him. However, one afternoon, she appeared deep in the jungle bathing in a pool under a waterfall. Fidelito had never seen anyone so beautiful. He tried to join her but she chastised him, telling him to go away. She said he did not belong there. Sad and disillusioned Fidel Castro left the beautiful Guajira and reluctantly returned down the mountain side to the hacienda of Angel Castro's dreams.

Later that summer, he remembered his dream about a just Hacienda of the Spirits. The realities of feudalism hit home hard as he observed boys and girls in the fields cutting cane from morning to night with no future in sight. In early August, Fidelito organized the Haitian Children and Raúl and Ramon into a small band to surround the perfect circle of sugarcane. Fidelito held up a sign he made which said, 'Your Land

Awaits You.' The ghosts were duly impressed. They were very familiar with Fidelito's rebellious and willful nature. Nothing would have come as a surprise to the ghosts or to Angel and Lina Castro. Angel Castro was at his wits end and he had no idea what to do with his son. Thus it was that Fidelito passed another idyllic summer on the hacienda of Angel Castro's dreams.

That summer, like so many summers before, Fidel took advantage of his free time and took to rereading all the books of chivalry he could get his hands on. He read all thirty-four volumes of the adventures of the greatest Spanish knight, Amadis de Gaula Then Fidelito decided to read all thirty-three volumes devoted to recording the exploits of Esplandian, son of Amadis. That summer on the Hacienda of the Spirits, the ghosts followed the reading of the Caballero Nino.

After reading dozens of books of chivalry, José Martí concluded that all in all over the years, Fidel Castro had read more books of chivalry than Don Quixote. When Don Quixote heard this remark by the Apostle, a mournful and sad look spread across his countenance. Never in all his days dead or alive did he expect anyone to surpass him in the reading of books of chivalry. The knight was completely taken aback and left speechless. José Martí and the veterans were terribly amused but did not dare show their laughter to Don Quixote.

# Chapter Seven

There was a terrible commotion in the household that summer among the Castros and the ghosts. The future of Fidelito had yet to be decided. Angel Castro was more troubled than ever about him. His other sons had settled more or less on their futures. Ramon was quite content to stay on the hacienda and help Angel Castro with the perfect circle of sugarcane. Raúl was dutifully enrolled en Colegio de Dolores. What lay ahead for the future Comandante en Jefe was a mystery.

José Martí was convinced now that Fidelito had a promising future if he could just get the proper education. Don Quixote kept consulting Ramon Lull's Recipes for the Perfect Knight Errant. He declared that what Fidelito needed was discipline. However, he did not really trust priests. Given the experiences the knight had in his former life, he felt that priests were the sworn enemies of Caballero Andantes. The knight was sure that Fidelito had come as far as he could at La Salle and Dolores in Santiago. The only school that represented a step forward was Belen Preparatory School in Havana.

José Martí had made it a point to go to Havana and examine the place. He observed the priests as well as the curriculum. He returned to Hacienda of the Spirits full of enthusiasm. It so happened at the same time Fidelito was thinking about his own future. He could see the value of a Jesuit education as he had blossomed at La Salle and Dolores both in terms of his physical prowess and his intelligence. He needed a school where he would be challenged in both of these areas. Angel Castro was not at all enthusiastic at first. He thought that Fidelito should come home and work on the hacienda alongside Ramon.

Fidel Castro had other ideas the summer he turned sixteen. He insisted that he continue his schooling in Havana. Don Quixote was convinced that the power of José Martí's wishes for Fidelito had influenced him and made him stand up to Angel Castro. José Martí thought that this was one of those circumstances which was ambiguous when it came to the influences between mortal and ghost. The veterans were sure that it was José Martí who had decided the future of the Caballero Nino.

Located in Havana, Belen was where the future leaders of many Cubans were being groomed. There he would get the best Jesuit education available in Cuba. Don Quixote had his doubts about priests and somehow feared them. These Jesuits were also Spanish like the Jesuits in Colegio de Dolores. However, their standards were even higher and their expectations of students much more rigorous. José Martí was confident that Fidelito would meet this challenge. The veterans also believed that Fidelito had physical strength as well as a keen intellect. They recognized these two attributes as the requirements of a great leader. Fidelito was well on his way to playing an important role in the liberation of Cuba. Don Quixote never stopped consulting The Perfect Knight Errant. Nor did the knight leave off comparing the exploits of Fidelito up to the mountains, to the rivers and to the sea with the exploits of the most famous knights when they were young novice knights.

Don Quixote and the veterans, who were now well versed in novels of chivalry, all claimed that Fidelito was a very advanced and accomplished novice knight. His education was beyond the formal education of most knights of old. Physically he was stronger and more powerful than his predecessors. Finally he had great mental powers which allowed him to read almost anything the ghosts put in front of him and to critically evaluate what he read. Now he was ready for his biggest challenge.

There was much hustle and bustle in the library as Fidel Castro was about to leave for Belen. Fidelito took some of his favorite books including a few books of chivalry that he thought he might read in his spare time. He took the train from Santiago to Havana and thought of all the challenges awaiting him as he looked out at the countryside. The hustle and bustle of Havana overwhelmed this country bumpkin from Biran. Fidelito was tall and lanky and towered over most people. He cut an impressive figure as he moved along Havana's busy streets.

He passed through the red light district on his way from the train station to Belen. Finally, after asking directions here and there, he arrived at the entrance of the massive building. It reminded him of the buildings he had read about in his history books as there were large illustrious columns and porticos. He pushed open the big door and went inside. Immediately he was met by some priests who welcomed him and showed him to his room. In the olden days the room had served as a priest's cell. Fidelito thought about the cell of the Padre Jesuita and wished he were here.

The young man was overwhelmed by his new circumstances. Colegio Belen was much larger than either La Salle or Dolores. Here there were two hundred boarders and a thousand students in all. Fidelito had never seen such a place let alone live there. He made friends quickly when they were giving out uniforms. Belen was like Dolores in that the school stressed both academics and sports. Fidelito had excelled in both areas before as duly noted by the ghosts. He looked forward to the challenges and proves awaiting him both in class and on the playing field.

José Martí had come to Havana and studied the curriculum of these Spanish Jesuits at Belen very carefully as he wanted Fidelito to have a well rounded humanistic education. Only the rich sent their children to Belen. José Martí and the veterans were very aware that Angel and Lina Castro were wealthy but simple people who lived and worked side by side with their workers. Fidelito was not the grandson of the owner of a hacienda but rather the son. He had grown up alongside the Haitians and he had never lost his love of the land. The young men at Belen were largely from Havana's upper classes. They had a different class consciousness than Fidelito who already sided with the peasants.

José Martí was confident enough in both the physical prowess and intellectual abilities of the Caballero Nino to know that he would fare well at Belen. As usual his predictions came true. Due to his incredible determination and will, Fidel Castro excelled in all sports as he did at both La Salle and Dolores. He worked very hard to become to best pitcher on the baseball team. He also tried hard at basketball but was not as successful, becoming the team's de facto captain. He played soccer and was a good boxer, but his favorite outdoor activity of all was one he began alone in the mountains of Pinar del Rio in western Cuba.

Fidelito would leave his studies and go off by himself to hike way up into the mountains. He was of course the happiest as a young man when he was in the thick of the jungles on some kind of adventure he had created in his imagination. He would hike for a long time and live on very little food. He would think of all the histories of the famous knights of old he read and how each of them did a penance. Isolated and alone, testing his own courage and will, Fidelito reveled in these long hikes up the mountains of western Cuba. He was a loner and needed a certain amount of solitude. Of course, during these times, Fidelito was not really alone. Don Quixote and the rest of the veterans went right along with him over rivers and streams. They too were in seventh heaven because they had fought as guerillas in these same mountains.

Soon after his arrival at Belen, Fidelito discovered a branch of the Explorers in Havana. These were the same Explorers he had led in Santiago. Here in the capital the group was much larger with many more members. Soon Fidelito was elected Explorer General because of his physical prowess in climbing mountains as well as his prodigious imagination. He always invented imaginative war games to play in the mountainous jungles. The veterans reveled in these games, thinking of those times in their past lives when they had prevailed as guerilla fighters against the Spanish.

One time, Fidel Castro and several of his fellow Explorers decided to climb the highest mountain in western Cuba. They mistakenly took the train south when they needed to go north. So they had to hike back three days to get to the foot of the mountain. Another two days was spent to climb to the top and come down again. Don Quixote and the veterans accompanied the boys on this five day journey and were exhausted by the end. The boys finally returned to Colegio Belen. The priests were very worried and very glad to see them.

Fidel Castro was the hero of the school. His skill at climbing mountains became legendary at Belen. All the other boys wished to imitate his adventures but very few succeeded. Fidelito had a great deal of self-confidence in this respect and felt very sure of himself whenever he was hiking up to an unreachable peak.

The Apostle recognized that this was a turning point in this veracious history. Fidel Castro's future depended on his being exposed to challenges and stimuli. He needed to grow and develop into a leader capable of changing the course of Cuban history. According to the veterans, he could not stay on the hacienda forever. He had to make his mark early in life according to Don Quixote. He had a very good start but had to continue his education. When José Martí was thinking about to which school Angel Castro should send his son he had two things in mind. He needed a place where he could keep on developing the physical prowess he had shown at La Salle and Dolores.

Fidelito was over six feet tall now and presented an imposing and charismatic figure wherever he went. He impressed both children and adults. Secondly Fidelito had such a keen mind, he needed a school that could continue to challenge his intellect. José Martí was aware that these Spanish Jesuits were rightists and pro-Franco. However, he felt that the Caballero Nino had developed such tremendous critical powers that he would not be unduly influenced by these conservative priests. Many of them were outstanding scientists and humanists.

José Martí was also tremendously impressed by the fact that the Belen curriculum followed the classical model. Fidelito would study the liberal arts or a broad range of subjects in both the sciences and the humanities. José Martí knew that the path would be difficult but that Fidelito would be equal to the challenge. Angel Castro was not so sure. He still was deeply disturbed by Fidelito's willfulness and stubbornness. Once he was determined to do something, no one could stop him. This characteristic combined with a need to always be first and the best at everything made him unique. Angel Castro resisted the idea of sending him to the Spanish

Jesuits but in the end gave in to the idea. He believed that these Jesuits would be capable of instilling great self discipline and a deep sense of personal honor which Angel Castro already possessed as a Galician.

Angel Castro was seated at the kitchen table as the veterans discussed how these Jesuits in Havana were even more demanding than the Jesuits at Dolores. The challenges that awaited Fidelito were far beyond those he had ever met. Máximo Gómez and Calixto García wondered whether or not he was up to the challenge. Antonio Maceo also had his doubts because he thought Fidelito was too willful to submit to the sometimes harsh discipline of the Jesuits.

It was with heavy heart that Angel Castro had finally consented to let his son attend Belen. One thing that convinced him was the fact that this school as opposed to the other schools did not accept students on the basis of whether or not they could afford tuition. Entrance through the portals of Belen depended on academic performance and a charismatic demeanor. Finally, shortly before his sixteenth birthday, Angel Castro decided that Fidelito would go to Havana. Fidelito was delighted when Angel Castro agreed to pay tuition and give him funds for buying books, clothes, and other expenses.

There was one more obstacle that the Caballero Nino need to overcome. In order to be accepted into the School of Oratory at Belen he had to deliver a ten minute speech that was well thought out and well presented. He had to present his first discourse to Padre Rubinos. He was sweating profusely and his knees were shaking. Nonetheless he managed to present a charismatic figure that was in full control of the situation. Padre Rubinos was duly impressed and the ghosts were ecstatic because they had tried to help the Caballero Nino prepare for his first big moment on the national stage. Fidelito had practiced the ten minute speech for hours in front of the big oval mirror in Angel and Lina Castro's boudoir with the ghosts gathered in a circle surrounding him. José Martí was confident that Fidelito would pass the oral exam. He did brilliantly to make his first mark at Belen to the sheer and utter delight of Don Quixote and the veterans.

During his first year at Belen, Fidelito had to overcome several obstacles. At first his classes were very challenging indeed. He had to study in an organized way which he did for the very first time. He soon however fell back into the bad habit of cramming at the last minute and depending on his prodigious photographic memory. His classmates were extremely impressed by his powers of concentration and ability to absorb ideas so quickly. During his first semester he started to study the Jesuit curriculum. José Martí noted the curriculum was close to the classical idea of the liberal arts, also known as the trivium and the quadrivium. Fidelito studied Spanish, rhetoric and logic along with philosophy, literature, history, mathematics, geometry and physics. At the end of the first semester he had flunked French and logic. Fidelito was horrified and had to do something to make up for his failure. He begged the priest in charge to let him take French and logic during the second semester even though he had failed to pass these courses during the first semester. The priest agreed when Fidelito promised to get one hundred percent on his final exams administered by the state.

For Fidelito, doing well in his courses was a matter of personal honor. He came through and passed the exams with one hundred percent. The ghosts were delighted. He did well in his other science and humanities courses during the first year. But he especially liked history and debating.

From the beginning of his second year, all his teachers noticed what a prodigious intellect Fidelito had developed. In the sciences he demonstrated in class the ability to solve problems that other students could not begin to understand. He also, at the age of sixteen, showed the makings of a fine speculative mind. He was often able to criticize the precepts and assumptions of the ideas of the great thinkers in his science and humanities courses. Some of the priests who were his teachers discussed among themselves what a fine analytical and theoretical mind their student exhibited in all the sciences and humanities.

It was not lost on the priests that Fidelito had the tendency to let his mind wander and that he was a bit a daydreamer. He liked to think about the lives of great soldiers of the past like Alexander the Great and Napoleon. He loved history because of the tales of great battles and military campaigns. He was fascinated by military strategies and would study Napoleon's failures and successes with equal interest. Fidel Castro also had a great interest in the Old Testament. He expressly liked the sacred history because of its fabulous content. He loved the story of Moses and the crossing of the Red Sea to the Promised Land, the destruction of the walls of Jericho by Joshua, and Jonah being swallowed by a whale.

During his third year Cuban history became one of his favorite courses. In these classes at Belen, he was again exposed to the works of José Martí. Like many of his classmates, he had read La Edad de Oro as a child. Now he read many of the Apostle's essays which discussed the interference of the United States in the affairs of Cuba. He came to fully understand that it was the gigantic del norte that had frustrated Cuba's attempt to achieve independence and social justice. Through his readings Fidelito came to distrust and hate the United States in a very conscious manner. Before reading José Martí's works, Fidelito was conscious of the effects of United Fruit on Angel Castro and the local sugarcane growers. He also understood the fact that social injustice prevailed in Cuba. Now Fidelito really did understand the history of the ghosts. José Martí and the veterans were delighted and surprised that the Caballero Nino had shown such an interest in the wars.

Don Quixote felt a bit left out, when José Martí reminded him that the Caballero Nino was still devoted to the adventures of Amadis. The Apostle claimed that Fidelito at this point knew more about books of chivalry than the knight. Don Quixote did not know whether to celebrate this fact or not. He had never had any competition before in this respect. When it came to books of chivalry even his enemies thought he knew more than anyone.

Fidelito took great pride in memorizing or picturing in his mind all the great battles of the Wars of Independence. He had a great imagination and loved the art of war no matter what the historical period. He was particularly enchanted with the guerilla strategies of the veterans. He saw the battles carried out by Antonio Maceo, Calixto García, Máximo Gómez and José Martí through the lens of the fantastical tales of the Old Testament. Fidel Castro studied all aspects of these battles and went to the school library to take out books on them not offered in class. He was especially interested in how the Mambises used guerrilla warfare as a tactic against the much larger and stronger Spanish army. The rebels had been far outnumbered by the enemy. He especially enjoyed the correspondence between the veterans where they discussed specific guerrilla strategies. He felt deeply the tragedy of José Martí's untimely death. He saw him to be a great hero on the world stage and certainly as great as the earlier heroes in history.

Every since Fidel Castro discovered the writings of the Apostle, Don Quixote talked about how José Martí was to become Fidelito's mentor and guide. The Apostle and his comrades were delighted no end at all this adulation. Don Quixote was of the opinion that the keen interest Fidelito took in José Martí's thought was a direct result of the influence of the phantoms. The knight would not accept the ambivalence José Martí felt at this point in the history towards his possible influence on the future Comandante. The Apostle pointed out to Don Quixote that the child had always shown a keen interest in military history and the great battles of the past. Hence it was only logical that he would be interested in the Wars of Independence in Cuba. Don Quixote would not be swayed. At times the knight too could be the master of oral argument. He got the Apostle and the veterans to admit that the influence between man and ghost was uncertain and ambiguous and often that influence seemed close at hand. Don Quixote was certain the historians would see things his way. José Martí wondered at the faith Don Quixote had in the influence of phantoms on mortals.

His first two years at Belen were a tremendous challenge for the future Comandante en Jefe. When he first got to Belen, Fidelito applied to be the monitor of the study hall where the boys studied at night between dinner and bedtime. This proved to be a very intelligent move on his part given his propensity to study and memorize at the last minute. Often Fidelito would stay after all the other boys left with the pretext of locking up. He would sit down and spend an entire night before an exam memorizing word for word all the assignments in the textbooks. As he had a photographic memory, he would recite a page word for word, not even omitting a hyphen. So powerful a memory did Fidelito display that he could recite verbatim all the theories in his science courses. He could recall in chronological order from memory all the Peloponnesian Wars in history class. The priests talked about his great philosophical mind and his penchant for philosophical speculation. José Martí and the veterans couldn't agree more. Don Quixote noted that Fidel Castro's intellect and imagination far exceeded the great Caballero Andantes.

One of his favorite courses at first was Spanish language and literature. When it came to understanding a literary work, the Caballero Nino only had to read it once. With his photographic memory he was fully prepared to comment on any topic related to the text. He had a wonderful Spanish teacher who saw that Fidelito had a keen literary mind and could write a better essay than any student his age. The young man reveled in the kinds of reasoning and analysis of the great philosophical thinkers stressed by the Jesuits. He loved the Spanish metaphysical poets like Jorge Manrique and Francisco de Quevedo. He loved the plays of Lope de Vega and Calderón de la Barca. He liked the arguments of Plato and Aristotle. Both his classmates and the priests noticed how the Caballero Nino dwelled on the existential questions posed by the great philosophers. The Jesuits were quick to pick up on the fact that Fidelito had a contemplative, philosophical side which must be developed. After his junior year they even thought that perhaps he might become a priest. Except for his rebellious ways, he fit the mold as far as his intellectual dynamism was concerned. He liked to dwell on philosophical problems presented by the priests and pose theoretical solutions.

In philosophy class, he would often take the role of Socrates in Plato's The Trial of Socrates. Never had the priests seen the role so well enacted by a student. The priests decided that they would present the dialogue as a student play for the rest of the students. Fidel convinced the entire school of Socrates defense and the importance of the willingness to die for an idea. The figure of Socrates enchanted Fidel Castro and would prove to have a direct impact on his future. In all his classes, Fidelito stood out as having the finest memory and greatest speculative mind of any student at Belen. Fidelito developed a thirst for knowledge going far beyond that of most of his classmates. He indeed had the reflective powers of José Martí.

Many a night the future Commandante en Jefe would sit up in the library and listen to the crickets outside, thinking about all the philosophical questions raised by the priests. At Belen more than ever, the Caballero Nino, like the Padre Jesuita before him, greatly enjoyed the contemplative side of knowledge. He was not religious but he could appreciate equally the magic of the religious tales typical of the Old Testament. Fidelito also liked the theories of the great scientists and classical philosophers. He studied the great thinkers of classical antiquity. He became more and more intrigued with universal philosophical questions, especially those for which there was no immediate answer.

Don Quixote and the veterans were very pleased at Fidelito's progress. They thought that the way his mind was developing would serve him well in a leadership role in Cuban history. Don Quixote noticed how contemplative he could be. He gave him some stories of the more spiritual knights of old whose histories were full of tales of spiritual fulfillment. Fidel Castro had shown that he was extraordinary in terms of physical strength, mental prowess and also in terms of analytical and speculative powers. Don Quixote went back to the library of José Martí's invention. He reviewed all the famous books of chivalry he had read in his former lifetime. He could not find one novice knight whose development compared with Fidelito's achievements.

From the time he was young on Hacienda of the Spirits; all the phantoms noticed Fidelito loved to talk. Even before he understood the meaning of words, he was formulating sentences and feeling the joys of language acquisition. The ghosts had a marvelous time watching his language skills grow. Of course his speaking skills were always put to good use when organizing the Haitians into adventures by the river, in the mountains or by the sea. Fidel Castro was known from the beginning of his studies at Belen as a student who got what he wanted by presenting a cogent oral argument. He was accepted into the prestigious School of Oratory due to his initial public speech in front of Padre Rubinos.

Often he would challenge his classmates to debate because he considered debating intellectual warfare. It was a matter of honor for Fidelio to win any and all debates. Fidel was attracted to art and to the glamor of public speaking. However, before he spoke, Fidelio had to overcome his shyness. Often his voice broke at the outset of an oral argument. He would practice his speeches in front of the mirror. When he became interested in his topic, he left his fear behind.

Soon Fidelito was debating so well that he won all the competitions in the school. This gave him a tremendous amount of prestige among his fellow students and the priests. He was indeed on his way to national recognition as far as his abilities went to formulate an argument, to manipulate language to his advantage, and to convince his audience of his point of view. Often in these early years at Belen, the Caballero Nino did not really care so much about what point of view he defended. Rather what was important to him was the ability to take a point of view and defend or negate the argument. By the fourth year at Belen, the Jesuits had taught Fidelito how to think so well that he could take the same idea and either defend or contradict the argument. But winning was everything to the future Comandante en Jefe. He had come from the countryside and ended up excelling beyond the wildest imagination of Angel Castro and the ghosts both in academics and sports.

During his first years at Belen, Don Quixote, José Martí and the veterans came and went. They preferred the atmosphere in the hacienda to the strict and ridged discipline of Belem. Don Quixote visited many of his classes in the sciences as well as the humanities. The knight felt that Fidelito was having his character shaped in ways consistent with the character of the perfect knight errant outlined in Ramon Lull's book. He was learning a great sense of personal honor. He was encouraged both intellectually and physically to seek self discipline. He was become more active and contemplative, which according to Ramon Lull was a prerequisite for becoming a great knight. Don Quixote was satisfied despite his suspicions about priests and their detrimental effects on Caballero Andantes. Although José Martí believed that it was the right thing for Angel Castro to have sent his son to Belen, he was also aware of the right wing philosophy of these Spanish Jesuits. He could see how their political persuasion influenced their approach to the liberal arts. However Fidelito had acquired a good amount of learning about the Spanish Civil War. Angel Castro and other Spaniards living on the hacienda sided with the Republicans. Hence he was shocked when one of his teachers coldly described the death of so many innocent partisans.

José Martí was shocked and dismayed when the priests gave the class literature on the nationalists in Spain. One priest, Padre Llorente, especially impressed Fidel Castro. He was a humanist but also against the Republican cause. While Fidel admired his incisive analytical mind, he soon learned that there was more to life than bare intelligence. The priest lacked heart and always espoused Spain's reactionary thinkers. He was a far cry from the Padre Jesuita who, after all, had both a great intellect and generous heart.

After reading all the wonderful poetry and essays by García Lorca and Antonio Machado the Caballero Nino had a hard time stomaching the lectures of these reactionary priests. Fidelito shut off the lectures from his mind and started to think of other things so as not to listen. He was, at age eighteen, a loyal Republican as were Angel Castro and the phantoms.

Belem educated Fidelito in the ways of the world. Simply being in Havana and walking through the streets of the city he learned a great deal. As he wandered on a Saturday or Sunday through Old Havana, he observed the social inequities prevalent in Cuba. There were women begging on the streets with children in their arms. There were prostitutes trying to sell themselves on street corners. He passed by the large gambling casinos on his way down to the port of Havana. The port was one of his favorite hangouts as he loved to talk with the sailors who had returned from far away exotic lands.

All that the Caballero Nino observed walking the streets of Havana reminded him of José Martí. What he saw collaborated with so much of what Martí had observed about Cuba. Martí often referred to the unequal distribution of wealth among the Cuban population. He also spoke of class warfare and the need for revolutionary armed struggle against the Cuban bourgeois supported by the Yankees. When Fidelito wandered around Havana walking the Malecón, Don Quixote and the veterans were always beside him. José Martí felt particularly close to Fidelito in those times. Fidel Castro was such a devout follower of José Martí's thinking along social and political lines that the two became inseparable. José Martí was up with Fidelito at dawn. He was with him in chapel and in all his classes. The ghost was so proud of Fidelito's ability to speak in class. The future Comandante en Jefe impressed his teachers and fellow students through his outstanding oratory on virtually any topic. He was exemplary as a public speaker during his last years at Belen. He had developed quite a reputation as such throughout the school. Often on weekends, when he wasn't wandering the streets of Havana with the phantoms trailing behind, he visited the homes of his classmates and became quite well known in upper-class social circles. Fidel Castro presented an imposing figure. He was so outstanding in sports, and he had such a way with words, that whomever he met was immediately impressed by the presence of the future Comandante en Jefe. During his second year at Belen, he was assigned to take a Spanish literature course where the principle reading was the History of Don Quixote. The students had to read this history in the original Renaissance Spanish which proved most difficult for Fidel Castro. But he muddled his way through the book and was soon reading old Spanish as well as the modern. Fidelito could see that the priest teaching the course was interested in the deeper, more philosophical questions raised by Don Quixote's author. That venerable old moor incorporated the ongoing enigma as to whether the old knight was more Platonic than Aristotelian. Fidel believed that Don Quixote placed all his faith in the world of ideas. It was after all the ideal of chivalry that enchanted the Caballero Nino. Fidelito then presented to the class a brilliant argument claiming Don Quixote was Platonic because of his steadfast belief in chivalry as a way of life. José Martí and the veterans agreed one hundred percent. The priest teaching the class was thrilled by Fidelito's argument in favor of Plato and could no waiting to tell his fellow priests.

During the summer months between the school years, Fidelito always returned to the hacienda of Angel Castro's dreams. There nothing had changed. All his Haitian friends were waiting for him. He noticed many of them now worked full time in the fields of the perfect circle of sugarcane. Still he found himself leading the Haitian children who were free up the Sierra Crystal to the villages of the Guajiros. Fidelito, who now was in full bloom adolescence, was always on the look out for that special Guajira he had known since childhood. Rarely did she appear during those summers, except when he went to the hidden pool under the jungle waterfall to see her bathing. She always looked so beautiful but he never let her know that he was there.

Fidelito spent an inordinate amount of time in the library during those summers reading the all the works of José Martí he could get his hands on. He was able to beg the priests at Belen to let him have some of the Apostle's essays to read over the summer. The magical library invented by José Martí supplied all the books Fidelito could ever want on any subject. Whatever book he wished for one day appeared on the shelves the next. This library was virtually limitless. Fidelito read many of the thinkers that he had learned about in his classes, both in the sciences and the humanities.

He spent a good amount of time reading Plato, Aristotle and other Greek and Roman thinkers. Like José Martí before him, the future Comandante en Jefe thought a great deal about the power of ideas on men. He loved the metaphor of Plato's cave as a means of making an inquiry about the nature and limits of knowledge. Fidelito was intrigued by the Greek concept of the city-state and speculated about such a concept for Cuba. He did not like the Greek idea of a slave-state. He was developing a great deal of independence as a thinker at Belen. He could absorb the good and leave the bad to one side. He read the great philosophers during those summers, including Hegel, and was fascinated by the concept of the dialectics of history.

During his senior year, Fidel Castro was named best all around collegiate athlete in Cuba. This was a great honor for Fidelito and a great boon for Colegio Belen. All his classmates were proud of him. Fidelito decided to go off on his own to the mountains to celebrate his victory. Don Quixote and the veterans as usual followed him over river and stream. He lived on nothing except herbs and grasses like the knights of old when carrying out a penance. These outings cleansed the souls of the ghosts and did the same for the Caballero Nino. During his senior year, Fidelito made it a point to keep going up the mountains in search of the highest peak.

All during his final year, Fidelito would challenge his classmates to debates. He would debate on all kinds of topics. Among his favorites was the history of the Wars of Independence in Cuba. Fidelito would come out with a perfect description of the battles of Máximo Gómez and Antonio Maceo. He had memorized all of Calixto Garcia's strategies against the Spanish. Fidelito would always know more facts than his classmates and hence he was better prepared than any of them. He debated in a highly sophisticated fashion, often imitating the rhetorical styles of the classical philosophers. The ghosts were enchanted with Fidel Castro's ability to formulate an oral argument on any topic at the drop of a hat. He had to win at all costs, and often sat up in the study hall at night, memorizing passages from the great philosophers that he could use during the competitions.

Fidel Castro made a great name for himself at Belen and was to be remembered there for many years. Looking back at the experiences, José Martí was quite satisfied that the Caballero Nino had used his time wisely at Belen. He had advanced in terms of his physical strength and endurance as well as his intellectual abilities. All the phantoms were quite satisfied that Fidelito was on his way to playing a great role in Cuban history. José Martí thought that despite all the discipline he had learned at the hands of the Jesuits, Fidel Castro remained a rebel with a cause. All through his humanistic training at Belen he had followed Cuba's political situation. There was tremendous corruption in the government. Upon leaving Belen, where the priests had taught him a strict sense of social justice, he was ready for a fight. Don Quixote thought that Belen had educated the future knight in ways consistent with tradition. In fact when compared to Amadis, Esplandian or Tirant lo Blanc, the Caballero Nino had received a much finer education than the knights errant. He had gone to school longer than any other knight, and had had much better tutors along the way. It was not lost to Don Quixote that virtually all these tutors and mentors were Spanish. Neither was this fact lost to Angel Castro who at the end of Fidelito's senior year showed that he was quite pleased with his son. He gave him a beautiful gold watch with thirteen semi-precious jewels.

Fidelito graduated with honors from Belen in the spring of 1945 and returned to the hacienda a changed man. Now he was grown up and ready to face his destiny. That summer, like so many summers before, the Caballero Nino divided his time between the library of José Martí's invention and the unparalleled beauty of nature.

By this time he had almost read everything José Martí had ever written. He loved both his poetry and his prose. Fidelito wished he could become half as good as the Apostle when it came to writing. He was equally impressed by his literary criticism. He adored his political essays and the critique of the Yankees at the center of his essays. He loved the poetry of José Martí and spent hours trying to write poems in imitation of the master. The ghosts would read these poems and wonder at the talent of the novice knight. He had a real flair with the pen that competed with his flair for the spoken word.

Early one morning Fidelito mounted his horse with Don Quixote seated comfortably behind him. The two of them headed for the Sierra Crystal and then on up the Guajiro village where they left Fidelito's big black stallion. From there they started to hike up to the highest peak. After a few days of sleeping on the ground and eating only wild fruits and berries, Fidel and the old knight from the Mancha grew weary and tired. They had to stop to rest every few minutes and it took hours to find the energy to make it to the top. Don Quixote could not have been more content because exploit could have come right out of a book of chivalry. Before all great battles, the great knights like Amadis and Tirant lo Blanc always went up deep into the mountains and lived off the land in preparation for battle. Fidelito knew full well the importance of training his men to sacrifice comfort to become a great guerrilla fighter. Here up in the isolated peaks of the Sierra Crystal, Fidel Castro hatched his plot for overthrowing the corrupt Batista Government. He and his fellow knights would fulfill the lost dream of Don Quixote. They would bring back to life that marvelous era of chivalry. In his dream society based on the values of chivalry, no one would go hungry. There would be free education for children, full employment and plenty of nutritious food for all. Don Quixote, who was lying right beside him on the ground, looked up at the stars. The old knight agreed with everything Fidelito had planned for the island. However, he realized that in the face of the vicious dictatorship, bringing back the golden era of chivalry would be difficult. Fidelito sensed the old knight's presence and was more determined than ever to make Don Quixote's lost dream come true.

# *Chapter Eight*

The summer of 1941 was both long and productive for the Caballero Nino. He spent an equal amount of time between the library up in the attic and the natural world. He again reverted to the habits and customs of his youth. He would take his favorite black stallion and head up into the high jungles of the Sierra Crystal to see the Guajiros. Whenever he was close to the Guajiros he thought about his new mission of reviving the age of chivalry. He and his companeros, along with his older brother Ramon and his younger brother Raúl, would go down to the Bay of Nipes and dive into the sea. This idyllic and bucolic life continued on into the late summer. Colegio La Salle, Colegio Dolores and Colegio Belen had had an extremely beneficial effect on Fidel Castro. Don Angel Castro was proud of his son. He wanted now to support his future education in any way possible. He noted that his son was autodidactic. He read the papers to stay abreast of current events as they affected the economics of running Hacienda of the Spirits. These things did not escape José Martí and the veterans.

With three papers arriving at the hacienda each morning, Fidelito became acutely aware of the struggle of the Spanish peasants. They had been locked within a feudal system for centuries. These working poor found their way out of poverty and ignorance through forming communes. There was real land reform for the first time in centuries. The Caballero Nino concluded that the situation in Spain at the time of the loss of the colonies was similar to that of Cuba. Both were countries where most of the people were landless.

Reading Primo de Rivera and other right-wing thinkers at Belen greatly disillusioned the Caballero Nino. These thinkers wanted Spain to turn away from modernization and away from the rest of Europe. They in essence advocated the enslavement of the working poor. They wished to live under a feudal system of land distribution that was outmoded centuries ago.

The Caballero Nino contrasted the thoughts of Primo de Rivera and others like him with the likes of Antonio Machado, Blasco Ibanez, and Miguel de Unamuno. These thinkers were on the side of socialists, communists and anarchists. During the Spanish Civil War they tried to deal with the problem of the working poor by forming collectives both in agriculture and in industry. These social experiments fascinated the Caballero Nino, and he studied their formation. Land reform was Spain's problem just as it was Cuba's biggest problem. The first social reform to be advocated by José Martí and the rest of the ghosts would be land distribution to the poor.

Perhaps the biggest influence on the future Comandante en Jefe of the Revolution was the Spanish cook. He still asked the now eighteen-year-old Fidelito to read the papers to him concerning the Spanish Civil War. Fidelito had read these papers out loud to the cook and the rest of the family often over the last six years. He was now well acquainted with all the battles and who won where and at what time. By virtue of reading these newspapers over a period of six years, Fidelito was well informed about every aspect of the civil war and truly interested in the outcome. That summer the Caballero Nino read Unamuno's poetry and prose. He loved Del Sentimiento Trágico de la Vida, the philosopher's existential treatise on death and the tragic end of the Republican cause.

José Martí and the rest of the veterans noted for future historians that Fidelito had a tremendous capacity to integrate knowledge from a wide variety of sources. He could sort through information in the newspapers and read the Spanish cook the essence of what appeared there. Don Angel Castro and Lina Castro were also autodidactic and had taught themselves to read and write. They were extremely proud of their son on so many levels. There was no longer any question that he would go to the university in the fall after his eighteenth birthday. So Fidelito spent that summer, like he had so many others, lounging around the hacienda. He spent an inordinate out on the back porch where he would sit for hours in the afternoon sun and under the occasional summer shower staring at the perfect circle of sugarcane. He was always reading books he had taken from the library up in the attic that summer. Like all summers before, the Caballero Nino reverted back to reading novels of chivalry. As he did so, José Martí, Don Quixote and the veterans followed suit. Everyone was back to reading novels of chivalry with the greatest of enthusiasm. The veterans and José Martí gathered in a circle on the floor next to the overstuffed easy chair where Don Quixote was seated reading volume after volume of the most famous exploits of Amadis de Gaula.

Don Quixote in those times could finish a volume of the knight's history in an afternoon and scrutinize and discuss all those infamous adventures and misadventures of the knight. And so it was that as June gave way to July and July gave way to August, the reader would find that Fidel Castro, for some inexplicable reason, had joined the circle of veterans. He was attentively listening to every word of the knight's latest take on Amadis de Gaula. It was obvious to those present that Don Quixote had complete command of each of those adventures and exploits. He was a veritable encyclopedia on the topic of chivalry and only became more knowledgeable in the course of this veracious history as did the future Comandante en Jefe.

Suddenly the phantoms stopped reading novels of chivalry and took to reading the Caballero Nino's only copy of the History of Don Quixote. As they gathered in a circle José Martí started to read the history out loud. All the veterans and Don Quixote were enchanted and demanded that the Apostle keep on reading. Each adventure read seemed more magical and colorful than the last. So it went throughout the rest of the summer. The veterans gathered in a reading circle along with Don Quixote, who was both surprised and delighted that these old veterans would take such an interest in his first lifetime. As José Martí read on, Don Quixote the ghost started to correct the author. The old knight claimed some of the adventures never happened in the first place, while with other exploits, Don Quixote praised the insights of Cide Hamete Benengeli.

During the course of the summer, Fidelito looked for his comrades, the Haitian children with whom he had grown up. He was sad to find that they were working alongside their parents on the perfect circle of sugarcane. Their plight was slightly better in those years immediately proceeding and during the Second World War. The prices of sugar were now guaranteed for the first time since the ghosts came to Hacienda of the Spirits. Don Angel Castro, the proud Galician who had built one of the largest feudal estates in Oriente Province, was keenly aware that his son had a brilliant future.

The historians disagree as to how it took place, but it was decided that Fidelito would study the law. He would enroll in the prestigious Law School at the University of Havana for a course of study lasting four years. The ghosts discussed the matter of his choice of careers at great length. It was agreed that he had developed great powers of persuasion. He had such abilities when it came to rendering an oral argument that Law School was the obvious choice.

That summer Fidelito often went off to explore the lands surrounding the hacienda. He frequented his old haunts like the Biran River, the Bay of Nipes, and the Sierra Crystal. He would mount his favorite stallion and wander up to the villages of the Guajiros. He would walk up from the villages to the highest peaks alone and relished the experience of being contained within nature. At these moments, the future Comandante en Jefe imagined that he was in a magical land out of a novel of chivalry. He imagined Amadis and Tirant lo Blanc riding through forests like these which were rich in green vegetation beyond what he could imagine.

How he loved the splendor of these great and verdant mountainous jungles. Little did the Caballero Nino know that years later he would find his skills at mountain climbing and exploring the jungles so useful to his survival. He walked the beach of the Bay of Nipes over and over again, drawing circles in the sand as he had when he was a child. He then dove into the aquamarine Caribbean Sea and looked for the fabulous fish of his youth. He knew something was changing.

No one was more aware of this silent transformation that summer than the ghosts. José Martí was the first to point out that Fidelito was filling out and that he was no longer so thin. The rest of the veterans and Don Quixote were delighted that Fidelito had achieved so much athletically. They felt certain that his physical prowess would hold him in good stead in the future. But it was his mental aptitude which truly amazed all these ghosts who had never left Fidelito since his birth. José Martí continued to be impressed with how much the Caballero Nino could read in an afternoon. He was ripping through books as fast as José Martí could wish them on the shelves. After books of chivalry, Fidelito started to read as much modern literature as he could get his hands on.

He read all the novels by Blasco Ibáñez and the great plays about the plight of women in the Spanish countryside by García Lorca, along with many other history books. He also loved the poetry of Lorca. But towards the close of the summer, throughout August that year, he returned to reading the works of the Apostle over and over in an attempt to understand his every word. José Martí would sit next to the Caballero Nino up in the library or out on the porch eager to help him understand his words. The other veterans stood by and laughed thinking the Apostle appeared to be more open than ever before to the possible influences between mortal and ghost.

After his eighteenth birthday, the Caballero Nino started to pack to leave for the University of Havana. He insisted that Don Angel Castro buy him a new car. Angel Castro accommodated his son's wishes by providing him with a brand new Ford. Fidelito was delighted. He first put several boxes of books in the trunk including one full of novels of chivalry. He packed his best black pinstripe suit and several fresh shirts and said his goodbyes. The veterans stayed behind but José Martí and Don Quixote could not contain their curiosity and hopped into the car as Fidelito took off for Havana. Don Quixote thought the car was a strange contraption meant to transport knights of chivalry on special adventures.

Oblivious to the ghosts, Fidelito took three days to get to Havana and learned how to drive on the way. As he entered Havana, the phantoms were mesmerized by the hustle and bustle surrounding them. Fidelito headed straight for a pension in Old Havana a friend had recommended the previous year. He had to walk up three flights of stairs where he found his room awaiting him. The place was quite large and had a balcony looking out onto the Malecon and the sea. Fidelito dumped his books onto the floor and left them in a pile.

Don Quixote and José Martí were impressed by the marvelous view of Havana. There was a staircase leading to the roof which had an even more fabulous view of the sea. All in all the phantoms felt quite comfortable in Fidelito's new home. They were however horrified at the personal habits of the Caballero Nino. Don Quixote in particular was beside himself and consulted The Perfect Knight Errant. Through reading this bible on knight errantry and from all his readings about the education of knights of old he was convinced that a sense of order was required. Fidelito exhibited none of these characteristics. The veterans continued to be upset by his apparent lack of organization. The Caballero Nino had a plan in mind. He was determined to attend all his classes and not cram at the last minute as he had so often in Belen. For the first three weeks, Fidelito went to all his classes and read all his assignments.

Meanwhile, José Martí sized up the university as a chaotic and violent place. He feared for the life of the Caballero Nino. He wished that he were mortal again so that he could protect him. Immediately Fidel Castro took an interest in both campus and national politics. He often stopped to listen at the scalinata, the famous university steps where politically minded students voiced their support for one cause or another, usually involving a critique of the government. Fidelito started to notice that his classmates in the first year of law school were dropping out. Soon there were barely any students in his classes. Sometimes the professors would fail to come to class as well. It didn't take Fidelito long to figure out that the university campus was both a chaotic and anarchistic place where indiscriminate violence ruled. He soon learned that most of the students carried guns for self protection. He found that instead of going to classes, he would spend all his time at the cafes around the campus getting to know his fellow students. He was both charismatic and charming and made friends easily. He learned about student government and during his first semester he ran to be the freshman representative from the law school. He won the election easily and soon had quite a following.

Fidel Castro then took to giving speeches on the escalinata. Slowly but surely more and more students and professors would stand and listen to his arguments about the corrupt Cuban Government. The public speaking skills he had acquired at Belen stood him in good stead now. After a few weeks the crowds swelled due to his inordinately fine abilities to present an oral argument. From the first Don Quixote and the veterans would always stand in front of Fidel when he was delivering an address on the escalinata. He reminded his audience of the ideas for social justice and national independence espoused by the Apostle. None of these things escaped Don Quixote or José Martí who followed him at all times. He gave more and more speeches on the escalinata and at Plaza Cadenas.

They were very conscious of the fact that Fidelito did not waste his time. Up in his room at the pension in Old Havana, he read all the books he could get his hands on on the history of the War of Independence. The veterans were thrilled. These books would help these old veterans connect their past lives to their lives as phantoms.

Fidelito was supremely confident he could do all the reading he liked and then at the last minute cram for his Law School classes. He was used to cramming and finished his first year of law school with flying colors. However he did not respect his professors as he had the Jesuits at Belen. He now turned his attention to other things. The university was autonomous and theoretically free from the intervention of the national police. Yet the student government was dominated by gangs. There were two major gangs who in essence controlled the students and professors. Fidelito refused to become aligned with any particular gang or organization. Rather he used his position as freshman year representative as a pulpit to deliver long harangues against the government of President Grau San Martín. He made it a point now to read all the papers and political pamphlets he could get his hands on. At first he would write out his speeches, but soon he learned to speak extemporaneously. Don Quixote and the veterans stood there listening to his every word. Fidel Castro delivered many speeches during his freshman year. In only one year he had developed quite a following as an impassioned and brilliant public speaker.

Students and faculty alike would stop to listen to his words and his impeccable rhetorical style. His Jesuit education had served the Caballero Nino well. He was eloquent and to the point. He was now drawing enormous crowds. He had the turn of mind to be able to analyze the national political climate, the corruption, the pay-offs, the gambling and prostitution, and the adherence of the Grau Government to the mandates of the Yankees. All these things the Caballero Nino articulated so well that by the end of his freshman year, he had gained some national recognition. The Grau Government and its representative gangs on campus recognized in Fidel Castro a potentially dangerous enemy. Everyday students were being killed for no reason. Fidel had a price on his head. He was in more danger speaking up on the escalinata and at

Plaza Cadenas than he ever would be later on up in the Sierra Maestra. Fidel Castro continued on with a deep existential commitment. He was disposed to paying with his own life if need be. Both José Martí and Don Quixote realized the seriousness of the situation. They followed him everywhere. Once up in his room on the third floor, they were amazed again by his lack of organization. He always wore the same black pinstripe suit and only came and went from his room to shave, bathe and change his shirt.

In his second year Fidelito got involved in the struggle for independence and social justice which was to characterize him throughout this lifetime. He was now a rising star beholden to no particular political party but rather representing a series of ideas.

At the tender age of twenty, through his own autodidactic style and his classical education, the Caballero Nino had come to believe in the power of ideas to move mortals. He was impassioned about the ideas of José Martí. In his speeches on the escalinata and at Plaza Cadenas he raised the ideas of José Martí for the audience to remember. The Apostle became his mentor and guide and this was evident from his earliest university public addresses. Fidelito began to feel that he had a role in history reserved just for him. None of these things were lost on José Martí and the ghosts who followed his every move unperceived.

Once in a while, particularly during the most difficult moments when Fidelito thought that his life was in danger, he felt that he was not alone. Certain historians are of the opinion that Fidelito could not have imagined the presence of the ghosts, while others agree that he was not far from doing so. Fidel Castro's thoughts were so aligned with José Martí's that at times the two were indistinguishable.

José Martí had noticed something significant during the Caballero Nino's time at Belen and his first year at the university, related to his giving one of his powerful speeches. The Caballero Nino actually was fearful and nervous before starting to speak. He began tentatively and slowly and was somewhat shy at first. Then once he became impassioned about his topic, the fear would disappear and would be replaced with enormous self-confidence. The strength of will that he had exhibited since childhood persisted unabated through his university career. By the end of his second year, he was one of the best known student activists. Undoubtedly through his eloquent public speeches on the escalinata and at Plaza Cardenas over these years he had achieved much attention. José Martí, Don Quixote and the veterans were pleased and astounded at the way the Caballero Nino had become involved in national politics. He had exceeded their wildest expectations. José Martí was not sure what he expected since he was beginning to believe that Fidel Castro had a great historical destiny reserved for him. Simultaneous to this thought was Don Quixote's own conviction that now the Caballero Nino was on his way to stardom. Indeed if this history had any veracity, he was destined to become a great Caballero Andante.

Don Quixote now reflected on all the books of chivalry he had read since coming back from the dead. He thought about the famous adventures of the knights of old he had ingested in his former life. Don Quixote was of the opinion that the life and times of the Caballero Nino would be the topic of inquiry of many historians, and perhaps even Cede Hamete Benengeli. As it turned out the old Moor had come back to life for that very purpose.

Don Quixote would stand out on the balcony and look out over the

Malecon staring at the Caribbean. Indeed he thought he was blessed to have come back to life. All the other veterans and José Martí felt the same way as they watched the Caballero Nino develop into an effective and convincing advocate for social justice and national independence. During his third year Fidel Castro faced the biggest crisis of his life. Many historians have noted the fact that the Caballero Nino faced numerous death threats due to his outstanding discourse on corruption. He had developed many enemies, and his life at no time before or since was in such danger.

Once he left campus and walked alone on the beach outside Havana trying to decide whether to go back to the university campus or not. The Caballero Nino did not really know the extent to which he represented a real danger to the status quo. Some sectors of the Cuban population had demonstrated against Grau San Martín. Fidel Castro had the power of the word and the word went out to all. He soon developed more and more of a following on the escalinata and at Plaza Cadenas. Alone on the beach Fidel Castro wondered whether or not to go back to the university and continue to be a visible opponent to Grau San Martín's Government. Fidelito turned within to face his existential crisis head on and with great courage. However, it was not only his courage that was so impressive. He was a young man barely twenty. He had developed many inner resources from which he could draw and in fact did draw from in moments like this one. He first remembered the Padre Jesuita at Colegio Dolores and all the ideas that he had first learned from this great mentor. In retrospect the Padre Jesuita was even more pivotal to his growth and development than he once thought.

He thought of his mentors at Belen and how he had learned so much about the power of ideas from them. Right then he thought of the figure of Socrates and his choice between life and death. Socrates seemed so relevant to the Caballero Nino at this moment. Finally he thought of the great writers of the Generation of '98, and of course José Martí who was also inspired by writers like Miguel de Unamuno, Antonio Machado, and Blasco Ibáñez. Right then the Caballero Nino thought most about how these writers challenged the spiritual degeneration of Spain after the loss of Empire. He remembered Unamuno's warnings against the paralysis of will that comes with political repression. Fidelito thought about Cuba and the lack of will on the part of the general populace which needed to be awakened because there was a will to independence just beneath the surface.

Fidel Castro went back to the university that day but he carried a fire arm due to the menace of the gangs who saw in him a person who could threaten their power. Don Quixote was never as frightened in this veracious history as he was at that moment. The danger was real. Fidelito had to move around the city from house to house, never daring to stay in one place. José Martí could see clearly now the importance of Fidelito's survival. More than ever did the Apostle feel the frustration of the limits of being a ghost. How he wished he could communicate directly with the Caballero Nino. Yet Fidelito could not have turned out more spectacularly if José Martí had written the recipe for his existence. Fidelito was pursued relentlessly by his enemies precisely because he was able to excite and inspire the crowds. His words broke through their apathy so that they would exert their will in the public arena. For Fidel Castro, life was living moment to moment much in the way prescribed by the great existentialist thinkers that he had read and grown to love.

Fidel Castro put his marvelous education use. For him there was no separation between word and deed. The more active he became, the more existential he grew in his approach to life. The contemplative side of him flowered and came to light. No one was more aware of the fact than José Martí. The phantom was convinced that Fidel Castro was born at this time and place to exercise a great role in history. José Martí and the veterans were of the mind that if he lived long enough, he would achieve great things on the national scene. The hopes of the ghosts for Fidelito rose during these university years. Although violence reigned on campus, the phantoms were used to the ensuing chaos and anarchy. They had faced such things in their former lives.

Cide Hamete Benengeli, the famous Moorish historian, was destined to write down all Don Quixote's exploits during his second lifetime. The old Moor was of the opinion that the ghosts were having considerable influence on the novice knight. Don Quixote observed that Fidel Castro had already achieved more than most novice knights. He had developed his mind and had the power to move the human spirit at an early age. He had had a much better formal education than either Amadis de Gaula or Esplandian or Tirant lo Blanc.

Don Quixote was of the opinion that José Martí and the veterans were influencing the novice knight. They were affecting Fidelito in ways they as yet did not understand but should accept on faith. José Martí found Don Quixote's faith inspiring as always and went along with him for now. Don Quixote thought that Fidel Castro was destined to have his history recorded by Cide Hamete Benengeli. He was sure that somewhere the Arab historian had risen from the dead for that very purpose. Don Quixote did not say anything to the other veterans about these thoughts. He feared they might think them too far fetched. However, the knight the remained certain in his own mind that this great historian of old would be inspired enough by the Caballero Nino and Don Quixote's own relationship with the novice knight to come back to life to write another history.

Fidel Castro was drawing the attention of many students at the escalinata at the end of his second year. But he was also the target of many bullets, which according to Cide Hamete Benengeli never hit their mark because he was under the protection of the phantoms. José Martí and Don Quixote were right by his side. José Martí wept many a tear thinking about the very real distance between mortal and ghost. The phantom was sure that Fidel Castro would be assassinated.

Finally, for a few months, Fidelito went to New York in a kind of self-imposed exile. The danger and threats to his life were so real that he had to leave Cuba. He crammed for a week for his exams at the law school and did very well. He then left for the Gigante del Norte. The ghosts of course were not far behind him and followed him all the way to Harlem. He rented a room and started to comb through bookstores in Manhattan. He was looking for books on all the topics that interested him. He was especially interested in politics and history. By this time, Fidel Castro shared to some degree the confidence that the ghosts had placed in him. He too believed it very possible and even probable that his future was tied up in the liberation of Cuba. During those short months inside the monster, Fidel Castro thought a lot about the Cuban problem and its complicated relationship with the United States.

There is no doubt that the future Comandante en Jefe had a love affair with Marx. He was so widely read that he was able to take the principles of Marx and apply them to Cuba's own unique situation. His historians have failed to grasp that the Caballero Nino had the ability to read things critically in such a way that it would add to his own sense of the world. Contrary to the opinion of those historians dedicated to defaming his image, Fidel Castro never blindly followed the precepts of those he read, and Marx was no exception. José Martí also had a love affair with Marx. The only thing that Fidelito did during those months was go to the bookstores and read, which was very fortunate as he had more challenges and adventures awaiting him in Havana.

The first thing Fidelito did when he reached Cuba was return to Hacienda of the Spirits for the summer. His presence proved to be a great relief to both Angel and Lina Castro. Both parents were well aware of the dangerous political activities of their son. Both of them had worried tremendously about him while he was at the university. Don Angel Castro begged his son to give up his role in national politics and come home and tend the perfect circle of sugarcane. Neither Fidel Castro nor Don Quixote agreed. José Martí and Don Quixote were more optimistic than ever. The Caballero Nino had survived the first two years at the university, which to them was like surviving a civil war. The government of President Grau San Martín was both corrupt and beholden to the United States. There was a terrible need for land reform. Land distribution was the greatest problem along with the control of the Cuban economy by the Yankees. No one was more aware of the social injustices and crippling colonial economy than was Don Angel Castro. He had to send his perfect circle of sugarcane off to the United Fruit Company each year. There was no alternative. The gringos controlled the whole economy.

The Caballero Nino, now twenty-one, took every advantage of his summer months to roam freely and safely about the hacienda. He still carried a sidearm. He never lost sight of the hatred of his enemies, not even during those times up in the Sierra Crystal or down by the Bay of Nipes. He then continued to dive into the sea and search for the fish of his youth. He went up into the Sierra Crystal alone on his big black stallion. He looked for the Guajira and to his delight found her in the magical pool bathing. She saw him and quickly ran off into the jungle. He never could find her. She remained a mystery to him for the rest of his life. When he was up the mountain accompanied only by Don Quixote and the veterans, he would think about the marvelous tale told by the old Moor, Cide Hamete Benengeli. Here up in the highest and most dense places on the mountain side, he would think about his secret desire to fulfill Don Quixote's dream of bringing back chivalry. He swore never to reveal his hearts desire to anyone.

When the Caballero Nino returned down the mountain he again saw the beautiful but elusive Guajira bathing in the pool close to the Guajiro village. She was as magical to him as one of those ladies in waiting out of a novel of chivalry. When he was not at the Biran River or elsewhere thinking about the elusive Guajira, the novice knight spent an inordinate amount of time reading to his hearts content up in the library. As usual he exhibited his autodidactic tendencies and read from a wide range of subjects including history, his favorite, along with agriculture which had become a more important topic of interest to him of late. He read more about the Spanish communes under the control of the revolutionary forces in the Spanish Civil War and thought a great deal about the problem of land reform in Cuba where, like Spain, there was such a problem with the landless poor. Fidelito never forgot to go and visit his friends the Haitians, even though most of them were married and had their own families by this time. Sadly they were repeating the tragic life of their ancestors.

Fidel felt this tragic sense of life deeply whenever he visited his Haitian friends. That summer he continued to read a lot of historical books including the works of Marx, Engels and Lenin. He was impressed by how much Marx and José Martí had in common. Both were on the side of the working poor and dispossessed. In one way or another, José Martí had articulated the terms of the class struggle but with a uniquely Cuban perspective. José Martí read Marx right alongside Fidel Castro with great interest. He did not believe in the fact that it was primarily the objective conditions of history that gave rise to man's revolt against oppression and injustice. Don Quixote agreed with José Martí. His past life was living proof that the objective conditions of history are what inspire men to stand up to injustice. Neither was the Caballero Nino convinced of this precept. But all in all, he was extremely moved by Marx and Lenin and the struggle of the Russian people against the Nazis. There was no doubt that the future Comandante en Jefe had a love affair with Marx, but he was so widely read that he was able to take the principles Marx espoused and apply them to Cuba's own unique historical situation. The Caballero Nino was so interested in history and especially social history that he managed to finish the complete works of the Apostle. José Martí and the veterans caught wind of his new passion and followed suit, reading and discussing the ideas of Marx in the reading circle in the library. José Martí would read Das Capital out loud many times over so that the veterans eventually grew sick and tired of hearing it.

The Caballero Nino as usual read one author passionately and with conviction and then turned his mind to other things as well. The earmarks of a classical education never left him as he was interested in everything from agriculture to poetry. He indeed was developing into a Renaissance Man. If left to his own devices he might have become a professor, an artist or a writer. Fidel Castro held the conviction that his destiny was now inextricably linked to the historical destiny of Cuba. Nonetheless he also found time to read a few books of chivalry each summer. The present summer was no exception. He picked up Amadis de Gaula and Tirant lo Blanc and remembered how much he enjoyed reading about those fantastic exploits of those knights of old. His pleasure from reading these books did not diminish when he was told they were tremendous exaggerations of the truth. The imagination of the authors and their ability to transport the reader off to magical and enchanted lands for all kinds of exotic adventures impressed him no end. Books of chivalry always took him back to his childhood where he remembered just how much he had enjoyed first reading them.

As in the case of Don Quixote, the spirit of chivalry had made such an impression on Fidel Castro that it was always to stay with him. The spirit of chivalry would inform everything he said and did for years to come. Don Quixote recognized the joy the Caballero Nino still derived from reading these books of his childhood. He shared that same delight. Whenever Fidel picked up a book of chivalry for fun, Don Quixote would do the same thing. Finally it was time to go back to the university where many challenges and exploits awaited him according to Cide Hamete Benengeli. José Martí was excited and worried. He knew the dangers that Fidelito would be facing. He was also aware of the attitude toward danger that the novice knight had developed. He had faced his own death at an early age. Fidel Castro had exceptional experiences for such a young man. The Apostle had faced death undaunted many times over in his first lifetime. He could appreciate fully the existential realities of the future Comandante en Jefe.

After summer, Fidelito returned to the old pension in Old Havana and made his way up to the third floor with all his belongings intact. He threw his books on the floor and took a shower, shaved and went out to one of the cafes nearby. There he found many of his friends who were talking about an exploit being planned at this very moment. The Caballero Nino listened attentively. One of his friends explained that there would be an expedition to Santo Domingo to overthrow the dictator Trujillo. Then they would liberate the people from one of the most oppressive governments in the Caribbean.

The Caballero Nino immediately wanted to join in this adventure and made arrangements with the people involved. He had to settle some scores with his sworn enemies. He did so successfully calling a truce with the members of the gangs. The lessons of Marx were not in vain. Fidelito was definitely now a believer in the international character of social struggle. After all, Maxim Gómez had come from the Dominican Republic to fight on the side of the revolution in Cuba. According to the historians, Maxim Gómez was present that day in the cafe. He was overjoyed that this group of Cubans, united with the Dominicans, were practically on their way to the Dominican Republic. There was a student organization of Dominican exiles in Havana. These exiles, along with a few idealistic young Cubans, were to go off to change the regime of one of the worst dictators in Caribbean history.

The group thought it was too dangerous to stay on Cuban soil since the government of Cuba was still under the control of the Yankees. Trujillo was supported by the United States. The expedition would be viewed as direct intervention in the affairs of the Gigante del Norte. Of course this would be viewed as an act of great insurrection. Fidel Castro and Don Quixote relished the thought of standing up to the Yankee imperialists. Fidel Castro was a firm believer that only through joining hands could Latin America and the Caribbean ever become independent. Don Quixote got incredibly emotional thinking that the future Comandante en Jefe was about to carry out a grandiose exploit. However the Apostle and the rest of the veterans were extremely worried. They thought this was pure adventurism and that if Fidel were killed it would mean the end of this veracious history.

The rebels went ahead anyway and so as not to remain on Cuban soil went in three small boats to Cayo Confites. It was a small key off the main island near the Bay of Nipes where Fidelito swam as a child. He knew these waters well and thank God he did. The small band of men waited there for fifty-nine days, burned by the relentless sun and bitten by mosquitoes. Finally the Yankees bore enough pressure that Grau San Martín sent a navel frigate to pick up the tiny regiment.

Most of the men gave up on overthrowing the dictator. Fidelito could not stand the thought of being taken back to Havana on a ship belonging to the very government he extolled for corruption. The ship was a ship belonging to the enemy. Fidelito and the ghosts did the only thing possible. They jumped into the shark-infested waters of the Bay of Nipes and tried to swim ashore. Luckily Fidelito was well acquainted with these waters having swum there as a youth. The official historians tell us that Fidelito swam with a semi-automatic weapon around his neck from ship to shore. However, what they don't tell us is that he was accompanied by José Martí and the veterans who often put themselves between Fidelito and the sharks. José Martí was convinced that as a phantom sharks could do him no harm and that he might well prove to be a distraction. Cide Hamete Benengeli, in describing this exploits, stipulates that the phantoms did provide Fidel Castro with protection from the sharks.

Don Quixote, who was not the best of swimmers, had a hard time keeping up. It was only with the help of Antonio Maceo who tugged him along so that he would not drown that the knight was able to come out in one piece. Don Quixote was worried that Cide Hamete would record this event. He shuddered at the thought of being caught dependent on another phantom. Finally they all reached shore and fell asleep on the beach. The knight was exhausted and still worried about how his historians would portray him in the shark-infested waters of the Bay of Nipes. José Martí and the veterans were glad that they had made it through this exploit. They hoped that Fidelito had learned his lesson when it came to adventurism. Soon they made their way back to Hacienda of the Spirits. Fidelito was welcomed with open arms by Angel and Lina Castro. Lina Castro swore that he would be killed and was amazed that he had survived. However, Fidelito was very upset because the expedition was frustrated from the start. He felt betrayed by his government and his comrades who had given in so easily to Grau San Martín's powers of persuasion. He was even more incensed and frustrated by the intervention of the United States and vowed never again to be caught unawares by the Yankees.

The Caballero Nino fell into a deep depression and revealed to the ghosts that he had become a bit of a melancholic. José Martí was concerned because he knew how dangerous it would be for the novice knight to continue to be depressed over time. Now more than ever he needed to fight back, not with the sword, although he was eager for action, but rather through the power of the spirit and the word. Fidelito used his spare time and Don Angel Castro's goodwill to write several meditations on national politics. He called for an end to corruption and an end to the influence of the United States. Through the written word and his eventual publication in several small underground newspapers, Fidelito had discovered a new medium which he would make good use of in the years to come.

He bounced back from his depression and the ghosts were well satisfied with the way he was spending his time up in the library organizing and writing down his thoughts. His mind focused on all kinds of things that had concerned the veterans most deeply, such as land reform, an end to governmental corruption and subservience to the United States, to say nothing of economic dependence, gambling, and prostitution. The ghosts were delighted that Fidelito had bounced back from failure so well. José Martí, the veterans and especially Don Quixote were no strangers to failure. Fidelito, like Don Quixote, was the object of his enemies scorn. Like Don Quixote, due to his idealism, Fidelito really took a pummeling. Yet he came out the other side with his ideals intact and like Don Quixote was even more dedicated to the cause of chivalry.

All the things on José Martí's agenda were now part of the agenda of the future Comandante en Jefe. Land reform, social justice, education, healthcare, a government for the people and by the people were all part of his childhood dream on the beach at the Bay of Nipes. Don Quixote saw no contradiction between these ideals which might now be carried out in history, and the ideals of those great chivalric knights. They too tried to bring about social justice and fight against those evil lords wishing to oppress and exploit the peasants. Knights like Amadis and Tirant lo Blanc were devoted to defending the weak and needy. Don Quixote and José Martí decided that this adventure, although a failure, was really a success in disguise. Fidelito had learned to deal with his enemies and to expect the worst from them. Yet his idealism and devotion to truth had grown tenfold. Don Quixote now was convinced that Cide Hamete Benengeli had come back from the dead to record these events and that indeed this adventure would be one that would be remembered by all his historians.

Fidelito had learned a very important lesson about the international nature of the struggle for justice stressed by both Martí and Marx. He believed even more passionately in the unification of the Caribbean states and Latin America for the purpose of standing tall against Yankee imperialism. So after a couple of weeks on the hacienda recovering from his experience on Cayo Confites, Fidelito returned to the university. He was now well into his third year. He had exams to worry about. Then there were national elections to be held in 1948 in the middle of his law school career. Fidel Castro faced the old dangers of sworn enemies continually threatening his life. Whilst Fidelito had to continue to move around Havana the ghosts continued to occupy his room on the third floor of the pension in Old Havana. All the veterans and Don Quixote turned now to José Martí for guidance and leadership. José Martí spelled it out clearly. The Caballero Nino was in grave danger. The whole history of Cuba depended on his survival. Yet the Caballero Nino did not think that far ahead. He was completely committed to the moment. The moment demanded that he face the new Auténtico candidate for President, Prio de Socorros as guilty of bribery and corruption.

About that time an event would occur that would change Fidelito's life. Eduardo Chibás, a senator, broke rank with the Auténtico party of Grau and the future president, Prio. With a small group of comrades including the young Fidel Castro, Chibás established the Partido Ortodoxo, or the Cuban People's Party. The party followed the ideas of José Martí to the letter as compared to the Auténticos. Fidel was ecstatic at the thought of being able to promote the ideals of Martí under the auspices of a new and idealistic political party. In 1948 along with Chibás, now his personal friend, Fidelito worked hard for all the Ortodoxos candidates, even traveling back to Oriente Province to campaign in small towns around Hacienda of the Spirits. José Martí and Don Quixote along with the rest of the veterans followed Fidelito on the campaign trail wherever he went. Again he proved his prowess for public discourse, giving moving speeches wherever he went. He worked tirelessly for months to make sure the Ortodoxos prevailed in the elections of 1948. The Auténtico candidate Prio won the election, however Fidelito and Eduardo Chibás continued to rally support for the ideas of José Martí related to social justice for the poor. All the while, Fidelito kept noticing certain similarities between the ideas of Marx and Martí. José Martí was enchanted with the comparison. However, he believed that his own specific ideas about national liberation were more relevant to Cuba than the ideas of Marx. Fidelito dedicated himself once more to public speaking on the escalinata steps to discredit Prio. During this period, Fidelito did not change his stance. Often he felt political repression deeply imbedded in the psyche of the people. He felt like Sisyphus rolling the stone up the mountain.

Soon he would recover his exuberant and idealistic philosophical viewpoint. His faith in José Martí and all things positive returned as did the exuberance of his childhood. No matter what they did to him, the joy of childhood would never leave him. Those closest to him or the phantoms would testify to this later on when recounting the history to Cide Hamete Benengeli.

During his fourth year at the university, the Caballero Nino heard about the student movement among certain Caribbean and Latin American states. The members planned to stage a protest at the meeting of the Organization of American States in Bogotá, Colombia. The protest coincided with the upcoming national election for the presidency of the nation. The liberal candidate, Gaitán was the favorite. Fidelito was a part of a student group that went from Cuba to Panama, Venezuela and Colombia.

Fidelito was horrified at the brothels and prostitution in the Canal Zone. In Venezuela he almost met the new left wing president, Rómulo Gallegos. In Colombia Fidel and a comrade booked into a local hotel. They were slated to meet the left wing hopeful for President, Gaitán. The meeting took place and then Gaitán was assassinated. Never had Fidelito experienced firsthand such anarchy and chaos compared to the Bogotázo. Fidelito was in the middle of one of the greatest acts of repression of the 20th century. The Caballero Nino now faced an existential challenge even more demanding than that he experienced with his own people. He was a stranger in a strange land. He did not know the cultural signals. He believed in the international nature of the struggle for social justice.

Fidelito got lost in the chaos of the enormous crowds. He ran in no special direction without the slightest idea of what was coming next.

There was a state of absolute anarchy new to the Caballero Nino. The hours passed in the wake of Gaitán's death, and Fidelito grew more scared surrounded by crowds in the streets. He never thought that he would survive the afternoon. The historians have tried to explain the fact that Fidel Castro did survive the Bogotázo. Cede Hamete Benengeli knew that without the intervention of the ghosts, Fidelito may well not have come out of this exploit in one piece.

Fidelito felt more existential angst than ever before in his life. His brush with death was closer than ever. José Martí, the veterans and Don Quixote were with him the whole way and saw firsthand all the violence. They later reported it to Cede Hamete Benengeli. The old Moor was well aware of the fact that the Caballero Nino might be killed at any moment. Up to now he had not faced moments as dangerous as these. The situation was changing moment to moment. It was hard to tell which side people were on. Afterwards Fidelito tells the tale of going to a police station and getting arms. Yet the supplies were scarce.

There was little hope for an armed uprising against the military. There were rumors of breaks in rank in the military but nothing was certain. The most likely scenario according to the future Commandante en Jefe was that the military would fire on the public, which is exactly what happened. In essence Fidelito lived through a military coup and another failed adventure. More than three thousand people were slaughtered in the streets of Bogotá. All the dreams of social justice in Colombia disappeared with the death of Gaitán. There was no organized armed struggle strong enough to overthrow the government.

Fidel Castro learned a great deal from the experience as did José Martí. The phantom had never had such a violent experience even in his past lifetime. Neither had the veterans. The whole experience made quite an impression on them. José Martí, the veterans and Don Quixote were shaken to the core. To the surprise of the historians, Don Quixote was quick to recover from the shock. The knight had adventures engineered for his demise by the Duke and the Duchess. Yet it left a terrible taste in the mouth of many members of the Organization of American States and contributed greatly towards discrediting the organization.

The Bogotázo as described by Cide Hamete was Fidelito's greatest existentialist challenge of his first lifetime. If the exploit was again a failure, it was also a great learning experience. José Martí was so relieved Fidel Castro had survived the experience that he was overjoyed. He really didn't think that he would live to tell the tale. When José Martí returned to the library on the hacienda he found the adventure recorded already by Cide Hamete Benengeli. The old Moor thought that this was an exploit worthy of being recorded with the greatest care. The Bogotázo provided lessons which would prove invaluable to the survival of the future Comandante en Jefe of the revolution. In the Bogotázo, Fidel Castro's first impulse was to act but there was nothing to be done. The situation was out of control. The military had won. Over three thousand people lay dead on the streets of Bogotá. The future Comandante en Jefe was lucky to get out when he did that night on a Cuban airliner bound for Havana.

Back at the University of Havana, on the Escalante, Fidel Castro proclaimed the government corrupted. He staged protests in front of the capital and other such symbolic monuments. He often honored the dead speaking at funeral processions that ended up on the Capitol Steps. Not only did he proclaim a new direction for Cuba but he also backed his words with a commitment to action.

From his earliest times at the university Fidelito was existentially committed to making the moment count. He lived every moment as if it were his last while still being wholly committed and positive towards revolutionary change. Fidelito's attitude towards death was mystical. Don Quixote was quick to point out to the veterans that Fidelito was on his way to becoming an exemplary knight. The most famous knights like Amadis and Tirant lo Blanc had to face death many times and at an early age. Don Quixote also emphasized the fact that Fidelito was like the knights of old who stood up against rich and powerful lords. Fidelito was fighting an enemy much more powerful than the lords had been. Don Quixote thought that like the knights of old Fidelito had many lifetimes. José Martí took solace in that thought, although he never believed in the veracity of those lying books of chivalry which had inspired Don Quixote to take up a life of knight errantry.

One event which Cide Hamete Benengeli felt compelled to recount was the defamation of the statue of José Martí in central Havana. One night some drunken American sailors stationed there climbed onto the statue and one of them urinated at its base. The Cuban people passing by were outraged. When Fidelito heard the news, he and some comrades formed a guard of honor to protect the statue. In the morning, they staged a demonstration outside the American Embassy. They hurled stones and demanded that the American sailors be handed over for trial to the Cubans. Fidelito and his friends accused the Americans of treating Cuba with arrogance and contempt.

José Martí witnessed the whole event incredulous. The phantom felt it was a very painful experience to see his image defiled by the agents of imperialism. Don Quixote and the veterans showed him all the sympathy they could muster. But he was stunned by the experience and did not get over it for several weeks.

Finally, in 1950 Fidelito graduated from the University of Havana with a degree in law. Don Angel Castro was extremely proud of his son having survived the chaos. He looked forward to having a practicing lawyer in the family to settle any land disputes. Don Angel Castro gave his son a beautiful watch with thirteen jewels which he wore for many years. Fidelito went home for the summer and again took advantage of the time to enjoy the wonderful countryside around Hacienda of the Spirits. The ghosts were delighted to be back on the hacienda. José Martí spent his time up in the library pouring over his own writings and gaining perspective on his own ideas. The veterans quickly fell back into their old routine of playing cards and drinking rum. At sunset they would all sneak a glass of rum from Don Angel Castro's liquor cabinet and join each other out on the back porch to see the yellow and orange sunset on the perfect circle of sugarcane. While he worried about their behavior, José Martí was more interested in taking advantage of this valuable time to continue his readings in the library. One afternoon, for some reason the historians never understood, José Martí put down his own writings. He then looked at the big green book with gold lettering on the desk. He had not thought of the History of Don Quixote for some time. Since Don Quixote's first appearance on the hacienda, all the print on the pages had gone blank. However, when José Martí opened the book he was surprised to see letters on the pages starting to surface as if there were another book in the making underneath. The Apostle squinted, trying to make out the words and sentences, and as he did so more words started to appear on the pages of the book. Now he started to read the book from the beginning. Much to his amazement, the book seemed to be recording the adventures of Don Quixote's second lifetime here on the hacienda of Angel Castro's dreams. Could it be, thought José Martí, that the Arab historian was writing a second history of the knight? But reading on more carefully, the Apostle could see that Cede Hamete Benengeli had recorded all the events in Fidel Castro's life up to the present moment. José Martí was surprised by the accurate description of events around Cayo Confites and the Bogotázo. The old Moor thought these exploits to be the basis for further adventures. Just then Don Quixote came up to the library and saw José Martí with the big green book in hand. Don Quixote could not contain his curiosity and peered over José Martí's shoulder in order to make out the letters on the printed page. To his amazement, all of his adventures and exploits since coming back to life were recorded with extreme accuracy.

As Don Quixote and José Martí continued to peruse the book together, they noted that some of the print would fade and then come back as they read the text. Some of the adventures would disappear while others would stay put. José Martí wondered if the author had a plan and was deciding which parts would stay and which would be eliminated. It seemed to the Apostle that this book had barely begun and was still very much in flux. Don Quixote read the text that was visible carefully. He noted the author's style, wit and turn of phrase. Immediately he recognized the author as the famous Moorish historian who had faithfully recorded the events of his first lifetime. José Martí was quick to agree with the knight that the style of this author was remarkably similar to that of Cide Hamete Benengeli. The brilliant conceits were too similar to be anyone else. As Don Quixote and José Martí read the parts of the book that were visible, they were amazed by how true to life these descriptions seemed. There was no question that this author had enormous talent.

As the two ghosts continued to read, all the print suddenly disappeared and the book was blank again. José Martí could not figure out how this could be and neither could Don Quixote. As it so happened, the rest of the veterans came up to the library. However, the book was already blank so they were not able to delight in the descriptions of their arrival on the hacienda. Nor could they enjoy the marvelous descriptions of Fidelito's formative years along with exploits like Cayo Confites or the Bogotázo. José Martí had a photographic memory so that he could recall all the adventures of the knight and the Caballero Nino recorded up to now. Because the book was divided into exploits, he believed that Cide Hamete Benengeli was intent on writing another book of chivalry. At the very least, he was trying to write another book recounting the adventures of Don Quixote. Then it occurred to the Apostle that this author was recording the exploits of Fidel Castro. José Martí was simply not sure at this point. However, the book stayed put on the table in the middle of the room. José Martí thought the better part of wisdom would be to leave the book alone for a while and see how things developed.

When the Caballero Nino came up to the library a few hours later, all the ghosts were asleep. He saw the big green tome with gold lettering on the desk and opened the book. However, there were only blank pages to greet him. The words and sentences that were visible to the ghosts were not visible to him. The Apostle awoke to find the Caballero Nino fingering the book in his hands. Fidelito somehow concluded that the words of this book, were they to become visible again, would only be visible to the ghosts. For the rest of the summer, the Caballero Nino continued to divide his time between the library and the natural world surrounding the hacienda of Angel Castro's dreams. He took his favorite black stallion and went up deep into the Sierra Crystal as if he were in search of some kind of mystery. He left his horse with the Guajiros in the village and climbed the highest peak accompanied by Don Quixote.

Nowhere was Fidelito more happy and content than when he was climbing a mountain peak. He loved to test his survival powers, and spent days without food, drinking water from a local stream. The Guajiros in the village began to worry about the Caballero Nino when he was gone for over a week. Then suddenly he returned looking stronger and more comely than ever. That summer the Caballero Nino often went up to the mountain pool where he would sometimes see the Guajira maiden bathing. He would look on too scared to greet her. Then she would inevitably disappear running into the dense jungle. Fidelito watched her disappear and then rode down the mountain beset by a certain sadness he did not understand. All the while, the Caballero Nino thought about his secret desire to bring back the era of chivalry.

Fidelito would also take his horse down to the Bay of Nipes and remember the whole Cayo Confites fiasco. He would lie down on the white sands and think about his university years for hours at a time. He was amazed that he had survived these times and wondered what dangers the future had in store. He was convinced by this time that his was no ordinary life. Often Don Quixote would join the Caballero Nino on the pristine white sands of the beach and lay down beside him.

Don Quixote was convinced that Fidelito had now completed his training as a knight. He was strong both mentally and physically and according to

Ramon Lull, had met all the requirements and then some to become a full fledged knight. During that summer, Fidelito also spent a lot of time up in the library reading Marx. He also reviewed and studied José Martí's essays. José Martí felt considerable frustration now at not being able to communicate directly with Fidel Castro who was so close and yet so far away. It made the ghost sad to think that while in some way Fidelito was very familiar already with his essays and poetry, there was no way to know him directly. José Martí also thought of the big green book often returning to it to see if he could make out any print on the pages. The print came and went and while some pages were legible others were blank.

All this seemed mysterious to José Martí who as yet could not decide whether Cide Hamete Benengeli was writing a second history of Don Quixote or the history of the Caballero Nino. This mystery would not be resolved for some time. Inevitably the Caballero Nino returned to his books of chivalry which provided a welcome respite to all the serious reading he had undertaken that summer.

Feeling relaxed and unafraid for the first time in a long time, the Caballero Nino would stretch out on the floor of the porch with a pillow to his head and reread all the books of chivalry of his youth. He read faster and faster these days, so it was easy for him to consume these books of fantasy in a single afternoon. He loved the descriptions of these knights of old fighting armies single-handedly and winning the battle. He loved the passages describing the allegiance of these knights to the ideals of social justice. Often Don Angel Castro saw him spread out on the porch reading. He would chastise him for wasting his time on these books of old. Yet he could not fault his son when it came to his intellectual development. He was more autodidactic than any of his children and the fact that Fidelito remained such an avid reader did not escape Angel Castro.

At the end of the wonderful and relaxing summer of 1950, Fidelito prepared for his return to Havana. He wanted to set up a law practice with some colleagues from the university where he could serve the needs of the poorest members of society.

Angel Castro was somewhat sympathetic but also hoped his son would find a more lucrative way of practicing law. Don Quixote, José Martí and the veterans were excited and elated by this turn of events and looked forward to taking up life again in Havana. Cide Hamete Benengeli tells us that all this time Fidelito held a secret he would tell no one. He would not even tell his closest confidant, his brother Raúl. His secret plan was to make Don Quixote's lost dream real and bring back the era of chivalry.

He wished to created the perfect chivalric society where everyone was employed or in school. The Caballero Nino also dreamed of education and housing for all. However, he did not say a word about his desire to resurrect chivalry. He made sure not to speak about his secret vow to bring back chivalry. He was convinced that if the leader of a rebel group told of the secret mission, the exploit would end in disaster.

# Chapter Nine

Fidelito had passed his summer feeling relaxed and reinvigorated after a difficult four years at the University of Havana. Yet the plans he had for the future would bring their own difficulties. He had decided with a couple of classmates to set up a law firm dedicated to helping the poverty stricken in Havana. There was no hope of his making a decent living. Fidelito was determined to continue his fight for social justice in any way he could. José Martí and Don Quixote went with him in his Ford to Havana. The rest of the veterans stayed behind on the hacienda playing cards and drinking rum. For the moment at least Máximo Gómez, Calixto García, and Antonio Maceo wanted to return to the lazy life on the hacienda. However events were to evolve in such a way that these gentlemen would inevitably be drawn back to Havana and the Caballero Nino.

Once back in Havana, Fidelito, José Martí, and Don Quixote went to the same pension where the Caballero Nino had lived during his university years. In fact, he returned to the same room on the third floor of the old pension. He and his comrades had set up offices in one of the poorest parts of Havana. Fidel Castro immediately became wrapped up in legal battles designed to defend the most defenseless. Fidelito started having money problems and could not pay the rent on time. The owner of the pension started to create problems for him. Don Quixote immediately flew into a rage. How could it be that this innkeeper was asking him for money? Then he remembered how innkeepers were the enemies of Caballero Andantes. Caballero Andantes did not carry money and were never asked to pay the rent. Don Quixote continued to be outraged as long as the innkeeper gave Fidelito trouble. Fidelito managed to evade him as he was so busy working for his clients that he practically had no time to sleep and always arrived late at night. Don Quixote and José Martí were both very impressed by Fidelito's choice of profession. They thought that for the moment he would be safer than he was at the university.

For now Fidelito seemed content to try and work within the system. He stayed active in the Partido Ortodoxo and was delighted when Eduardo Chibás decided to run for president in the elections of 1952. Fidelito spent whatever spare time he had working for Chibás. He was so excited about the future of Cuba under a decent president who followed the dictates of José Martí. The Caballero Nino decided to run for congress. He quickly became the candidate in one of the poorest areas of Havana. José Martí and Don Quixote were delighted. However both of them saw problems ahead and knew on some level that it would not be smooth sailing for the Caballero Nino. They knew that his idealism and hopes for the future would suffer. However, neither of them knew precisely how.

The two ghosts followed Fidelito around wherever he went in those days. After he decided to run for congress, José Martí felt that he again was in danger. Don Quixote agreed. Fidelito, on the other hand, just kept on plugging away confident that the future would bring something better. He was convinced that Eduardo Chibás, who after all had been a senator, would be elected president in the elections of 1952. Then the drama began which was to compel Fidel Castro into the future, but not in the ways that he or the ghosts could have imagined. Eduardo Chibás had a radio show every Sunday night. Fidelito and the ghosts listened to him religiously up in Fidelito's room in the pension. One week in 1951, Eduardo Chibás accused a government official of taking government funds for his own use. The official publicly challenged Chibás to prove his accusations. Apparently Chivas could not come up with the necessary proof. He then committed suicide on his radio show. Fidelito and the ghosts were horrified and stunned by this turn of events. Don Quixote and José Martí realized that it was Eduardo Chibás' sense of honor that betrayed him. Don Quixote thought that had he lived he too might have become a great Caballero Andante. He too might have changed the course of Cuban history. Fidelito was wounded to the core.

Eduardo Chibás was the most popular political leader in Cuba. The future Comandante en Jefe thought that he was exemplary in every way. Fidelito knew at that moment the course of Cuban history would be forever changed. There was an elaborate funeral for Eduardo Chibás attended by a large portion of the Cuban people. He was loved by all. Fidel gave one of the most moving eulogies ever given in the history of Cuba. The eulogy was also a tribute to the ghost, José Martí, who was present along with Don Quixote and the rest of the veterans.

Fidel evoked the memory of the veterans and their ideas about social justice and the need for national independence. The eulogy was published and distributed to the Cuban people. Fidelito was not the same for a long time after the death of Chibás. José Martí believed that the death of Eduardo Chibás would inevitably lead to a coup d'état before the upcoming elections. Don Quixote listened to the Apostle. All the veterans had come from Hacienda of the Spirits to Eduardo Chibás' funeral. They were now ensconced in Fidelito's room in the pension in Old Havana listening to the radio. José Martí was convinced that there would be a military coup. The Caballero Nino was as yet unaware that such a thing could occur before the upcoming elections. After all he was a candidate for congress. He worked tirelessly and long to win over his constituency. He was destined to win and take his place in congress when the coup d'état occurred.

José Martí had foreseen history and predicted accurately what would happen. There was a military coup d'état supported by the United States and lead by Fulgencio Batista. Fidel Castro was crushed, as were the hopes of the Cuban people. Fidelito remained convinced that the death of Eduado Chibás had led directly to the coup d'état.

All the ghosts and Fidelito returned for a time to the hacienda. Fidelito moped about the house-on-stilts seemingly beyond pain and hurt. Don Quixote was very worried about him and wished he could diminish his disillusionment. Hopes of achieving José Martí's goals of social justice and national independence through the electoral process were dashed. The morning following the coup d'état, Fidel Castro presented a denouncement in court. He accused Batista of violating the Constitution of 1940. At the same time, he published a message addressed to the Cuban people. Among other things, he said "There is not a sadder spectacle than a people that goes to bed free and wakes up enslaved ... Another time the boots, another time force against human reason ... Another time tyranny in Cuba, but there are also José Martí, Antonio Maceo, Máximo Gómez and Mella. Onward Cubans, if life is lost, nothing is lost, 'To Die for the Homeland is to Live'." These words made Fidel Castro a national hero.

The Caballero Nino and the ghosts came to the conclusion that change in Cuba would not occur by peaceful means and that armed struggle was the only solution. Don Quixote knew everything the Caballero Nino had experienced up to now was only a preparation. The first adventures were but a preface of the adventures to come. The veterans agreed with the knight and concluded that Fidel Castro's greatest adventures still awaited him. José Martí lectured the circle of ghosts up in the library about possible outcomes for the future. He knew that the moment had come for Fidel Castro to make his entrance onto the national scene. He was on his way to becoming a great leader and presented a real threat to Batista.

The Caballero Nino spent a lot of time up in the Sierra Crystal that summer. Don Quixote always accompanied him in those days and kept him close as never before, knowing that some of his most fantastic adventures awaited him shortly. The two of them would ride up to mountain on Fidelito's black stallion. They would stop at the Guajiro village and search for the magical Guajira maiden by the pool. Then Fidelito would leave his horse in the village. With the knight in tow, he headed up for the highest peaks he could find. He again imagined that he was in a magical land out of a book of chivalry. Here he felt closest to the lost dream of Don Quixote up in these remote mountains. Up in those deep jungles, he would concentrate on his desire to realize the unfulfilled mission of Don Quixote. The future Comandante en Jefe was certain he could restore chivalry to the world. However he knew he needed help. At some point he would have to unite his comrades and plan a sneak attack against Batista's army. He knows he would be outnumbered. He would have to train his comrades in the art of guerilla warfare. Guerilla warfare was the same strategy used by knights like Amadis and Tirant lo Blanc.

The Comandante en Jefe knew that secrecy was of the utmost importance. Those knights of old were the first to use guerilla tactics against a much larger and stronger enemy. Fidelito still had a childlike fascination with the vegetation of the pristine jungle. Fidelito imagined he saw Amadis dressed in a perfect suit of sixteenth-century armor made of shining silver that sparkled in the sun. Don Quixote imagined all kinds of knights in this magical land, just like ones described in books of chivalry. The two fasted and drank from the local streams and slept under gigantic mahogany trees. These sojourns with Don Quixote that summer would last for a week or more. José Martí and the veterans would start to worry. However, they realized that these trips did him good and that the coming months would be difficult for the Caballero Nino. He would soon enough return to Havana and get into the thick of things. The veterans were concerned about whether or not he was safe up in these mountains. However they were glad that he had some time to be alone in the places he loved the most.

As always, that summer Fidelito returned to the library of José Martí's invention. He read all kinds of things including novels and poetry. Ultimately his sense of duty took him back to Marx and Engels along with José Martí, his favorite author after Cervantes. He grew very sentimental and picked up La Edad de Oro and reread the tales of his youth. He returned to his love of philosophy, and read some of Plato's dialogues as he had done at Belen so often with the priests. He reread the Death of Socrates, by now one of his favorite dialogues and thought again about the need for revolutionary struggle against Batista. He read the great play by Lope de Vega, Fuenteovejuna and other great plays by Lope advocating the uprising of the poor and defenseless against an unjust dictator. Fidelito thought about the need for the Cuban people to rise up against tyranny and social injustice of Batista. He was convinced that the Cuban population was ready for insurrection against the dictator.

They had suffered enough.

That summer, up in the library of José Martí's imagination in the company of the ghosts, Fidel Castro started to think about how to get control of the Cuban army. He and his comrades needed to devise a plan by which they could take control of a military post like the Mambises did in the Wars of Independence. If he could take arms away from the enemy and arm his own guerilla force, the rest of Oriente Province would follow and then the rest of Cuba. The Caballero Nino talked to no one about his ideas but rather wrote them down in a journal. Most of his ideas followed José Martí's precepts on land distribution and the need to free Cuba from the Gigante del Norte.

José Martí looked at the journal and was convinced the Caballero Nino was on the right track. He was also extremely flattered that Fidel Castro was such an avid follower of his ideas on social justice. The idea of the armed struggle against the Batista dictatorship responded to the same criteria that José Martí sustained when he convened what he called "the necessary war" against Spain in 1895. The Caballero Nino was fearless. He had an iron will which all the veterans knew would stand him in good stead. Don Quixote could see a great chivalric adventure in the making.

It was about that time that Fidelito returned to reading novels of chivalry and the tales of the battles of the great knights of old who constantly faced death and an enemy much stronger and with many more resources than they. Fidelito loved these tales which reminded him of David and Goliath. He was up against an enemy far greater in size than he and was counting on the support of the Cuban population. Don Angel Castro was in some sympathy with his son and recognized his potential for leadership. He had his doubts about the outcome of events, but did not speak of these doubts to anyone. Angel Castro even provided Fidelito with financial support for his undertakings. No one knew better than Don Angel Castro and the sugarcane growers in Oriente Province of the damage being done by the Gigante del Norte. After all, Angel Castro had sent the perfect circle of sugarcane off to the mills of United Fruit Company every year. The foreigners controlled the economy of the island and were continually extracting its wealth. Fidelito kept reading José Martí over and over especially when it came to the role of the Yankees in Cuba.

Once back in Havana, Fidelito and the ghosts went to the pension in Old Havana where he had now lived for years. Don Quixote, José Martí and the rest of the veterans had all followed him to Havana. They crowded into the large room and spent a considerable amount of time out on the balcony looking at the sea. Fidel was rarely there in those days for he spent the majority of his time with his friends Abel Santamaría and Haydée Santamaría in their apartment in the Vedado neighborhood of Havana. There Fidel outlined his plans to form a movement through the mechanism of cells. Each cell was made up of about ten to twelve like-minded people who often joined as a group.

Castro was the only one who knew of the existence of the newly formed individual cells. He would go from cell to cell in Havana and to other places such as Pinar del Río and Santa Clara. He would speak in a low but passionate voice of the need for political change. He fostered the idea among the various cells that armed rebellion was the only way to bring back the rule of law and the Constitution of 1940. All his followers were mesmerized by his breathtaking intellect and magnificent oratory skills.

In those early days Fidel Castro started what came to be known as The 26th of July Movement. He was always dressed in a black suit, fresh shirt and tie. As he espoused his revolutionary ideas he looked very conservative. He outlined for each cell José Martí's agenda for national independence and social justice. Martí and Don Quixote were extremely pleased by this turn of events which started in 1952 and moved into 1953. By the spring of 1953, there were more than one hundred cells in the movement and each member was sworn to strict order and discipline. The members of each cell led austere lives, leaving behind drink and other amusements to focus on the common goal of overthrowing Batista. The veterans along with Don Quixote were more than impressed, and in fact dumbfounded, by Fidel's ability to both organize and inspire people. He had started with a single cell and now there were more than one hundred throughout the island. The ghosts continued to be captivated by Fidel's organizational powers as well as his powers of persuasion.

The people who participated in the first year of The 26th of July Movement were not intellectuals. There was a doctor, a few lawyers and some professionals but the rest were working class people like bakers, bus drivers, maids, peasants and other like-minded people. Fidel was able to take José Martí's ideas and put them in terms that would be understandable to men and women from all walks of life. As the Movement began to take on momentum, two wings developed which were to have significant consequences for the future of Cuba. First there was a political wing, with six members drawn from various cells in Havana to organize political activities against the Batista regime. Abel Santamaría and Jesús Montané found an old second-hand printer and bought it for a pittance. Immediately they set up the underground paper, El Acusador. Fidel Castro wrote articles for this paper which had a distribution at one point of ten thousand copies per edition. He wrote under the pen name of Alejandro, his little-known middle name. He called for an end to the abusive treatment of workers and peasants. He also called for improved wages and respect for the rights of women. Alejandro wrote to the Cuban people that after the revolution and return to the rule of law and the constitution of 1940 the land of the big absentee landlords would be returned to the peasants.

Don Quixote and José Martí, as well as the rest of the veterans, were ecstatic about the Caballero Nino's activities, ideas and goals. José Martí was touched that Fidel was following to the letter so many of his ideas on social justice and national independence. Although the Caballero Nino did not show it early on in those times, he knew that his biggest enemy was the United States. Eventually not only would he have to confront Batista but also the Gigante del Norte. Fidel Castro refrained from speaking to anyone about his secret desire to resurrect chivalry. He followed the precept of José Martí that to achieve one's goals, one has to hide them in the beginning.

Secrecy was paramount against an enemy much stronger and more powerful than his movement. To organize the military objectives of the movement, many members sold personal items like cars and furniture to raise funds to purchase arms. The only arms available to them on the black market were .22 rifles and other light arms. Fidel would organize the cells for target practice after dark. No one knew the precise nature of the objective of the practice. There was the utmost secrecy in keeping with José Martí's precepts. The individual cells were armed by the Caballero Nino with José Marti and the ghosts following him everywhere he went. The cells would undertake target practice in the basements of abandoned university buildings or on farms outside Havana after dark.

Everything was done with the utmost secrecy and organization. Nothing was left to chance. If anyone were captured and questioned by SIM, the Batista secret police, no one would know enough to compromise the mission. Fidel Castro had learned about the importance of secrecy from earlier exploits like Cayo Confites and the Bogotázo. The participants had failed to use surprise as a weapon. He had also learned the very hard lesson that lawful means could not be effective any longer in Cuba. Fidel Castro and the 26th of July Movement participated in the centenary of the birth of José Martí on January 28th 1953. Batista organized lavish official celebrations starting at the presidential palace. Opposition groups organized counter-celebrations.

Fidel Castro, who according to José Martí was his true heir, staged a great demonstration leading a mass torchlight parade through the streets of Havana. However no one suspected that Castro had a secret army. Batista didn't think the demonstration of torch lights to be significant enough to disrupt the activities he had planned around José Martí's birth. José Martí, Don Quixote and the veterans were deeply touched by the display of affection for the Apostle. All the veterans embraced him as did Don Quixote who congratulated him for having had such a positive effect on the living.

Don Quixote made the observation that José Martí was so alive in the minds of the Cuban people that he was more alive dead than most mortals. José Martí and the veterans laughed at Don Quixote's conceit and appreciated the thought. Meanwhile plans continued on the military side of the movement. Fidelito was taken up with organizing an attack which he had clearly planned in his mind as a result of reading José Martí. Fidel knew that if he were to succeed against the illegal Batista regime supported by the Yankees, he would have to steal arms from the enemy. Like the Mambises before him, Fidel remained convinced that he would have to attack an army post that was well armed and fortified by an even greater enemy. He would have to look for a post where perhaps he might find an advantage as far as numbers were concerned. If the army being attacked had more men, then there would have to be the element of surprise to compensate.

That is why the element of surprise was so important as far as José Martí and the veterans were concerned. José Martí could literally read Fidelito's mind in those days. He was perfectly aware of his thought processes as he had gone through the same thing during the Wars of Independence. Often during the spring of 1953, when Fidelito was alone in his room in the pension in Old Havana, he felt as if he were in the company of the great heroes of the Wars of Independence and that somehow they were right by his side. The Caballero Nino believed in the presence of these great soldiers all through the time he was organizing the 26th of July Movement. The ghosts were delighted as they followed Fidel Castro from cell to cell and heard him tell the members of the Movement that what they were fighting for in terms of social justice and national liberation was a continuation of the Mambises.

José Martí and the veterans were the models for the movement. Don Quixote thought that Fidel Castro's dedication to the ideas of José Martí was admirable. He too delighted in all the times that Fidelito brought the ideas of the Apostle to light in his talks with the more than one hundred cells by the spring of 1953. Still Fidel had not named the army post that would be attacked. Only the ghosts were able to follow his train of thought that far. They knew the element of surprise was paramount. They realized that there had to be something in the circumstances which gave an outnumbered group of rebels some advantage. Finally, for this reason and for the reason that they were located in Oriente Province, Fidel Castro chose the army garrison called Moncada in Santiago de Cuba. Moncada was the second largest fort on the island. At the same time, a smaller group would attack the Bayamo garrison, also located in Oriente Province.

The barracks at Moncada contained 380 men. However, it was carnival time so Fidelito thought that many of these soldiers, especially the officers, would be off celebrating carnival away from the barracks. Another reason for choosing these barracks was that they had an armory with plenty of arms and ammunition. With these arms, the hundred and thirty-eight members of the Movement participating in the action would immediately become a significant force. Castro believed that the population of Oriente would support and follow them. José Martí was delighted with the plan as well as the fact that everything had remained a secret. None of the participants knew of the plan until hours before it was to be carried out. All was coordinated in the mind of the Caballero Nino.

Suddenly, one morning shortly before the two attacks on Moncada and Bayamo, Don Quixote announced that this would surely be one of the greatest adventures of chivalry ever set down by Cide Hamete Benengeli. All the goals of José Martí, the veterans and the Caballero Nino were perfectly in keeping with the spirit and even the letter of chivalry.

The notion of liberating the peasants and giving them land, along with the end of their abuse by an evil and greedy lord, was well within the thinking of the knights of old. José Martí and the veterans agreed with the knight which made him very happy for the moment. He sincerely believed that Fidel Castro was to have his history recorded by Cide Hamete Benengeli. Moncada would be one of the most significant and famous exploits ever to be recorded in any book of chivalry. As it turned out, Don Quixote was absolutely right as will become evident later on in this veracious history. Finally, on the afternoon of July 24th 1953 all of Fidel's comrades followed him to Siboney Farm in Oriente not far from Santiago de Cuba. Fidelito had arranged to rent the farm three weeks earlier in order to store uniforms and weapons.

The members of the Movement came from Havana in cars, buses and trains. These comrades secretly made their way to the farm. The secret army was gathering there to learn the plan of attack from the Knight of the Great Colored Green Coat. Fidel Castro stuck to his beliefs based on the French Revolution. The future Commandante en Jefe believed that boldness and the element of surprise were the secrets of success. He started with these ideas as he proceeded to give a lengthy explanation of the upcoming operation. First there would be one hundred and thirty-eight participants in Moncada and twenty-seven in Bayamo. He was out to prove Batista's assumption that his army was invincible was wrong.

His youngest brother, Raúl, was also part of this group of rebels. From his descriptions of the barracks Don Quixote thought it sounded like one of the medieval castles described in books of chivalry. As it turned out, the knight was not far off the mark. At first glance Moncada, with its high walls and turrets, looked very similar to a medieval structure. The 27 men in Bayamo would also depend on the element of surprise to gain the advantage against an enemy far greater in number than they. The Carnival in Santiago was scheduled for the 25th of July when everyone would be out celebrating and getting drunk. On the morning of the 26th at 4.00 am an armed convoy of sixteen cars filled with armed men dressed in military uniforms was about to leave Siboney Farm. Fidel Castro gave one last speech to explain the operation to his comrades. He told the members of the guerilla force that they were ready for the fight. He expected it to be bloodless with no deaths. If they succeeded then the ideals of José Martí would be realized sooner. If not, and if they failed, then others would lift up the banner and Moncada would serve as an example to future generations.

The idea was to attack and occupy the garrison and to incite the Cuban people to insurrection. If need be, they would go to the Sierra Maestra to continue to resistance from there. As soon as the procession got underway, one car had a flat tire. Unfortunately there was no spare tire. Four of the guerillas found spaces to sit in other cars while four men had to give up and return to Siboney. Then a car with eight men took a wrong turn only to get hopelessly sidetracked. They got upon entering Santiago never to get back in line again. A car with six guerillas, including Raúl Castro, bound for the Palace of Justice also took a wrong turn and got lost.

Abel and Haydee Santamaría along with Melba Hernández took the hospital overlooking the Moncada fortress without incident. The first cell to approach the entrance to the barracks had no problem. Dressed in military uniforms, three men jumped out and shouted the general was coming. The soldiers guarding the fortress took down the chain blocking the road. The members of the first cell entered and went directly to the barracks where they surprised a group of drunken soldiers whom they ordered out into the yard.

Meanwhile, Fidel had spied two uniformed soldiers with automatic weapons walking along the street in front of the car he was driving. One soldier turned around and looked at Fidel Castro and Fidel's comrade shot him. With that the alarm sounded in the barracks and a whole new regiment of soldiers streamed out into the courtyard. Now Fidel Castro and several more cars were inside the fortress. They were being fired upon by the battalion of men that had just come out of the fortress building. Both sides took cover and started to fire on each other. All hell broke loose and right then Don Quixote, José Martí and the rest of the veterans jumped into the fray. Don Quixote drew his sword and went after two soldiers at once. He swiped his sword right through the neck of a soldier. The soldier reached for his neck as if he felt something. Just then one of the rebels aimed and shot him

According to Cide Hamete Benengeli in the second history of Don Quixote visible only to the ghosts, Don Quixote slashed through Batista's soldiers, wounding them as he went, as did Calixto García, Antonio Maceo and Máximo Gómez. These phantoms were jubilant about being able to participate in a guerilla action against an evil dictator supported by an even more evil lord. These phantoms loved going against a much stronger enemy and knowing the thrill of doing so went beyond pain and hurt.

All the ghosts enjoyed the heat of battle because they were beyond death. Bullets meant nothing and went right through them. Fidel Castro kept right on fighting against the regiment that had come out of the barracks to surprise them. Don Quixote in the heat of battle saw all the great knights of old, swords raised, headed into the fray. He saw Amadis and his son Esplandian, along with Tirant lo Blanc and Palmerin. Despite the fact that they were outnumbered, Fidel Castro and the rest of his men kept right on fighting inspired by the spirits of the veterans. Fidelito did not feel alone. He did not worry that his side was so much fewer in number than the enemy. He just kept on fighting in good faith along with the veterans. They had fought many battles like these during the Wars of Independence and felt well prepared to take on the enemy. During the prolonged battle that was never before recorded in a book of chivalry, Don Quixote continued to see all the knights of old raising their swords against Batista's soldiers.

Later on Cide Hamete Benengeli would record these events just as they occurred. He also recorded the fact that José Martí and the veterans shared to some extent Don Quixote's frame of mind. They were enjoying the battle for the fighting made them feel very much alive. They too thought of the fighting of the great knights of old. About thirty men were killed and others taken prisoner. Fidelito and his guerilla fighters fell back and left the courtyard. Meanwhile, Batista's soldiers had discovered the guerillas in the hospital. Immediately they began to torture and kill them. In all twenty-two were tortured mercilessly and murdered in cold blood. Abel Santamaría had both his eyes gouged out by a bayonet. Antonio Maceo and Calixto García witnessed these atrocities committed against the much weaker guerilla force and wept. Later they would provide testimony on the torture of the members of the 26th of July Movement to Cide Hamete Benengeli who would record these events.

Meanwhile, Fidel Castro with no more than forty men fell back to

Siboney Farm. Nineteen guerillas remained there. Fidel followed his old habit and custom and headed with them to the mountains of the Gran Piedra. There he planned to regroup and set up a new guerilla base. Don Quixote and the veterans followed Fidel Castro up the mountain as they had when he had gone up into the Sierra Crystal during his youth. All the trips that Don Quixote had taken with Fidelito were but a preparation for the present exploit. Don Quixote and the veterans felt more alive than ever as they climbed the mountains behind Fidel. He kept climbing up the mountain with his followers but within a few days most of them were taken prisoner including Raúl Castro who tried to make his way back to Hacienda of the Spirits. Only three remained including Fidel. They would go from peasant hut to peasant hut as they climbed higher and higher into the jungles of the mountains trying to escape

Batista's infamous Rural Guard was known for their bloodthirsty tactics. After seeking refuge in the hut of a Guajiro and his family, sixteen members of the Rural Guard caught Fidel Castro and his companions. José Martí, Don Quixote and the veterans who had followed Fidelito into the mountains and surrounded him at every turn were now keenly aware that he was in danger of being slaughtered. The phantoms did the only thing they could which was to surround Fidelito and think positive thoughts. For a few minutes the soldiers who contemplated killing him started shouting "let's kill them, let's kill them," but then Lieutenant Sarria appeared on the scene and saved the day as the Guajiros looked on thinking Fidelito was a dead man. Oddly enough, an official of the army of the black race captured Fidel but he prohibited them from killing him saying "ideas cannot be killed."

Perhaps he was acting under the influence of the invisible phantoms that surrounded Fidel Castro. By that time the Archbishop of Santiago also appeared and ordered an end to all killings. Then Fidel Castro and the ghosts were lead down the mountain by Batista's Rural Guard. The Archbishop asked Lieutenant Sarria to take Fidel and his comrades to the local jail instead of Moncada. There the infamous Colonel Chaviano questioned Fidel Castro in front of the Cuban press. Fidelito confessed to having organized the 26th of July Movement. He admitted to trying to overthrow Batista's illegitimate government and restore the rule of law and the 1940 constitution. He openly told Chaviano that he wanted to install an entirely new system of government free from colonial rule. Chaviano realized he had made a big mistake in allowing the press to witness Fidel's confession. He was in the newspapers all over Cuba. José Martí and the ghosts knew there was nothing that could stop him now short of assassination. He had become a national hero overnight and even achieved some international recognition due to his armed opposition to a regime supported by the United States. Soon Chaviano and Batista cut off all communication from the outside world and put Fidel Castro in solitary confinement in a prison forty miles outside Santiago de Cuba called Boniato. There he remained in solitary confinement until the 21st of September, completely incommunicado. If it hadn't been for the ghosts, the Caballero Nino might have gone quite mad. José Martí and Don Quixote were sure to bring him all kinds of reading materials. Fidel Castro remembered back on his days up in the library of José Martí's invention reading to his heart's content.

The Caballero Nino never questioned how the books he wished for reached his cell. He was aware of a force far greater than he was supporting him in his hour of need. He thought of it as a just force. He was reminded of his days at Belen where he would sit and read in his cell for hours. He prepared the defense of the attack for the 21st of September. The defendants would be brought before the judges in a trial that all of Cuba would be watching. As he sat in his cell from August through September, Fidelito thought back on the idyllic days on the hacienda and wished for his books. He thought of the library. The ghosts appeared along with all the books he wished for so that the Caballero Nino was never alone. He thought back on all the famous men in history who were unjustly imprisoned. No one came to mind faster than the figure of Socrates and his willingness to die for an idea.

All through August and September, José Martí, Don Quixote and the veterans were convinced that his jailors were going to kill Fidel Castro. Fidelito was well aware of the danger. In a highly disciplined manner reminiscent of José Martí and the Mambises as well as the knights of old, he put all his attention on his readings in preparation for the defense of those who had participated in Moncada. Finally the day came when the future Comandante en Jefe, along with his comrades, came before the court in the Palace of Justice in Santiago. The defendants were accused of organizing an uprising of armed persons against the Constitutional Powers of the State. Fidel Castro defended his actions by stipulating in the most eloquent language possible that he had led an uprising not against the Constitutional Powers of the State, but against Batista who had illegally seized power. The trial quickly became a trial of the army and Batista. The journalists present reported Fidel Castro's brilliant defense of the Moncada attack as an attempt to return to the rule of law and the Constitution of 1940.

Witnesses on both sides revealed the tortures and murders committed in the Moncada barracks. Don Quixote, José Martí and the veterans had witnessed these atrocities first hand. They all sadly and incredulously could testify to the fact that Abel Santamaría had both eyes gouged out with a bayonet. Fidel Castro eloquently and persuasively summarized the various atrocities committed on those brave souls who had participated in the 26th of July Movement at Moncada. He argued that the authorities had committed serious criminal offences. He asked the judges to collect evidence to bring about the appropriate prosecutions. The flustered judges begrudgingly accepted the petition of Fidel Castro.

The trial thus far was a public relations disaster for the Batista Government. Fidelito and his comrades, both dead and alive, were quickly becoming national heroes. The trial was on the minds of all Cubans and represented the wave of the future. Then suddenly all public contact with the accused was cut off. Fidel Castro was returned to his cell under solitary confinement. There was a general suppression of the newspapers and radio. There was also a blackout of all information in the press about Moncada.

On the 26th of September 1953, the trial of the Moncada group resumed in the Palace of Justice. All the ghosts were present and seated in the front row but unexpectedly and inexplicably Fidel Castro did not appear. The infamous Colonel Chaviano claimed that Fidel Castro was ill and presented a phony medical certificate signed by the appropriate doctors. At the same moment Melba Hernández stepped forward and pulled out a note smuggled to her in prison from Fidel Castro. The note stipulated that the medical certificate was a way of keeping him from returning to court and speaking his piece to the public. He also told the judges that Chaviano, at the request of Batista, was about to have him killed. Castro's note finished with a quote from José Martí stating that "...a just cause from the depths of a cave is stronger than an army."

The Apostle was delighted when he heard his words quoted in the note. The judges now paid close attention. Once again Fidel Castro's eloquence avoided disaster. The judges ordered an independent medical examination and that Castro be tried separately the following month. The ghosts were disappointed that the judges had not permitted him to appear in the courtroom right then and there. They realized there was a limit to their power. Raúl Castro remained on trial with his comrades. He was sentenced to thirteen years in prison along with some other participants. Other comrades were sent away for three to ten years Haydée Santamaría and Melba Hernández were sentenced to seven months in prison. Fidel Castro was again forced to wait in his cell almost another month before resuming his defense of the Moncada attack.

On October 16, 1953 Fidel Castro was not taken to the Palace of Justice as all the other accused had been. In order to go along with the fiction that he was sick, the so-called trial was held in the nurse's lounge of the civilian hospital next to Moncada. Here was where all the terrible tortures had occurred. The trial was held in the utmost secrecy. However, six journalists were present when Fidel Castro was escorted into the room.

All the ghosts were present and seated as close to the front and as close to Fidel Castro as space would allow. Fidel launched into his defense. He did it all from memory. He had no notes. The journalists present observed that he had nothing but his recollections and sense of justice to guide him. At no time was Fidel Castro closer to José Martí than he was at this moment. He started his address by denouncing the authorities for not allowing him to have a fair and public trial. He protested the fact that he was kept for all this time in solitary confinement and not allowed to speak to a lawyer except in front of SIM, the Batista secret police. The ghosts were horrified at this state of affairs. Fidel Castro went on to explain that the government had issued a fraudulent medical certificate to keep him away from the main trial. Here was a regime that shrank in fear of the political and moral convictions of a defenseless man. As he continued the defense of the Moncada attack, Fidel grew more and more eloquent and more convincing to his audience. José Martí and Don Quixote thought that all Fidelito's actions exemplified the best of chivalry and the best of the knights of old. Don Quixote went on at great length about the fact that there had never been a knight so eloquent nor memorable to his audience.

Once again Fidel described the torture and murder of his colleagues and noted how their bodies were thrown into unmarked graves. Fidel Castro proclaimed proudly that one day these brave men would be disinterred and carried to a place beside the tomb of José Martí. The Apostle was very touched by these words as were the veterans. Fidel Castro went on to ridicule the efforts of Batista to claim that the 26th of July Movement had no popular support. José Martí was furious about this point because he realized that the Movement had overwhelming support from the 700 000 unemployed, the 500 000 impoverished farm workers, the 400 000 underpaid and ill-housed industrial workers, the 100 000 tenant farmers, the 30 000 underpaid and underappreciated teachers, the 20 000 small businessmen burdened by debt and the 10 000 doctors, engineers, lawyers and other professionals unable to practice their professions.

The ghosts sat by as proud as could be, especially José Martí because he recognized his own thoughts in the thoughts of the Caballero Nino now defending the future of Cuba. Fidel Castro then launched into a description of a political program starting with five Revolutionary Laws. These new laws would be promulgated when the people of Cuba again took power. These Laws involved land redistribution and profit sharing for workers. José Martí, Don Quixote and the veterans were delighted. Don Quixote was on top of the world because he was convinced that the Caballero Nino was taking the laws of chivalry to a new level. These laws represented the essence of a future society based on chivalric values. José Martí and the veterans were ecstatic because they saw their own values being carried out. The five Revolutionary Laws did not go along with the idea of absolute free enterprise, the law of supply and demand, nor traditional guarantees to investment capital. Fidel Castro explained that measures to be introduced included radical educational and health reforms and the nationalization of utilities and telephone companies. He closed his remarks with another quote from the Apostle, "The dream of today will be the law of tomorrow."

He returned to the theme of just force to overthrow an illegal government. He stressed that the 26th of July Movement had nothing against the ordinary soldier. Their argument was with Batista. Fidel Castro again asserted that the attack on the Moncada garrison was to provoke an uprising in Oriente Province against Batista. José Martí grew very emotional when Fidel said that he was the author of the Moncada attack. Again Fidel Castro thought back to his many readings and remembered the defense of Socrates when he declared at the end of his speech "Condemn me, it does not matter, history will absolve me." The ghosts were overwhelmed with Fidel Castro's eloquence as were all the other people in the room, including his enemies. José Martí was still worried about his safety and Don Quixote was convinced that Colonel Chaviano was out to kill him. The judges took only four hours to deliberate and gave Fidel Castro fifteen years in prison, the harshest sentence of any member of the group who had participated in Moncada. The ghosts were brokenhearted and immediately returned to Hacienda of the Spirits.

José Martí was eager to read the history being recorded by Cide Hamete Benengeli so he went up to the library to see if the distinguished Arab historian had recorded recent events. As he struggled to read the print came to the surface and the ghost read about the very adventure that he and his comrades had participated in just months ago. The veterans had to admit that it was indeed strange to read about themselves. The Apostle quickly formed a reading circle and read the adventure of Moncada to all the veterans who were absolutely dumbfounded but fascinated by the insights of Cide Hamete Benengeli. As José Martí sat there reading the description of events, he couldn't help but be struck by the accuracy of the account. The old Arab had included a fabulous description of the battle inside the Moncada barracks. All the veterans had participated along with the knights of old that Don Quixote had visualized clearly in the most heated moments of the battle.

Don Quixote was amazed that Cide Hamete predicted the same thing he had foreseen. The veterans thought that Moncada was an immediate failure in terms of not achieving its goals. However, the battle would still go down in the annals of chivalry as one of the most memorable exploits ever recorded. All the participants stayed with the Caballero Nino to the end without giving in to the enemy. They were great chivalric heroes. In fact those brave men and women who had carried out the Moncada attack brought the values of chivalry alive.

The reading circle of ghosts, with José Martí leading the group, read Cide Hamete Benengeli's account of Fidel Castro's defense. His defense sounded even more eloquent and more convincing than when they had witnessed it firsthand. Cide Hamete seemed to have a particular predilection for the Caballero Nino, believing in his abilities for leadership. He noted the tremendous sacrifice and discipline required to have organized such an exemplary action. He stressed that the action was exemplary as far as the annals of chivalry were concerned. He asserted that this exploit would be read about with great pleasure by the audiences of the future. A small group of men had taken on a much stronger enemy willing to sacrifice their own lives. Many lives were sacrificed and those who died did so with honor. According to Cide Hamete, all the participants' actions would be recorded by the historians in the near future. He named all the participants one by one so that no one would ever forget them. The old Moor wrote some tantalizing tidbit of information on each person to highlight their existence. After reading Cide Hamete Benengeli's account of this history, it seemed that he had a better understanding of events than he would have by simply participating in them.

The Apostle looked upon this book-in-the-making as an incredible feat. At first he doubted that Cide Hamete Benengeli could have come back along with Don Quixote. But judging from his literary style and penchant for the truth of the matter, by the end of this first reading session, José Martí was convinced that the book he had just read to his comrades was in fact true to life. Fidel Castro was described as exemplary and ahead of his time. Just as José Martí was finishing up the description of the speech

Fidel Castro had just delivered, the print started to disappear from the page and the episode ended in the middle of a sentence. All the veterans were highly disappointed. They held the illusion that they might be able to find out about future events. José Martí thought that perhaps Cide de Hamete had the ability to foresee exploits, though he was not about to let the ghosts share in those insights for now.

José Martí suddenly noticed Don Quixote seated over in a corner of the library in the attic. He went over to him as did the other veterans because the knight looked disturbed and out of sorts. He seemed particularly melancholy. José Martí asked what was wrong but the knight refused to speak. Instead he disappeared completely from the attic, much to the chagrin of the ghosts. After dinner and after the family had gone to bed the ghosts were back up in the library. Don Quixote reappeared in his suit of sixteenth century armor still looking disturbed. Finally José Martí got out of the ghost what was disturbing him. Don Quixote had at first thought that Cide Hamete Benengeli had come back to life to write his second history. However, after reading the description of all the events leading up to Moncada and the attack, the knight was convinced that the old Arab historian was not writing about his second lifetime. Instead he was completely taken up with Fidel Castro as a knight. Tears streamed down his face as he realized that the old Moor was more interested in Fidel Castro than himself. A tear came to his eye as he reluctantly related to the group that his portrayal in this book was indeed secondary to the future Comandante en Jefe.

As José Martí flipped through the earlier parts of the book being written by the Arab, the print would appear momentarily then disappear as if to tease him into reading. The Apostle started to read about the Caballero

Nino's childhood. After five minutes or so, just as he was getting interested, the print would disappear. One thing for certain the Apostle realized was that this book was still in the process of being written and was meant exclusively for the ghosts. José Martí's suspicions in this regard were confirmed one day when Lina Castro came up to the attic to dust and found the library. She didn't seem that surprised and picked up the big green tome on top of the desk. All the pages went blank immediately before she could notice any print. José Martí observed this phenomenon and was convinced that the book was written solely for the ghosts.

Angel Castro and Lina Castro were extremely upset that their children were condemned to prison. They had watched the trial religiously in the papers and through friends who were present during the proceedings. Some journalists came to the hacienda to interview Don Angel Castro, who defended his son as nothing but patriotic. Lina Castro did the same. Yet for all their public decorum, they were terribly worried and sad. Angel Castro remained convinced that Batista would kill both his sons but Fidelito was the one in the most danger. He could be murdered by his jailors at any moment and it was likely that he would be soon. His reputation as an orator and as an exemplary man of action bound to eternal principles was alive and well in the hearts of the Cuban people. Batista would not have killed him because he did not want to make a martyr out of him. But after Moncada and the trials and Fidel Castro's defense, Cede Hamete Benengeli named the defense 'History Will Absolve Me'. Whenever the veterans around the card table in the kitchen started to worry about Fidelito, José Martí reminded them that to murder him would mean making a martyr out of him. He represented now the wave of the future, and the dreams of the Cuban people were in his hands.

Meanwhile all the phantoms except José Martí continued to feel depressed and hopeless. The veterans sat around the kitchen table playing cards and drinking rum way into the night. José Martí went to the library of his own invention. There he sat in the overstuffed easy chair and stared out at the moon. He fell asleep and did not awake until the moon was high and full in the night sky. He opened his eyes sometime later and his attention immediately went to the big book bound in green leather with gold lettering. He walked over and picked it up and read the last part of the Moncada adventure composed by Cide Hamete Benengeli. There he saw described in the most fantastic of terms the speech given by Fidel Castro in his own defense. The description was so eloquent and timely that José Martí could hardly believe his ears. He went back to the overstuffed easy chair and sat down book in hand and read on. Then he put the enormous tome down in his lap. The Apostle thought that Moncada would now be one of the greatest adventures ever recorded in the history of chivalry. The knights of old that Cide Hamete portrayed as having participated in the battle made it that much more interesting. The veterans and Don Quixote were portrayed in the heat of battle in ways that would make them memorable to the reader. One again Fidel Castro was portrayed as the great Caballero Andante he would turn out to be.

José Martí and the phantoms were sure now that Fidel Castro had changed the course of history in Cuba forever and that the Cuban people would never be the same. Meanwhile there was a great sadness that fell over Hacienda of the Spirits when Fidel Castro was transferred from Boniato Prison in Oriente Province to the new prison recently built on the Isle of Pines. Doña Lina Castro spent many mornings next to the kitchen stove weeping in silence. Angel Castro looked like he had the weight of the world on his shoulders. He worried incessantly about his son and whether or not he would survive. He firmly believed that Batista wished to see him dead and remained convinced that he would receive word that Fidelito had been killed soon. José Martí did not dwell on the past. He sat in the overstuffed easy chair thinking about how he and the veterans along with Don Quixote would go about helping the Knight of the Great Colored Green Coat as he faced the future. For now the phantoms stayed on Hacienda of the Spirits and waited for news as will be recounted later on in this veracious history.

According to Cide Hamete Benengeli, Fidel Castro was condemned to prison as a result of having tried to restore the rule of law in Cuba. Shortly after his sentencing, he and his comrades were moved to the new prison on the Isle of Pines in southern Cuba. Here he soon concluded that the jailors who ran this prison were more intelligent and decent than those who ran Boniato. Here the administration had goodwill. Fidel Castro immediately went about planning how he and his comrades could best use their time in prison. They were housed in a hospital ward in the prison which gave them plenty of room and plenty of contact with each other. As usual Fidelito's imagination and experience came together to create a program of education for those who would participate in the struggle against Batista in the future.

Fidelito first thought back on his education at Belen College in Havana. There he was exposed to the ideals of a classical education. He saw the value of bringing as many disciplines to bear when trying to understand a topic. Here he wanted to perfect the meaning of his life. He wanted the same thing for his comrades. He enforced a ridged Spartan discipline and soon had a daily routine worked out for those who carried out the Moncada attack. He started a school based on the teachings he had received at Belen. Each morning Fidel formed a reading circle reminiscent of the reading circle started by José Martí and the veterans. Fidel thought of the library of José Martí's invention as he went about formulating the new curriculum for the school.

Each morning Fidel lectured the circle of comrades on philosophy and history. He told the group that he wanted them to understand the ideas of all the great thinkers. He encouraged them to take advantage of the time to educate themselves in preparation for the future. Other comrades taught grammar, arithmetic, geography, Cuban history and English. At night Fidel would discuss topics in political economy and rhetoric. All in all, the curriculum was reminiscent of the classical era or the trivium and quadrivium. Fidelito was well aware that he was using this invaluable time to educate his comrades well beyond those things needed to carry out a revolution. Fidel again exhibited a strong desire to acquire knowledge for the sake of knowledge. He had by now developed a deep, almost mystical respect for learning.

Soon the phantoms of Hacienda of the Spirits had joined the Moncada veterans and were participating in the learning circles provided by Fidelito. José Martí of course provided all the books for the school. As soon as Fidelito wished for a book, he would have it in hand. The rebel leader would not have been able to organize such a sophisticated school for his comrades without the guidance of the Apostle.

As the months passed, the veterans seated in the learning circle listened to Fidelito each morning lecture on the famous philosophers. The comrades grew more and more interested in reading for the sake of reading. Soon all the comrades were reading vociferously. Fidel and the ghosts were delighted. By Christmas time the library in the hospital of the prison contained more than three hundred volumes of first rate books. Fidel started his lectures with the Greeks and the Romans and discussed the great Dialogues of Plato including The Republic and The Apology. The Apology was a particular favorite of Fidel Castro's. Socrates exemplified how a man could give his life willingly for an idea. Fidel had always lived his life up until now in the spirit that Socrates intended. At the same time that he organized the school for the veterans of Moncada, Fidel wrote to his comrades on the outside beseeching them to denounce the tortures by Batista's henchmen. However, soon José Martí sadly realized that Fidel's efforts to publicize his plight were fruitless. Fidel Castro reluctantly concluded that he would not be able to organize armed resistance on the outside from inside prison.

The school progressed over several more months and the prisoners were using their time well. Fidel did not forget the importance of the History of Don Quixote. He formed a special reading circle where slowly he read about all the adventures of Don Quixote. His comrades were all delighted with the many colorful and delightful adventures. Fidelito reached the end the book and found Don Quixote on his death bed. All the veterans and especially José Martí grew sad at the thought that the old knight had not resurrected the era of chivalry. He died leaving his mission of bringing chivalry alive unfinished.

On February 12th, 1954, Batista came to visit the prison and to dedicate a power plant. He and his fellow officers were wearing full dress uniforms. Fidel decided that he and his comrades should sing the 26th of July Hymn when Batista was within range. In the end this decision had negative consequences, for Batista ordered an immediate end to the school. He sent Fidel Castro into solitary confinement which was to last for the remainder of his prison term. He was immediately banished to a small cell with no lights and no contact with his fellow prisoners. He managed to get an oil lamp from a guard so he could read and write.

The phantoms of Hacienda of the Spirits immediately joined Fidel Castro in his isolated cell. Surrounding him, they did all they could to console him and to calm him down. Never had José Martí and Don Quixote seen Fidel Castro so disillusioned. A great sadness came over mortal and ghost alike in this cell so far removed from the rest of the population. Fidel soon began to regain his strength and composure. He again thought that he needed to chart a course of action to achieve his long term goal of overthrowing the dictator. Once more he turned to his readings and thought about the fact that he wanted to carry out Don Quixote's mission of bringing back chivalry and of turning Cuba into the perfect chivalric society. He was delighted with the fact that he had brought the only copy he had of the History of Don Quixote.

Don Quixote was overjoyed that the future Comandante en Jefe was so intent on carrying out his mission. The old knight was saddened by the fact that he had failed to bring forth the era of chivalry. The ghosts had brought all the books formerly in the hospital ward school to Fidelito's cell. Subsequently Fidelito developed a reading schedule that was really beyond the abilities of most men and more in tune with the reading abilities of the phantoms. José Martí would make the long journey back and forth from the library of his own invention in Birán to the prison on the Isle of Pines just to provide him with the right books. Cide Hamete Benengeli, in his history of the Caballero de Birán, tells us that Fidelito embarked on reading the great books from Plato to Dostoevsky. He overcame his depression and sadness each morning by picking up one of the great philosophers and making a promise to finish the book before nightfall.

The ghosts were astounded by the quantity and caliber of Fidelito's consumption of the great books in solitary confinement. One of Fidel Castro's greatest achievements was reading the History of Don Quixote cover to cover in a single reading. The ghosts were stunned once more at the rapidity with which the Caballero Nino could digest books. Again he was reminded of his secret vow to resurrect chivalry. In the spirit of chivalry he would wipe out illiteracy, make sure there was full employment, good housing and medical attention for all. For the moment the future Comandante en Jefe did not speak of bringing chivalry alive to anyone. Once Cuban society was transformed into the perfect chivalric system, nothing could turn the clock back on history. In his isolated cell, to avoid solitude Fidel continued with his readings. He read about the great battles of the past and the great historical figures just as he had in Belen. His favorites were still Alexander the Great and Napoleon. His tastes for fiction had matured. He set about reading all of Dostoevsky's novels. His favorite was The Brothers Karamazov. He also liked the English Writers and read Shakespeare religiously, enjoying the delights to be had from King Lear and Hamlet. He also read W. Somerset Maugham, Honoré de Balzac, Thackeray, and Turgenev, to name only a few on the future Comandante en Jefe's reading list.

Amid all this serious reading, José Martí and Don Quixote did not forget to take all thirty-one volumes of Amadis de Gaula off the shelf in the library and bring them to the Caballero Nino's cell. Once he laid eyes on Amadis, a broad smile came across his face. He was delighted with his old books and delved right into Amadis. He found the knight was the victim of an evil enchantment by some foreign giant hell-bent on keeping him from resurrecting chivalry. Amadis was confined to a cell which was a cave. He was frozen and could not turn around and was condemned to watch the shadows of his jailors cross the back walls of the cave. Fidelito was convinced after reading about his favorite knight that he too was condemned to seeing shadows on the walls of his isolated prison cell. Don Quixote was delighted with the fact that Fidelito was reading books of chivalry again. He wished to keep the chivalric ideals alive in the Caballero Nino. From his own experience, he knew that Fidelito would have to continue to read about these knights of old were he to carry out a chivalric revolution.

After several months Fidelito was leading the most Spartan of lives. He was cut off from the outside world. His only company was that of the phantoms of Hacienda of the Spirits and he again decided to try and make contact with the outside world. This time he wrote a political tract based on his defense of the Moncada attack. He composed the tract line by line, recreating his speech before the judges some months ago. He wrote his thoughts down between the lines of correspondence to Lina Castro and Melba Hernández. One way or another the two women were able to reconstruct the lengthy manuscript that would become Fidelito's first and best known statement about revolution. Melba Hernández found a printer that would produce twenty-seven thousand copies. Fidelito had asked for one hundred thousand. In describing this political tract later on in his history, Cide Hamete Benengeli referred to the writings of Fidelito as a treatise on social justice. There, according to Cide Hamete, Fidel outlined the parameters of the perfect chivalric society he wished to create.

He stressed the need for the redistribution of land. He spoke of such measures as improved crop production, decent housing, agricultural and technical schools, sanitation measures, and the equality of rich and poor before the law. Fidel wrote, "There is no reason for poverty. The markets should be overflowing with goods. Everyone should be working and producing. What is inconceivable is that men should go to bed hungry while lands remain uncultivated. He went on to stipulate that thirty percent of the farmers were unable to write their own names; that ninety percent should know nothing of the history of Cuba; that the majority of our rural families should have to lived under conditions far worse than those when Columbus discovered 'the most beautiful land'. To those who call me a dreamer, I offer the words of José Martí: a true man does not look around to see where he can live better, but rather where his duty lies."

José Martí read the treatise out loud in its entirety to the veterans and Don Quixote. He could see how all the reading Fidel did in his isolated prison cell had fed into this discourse. The treatise was nothing if not eloquent and timely. Don Quixote thought that it was one of the best treatises given by any knight. He was certain that Cide Hamete Benengeli would include it in its entirety within his new work. However, be that as it may, it happened that the treatise Cide Hamete called 'History Will Absolve Me,' did not reach as many people as Fidelito wanted. The more time he spent in his cell isolated alone, the more frustrated and disillusioned he became. He finally realized once and for all that he would never be able to organize a movement to oust Batista from his prison cell. He felt hopeless and helpless in the face of his incarceration. Sometimes late at night he felt it really wasn't worthwhile living any more and he would weep to himself for hours. When the sun came up, the future Comandante en Jefe would recover from his feelings of depression. Fidel Castro became the Knight of Iron in prison.

In November 1954 Batista held phony elections he was guaranteed to win. Feeling confident, he then declared a full amnesty for all political prisoners "in order to contribute to the return of harmony in the Cuban family." Public opinion was strong in favor of those who had carried out the Moncada attack. Batista was finally convinced to give in and provide them all with amnesty. He had decided that Fidel Castro posed no threat to him. As dreams of release from prison became real for him, Fidelito began to think about his life outside prison. He was determined to take up the cause against Batista. He had become accustomed to the Spartan life in prison. He wrote Lina Castro and Haydée Santamaría that he would need little more than a room in a pension where he could throw his cigar butts. He was released from the Isle of Pines amidst the cries of reporters from around the globe. He declared to them that he was still tied to the ideals of Chibás and José Martí. He promised to fight the government openly for new and honest elections from the moment he was released and went about writing articles in Bohemia and La Calle.

His newspaper and magazine articles were widely received and influential. Batista was well aware of just how effective Fidel Castro had become in prison. He grew even more fearful of the Caballero Nino than he was previously. The number of bombings in Havana had increased recently with the call for new elections. However the government grew more paranoid about the Castro brothers. Raúl Castro was accused of complicity with student terrorists and had to leave Cuba for Mexico. Fidel Castro decided that there was no more hope for peaceful elections or peaceful change in Cuba. With no access to the news media and SIM making arrests daily, Fidel Castro was forced to follow his brother into exile in Mexico. Before he did, he thought about returning one more time to Hacienda of the Spirits. How tempting a few days on the hacienda were to him at that moment. But reason prevailed and he decided that he must leave Cuba immediately to achieve revolutionary change later on in this history.

On July 7, 1955, just two years after the attack on Moncada, Fidel Castro boarded a plane for Mexico. As he said his last goodbyes, he evoked the words of José Martí. "From trips such as this, one does not return, or else on returns with the tyranny beheaded at one's feet." All the phantoms climbed on board the airplane to go into exile along with Fidel Castro. Don Quixote reminded the group that many a Caballero Andante had gone into exile only to return to his native land having triumphed over evil. This was not the first time José Martí had gone into exile. At this point in the history he was looking forward to his time in Mexico.

# *Chapter Ten*

Cide Hamete Benengeli tells us Fidel Castro arrived in Mexico City on a typical grey rainy afternoon. The smog made it hard to breathe at first and together with the altitude it took him several days to become acclimated. Alone and feeling a tremendous amount of solitude, solitude worse than he had experienced in prison, he stayed at a cheap pension near Insurgentes. Don Quixote and the veterans had a terrible time breathing due to the smog but never left the Caballero Nino's side. Don Quixote reminded the group that all great Caballero Andantes had to face exile in strange lands.

There Fidel spent his first days lost in sadness and deep reflection about what had brought him to this juncture. All the ghosts had come with him and settled right down in his room, much like they had in the pension in Havana. Fidel thought first about the carefree days of his childhood on Hacienda of the Spirits. He knew he had had a privileged upbringing, a stellar education. Despite his circumstances, he felt that he had great adventures awaiting him. Indeed over time he would be able to change forever the course of Cuban history. But just as quickly as he would feel uplifted about the future, he would sink into a deep depression and terrible feelings of solitude would again overwhelm him. The first week in Mexico was full of these ups and downs, but mostly downs as he had no one with whom he could communicate his thoughts.

He took to wandering along the Avenida de los Insurgentes and stopping in at small cafes for coffee. He missed his Cuban cigars. At night he took to reading as he had done all his life. José Martí did not forget to bring a few of his favorite books with him from the library of his own invention. Among them was The Brothers Karamazov, his favorite novel, along with a few books on Napoleon. Don Quixote did not forget to bring along the first few volumes of Amadis de Gaula for when the Caballero Nino needed some lighter reading. According to Cide Hamete Benengeli, the future Comandante en Jefe wandered the streets of the capital. He would return to his room in the pension and pick up a volume of Amadis to ward off his depression.

Amid all this sadness, the Caballero Nino within him took great joy in reading about the battles of the famous knight of old. He loved reading about how the knight always prevailed over a much stronger enemy. Fidel Castro identified with the plight of these ancient knights pitted against much larger forces. He knew the enemy awaiting him in Cuba was much larger and stronger than he. Then of course he would take out his only copy of the History of Don Quixote gifted him by the old Padre Jesuita. The book was his most prized possession. Again he thought about how important it was to keep the fact that he dreamed of bringing alive chivalry in the modern era a secret. He took note of the fact that knights of old like Amadis always kept their plans to themselves, only confiding in their comrades on a need to know basis.

As the future Commandant en Jefe wandered Insurgentes over the course of the first couple of weeks, he reformulated a plan in his mind that he had conceived much earlier in Cuba. He came to Mexico with the express objective of gathering an armed force of exiles to invade Oriente Province. He wished to establish a guerrilla camp in the Sierra Maestra. The people in the cities and provinces of Oriente Province would rise up against Batista and there would be a general strike. Frank País in

Santiago de Cuba and the leader of the Directorio Revolucionario Estudantil, José Antonio Echeverría, had committed themselves to supporting the landing of Fidel Castro with armed action in the principle cities of the island. José Martí, Don Quixote and the veterans were ecstatic as Fidelito put his plans down on paper, seated at the tiny desk against the wall in his solitary room. As he sat there putting his ideas into writing, he suddenly felt as if he were no longer alone. It was the strangest feeling according to Cide Hamete and one he did not forget for a long time. Fidelito felt as if he were accompanied by some force much greater than he. At these times, he would read José Martí and the ghosts would stay close to him.

Not long after this initial phase, Fidelito met up with Raúl who was staying at the home of a Cuban exile, Maria Antonia González. She was a strong and competent woman who had fled Cuba years ago. Her apartment served as the headquarters for all Cuban exiles in the capital. She provided food and shelter to as many exiles as she could. There in her apartment Fidel's work began. He again turned to the power of the word in order to recruit Cuban exiles willing to take up arms against Batista. Learning from his Moncada experience, Fidel never divulged the exact nature of his plan to invade Oriente Province. He wished to establish a guerrilla base in the Sierra Maestra. As usual his eloquence proved to be a critical tool to convince the newly arrived exiles from Cuba to join in his planned adventure. Now Fidel Castro was in his element speaking to important Cuban exiles. He also went in search of funding but with limited success.

One afternoon Fidel met Alberto Bayo, a Cuban living in Mexico who had fought on the side of the Republicans in the Spanish Civil War. The old man was an expert in guerrilla warfare. Fidel Castro described his plans and the need for someone to train his men in guerrilla warfare strategies. Fidel told the old man that it would be an extended war lasting for some time and that his recruits needed to know how to survive in rough mountain terrain. Bayo was impressed by Fidel's planning. He could see he had given it a great deal of thought. However, Bayo was also taken with the fact that Fidel was projecting an exploit that was no more than pure fantasy. Whether or not he would be able to transform his dream into reality and change the course of Cuban history remained doubtful to the old man.

Meanwhile, the veterans were very enthusiastic about Fidel Castro's dream for Cuba. José Martí recognized clearly that Fidel Castro was carrying out his own dreams for the island. In his talks to potential recruits at the home of Maria Antonia González, Fidelito always spoke of the dreams and aspirations of the veterans. The veterans were usually with him. They took great delight in knowing that the future Comandante en Jefe was planning adventures that mirrored their own exploits. José Martí and the veterans often commented on how much Fidel Castro's ideas reflected their own thoughts. José Martí wept at times because he had had the good fortune of finding a mortal who supported his ideals. This made the old Apostle believe in the connection between man and ghost. Don Quixote and the other veterans felt the same way.

Don Quixote felt sure that Fidel Castro was destined to become a great Caballero Andante and bring back the era of chivalry. The old knight felt that Fidelito was destined to liberate Cuba through a chivalric revolution. All the while he was in Mexico drumming up enthusiasm for his cause in exile he had not forgotten the place of the 26th of July Movement within

Cuba. Exile was like prison. The future Comandante quickly realized as he had in the aftermath of Moncada just how difficult it was to mobilize the masses from a distance. Nonetheless he continued trying through the power of the written word. His eloquence was never lost to his readers and so it was with 'Manifesto No. 1 to the People of Cuba'. This political tract was more radical than 'History Will Absolve Me'. Fifty thousand copies were distributed in Havana and Oriente. The Manifesto proclaimed the 26th of July Movement was not a political party but rather a revolutionary movement with a program. The program outlined by the future Comandante called for an end to the latifundia system, land distribution, and worker participation in profits in industry along with a call for state housing, state managed industrialization, rural electrification, education, and finally and most importantly, an end to Yankee imperialism.

The treatise was anti-imperialistic in tone and pleased the ghosts enormously. Don Quixote read and reread the document several times out loud in a reading circle to the veterans. He extolled to them on just how much the Commandante was influenced by chivalric ideals. They pointed to Amadis and Tirant lo Blanc as examples of those famous knights of old who favored land distribution for the peasants. Many a battle was fought along such lines by these knights. José Martí and the veterans of course recognized their own ideas. The admired the treatise and felt that it was worth coming back from the dead just to have read it.

The veterans and Don Quixote, according to Cide Hamete. grew more excited by the moment about Fidelito's plans for the future. One afternoon Fidel Castro was delivering one of his most eloquent appeals for support of his enterprise. A young, thin, dark-haired individual with an unforgettable face entered the room. He sat down on the floor and stared up at Fidel Castro. As their eyes met; there was a mutual and immediate recognition that they were to play an important role in each other's lives. Raúl introduced Che Guevara, a young Argentinean doctor, to his brother. They embraced as if they already knew each other. Che was mesmerized by Fidel's passion and enthusiasm. He shared his anti-imperialist attitude towards the United States. This fact alone would have united them. However, there was so much more they had in common.

As Fidelito spoke late into the night, Che was captivated and already a recruit. Che explained to Fidelito that he was a medical doctor raised in Buenos Aires and Cordoba, Argentina. Despite his bouts with asthma, he had climbed mountains and spent a lot of time in the great outdoors. He explained his long trip through Latin America and his recent experience of fighting for a popular government in Guatemala. The rebels were defeated by an invasion supported by the Yankees. He was prepared to participate in the Comandante en Jefe's next exploit. Fidelito described it in such dramatic and fantastic terms, that Che fell in love with the notion of the expedition immediately.

Part of the attraction of Fidel and his plan for future exploits along the coast of Oriente Province was that it was nothing more than a dream. Could Fidelito transform Don Quixote's dream into something real? Could he change the course of Cuban history forever? Che was convinced that he could. The young Argentine was determined to follow him all the way to the Sierra Maestra. Then the most amazing thing happened. Fidel spied a torn and tattered copy of the History of Don Quixote on Che Guevara's bookshelf. Soon the two of them were discussing all the episodes and exploits of the knight. Both parties were enamored of him and his love for justice. It was then, and only then, that Fidel told Che about his secret desire to realize the lost dream of Don Quixote. Fidel told Che, who agreed, that Don Quixote had failed in his mission to bring back the era of chivalry. Che was delighted and told Fidel that his plan was ingenious. No mortal had ever succeeded where Don Quixote failed. Of course Don Quixote and the veterans were ecstatic at the thought of a society built on chivalric values. Fidel claimed that it would not be too hard because the whole Cuban population was well acquainted with the exploits of Don Quixote. By far the History of Don Quixote was their favorite book and a copy was to be found in every Cuban household, read by young and old alike. The old knight's adventures were pleasing to everyone.

Now that Che knew about Fidel's war plan as well as his intention of taking the battle to the enemy, he was enthralled with Fidel Castro and was to remain a loyal follower. Raúl was delighted at their new recruit, as were the ghosts. Don Quixote ran around the room proclaiming that here was another knight in the making. None of the knights of old had succeeded in bringing back the age of chivalry. José Martí and the veterans laughed at the knight thinking again that he had lost his mind.

José Martí and the veterans had many doubts about Fidelito's plans for the expedition. As yet he lacked a following with the loyalty and training required to become an effective guerrilla force. He also lacked funds for such an enterprise. José Martí was very much aware that at this point, revolution in Cuba was little more than a dream. José Martí and the veterans also doubted the fact that the Cuban people were ready to rise up against Batista. For the ghost, Fidel Castro's next exploit in Oriente and the Sierra Maestra bordered on adventurism. How could he and his comrades prevail against the strength of Batista's military force of over fifty thousand men? Fidelito kept stressing the importance of his plans remaining a secret. However, unbeknownst to him in the beginning at least, Batista had sent his secret police to Mexico.

SIM, in conjunction with the Mexican police, were planning to assassinate Castro as soon as possible. They planned to send two Mexican policemen to arrest him on the street. Before killing him, they would force him to send a message to his comrades that he had been sent away on urgent business. The attempt failed in the end. Castro became acutely aware that because he was so outspoken in the exile community about the need for armed insurrection, he now represented a real danger to the Batista regime. He never slept in the same place twice after the plot against him was discovered. The phantoms were with him at every moment on the look out for assassins. His comrades received him in their apartments or he would book into a cheap pension on Insurgentes. In this way he avoided assassination. He was now leading a moment to moment existence again.

Soon Fidel Castro was invited to the apartment of Che Guevara. The first thing that caught his attention was the enormous number of books on the shelves of his library. Immediately Fidelito thought of the library back on Hacienda of the Spirits. As he perused the bookshelves, Fidelito was astonished by the fact that so many of these books were the same as those on the shelves of the library at Hacienda of the Spirits. Several tomes immediately caught his attention including the Dialogues of Plato, the complete works of Hegel and Kant and all the great Spanish poets, both classical and modern, along with Marxist literature. These were only a few of the books that both Che and Fidel held in such high regard.

Then low and behold, Fidel Castro came upon a shelf full of books of chivalry, including a complete set of the adventures of Amadis de Gaula and his son Esplandian. For the next several hours, the two guerrillas talked about the most famous adventures of the knights of old.

Fidel's eyes fell on a green leather tome with fine gold lettering. The future Comandante en Jefe immediately recognized the book to be the History of Don Quixote. Therein started one of the longest and most passionate discussions about the book as ever happened anywhere. Each of these two gentlemen had read the book so many times they knew it by heart. They discussed all their favorite adventures along with the more complex philosophical issues raised by Cervantes. The two men agreed that they could take chivalry further than it had ever been taken in the past. They wished to create the perfect chivalric society where everyone would eat well. No one would beg or go to bed hungry at night. They wished for a chivalric world where everyone had an education and healthcare. The two of them continued talking about these things until the wee hours of the morning. Both were convinced that they could not tell their comrades yet about their plans to resurrect chivalry.

As it turned out, Che had read novels of chivalry since he was a child in Argentina. He too was a veritable encyclopedia on all the exploits of the famous knights. He and Fidelito were enchanted with each other because each had such specific knowledge about these ancient knights. Don Quixote was filled with enthusiasm by the presence of Che. They started a long practice of Fidel arriving at Che's apartment, book in hand ready to discuss the contents.

They discussed the Brothers Karamazov and whether or not either of them resembled Demetri, Alyosha or Ivan. They also discussed

'J'accuse...! by Émile Zola. These late-night discussions of all the famous books would go on until the early hours of the morning. According to Cide Hamete Benengeli, the two revolutionaries debated the ideas and merits of most of the great thinkers within just a few months. Both of them read with the rapidity and depth of the ghosts. The two men also frequented the best books stores in the capital in search of new books. Fidel was so delighted to have someone with whom he could discuss the ideas of the great philosophers. Soon these two men were soul mates and locked at the hip.

Fidel had confidence in Che and told him about the plans for invading Oriente Province. Che was enchanted with the notion of becoming a guerrilla fighter and read everything he could on the topic. Fidelito gave him a copy of the complete works of José Martí for Christmas. Che was taken up with the thoughts of the Apostle for weeks after receiving his present.

All the ghosts were enchanted with Che Guevara's magical library. Like Fidel Castro, José Martí was struck by the fact that so many tomes were also on the shelves of the library of his own invention. Fidel and Che discussed a great variety of books. The ghosts listened and were always fascinated by how the two really had met each other's match. Che had just as much intellectual curiosity and prowess as Fidelito. Fidel Castro recognized that Che knew Marx and Lenin better than anyone he had ever met. He was much more advanced in his thinking along Marxist lines. Everything interested him. He was equally at home with history, philosophy, literature and politics. Don Quixote meanwhile was thinking something quite different. He was struck by the fact that Fidelito and Che had so many of the same character traits. Both men had enormous strength of character and will, great empathy with the poor, a sense of social justice, and a deep sense of personal honor. All these things made Don Quixote conclude that here was another great Caballero Andante in the making. All the veterans and especially José Martí realized that Che, like Fidelito, read with the focus and concentration of the ghosts. Che's reading powers were greater than most mortals. Che Guevara had a love of knowledge for the sake of knowledge like Fidel Castro. Both were truly Renaissance men.

In October 1955, Fidelito embarked on a tour of the United States to raise funds for the expedition. As usual his gift for public speaking drew enormous crowds of Cuban exiles. He spoke of the need for armed resistance against the Batista regime. He spoke across the eastern seaboard. He made a special impact in New York where he drew over eight hundred people. He then went on to Tampa and Key West. Of course all the ghosts followed the Caballero Nino to the United States and accompanied him on his tour. José Martí grew especially nostalgic because he had made the same journey in his former life to raise money for the Mambises. In all Fidelito's eloquent presentations to the public, he never failed to mention the figure of José Martí. The Apostle and the veterans were delighted with all the attention they were getting in these speeches. As they sat there in the auditorium of Tampa, the veterans felt as if they had returned to a moment in their former lives. They all had passed through Tampa and Key West many times on their way to Cuba. Don Quixote was enchanted with Florida and the beautiful coastline near Tampa. The place looked to him to be right out of a book of chivalry.

When Fidelito reached Key West, he had raised enough funding to start a chivalric revolution. At this point, Batista started rumors to the effect that

Fidel Castro was using donations for his own personal gain. In another manifesto, entitled 'Manifesto No. 2', Fidelito defended his reputation against these unjust accusations. He knew the dictator had started a defamation campaign against him. Most of all, Batista wished to discredit Castro in the eyes of the Cuban people in order to prevent mass uprisings against the government. By this time Batista was well aware of Castro's plans to invade the island. He knew that the future guerrilla would make a landing near Oriente Province. With plenty of financial backing in hand, Fidel Castro returned to Mexico. There he found Raúl, Che and his other comrades awaiting him.

Immediately Fidelito flew into action and predicated his actions on his experience with planning Moncada. He first established several safe houses or cells for the participants of the expedition. As usual secrecy was of the utmost importance. Only Fidel Castro and the ghosts knew of the locations of the safe houses as well as the identity of the members. Now that he had funding, he instructed his men to find a hacienda where they could train a guerrilla force for the invasion. They found Hacienda Santa Rosa just twenty miles south east of the capital. The hacienda was ninety-six square miles and included mountains and a grand manor which could house fifty combatants. The house was surrounded by a great cement wall with turrets. Don Quixote thought it was a medieval castle and that this was the beginning of some grandiose exploit. There were also mountains on the hacienda where Fidelito and Alberto Bayo took the men on long treks lasting for weeks. The ghosts always went along because they were well aware that they would have to be in shape to survive the Sierra Maestra. Besides, all Caballero Andantes undertook long and difficult treks up the mountains in order to train as capable guerilla fighters. Fidelito warned his men that like the great knights, they were out numbered by a superior, well-armed force. As in the times of Amadis and Tirant lo Blanc, all great knights had to be tested for their stamina and heart when going against more powerful enemies.

Don Quixote had a hard time keeping up at first. His armor was so rusted that he creaked as he walked along behind the veterans. When they had to swim small rivers, Antonio Maceo always had Don Quixote in tow. The knight had a terrible time swimming with his heavy armor. Alberto Bayo trained the men in guerrilla warfare tactics. José Martí, Don Quixote and the veterans participated in the maneuvers thinking of former battles won and lost.

Back in the capital, Fidelito welcomed more than forty recruits from Cuba. Immediately he went about establishing more cells or safe houses for the new men. They were secretly transported to Hacienda Santa Rosa in order to prepare to be effective guerrilla fighters. Always on these long journeys up in the mountains the phantoms were willing participants. They realized these vigorous exercises were preparing them for the long struggle against Batista up in the Sierra Maestra. José Martí was impressed with Alberto Bayo's knowledge of guerrilla war tactics. The men would stay up in the mountains for weeks, soaked by the rain and with little or nothing to eat or drink. Don Quixote thought the mountainous terrain looked like land described in novels of chivalry. He was certain that Fidelito had planned some great chivalric adventure and that Cide Hamete Benengeli was recording all the events in the here and now.

As it turned out there was an unexpected turn of events in the proceeding weeks that created great problems for the Caballero Nino. As he was leaving a safe house in the capital one rainy night, the Mexican police caught him, Che Guevara and some other comrades. They were immediately taken to prison. The comrades were questioned about Hacienda Santa Rosa. Fidel Castro gave away the location to avoid bloodshed. Fidel Castro told the police that they should take him with them when they went to raid the hacienda. In this way, no one would be killed. There Fidel Castro told his men to give up peacefully. All the comrades were taken to prison. Fidel Castro was again given solitary confinement. All the ghosts followed the Caballero Nino to his cell. They made a circle around him and concentrated all their energies on making him feel better. Of course Fidel brought his torn and tattered copy of the History of Don Quixote gifted him by the Padre Jesuita. To avoid depression, he would dip into the adventures he liked best. Fidelito wept at the prospect of living in solitary confinement.

Don Quixote remembered how many times the knights of old had to spend in dungeons awaiting an unknown fate before they triumphed over evil. The outlook for the future indeed looked bleak. Fidelito was finally allowed out in the prison courtyard to mingle with the other prisoners. There he saw Che and Raúl and they all embraced. Again, Fidel was dressed in a dark suit and looked the part of a great orator rather than a revolutionary guerrilla. Many of the safe houses had been raided by the Mexican police in conjunction with Batista's secret police.

Fidel and the ghosts were well aware that Batista wanted the Caballero Nino assassinated before he could carry out an invasion. All the arms and uniforms were confiscated from Hacienda Santa Rosa. He was finally was released from prison with the intervention of ex-President Cárdenas of Mexico. Sadly, Fidelito found that he had to start all over to plan the invasion of Orieinte Province.

This was indeed a somber moment for the future Comandante en Jefe of the Revolution. Much valuable time was already lost. There would be a need for more financial backing because all the arms and many of the men were lost. Fidelito moved around the capital, again never sleeping in the same place twice. He was all too aware that there was a price on his head, and so were Raúl and Che. Finally, Fidelito traveled north to the United States in search of funding for his future exploits. He met with the old Cuban President, Carlos Prío Socarrás who was defeated by Batista. He contributed one hundred thousand dollars to the cause. This was a great stroke of luck for Fidelito and he was very grateful. He returned to Mexico and again set up a variety of safe houses throughout the capital. Once more he bought arms on the black market. Then he traveled to Veracruz in search of a vessel to carry the men to the Oriente coast. He settled on a pleasure cruiser named the Granma. The boat had sunk once in a storm so it needed lots of work. Fidelito brought several men from the capital to Veracruz to make the vessel seaworthy.

When Raúl and Che saw the Granma they were stunned. They couldn't believe their eyes. The boat could hold only about twenty-five men. They wondered how all the men destined to go on the expedition would ever survive in the Gulf of Mexico. The Mexican police and Batista's secret police in Mexico were still after Fidel Castro and his men. Fidelito decided that they had to move fast. All the safe houses were emptied of men and arms. They were taken in a caravan to Veracruz for the planned departure. Then word came from Frank País and Celia Sánchez in Oriente Province that the Cuban people were not yet prepared to rise up against Batista. Neither would there be a general strike as Fidelito had always anticipated.

Che and Raúl thought the expedition should be postponed. Che even quoted José Martí when he advised his men to wait to invade Cuba until the right moment. Fidel ignored these warnings. He had promised to invade the island by the end of 1956 and he always kept his promises. His message to the Cuban people was "in 1956 we well be free or die as martyrs". Also the Mexican police and Batista's henchmen were biting at his heels. So Fidelito brought all the men and arms he could gather in a fortnight from the capital to Veracruz. There, eighty-two men were assembled to embark on the expedition. Fidel had received the proper naval coastal maps of Oriente. In this sense he was well prepared.

But the Granma was a problem. Don Quixote looked at the strange boat and thought that it was some magical contrivance out of a book of chivalry. In fact at that moment he remembered the adventures of Amadis and the enchanted bark. In these the knight was magically transported from the mainland to an island using some kind of fantastic contrivance. Don Quixote at that moment thought the Granma was a magical scheme designed to take knights to faraway islands. José Martí and the veterans were amused at Don Quixote's explanations. They were also horrified at the prospect of boarding this strange boat which indeed had an otherworldly appearance.

As Fidel prepared to leave, José Martí and the veterans had serious doubts about the outcome of this exploit. José Martí felt strongly that Fidelito should wait until the people of Cuba were prepared to rise up against Batista. The Apostle thought it was a grave mistake to invade Cuba now. Don Quixote on the other hand had never been so enthusiastic about a future exploit. He immediately told the veterans about the Adventure of the Enchanted Bark, the strange and fantastic contrivance that carried Amadis from island to island. José Martí and the veterans understood the analogy and laughed uncontrollably at the knight. Then it was time to board as all food, arms and provisions were already on the boat.

When all the men were assembled Fidelito gave them a magnificent speech about how they were following in the footsteps of the veterans. José Martí was touched as Fidelito mentioned him over and over again along with the rest of his comrades. The crossing of the Granma from the Yucatán Peninsula to the Oriente coast was a nightmare lasting seven instead of five days. For the expedition, the horror began the instant they entered the Gulf of Mexico. The sea attacked the small boat weighted down well beyond its capacity. Already the Granma was taking on water. Immediately, most of the men grew violently seasick. Che Guevara said later that the entire boat had a ridiculously tragic aspect. Men with anguish reflected in their faces grabbed their stomachs. Some had their heads inside buckets. Others had fallen into the strangest positions, motionless, their clothes filthy from vomit. All the veterans were seasick and so was Don Quixote. They lay on top of each other holding their stomachs trying not to be sick. Don Quixote told the veterans that they were on some kind of enchanted bark. If this adventure was like the adventures of the enchanted bark in Amadis, they were bound to crash on rocky seashore soon.

Fidel Castro and Che Guevara did not succumb to seasickness. They fixed the leak. The storms raged on. The ghosts had a terrible time due to the tossing and turning of the waves that hit the tiny boat. The expedition sailed towards the Cayman Islands and ran two days late. Frank País organized an uprising in Santiago which was supposed to coincide with the landing of the Granma. The uprising was very important but it did not coincide with the landing of the Granma, delayed two days now.

According to Cide Hamete Benengeli, the last two days of the trip were unbearable. The ship kept taking on water. Food, guns, and most ammunition were soaked and rendered useless. The men continued to be sick as high waves made for rocky seas. The phantoms had a hard time. To remain standing turned out to be quite a feat. Antonio Maceo kept vomiting into a bucket and then throwing it overboard. Calixto García remained bent over holding on to his stomach, as did Máximo Gómez.

In the dark, the Enchanted Bark hit the shores of Oriente Province in a grand shipwreck. Cide Hamete Benengeli later recorded the event as reminiscent of the grand shipwreck of the magical contrivance that carried Amadis across stormy seas. As they hit the coast and the ship splintered into pieces, José Martí and the veterans held on to each other for dear life. Don Quixote was holding on to Antonio Maceo who tried to steady him. The veterans and the knight were convinced that this was to be the end of this veracious history. According to José Martí, at that moment all was almost lost. Don Quixote however regained his equilibrium and his enthusiasm at the same moment.

The knight announced to the veterans that this was the beginning of the greatest adventure so far. He assured them that the exploits that awaited them in the Sierra Maestra would surely go down among the greatest exploits ever in the history of chivalry. José Martí and veterans would not be consoled. The Apostle understood the gravity of the situation. All food and provisions were lost, along with most of their arms. Fidel Castro asked the man at the helm if Cuba was in fact on the horizon and ordered him in that direction. Then the Granma crashed on the rocks lining the shore. The shipwreck of the Enchanted Bark was a total disaster for the expedition and for the ghosts.

# Chapter Eleven

The enchanted bark crashed on the rocks and the eighty-two men onboard were thrown every which way. The food and supplies were lost with only some guns and ammunition remaining. Soon after falling into the choppy waters surrounding them, the men found themselves in the middle of an enormous mangrove swamp. They waded for hours with the putrid waters of the swamp up to their shoulders. The ghosts had a particularly hard time of it as the heavy waters kept pulling them downward. Don Quixote was the worst off. Like the men, he was being eaten alive by mosquitoes. Soon mosquito bites covered his face and hands. His armor became so tangled up in the mangrove plants that Antonio Maceo and Calixto García had to spend a good hour untangling him.

Finally, after more than forty-eight hours of intense struggle, the men came to the end of the swamp and headed for dry land. Batista's henchmen were all around them. Several men were killed as they headed for the nearby hills. José Martí, Don Quixote and the rest of the phantoms were horrified and thought for sure that the men wouldn't make it up to the Sierra Maestra. Just then Fidel Castro shouted to the group to head for the cane fields further on up the hillsides. Batista's airplanes started to bombard the men as they tried to reach the cane fields. Don Quixote looked up and was convinced that the airplanes were great flying monsters out of a book of chivalry. Several more men were killed, but finally Fidel Castro and another small group, including the ghosts, were able to hide in the tall cane break. Batista's men followed them and surrounded them. After several hours they gave up, although the bombardments continued for some time.

The men scattered so as to not make a clear target and Fidel Castro had only three men by his side. They did not dare move a stitch for hours on end. As darkness came, Batista's henchmen combed the cane fields. Fidel and his men were far outnumbered and with only a few guns between them. As Fidel and his companions lay there motionless in the dark, they could hear the screams of dying men around them. José Martí and the veterans were convinced all was lost. Don Quixote tried to assure them that this was only the beginning of a great adventure for the Caballero Nino. José Martí and the veterans threw themselves over Fidel Castro and his three companions. They thought that if there was any hope at all, Fidel Castro had to survive. When the bullets flew past the men, the ghosts concluded that their efforts to protect these mortals had worked. So did Cide Hamete Benengeli when he faithfully recorded the exploit in his second history of Don Quixote. The phantoms would read the account upon their return to Hacienda of the Spirits.

For over a week the men lay in the canebreak motionless. Batista's soldiers started to burn the cane fields. However, they failed to set on fire the cane field where Fidel and his companions were hiding. The men stayed alive by sucking on the cane stalks around them so they would not die of thirst. Finally Batista's army left the scene and the planes disappeared overhead. Don Quixote told José Martí and the veterans that the same thing had happened to Amadis when the Enchanted Bark crashed on the shores of some unknown island. Amadis was attacked by giant monsters flying overhead and he survived. It was only appropriate to this adventure that Fidel should survive as well. José Martí was in no mood for tales of chivalry. He and the veterans were very concerned about how many of the men had in fact survived the wreck. Finally Fidel was able to locate all the surviving men. There were a total of twelve out of the original eighty-two men left, including Raúl Castro, Che Guevara and a very charismatic Cuban soldier named Camilo Cienfuegos.

Fidel Castro was delighted that these companions had made it but he was greatly saddened by the tremendous loss of life among his troops. José Martí and the veterans felt terrible that they had not been able to be in more places to guard the men and save lives. They had only succeeded in protecting a handful of men. Just then Fidel Castro shouted out that they had achieved victory with just twelve men and five guns. Many of those present thought Fidel was crazy in affirming victory with such few resources. Fidel believed it was possible and told his troops not to loose the faith. In the end, they would defeat Batista.

José Martí, the veterans and Don Quixote were stunned. Don Quixote declared that Fidel Castro's faith was exemplary and unprecedented and would be recorded faithfully by the historians in the annals of chivalry. He told his ghostly counterparts that he could not think of a single instance where a knight had shown such faith against such overwhelming odds. Don Quixote took this as a sign of great adventures yet to come. He told the ghosts that many a great exploit was reserved for Fidel Castro and that these exploits would be more fantastic than those recorded thus far in any book of chivalry. José Martí and the veterans did not share Don Quixote's enthusiasm and were worried about the survival of the men. Surely Batista's men were scouring the foothills of the Sierra Maestra. Just then Fidel Castro gathered the men around in a circle. The future Comandante en Jefe explained that they had to get to the upper reaches of the Sierra Maestra in order to carry out the war from there.

The journey up the Sierra would be dangerous and tricky given the fact that Batista's army still surrounded them. Fidel thought that Batista had concluded that he had killed them all. In one sense the hardest part of the trek up the mountain would be climbing up the foothills of the Sierra. There were many villages of Guajiros on the way. Fidel knew that if they stopped and asked them for food he would be putting them at risk. He realized that some of the Guajiros were so afraid of Batista's soldiers that they might turn them in if discovered.

The first part of the adventure began with the men traveling by night only and hiding during the daytime to avoid detection. They would scatter out for fear of being all found at once. They slept on the cold damp earth and crept through several Guajiro villages during the first week in search of food. Often the Guajiros would awaken at night and provide the men with a meal of pork, rice and beans, and yucca. This was extremely dangerous but they hated Batista's soldiers. These soldiers routinely invaded their homes, raped their women, and killed at random. Don Quixote and the veterans continued to try and protect the men by throwing themselves over their bodies as they slept. Once the enemy soldiers came dangerously close to Fidel Castro so Don Quixote and José Martí piled on top of him in an effort to keep him alive. The experience made the Apostle reflect even more on the possible influence of phantoms on mortals.

As the men reached the upper areas of the Sierra Maestra, José Martí and the veterans recognized the rich tropical vegetation. They had all awaked from the dead in these parts so the terrain seemed very familiar to them. They left Batista's army behind them in the lowlands as they penetrated the thick fog and mists of the upper part of the Sierra. Fidel Castro's plan had worked as the army lost track of them in the lowlands. Trekking up the mountainside, they would often come upon waterfalls and clear pools. The men stripped themselves of their clothing and dove into the crystal clear pool. This came as a great relief since they had not bathed for a week. Don Quixote was embarrassed as the veterans stripped him of his armor and made him take a bath in one of these wondrous pools. Don Quixote looked at the rich green vegetation around him and was convinced that he and the men had reached a magical land described in Amadis. The fogs and mists surrounding them as they marched on contributed to his impression. The veterans found Don Quixote's proclamations very amusing. They could see why the knight would come to this conclusion as the magical world of the upper Sierra indeed seemed like the fantastic lands portrayed in books of chivalry.

After climbing upwards for over a week, Fidel Castro found a nice hiding place among the thick vegetation next to a waterfall and beautiful pristine pool. The comrades were absolutely starved having left the Guajiro villages far behind them. The hunger of the ghosts was insufferable. Don Quixote knew that if help did not arrive soon, all would be lost. The men would soon starve to death. Fidel Castro and rest of the group grew thinner and thinner. José Martí and the veterans were also shrinking. The situation was intolerable. The men took to sleeping on the ground most of the time. Some were struck by fever as the ground was so damp that they could not avoid getting sick. Several men did suffer from fever and other diseases. Che Guevara did his best to help them.

Then something miraculous happened which Don Quixote took to be the beginning of great exploits yet to come. Celia Sánchez and Frank País, two comrades who were in contact with Fidel Castro when he was still in Mexico, somehow made it up the Sierra with food, arms, supplies and soldiers. Fidel's lookout spied them and their men coming up the mountain and at first thought it was the enemy. Don Quixote and the veterans concluded something quite different as they saw them coming. Luckily Fidel recognized Frank País, a comrade from Santiago who had planned an uprising in the city in conjunction with the landing of the Granma. The uprising failed and País and Sánchez headed up the mountain in great secrecy based on the faith they had in Fidel Castro's ability to survive. They were not at all sure they would find anyone alive and were delighted when Fidel Castro stood up in the middle of the rich tropical vegetation where he had hidden to greet and embrace them.

Don Quixote was stunned at seeing a woman dressed in battle fatigues. He tried to think back on examples of such a thing in novels of chivalry. Finally, the knight concluded that this small woman with dark brown eyes had to be some kind of seer or priestess. José Martí and the veterans broke out in laughter. Fidel Castro and his men embraced the newcomers. Never had Fidel been so happy to see anyone. Not only did Celia Sánchez and Frank País bring much needed food and supplies along with guns and ammunition, they also brought hammocks for the men to sleep in. Fidel and the ghosts were ecstatic since sleeping on the ground had caused them so much trouble. Don Quixote was sore all over from sleeping on the wet earth in a full set of rusty armor.

It was about this time that Fidel Castro and his brotherhood became aware that Batista had claimed to have killed them all. Newspapers around the world carried stories of Fidel's death at the hands of the dictator. The bombs had found their mark according to the official version of the history. Fidel Castro had to do something, and quickly, to quell this myth and put aside these lies. It was about that time that a journalist from the New York Times made it known to Fidel Castro that he wished to interview him to prove that he was alive. Fidel and Che found out about Herbert Matthews and his desire to come up into the Sierra to interview the future Comandante en Jefe through the radios they had gotten from Sánchez and País. In this way, Fidel kept abreast of events as they were happening in the big cities like Havana, Santiago and Santa Clara. There were even rumors of a general strike to stop the country's economic engine. Fidel thought this was a great idea but that the time was not right yet. Batista's army, although greatly weakened from the attacks by the new knights, was still a moving force to be feared by the general population.

In February 1957, Herbert Matthews quietly made a trip to Cuba. He landed in Havana and traveled by car to Santiago. There he was met by members of the Cuban underground who carefully planned a secret trip up to the base camp in the Sierra to prove once and for all that Fidel Castro was alive. The trip was difficult and took over a week, but finally Herbert Matthews met Fidel Castro. He conducted a long interview and took many pictures of Fidel. Don Quixote always inserted himself in front of the camera and even in front of Fidel at times. According to Cide Hamete Benengeli, when the pictures were published in the New York Times, Don Quixote remained invisible. In the coming weeks, the old knight complained that he was not visible. José Martí and the veterans tried to console him. Don Quixote could not be convinced that he ever would be visible to mortals.

Herbert Matthews wanted to know how many men made up the new brotherhood called the 26th of July in honor of Moncada. Fidel Castro had few men as so many had perished at the hands of Batista's forces. So all the veterans stood in line and the newly formed brotherhood marched in a circle in front of the journalist. The guerillas moved in and out of the thick vegetation which protected them from view and they were only visible momentarily. As they continued to weave in and out of the vegetation, Herbert Matthews got the impression that there were many more men than were actually present. The veterans of course helped out in this very important event according to Cide Hamete Benengeli. Herbert Matthews returned to New York with the impression that Castro had a significant army which would not easily be reckoned with by Batista's forces. It was Matthew's opinion that Batista was slowly losing the war. His headlines made their way to Havana and Santiago as well as the other cities on the island. Spirits soured as news of Fidel's exploits reached the eyes and ears of the general population.

Soon the men had settled back into a more normal routine. Sleeping at night in the hammocks made life so much easier, as did having a regular square meal. Celia Sánchez tended to the needs of the men. Don Quixote again thought she was some kind of seer or priestess out of a book of chivalry. The men followed Fidel's example and tied the hammocks between trees. José Martí and the veterans soon realized that Fidel Castro would soon long for his beloved books. José Martí and Máximo Gómez decided to make their way down the Sierra to the lowlands where Batista's army was still located. Being invisible had its advantages as they passed right through the camps of the soldiers on their way to Hacienda of the Spirits. When they finally arrived at the hacienda, they were exhausted and slept for some time before getting up the next morning. Máximo Gómez was delighted at the chance to do his toilette in the bathroom. Meanwhile José Martí went up to the library and out of curiosity started to read Cide Hamete's account of Fidel Castro's latest adventures. The ghost was very impressed by the truthfulness with which Cide Hamete Benengeli had traced the latest exploits. Then José Martí gathered all the books he could with the help of Máximo Gómez.

The two of them started the long journey back up the Sierra Maestra. The books in hand included many novels of chivalry which José Martí knew would inspire Fidel. He had become a great aficionado of such books and had enjoyed them so in Mexico. The ghosts passed through the camps of the enemy army carrying all the books they could, including a complete collection of José Martí's own writings. They passed through the Guajiro villages they had been through before with Fidel and his comrades. They stopped to enjoy some rice and beans leftover in a pot hanging outside the hut of some Guajiros. Then they hit the upper reaches of the Sierra Maestra and walked on for two days before reaching Fidel and his men. They neatly stacked the books with the novels of chivalry on top in the middle of the encampment.

Soon Fidel Castro discovered his beloved books but could not explain how they got there. He did not worry about it much. However, he delved into reading some essays by José Martí that outlined the goals of those who led the Wars of Independence. Che joined him, as did the other men, and soon the encampment was transformed into a school, much like the one Fidel Castro organized when in prison. Fidel would lie in his hammock day after day and lecture the men on how José Martí's goals and plans for a new Cuba were exactly those which they should follow as revolutionaries.

One night under a full moon, when it was possible to read, Fidel and Che started to read books of chivalry. Soon they were reading the fantastic adventures of Amadis and Esplandian out loud. The men were intrigued and gathered around in a circle listening intently to every word. José Martí and the veterans were again struck by the fact that the goals of knighthood were very similar to the goals of José Martí and the revolution. Things like land reform, healthcare, education and decent housing for all were goals which were shared by the great knights and revolutionaries alike. Don Quixote grew very enthusiastic listening to Fidel and Che remember and recite by heart the adventures of the great knights. He was sure this was the beginning of a series of great and magical exploits by Fidel to bring back the era of chivalry.

Don Quixote was certain now that this was the goal of all the comrades as they sat around in a circle. Fidel Castro was in the middle reading books of chivalry to his heart's content. Suddenly Fidel grew more enthusiastic than ever about achieving the revolution as quickly as possible. He told Che Guevara that he thought Carlos Marx was wrong. The ability to carry out the goals of the revolution did not depend mainly on the objective conditions. Rather, the hearts of those wishing to bring about lasting change determined the outcome of the struggle. Guevara thought about this point for some time and concluded that he was in complete agreement with this kind of thinking. Don Quixote and José Martí agreed it was the desire of the people to overthrow Batista which would make the difference. Don Quixote went on at length to the veterans and anyone else who cared to listen about all the great knights. Amadis was his favorite knight who won battles against overwhelming odds and never gave in to the enemy when it came to implementing social justice. He cited the example of Amadis fighting an enemy army of thousands alone. When the enemy cut off his head, the knight calmly picked it up off the ground and put it back on his shoulders.

At this point, José Martí and the veterans broke into uncontrollable laughter at the fact that Don Quixote took these fantastic tales to be true to life. Their doubts did not affect the knight. He went on at great length about the fact that all kinds of magical events had already transpired in this veracious history and that there would be many more to come. The knight asserted that Fidel Castro had survived and thrived up to this point. There was enough proof that he was a great knight. He was certain that Fidel's adventures were being recorded faithfully by Cide Hamete Benengeli.

The men continued to gather around in a circle to listen to Fidel Castro and Che Guevara read and discuss various adventures of the great knights. Fidel's favorite knight of course was Amadis while Che had preferred Tirant lo Blanc since childhood. Again Fidel Castro pointed out to the men over and over just how similar were the goals of chivalry and the goals of the revolution. Sometimes when Frank País and Celia Sánchez brought food, supplies and ammunition they would join the circle of listeners. Celia was fascinated by Fidel Castro's obsession with the tales of great knights and immediately concluded that these books would influence him in the future. Don Quixote, on hearing her comments, concluded that she was indeed a seer or a priestess found in books of chivalry. These seers often served as consorts and advisors to the great knights and he was sure that this would become true.

One evening, under the light of a full moon, Che and Fidelito started to reminisce about their love of books of chivalry since childhood. Each had identified with different knights. Che liked the first Spanish knight who had his history recorded, one Caballero Zifar. Fidel liked the Caballero de Hierro whose identity was forged in the fires of war between the early Celtic people and the barbarians. But it was Amadis that Fidel was most taken with and for Che it was Tirant lo Blanc. The two soldiers often argued about who had the most fantastic adventures, who had fought the hardest battles, who had undergone the most enchantments, who had brought the ideals of chivalry to bear on the weak and needy peasants of their time. Fidel Castro argued that it was Amadis who was the most socially conscious of the two knights, while Che never lost faith in his chosen knight and maintained it was Tirant lo Blanc who identified more strongly with the peasants. They never settled the question. Cide Hamete Benengeli failed to settle their differences regarding the two knights. He recorded this adventure in the second history of Don Quixote which even now remains invisible except to phantoms.

After several weeks of reading books of chivalry, Fidel grew worried about the strength and stamina of the men to do battle. Batista's army did not dare to come up to the higher reaches of the Sierra where the men had now made permanent camp. It became obvious to Fidel that the men would have to resort to guerilla warfare of the kind they had trained for in Mexico. He feared his men were growing weak lying around in hammocks. So he suddenly announced that the men would start to take long treks up to the very top of the mountains to a place called Pico Turquino.

In the months that followed, these long marches would become a regular event as preparation for going down to the lowlands to attack Batista's regiments. Don Quixote was at first delighted by these turn of events. He longed to do battle. The knight said it was in keeping with tales of chivalry. The higher up they climbed the better prepared they would be to do battle in the lowlands. Don Quixote firmly believed that these long marches were a way of doing penance just like Amadis had done always before a great battle.

On these long marches the men suffered a great deal. They went for days at a time, and led by Fidel the men had a hard time keeping up with him. The more they complained the harder Fidel pushed them on. These long treks were so exhausting that it was commonplace for the new knights, as Don Quixote liked to call them, to hallucinate and have visions. Fidel and Che were the first to see all the great knights of old coming out of the fogs and mists to accompany them on their marches. Then all the men started to see the knights of old they had heard about when listening to Fidel and Che. Fidel saw the first Spanish knight ever to have his history recorded in a book of chivalry, the Caballero Zifar. Then there was Amadis in his shiny suit of silver armor. There was the Knight of Iron in his iron suit of armor, followed by the son of Amadis, Esplandian, with his armor fashioned out of bronze. The Knight of the Sun and the Knight of the Moon were also marching beside the men. All these knights and more joined the march on their trusty steeds. Amadis had a beautiful white stallion which magically appeared with its rider alongside Fidel, accompanying him up the mountainside. Fidel and Che were sure that these hallucinations were not real, but appreciated being accompanied by the knights nonetheless. Don Quixote of course was absolutely sure they were real and true to life. He was convinced that the spirit of chivalry was so alive in Fidel Castro and Che Guevara that they rose from the dead to join them.

At first the only one to see the knights of old emerging out of the mists in this magical land was Don Quixote. The hallucinations came from hunger and exhaustion. José Martí and the veterans were convinced what they were seeing was real. At least this much was true while they were hallucinating. Then they returned to base camp and recovered their senses. José Martí and the veterans were not so sure they were not real. Of course Don Quixote tried to convince them. He stipulated that all the exploits of Fidel Castro and the new brotherhood were totally in keeping with those described in books of chivalry. José Martí and Máximo Gómez smiled in amazement. However, Calixto García and Antonio Maceo weren't so sure but tended to believe Don Quixote.

Between the long marches and hallucinations, the new knights went to the lowlands to attack Batista's troops. Again the reader of this veracious history would see Fidel Castro and Che Guevara in their hammocks swinging back and forth in the gentle breezes of night. They were reciting adventures from books of chivalry which were pertinent to their present circumstances. Then Fidel Castro took out his torn and tattered copy of the History of Don Quixote gifted him by the Padre Jesuita. He started to read the adventures out loud and all the comrades remained absolutely enthralled with the knight. They all loved the chapter of the history which tells of Don Quixote reading books of chivalry in his library. They adored the adventure of the windmills where Don Quixote mistakes windmills for giants. Everyone was in stitches because the thought of turning windmills into giants amused them no end. Then there was Maestro Pedro's puppet show where Don Quixote mistakes puppets with real soldiers. Then they died laughing when Fidel read the chapter where Don Quixote mistakes two bands of sheep for two great armies out of a book of chivalry.

All in all, when everything was said and done, Fidel told his comrades that he wished to make Don Quixote's lost dream come true. The future Comandante en Jefe told them that their mission was to bring back the era of chivalry. All the comrades were delighted and enthusiastic about realizing Don Quixote's lost dream. All were in agreement that this mission left undone by Don Quixote had to be finished. The moon was full again and the men formed a circle around their two leaders asking them about their hallucinations. Che told them that if they believed they were true, then they were so. Don Quixote took such a liking to Che and his faith in the ideals of chivalry that he let loose with a whole string of absurdities directed at the veterans about how Che would go down in the history of chivalry as one of the greatest knights to have ever lived. Don Quixote believed that he was to play an important role in the revival of chivalry described in the history of Fidel Castro presently being written by Cide Hamete. However, everyone agreed that Che Guevara deserved his own history.

It was about this time, shortly before the new knights journeyed down to the lowlands to attack Batista's troops, that Fidel Castro started to return to his dreams of childhood. He would dream of the adventures read by the ghosts as if he were still a small child. The knights seemed larger than life in his dreams and more real than when he was awake. These dreams had a calming effect on Fidelito when he was a child as they did now. One night Fidel dreamed of Amadis being dubbed a knight in front of a small medieval chapel. Fidel was behind him in the dream. He was waiting in line to become a full-fledged knight like Amadis. He thought of Amadis's perfect white skin and classic features with long golden locks. Then in the dream, Fidel Castro walked around and faced Amadis. He lifted his visor to see his face. To his surprise it was not the face of

Amadis at all but rather his own countenance staring back at him.

Fidel was caught by surprise and awakened with a start. He looked around him from his hammock but all the men were asleep except for the lookout. It was at that moment under the light of a full moon up in the Sierra Maestra that Fidel Castro realized that these adventures represented his initiation into knighthood. He lay awake the rest of the night thinking and planning ahead about all the things the chivalric revolution and the new knights would accomplish once the war was won. There would be first a grand literacy campaign since Cuba was over eighty percent illiterate. Then there would be housing for all, good food, free medical attention and free education. He had absolute faith that the war would be won and in the not so distant future.

Celia Sánchez and Frank País continued to make their way up the Sierra Maestra to the base camp of the new brotherhood of knights led by Fidelito. There they would report on the location of Batista's army and the different forts and garrisons which housed them. The one thing they were certain of was the fact that Batista's army would not follow them up to the highest reaches of the Sierra where the base camp was located. Now it was time for the new knights to descend the mountains and go in search of the enemy army. Fidel Castro, Che Guevara and Raúl Castro led the first band of men down into the lowlands to attack the army using the guerrilla tactics they had practiced in Mexico. Of course the veterans were already well familiar with guerilla warfare, as they had used these tactics against the Spanish during the Wars of Independence. They felt well prepared to participate. Given their experience helping the men survive in the cane fields, they hoped that they could take some bullets directed at Fidel and his men. According to Cide Hamete Benengeli, it happened that the new knights attacked an important fort in the lowlands. At first they approached the fort head on. Then, when chased by enemy soldiers, they retreated into hiding. The second contingent of new knights attacked the enemy as the first were in retreat. These second attacks were led by Fidel Castro and Che Guevara along with Don Quixote.

According to Cide Hamete Benengeli, in the first true history of Fidel Castro called The Caballero de Biran, these second offensives were successful. Taking the enemy by surprise, they wounded or killed most of Batista's henchmen before they knew what happened to them. José Martí stood in front of Fidel Castro and took many a bullet for him. He could feel these bullets pierce his heart and lungs. The pain soon went away and he always survived to live another day as a ghost. The same was true for Don Quixote who with great effort protected Che Guevara. The other veterans did the same falling on top of the men who were in most danger. According to Cide Hamete Benengeli, Fidel, Che, and many of the new knights survived the battle because of the phantoms. The phantoms' courage and protection made it possible for Fidel Castro to survive.

A year passed quickly for the comrades up at the base camp in the Sierra Maestra. They had gotten used to the long treks up the Sierra Maestra to Pico Turquino. Frank País was killed suddenly in Santiago de Cuba. It was too dangerous for Celia Sánchez to come and go from the Sierra now. Fidel Castro decided that she had to come up to the base camp permanently. It was about this time that it occurred to Fidel to build a treehouse in a giant mahogany tree near camp. This was to be Celia's new home. She would have some privacy there. The treehouse would be the perfect place for the men to plan their next adventure in the lowlands.

Don Quixote was delighted with her presence. The knight spent as much time as he could following her around camp and back up into the treehouse. Supplies were dwindling since Celia no longer was going back and forth from Santiago. The whereabouts of Batista's army was also a mystery as Celia had provided knowledge of their location before being exiled to the Sierra.

Now Fidel had to send out search parties to find the most important places to attack. Sometimes these men were caught and shot. Sometimes the men would learn of Batista's army's whereabouts from the local Guajiros. This too was also highly dangerous, as many of the Guajiros who tried to help the new brotherhood were tortured and killed. Nonetheless, the sojourns to the lowlands to attack Batista continued and with great success. They always used the same guerilla tactics of attacking the enemy and then falling back only to have a second contingent of men waiting to attack the enemy in retreat. During these battles, Don Quixote saw many famous knights of chivalry joining the fray. Whenever they would attack a garrison or fort, Amadis and Tirant lo Blanc would head up the attack. Cide Hamete recorded these events, stipulating that the spirit of chivalry was so alive in this new brotherhood that the knights of old could not resist coming back to life. Many new knights perished in these undertakings. Some were tortured mercilessly. Fidel and Che always managed to escape. According to Cide Hamete, it was due to the fact that José Martí, the veterans and Don Quixote were always by their side ready to take a bullet.

Thes attacks on Batista's army went on for many months. The new knights were usually successful, although they took their fare share of casualties. Batista's army was unable to beat Fidel Castro and his brotherhood in the lowlands. They were unable to reach the upper parts of the Sierra Maestra for lack of training. Batista decided to try and bomb the base camp using airplanes. The new knights took many casualties and bombings became more and more frequent. Fidel had to move the base camp and training sites often to avoid being killed. As usual, Don Quixote took the airplanes to be giant monsters like those described in books of chivalry. For a change José Martí and the veterans went along with him. As José Martí said many years later, they might as well have been giant monsters for all the harm they did to Fidel Castro and his comrades.

The time for a general strike throughout the island was near and the conditions were ripe. By this time, Fidel Castro had established Radio Rebelde with the radios brought to the base camp by Celia Sánchez and Frank País. As Cide Hamete Benengeli described it, Radio Rebelde was the perfect mechanism by which Fidel could voice the goals of the revolution and the values of chivalry to the general population. Everyone on the island listened intently to his every word.

The war was prolonged and difficult. Fidel decided to expand the presence of the Rebel Army throughout the island. He sent his brother Raúl to open a second front in the center of Oriente Province. He dispatched Comandante Juan Almeida to open a third front in eastern Oriente. He ordered Comandante Che Guevara and Comandante Camilo Cienfuegos to advance with their columns toward the western part of the island. They had to travel more than a thousand kilometers in very difficult terrain to get to their destination.

Batista's army attempted to deal a mortal blow to Fidel Castro in the

Sierra Maestra. He sent thousands of soldiers to the mountains in an operation called the 'final offensive'. After several fierce battles in the Sierra, Batista failed in his objective. Raúl Castro and Juan Almeida had by this time consolidated their positions respectively. Che Guevara and Camilo Cienfuegos arrived at the center of the island. Along with the other revolutionary forces they won many important battles including the Battle of Yaguajay and the Battle of Santa Clara. In these conditions, Fidel Castro decided to surround Santiago de Cuba and promote insurrection among all the revolutionary forces fighting to resurrect chivalry. Within a few months, Batista's army had dispersed and almost disappeared. The battles in the lowlands were easier now as there were not as many soldiers. Those left were terribly disorganized, tending to run away at the end of a battle. The new knights followed them. Batista's forces took more and more casualties. Finally they showed themselves unwilling to do battle at all.

The war was won and the spirit of chivalry more alive than ever in the hearts and minds of the new brotherhood. Fidel and Che were ecstatic at the thought of finally being able to leave the Sierra Maestra. They were there for almost three years. On the short wave radios the good news came that the general populace was ready for a coordinated strike throughout the island. The members of the 26th of July Movement had organized the people well. All that remained was for Fidel Castro and the new brotherhood of knights to come down off the Sierra Maestra.

According to Cide Hamete Benengeli, on January 1, 1959, the knights of old followed the new knights down the mountain. As they passed through many Guajiro villages, the people cheered them on. Batista was preparing to leave the island and go into exile. Many of his henchmen were left behind. Fidel Castro slowly made his way towards Havana, stopping in cities and towns along the way. Don Quixote was certain that this was to be the beginning of a new era. In some of his speeches, Fidel Castro made reference to the great heroic knights of old. He told the people that the goals of the revolution were reminiscent of the goals and values of chivalry. The crowds cheered with enthusiasm and Don Quixote rode alongside him in his jeep all the way to Havana. Cide Hamete Benengeli later faithfully recorded these events. The ancient Moor was of the opinion that the exploits in the Sierra Maestra these last three years would go down as among the greatest in the history of chivalry. Don Quixote and the veterans were certain that defeating Batista was one of the greatest adventures ever carried out by any knight. The people and the phantoms believed that Fidel Castro was 'Larger than Life.'

In Havana the general strike was underway. The people had already started to destroy the casinos and gambling dens. The mafia who ran the casinos were on their way into exile. Fidel Castro and his new brotherhood of knights reached Camp Colombia. The place was Batista's fort on the outskirts of Havana. The future Comandante en Jefe gave his final speech of the afternoon on the values of the revolution and of chivalry. As he spoke of the new era of chivalry, a paloma landed on his shoulder and everyone gasped. The many photographers present took Fidel Castro's photograph with the paloma. Don Quixote was quick to jump into the picture. Cide Hamete Benengeli pointed out in The Caballero de Biran that Don Quixote had managed to get into the picture.

# Chapter Twelve

According to the ancient Moorish historian, Cide Hamete Benengeli, after his final speech of the afternoon Fidel Castro retired to the top floor of the Havana Hilton. He quickly had the sign 'Havana Hilton' removed and put in its place a new sign. He renamed the hotel 'the Habana Libre'. Don Quixote and the veterans were delighted to see the Caballero Nino move into action so quickly. The ghosts immediately found a large room with several beds to accommodate their need to sleep next to Fidel Castro's room in the newly named hotel. The phantoms wished to remain close to Fidel in order to protect him.

There was a large room with an enormous round table on the top floor of the Habana Libre. Fidel renamed the large conference room 'Pico Turquino' after the highest peak in the Sierra Maestra. Fidel immediately called for the presence of the members of the rebel army and the 26th of July Movement who had come down from the Sierra Maestra. The men met for several weeks. The spirit of chivalry was so alive in the new knights that all the great knights of old came alive. Don Quixote was convinced that these meetings were held to think about how to bring back the era of chivalry. The topics of conversation were like those held by the rebels up in the Sierra Maestra.

Seated comfortably around the round table overlooking Havana, Fidel and Che started the discussion. The first thing they suggested was a literacy campaign. Over forty percent of the population in Cuba was illiterate or semi-illiterate. Fidel had the idea that all the population would participate. Those who knew how to read and write even a bit would teach those without any education. Hence sixth graders would teach fifth graders, and fifth graders would teach fourth graders and so on. Don Quixote and José Martí, seated on either side of Fidel Castro were ecstatic at the thought of everyone learning to read and write. The knights of old thought this was a way of taking the values of chivalry even further than in the past.

According to Cide Hamete Benengeli, the truthful and wise Arab historian, Amadis got up and lifted his visor to compliment Fidel and Che on their brilliance as well as their devotion to chivalry. Then all the knights of old stood up from their places at the round table and cheered at the thought of the literacy campaign. They discussed among themselves how literacy among the peasant population in their own times had been ignored. Amadis and Tirant lo Blanc agreed that this was a great step forward for chivalry.

Next Fidel and Che hit upon the topic of land reform. Ninety percent of arable land in Cuba was in the hands of foreign investors. The majority of Cuba's land belonged to the Yankees. These lands had to be expropriated and turned into state farms, cooperatives and small partials for the peasants. The new knights were aware that there would be tremendous opposition to any kind of land reform. The kind of radical land reform Fidel and Che were suggesting would be especially threatening to Cuba's upper class. Don Quixote and the veterans were delighted with the progress being made. José Martí had expressed in his writings the need for land reform as the basis for a new chivalric society. Don Quixote of course was ecstatic because he had seen first hand during his first lifetime the terrible suffering of the peasants without land.

As the ideas of the new knights were laid out on the table for all to see, the old knights grew more and more excited. Amadis proclaimed that Fidel Castro was well on his way to bringing the values of chivalry to life. He proclaimed that the new society would bring back chivalry in ways the knights of old could only dream about. All the other knights joined in the enthusiasm and delight of Amadis.

Next on the agenda were several important goals articulated beautifully by Fidel Castro. Firstly the new government had to close down all the gambling casinos and exile the Yankee mafia. Fidel also stipulated that it was high time they put an end to prostitution which had been rampant during the era of Batista. Next the new knights projected their plans to build new schools throughout Cuba. All private schools were to be shut down, including Catholic schools. All lands of the church were to be nationalized. Then Fidel Castro called for the nationalization of all public utilities. Electricity and gas would be provided to the population at fair prices instead of the high prices demanded by the private sector. Fidel also called for the nationalization of foreign banks. José Martí was ecstatic seated next to Fidel Castro at the round table. It felt to José Martí that he were actually talking to the new Comandante en Jefe instead of just sitting beside him.

Next Che Guevara spoke of the need for hospitals and the training of new doctors who could provide healthcare to all Cubans. Don Quixote jumped up out of his chair. He had seen so many peasants perish during his first lifetime from preventable illnesses due to lack of healthcare. Amadis again pointed out to the knights of old that chivalry was never perfected to such an extent during their times. All the other knights in attendance agreed enthusiastically with Amadis, including the Caballero Zifar and Esplandian. Fidel went on to stipulate the importance of nationalizing all private investments in the hands of foreigners, which amounted to over one billion dollars. José Martí was horrified at the thought of so much investment in the hands of the Yankees. Máximo Gómez, Calixto García and Antonio Maceo clapped their hands together in agreement. Don Quixote sat quietly next to Fidel Castro in these discussions of nationalizing utilities and foreign investments. The knight really didn't understand what these things entailed. During his first lifetime, he had never heard of utilities or investments and these ideas remained foreign to him.

Che Guevara, who after all was a physician, returned to the topic of healthcare on the island. Up in the Sierra Maestra and in other places on the island he had witnessed the death of many peasants from diseases that were completely curable. He again reiterated the need for training hospitals to produce doctors who could go to the countryside and care for the sick. Che and Fidel also spoke of the need for decent housing for all Cubans. There was to be a great campaign to build public housing for the entire population. The people would pay only ten percent of their salaries for housing.

José Martí was sitting next to Fidel Castro, as was Don Quixote. Don Quixote reminded José Martí and the veterans that chivalry had always had many enemies, especially those who believed in private property. Don Quixote was worried and told the veterans that there had to be some mechanism to defend the revolution. Just at that moment Fidel Castro turned to the group and suggested forming in each block of every town a Committee for the Defense of Chivalry. Don Quixote and the veterans were delighted. It was as if Fidel had read their minds. The knights of old were also ecstatic at the thought and committed themselves to the defense of chivalry. The Caballero Zifar, Amadis, Esplandian, Tirant lo Blanc, the Knight of the Mirrors and Palmerin stood up and raised their swords simultaneously. They all swore to uphold all the ideas that Fidel and Che had articulated that afternoon.

Soon after the meeting on Pico Turquino in the Habana Libre, the large landowners heard about the idea to expropriate large land holdings and the great haciendas belonging to the Yankee imperialists. It was then that the privileged class of large landowners, many of whom had mansions in Havana, decided to take their funds out of the bank and leave Cuba behind. Most of them headed for Miami, while others went to other Latin American countries or Spain. This came as no surprise to Fidel because he knew their lives were to be altered forever by the new Agrarian Reform Laws. Still he felt sad that these people would not become part of the revolution. In fact, he suspected that from Miami they would conduct many anti-revolutionary acts of terror. As it turned out he was absolutely correct. What did surprise Fidel was that not long after the changes started being enacted many professional middle-class people like doctors, lawyers, teachers and engineers left for Miami. He found out that many of these people were forming paramilitary forces to later commit terrorist acts against the revolution. This saddened Fidel, Don Quixote and the ghosts much more than the leave taking of the great landowners. Why a doctor would leave the country when the new government was about to establish a stellar healthcare system was beyond their understanding. Why a teacher would leave when a new educational system was being formed was also beyond their comprehension. No one was more miserable or disappointed than José Martí. He had believed that the middle class professionals would stand by the new Comandante en Jefe. The phantom was clearly disillusioned by their lack of enthusiasm for chivalric values. He thought that this grand exodus of middle class professionals would be very detrimental to the revolution.

Soon after the meetings and initial planning sessions of the revolution ended, Fidel Castro made a trip to Washington, D.C. to meet with President Eisenhower. Don Quixote and the veterans accompanied him on his journey abroad. However, José Martí had his doubts about the United States and its willingness to support the new ideals of the revolution. His doubts became more intense when Fidel learned that Eisenhower preferred to play a game of golf rather than meet with him. He sent his vice president, Richard Nixon, to meet with Fidel instead. The meeting was cordial, but José Martí observed Nixon closely and concluded that neither Nixon nor President Eisenhower would befriend Cuba. In the end, José Martí was correct in his assumptions. Soon after this meeting, the United States stopped buying its quota of Cuban sugar, a very important source of income for the island. This was a big blow to the Castro Government. Neither would the U.S. provide Castro with any more oil.

At this point Fidel turned to the Soviet Union for economic aid. The Soviets were delighted and promised to supply Cuba with much needed oil and buy all the sugar Cuba could export. José Martí and the ghosts were delighted. Martí had some reservations about doing business with such a large and powerful nation as the Soviet Union. Don Quixote reminded the veterans that the Soviet Union was a good giant. According the knight, good giants were always on the side of knights errant and very supportive of chivalry. These good giants had often once been knights themselves. José Martí and the veterans again marveled at Don

THE LOST DREAM OF DON QUIXOTE

Quixote's knowledge of chivalry. They marveled at the knight's ability to apply what he had learned about chivalry to the present historical circumstances.

Soon after his problematic visit to the United States, the U.S. Government made it clear that they would not provide Cuba with oil. Then the promised oil from the Soviet Union started to arrive. The Comandante en Jefe asked the many Yankee refineries to refine the oil for Cuba. The refineries refused to do this. It was then that José Martí saw the need to nationalize oil companies such as Texaco, Esso and Shell Oil. As if he were reading José Martí's mind, Fidel immediately did so, and so Cuba had oil once more. Fidel Castro then made a long trip throughout the island visiting all provinces, cities and towns. He also spent ample time in the countryside. He took his jeep and left Havana with Don Quixote in the front seat and the veterans crowded in the back.

He first went to Holguín and then to the properties of the United Fruit Company, just in time to see the rebel army expropriate the lands off these usurpers. Fidel remembered how Don Angel Castro, who had since passed away, took his perfect circle of sugarcane to be processed each year at United Fruit. This would happen no more and the phantoms took great delight in this fact. After seeing the vast lands of United Fruit Co expropriated, Fidel Castro and the ghosts drove on to Hacienda of the Spirits in Biran. Doña Lina greeting them and as usual had a warm pot of rice and beans on the stove plus a large pot of coffee. Fidel was delighted to sit down at the round table in the kitchen along with the ghosts to enjoy a sumptuous meal of pork, yucca and rice and beans with a beautiful flan Doña Lina had prepared for dessert.

Then Fidel broke the news to his mother that the lands of Hacienda of the Spirits would soon be expropriated in accordance with the new Agrarian Reform Laws. Doña Lina took the news extremely hard. The thought of the perfect circle of sugarcane no longer being hers made her heart sink. Fidel quickly responded that he would leave the house, the library and the perfect circle of sugarcane in her hands. Doña Lina rested much more easily. She understood that Fidel had such affection for Don Angel Castro that he was willing to make an exception to the rule. Meanwhile all the veterans went up to the library and were delighted to find everything was just the same. So much had happened to them since first coming to Hacienda of the Spirits. All José Martí wanted to do was sit down in the overstuffed easy chair and look out on the Sierra Crystal. The veterans rested on the floor while Don Quixote stretched out on the large divan where he had first awakened from the dead. These were happy times and he took great pleasure in knowing that the era of chivalry would soon return. He was so happy to have a second lifetime. All the veterans reminisced about the Wars of Independence and how their aims and goals fit in perfectly with the goals of chivalry. The phantoms couldn't have been happier.

All the ghosts took a long nap and did not awaken until the moon was high over the Sierra Crystal. The moonlight illuminated the entire library. Suddenly José Martí remembered the book on the desk by Cide Hamete Benengeli. He went over and picked it up and sat down in the overstuffed easy chair once more. Don Quixote remained on the divan wide awake. The veterans sat in a circle on the floor around José Martí. He was now thumbing through the volume looking for various passages to read aloud. Finally he found his place in the book and started to read to Don Quixote and the veterans. He picked up the story at the time Fidel Castro was exiled to Mexico and the description of the terrible crossing of the Gulf of Mexico on the Enchanted Bark. He read about all their adventures in the Sierra Maestra. He enjoyed the old Moor's tale of Fidel and Che reading books of chivalry to their comrades in the moonlight. He took delight and special pleasure in reading Cide Hamete Benengeli's account of Fidel Castro's entrance into Havana on January 8, 1959. He read with glee about the paloma that landed on Fidel's shoulders in Camp Colombia. Don Quixote pricked up his ears as Martí read about how Don Quixote was in the pictures taken by photographers. Don Quixote appeared both up in the Sierra when Herbert Matthews visited the base camp and when the paloma landed on Fidel's broad shoulders. Then José Martí read the episodes of the planning of the revolution and the description of all the knights of old gathered around the round table at the top of the Habana Libre. The ghosts delighted in the descriptions of the knights of old and their desire to take part in forming a perfect chivalric society. Then as the sun came up the text came to an end and there were only blank pages. Yet the book was large and there was plenty of space for more writing. Don Quixote took this to be a sign that the Caballero Nino, as he liked to call him, was destined to have many more exploits. Don Quixote went on at great length about the fact that Fidel Castro had single-handedly taken chivalry far beyond the wildest dreams of knights like Amadis, Palmerin, or Tirant lo Blanc. In his hands, chivalry would soar to unknown heights.

Shutting the book, José Martí noted that the gold lettering of the original title had changed. Instead of Don Quixote de la Mancha the book now carried the title The Caballero de Biran. This gave the veterans some pause. Whether or not Cide Hamete Benengeli was writing a second history of Don Quixote was now clear. Although Don Quixote had a pivotal role, the history being written by that ancient Arab historian was definitely the history of Fidel Castro. Don Quixote seemed somewhat disappointed. A mournful look crossed his countenance for a few minutes. He told the veterans that he felt badly that another history devoted exclusively to his exploits was not being recording by the old Moor. But then the mournful look disappeared and a happier face took its place. José Martí and the veterans had to put their hands over their mouths to keep Don Quixote from sensing their amusement.

The ghosts then went down the circular staircase and saw that Fidel Castro was still in the kitchen with his mother talking about Angel Castro and the incredible life he had led. Angel Castro had died shortly before Fidel came back to Cuba to establish a camp of rebels in the Sierra Maestra. Both Lina and Fidel seemed very sad as they reminisced about Angel and his struggle to build Hacienda of the Spirits. The ghosts helped themselves to the pot of coffee on the stove. They sat down at the round wooden table Angel had crafted with his own hands. Ramon came in from tending the perfect circle of sugarcane and embraced Fidel. He was saddened by the news that Hacienda of the Spirits would be nationalized in short order. Being a just man by nature, Ramon felt good about the fact that the Haitians would now be able to grow their own food. He was also relieved to hear that the perfect circle of sugarcane, the house, and the library would remain within the family. The ghosts were also relieved.

Shortly after breakfast, Fidel and the ghosts took leave of Hacienda of the Spirits and headed back to Havana. On the long journey back, Fidel and the ghosts saw the campesinos working in the newly formed cooperatives. Don Quixote, to his surprise, saw Amadis and all the knights of old ride through the fields attending to the needs of the peasants who worked the land. It was a beautiful sight. Don Quixote spoke of the knights of old riding up and down in the fields. José Martí and the veterans laughed but thought he was right in spirit. The new land would be the kind of place the knights of old would return to if given the chance at a second lifetime. Once in Havana, the group returned to the Habana Libre. The ghosts went to their room on the top floor next to the large conference room.

Don Quixote and the veterans spent the next several weeks walking around Havana. They saw all the old casinos fall. The people were happy and gainfully employed in building new housing, schools and hospitals. José Martí couldn't be more content but wanted to keep an eye on Fidel Castro. So at one point, he suggested to Don Quixote and the veterans that they return to the Habana Libre and to Fidel Castro's room. This they found to be a mess with clothing strewn around. He was living like he had lived when he was a student at the university. José Martí was horrified and felt it very important that he make an effort to organize the new Comandante en Jefe.

The ghosts went about picking up his clothes and hanging them in the closet or folding them neatly and putting them in the drawers. When Fidel Castro came in later that evening he assumed that Celia Sánchez had done all this work. He went to thank her in a nearby room. Celia said that she had done no such thing. Fidel and Celia were mystified at who it could be that had cleaned up the messy room. Celia immediately called for more security around the new Comandante en Jefe.

In the weeks that followed, Fidel and the ghosts continued to ride around the island in his jeep witnessing all the progress being made towards the big government cooperatives. The veterans went along with Don Quixote when he pointed out the things that made the new society exemplary in chivalric terms. Fidel would stop in villages and towns and speak of the goals of the revolution and just how much progress was being made in such a short amount of time. The people were delighted to be employed in the literacy campaign, the rebuilding of roads and bridges, and the construction of schools and hospitals. Already there were more children in school than ever before in Cuban history.

Suddenly Don Quixote had the urge to return to Hacienda of the Spirits and so he did, by taking buses and walking a fair amount. He had a bad feeling that he could not quite pinpoint. As was his usual custom, he took a horse from the barn and rode down to the Bay of Nipes. There he saw a dark cloud coming from the north and he feared for Cuba and chivalry. It seemed to him that the Gigante del Norte was about to raise his ugly head and do something to pervert chivalry on the island. As he rode back towards the hacienda, he suddenly saw the fields of a cooperative on fire. The campesinos were doing everything in their power to put out the fire. However, the enormous fire was quickly spreading. Don Quixote rode towards the fire and felt absolutely helpless. He knew this was the work of traitors. The fire was the first terrorist act by the Gigante del Norte that the famous knight witnessed. He would see many more before the year was up. All the newly planted fields burned to the ground. Don Quixote quickly returned to Hacienda of the Spirits where to his satisfaction everything was in place and there were no signs of violence. He then put his horse away and walked to Holguín where he caught a bus to Havana. He quickly walked from the bus station to the Habana Libre where all the new knights were assembled around the large round wooden table in the conference room which had been renamed Pico Turquino. Fidel Castro and the new brotherhood had heard of many fires being set on cooperative farms throughout the island. These were the first acts of terrorism, and were to be followed by many more in the coming months. Fidel, Don Quixote and the phantoms went out on a long journey around the island assessing the damage. It was far beyond what Fidel Castro and José Martí expected. It was hard to believe that the evil Gigante del Norte could do so much damage in such a short period of time.

News of the death of many of the young literacy campaign workers reached the Comandante en Jefe in Pinar del Rio. In Santa Clara he saw the remains of what was a newly built school. In Santiago de Cuba he and the ghosts witnessed a new hospital burn down to the ground. In Havana the enemies of chivalry had torched the new housing project on the outskirts of the capital. Fidel Castro's heart sank and he started to weep silently, as did José Martí. Don Quixote also had tears streaming down his face. He thought that the enemies of chivalry were much worse than in his own times. He concluded that the Yankees were fearful of the example set by the Cuban people in forming the new chivalric society. Fidel Castro feared once more for his life.

Back in Havana, Fidel Castro once more called for a meeting of the new Knights of the Round Table. He was concerned with the terrorist activities of the Gigante del Norte. They needed to bring all their brainpower to bear on how to stop the gringos from destroying the revolution. Fidel realized that while the Committees for the Defense of Chivalry were a big help in stopping terrorism, something further had to be done. José Martí, the veterans and Don Quixote agreed that some drastic measures needed to be taken right away. This was when Che Guevara chimed in that the army had to be mobilized throughout the Cuba to protect the state farms, cooperatives, the schools, hospitals and newly constructed housing developments. The Comandante en Jefe agreed and immediately dispatched Raúl Castro to mobilize the army into defense units. Raúl set up these defense units throughout the island. He wanted to guard the countryside and the Sierra Maestra, the Escambray and the Sierra Crystal.

Not long after Raúl had mobilized the army to protect the people and the revolution, Fidel Castro's intelligence service informed him that the Central Intelligence Agency of the U.S. Government, in conjunction with a large group of Cuban exiles, was planning an all-out invasion of Cuba. They had already made several attempts on the life of the Comandante en Jefe. Fidel took matters into his own hands and mobilized his troops. Seated on top of a tank, he and his men headed for Playa Girón where the invasion was to take place the next morning. Fidel organized his army around the swamps of Girón. He quickly learned that the enemy was bombing the airfields with the hope of doing away with the Cuban airforce. The enemy bombings did not destroy the airforce, which was very lucky for Fidel and the ghosts. They would need to bomb the enemy troops now landing on the beach.

The battle lasted three days, with Don Quixote riding right beside Fidel on his tank. Fidel was giving orders to his men faster than the ghosts could comprehend them. As they went into the heat of battle on the beach, Don Quixote saw all the knights of old enter the fray. Amadis led his counterparts with his sword raised on his beautiful white stallion. The knights fought long and hard for three days and nights. According to

Cide Hamete Benengeli, it was enough to do the trick. At the end of three days, the enemy gave up and realized they were beaten once and for all. Out of the more than fifteen hundred Cuban exiles, one hundred and nineteen had perished in battle and over a thousand men were taken prisoners. The news quickly reached the Cuban exile community in Miami. The terrorist groups who had planned the invasion with the help of the CIA ended up disheartened and disillusioned. Their hopes of returning to Cuba were lost. On the other hand, there was great celebration in Havana as people danced in the streets and welcomed Fidel and his army with open arms. The celebration among the people went on for several days. The enemy combatants filled the Cuban jails and prisons. Fidel, however, did not feel as jubilant as his people. He was worried that the great terrorist to the north would try another even bigger invasion soon. Fidel Castro and the ghosts hopped into his jeep and headed for Oriente Province. Fidel and the ghosts stopped briefly at Hacienda of the Spirits to have a square meal served up joyfully by Doña Lina Castro who was always grateful to see her son. The ghosts helped themselves to some Cuban rum from the liquor cabinet and watched the yellow and orange sunset on the perfect circle of sugarcane. Then they went inside for the delicious dinner awaiting them. Fidel was tired so he decided to spend the night. The ghosts headed for the library where José Martí was amazed to read about the attempt to invade Cuba by the Yankees. He thought how quickly this humble Arab historian was able to record the Comandante en Jefe's exploits. Why he practically recorded the events before they happened. José Martí and Don Quixote were convinced that Cide Hamete was somewhat clairvoyant.

The next morning both Fidel and the ghosts hopped onto the jeep that had carried them to so many places on the island and headed back to

Havana. When they passed the old sugar refinery of United Fruit Company they all smiled and cheered with such joy on seeing the results of expropriation. The cooperatives were in full swing that time of year and all the peasants were hard at work in the fields. Don Quixote saw Amadis, his son Esplandian, Tirant lo Blanc, and Palmerin along with the Caballero Zifar riding back and forth in the fields tending to the needs of the peasants. Don Quixote thought it made a beautiful picture. He felt such joy at seeing these knights participating in the building of the new chivalric society. José Martí and the veterans wondered what was up. Don Quixote told them to have a look. The veterans again covered their mouths to avoid showing their laughter. Calixto García half believed Don Quixote, as did Antonio Maceo. José Martí said that it was true in spirit. The Apostle went on to say the spirit of chivalry was so alive on the island that it made sense to have these hallucinations. Don Quixote did not say a word and kept his own council, preferring not to comment on these disbelievers.

Several months passed and back in Havana the ghosts finally fell into a routine. They awoke in their comfortable room on the top floor of the Habana Libre and stood in line in front of the bathroom waiting to do their toilette. They particularly enjoyed shaping their mustaches and trimming the bottom of their beards. Don Quixote had no such interests until the veterans forced him to take a shower each morning and trim his beard. Then they would go down to the dining room on the first floor for some fresh Cuban coffee. The smell of coffee always made Don Quixote swoon. Then it was back up stairs to the conference room known now as Pico Turquino, where the brotherhood of new knights would gather to make important decisions regarding the revolution.

One morning when Don Quixote entered the room he saw the knights of old with their swords raised and mournful looks on their faces. José Martí sensed something was in the air as did the other veterans. Fidel Castro made an announcement which was to change the course of Cuban history. The Yankees had decided to blockade the island. It was February 1962, just three years after Fidel had taken power. The blockade came in the form of a commercial, economic and financial embargo. Not only would the United States no longer trade with Cuba, but they would do everything within their power to keep other countries from trading with the island. The embargo included much needed items. So Fidel decided after much thought that he would trade the captives from Playa Girón for food and medicine.

The Cuban people were aghast at the news of the embargo and Fidel Castro drew the population together by delivering a long speech on television. He was to deliver speeches quite often. He explained that part of the purpose of the embargo was a news blackout. Nothing coming out of Cuba would be known to United States citizens. No news would come in from the outside world. Fidel explained to his people that the gringos were afraid of the example being set by the new chivalric society. The new healthcare system was almost in place, as were schools and housing. There was no more starvation in Cuba as there was in the rest of the Caribbean and Latin America. The example of all the Cuban people had accomplished scared the Yankees. For the cost of five jet fighters Castro had carried out an exemplary revolution and for all intents and purposes ended human suffering. The chivalric value system was in place and the gringos wanted no part of it since it presented a grave threat to the capitalist system.

After a few months had passed, surprisingly enough, the news blackout imposed by the embargo wasn't working. News about the Cuban revolution reached Europe, Latin America and even the United States. Many countries continued to trade with Cuba. The embargo imposed a great deal of hardship on the Cuban population. The Comandante en Jefe was worried that the great terrorist to the north would try another big invasion. His trusted intelligence inside the CIA brought news that the army and navy were carrying out maneuvers for the purpose of destroying the revolution. Fidel was at his wits end. He dispatched Raúl Castro to Moscow. The Soviet Government offered a great amount of military assistance and sent planes, tanks and ammunition. Yet Fidel was still worried and disillusioned. He concluded that more would be needed to stave off the Yankees. José Martí and the veterans were convinced that Fidel was correct and that something disastrous was about to happen. The Soviet Union then offered to send missiles to Cuba where they would be placed strategically around the island. The missiles would be capable of hitting the United States and could therefore act as a deterrent. Fidel Castro accepted this strategy as required to save the revolution.

The Yankees regularly sent spy planes high over the island to see where they might next attack. President Kennedy was surprised that these planes had spotted the location of the many missiles. There was indeed a crisis looming and José Martí was particularly worried. He knew that the Yankees could easily destroy the island and Don Quixote's dream. Behind the scenes, Kennedy negotiated with the Soviets to end the crisis and have the missiles removed. Fidel Castro knew nothing of these negotiations until much later on in this history.

The United States navy sent warships to form a blockade around the ships coming from the Soviet Union with missiles and planes aboard. There was a standoff but eventually the Soviets gave in and turned back their ships. Fidel Castro was horrified that a secret accord had been reached between the Soviet Union and the Yankees. The agreement stipulated that in exchange for removing the missiles on the island, the United States would remove its missiles from Turkey and Italy. They would do this at some unknown future date. The United States also promised to never again invade.

Furious and disillusioned, Fidel Castro did what he always did when upset. He took his jeep with Don Quixote in the front seat and the veterans crowded in the back. He drove as far as he could up into the Sierra Maestra. He could only go so far with his jeep. So he stopped and left it in a Guajiro village. He took some provisions from the Guajiros and headed up the mountain with José Martí, Don Quixote and the veterans in lockstep behind him. They headed for Pico Turquino, the highest point of the Sierra. They passed the old base camp where they stopped and rested awhile. Then they kept going upwards through the fog and mists of the Sierra. Once they stopped to bathe in a mountain pool, just as they had done when fighting as guerillas in the time of the war against Batista.

Finally they reached Pico Turquino where they slept on the damp ground for the night. Don Quixote was particularly uncomfortable as his armor was getting rusty from exposure to the elements. Fidel lay awake looking at the stars and remembering his childhood. He thought of the bucolic days of his youth when he and the Haitian children would ride up into the Sierra Crystal to the Guajiro villages. He remembered the beautiful Guajira bathing in the mountain pool next to a waterfall. The

Commadante en Jefe finally fell asleep. Soon he fell to dreaming of all the great knights of old whose histories he had read many times over. He dreamed of Amadis with his long blond locks of hair, penetrating blue eyes and white skin. He then fell to dreaming about other knights. Towards the end of the dream, he saw the Knight of the Mirrors coming towards him. The knight stopped right in front of Fidel. He was covered in tiny round mirrors along with his headpiece which was also a mirror. Fidel Castro saw his own image fragmented into a thousand pieces reflecting back at him. He saw his face reflected back from the head piece and he had a terribly mournful look on his countenance.

Suddenly the Comandante en Jefe awoke in a cold sweat. He was still shaking when José Martí and Don Quixote awoke to see such a strange and unusual sight. The dream frightened Fidel, and for the first time in his life, he felt some lingering doubts about his identity. He felt as fragmented as he appeared in the dream. He knew this was linked to his feelings about the Soviet Union's betrayal. He and the phantoms headed back down the mountainside. He still felt fragmented and disillusioned. By the time they reached the old base camp, he felt better. This came as a tremendous relief for Don Quixote and the veterans. José Martí wondered at the fact that he wasn't more pleased with the Yankee's promise not to invade Cuba. Yet Fidel was wary. He felt that his relationship with the Soviet Union had its negative side and that he needed to be very careful in dealing with them.

When Fidel Castro and the ghosts reached the Guajiro village they found their jeep waiting for them with children playing around the vehicle. Fidel spoke with the men and women of the village for a while. The phantoms played with the children. Then they were on their way. They stopped briefly at Hacienda of the Spirits to have a meal with Doña Lina Castro. She was always delighted to see her son. The phantoms helped themselves to some Cuban rum from the liquor cabinet and watched the familiar sunset on the perfect circle of sugarcane. Then they went inside for the delicious dinner that awaited them. After dinner the ghosts headed up to the library where José Martí was amazed to read about their latest sojourn up the Sierra Maestra. He read about Fidel's encounter with the Knight of the Mirrors. He thought again how quickly this humble Arab historian was able to record the Comandante en Jefe's exploits. José Martí and Don Quixote were convinced that Cide Hamete could see the future.

# Chapter Thirteen

Not long after the Comandante en Jefe carried out the initial phase of the 26th of July program, the revolution made use of the Palace of the Revolution and the Plaza of the Revolution built by Batista. In the Palace of the Revolution, Fidel Castro had his new offices. The walls were lined with wooden bookshelves and famous Latin American paintings which made the large room that much more attractive. The ghosts were delighted when they accompanied him there to find a grand library not unlike the library of José Martí's invention. Don Quixote was overcome with joy when he found a complete collection of his famous exploits on the shelves. He found an entire bookshelf with his history in many different languages given to the Comandante en Jefe by leaders around the globe. The first book published after the revolution was the History of Don Quixote. Now the whole Cuban population would be able to read about his exploits. There were also the great philosophers, novelists, poets and of course the works of José Martí. Don Quixote stood a long while fingering through Amadis de Gaula while José Martí took a good long look at his own works. There were also many books that Fidel Castro had had in prison and up in the mountains. All in all, it was a spectacular library that both in scope and breadth went beyond the libraries of most world leaders. Just outside the office of the Comandante en Jefe was a small office for Celia Sánchez, now his executive assistant.

From his offices in the Palace of the Revolution, the Comandante en Jefe conducted most state business. He was called upon to give an inordinate number of interviews to journalists from all over the globe. Jean-Paul

Sartre and Régis DeBray were among the first to interview Fidel Castro. Usually these interviews would last several hours, if not longer, as the Comandante en Jefe explained the advances of the revolution. These included agrarian reform laws, the literacy campaign, schools, hospitals and the grand housing projects designed to provide all Cubans with a decent home. Fidel was proud of all these achievements and also enthusiastic that these goals had been achieved in record time. The journalists were duly impressed.

Don Quixote and the veterans were always present during these interviews and always had some words of wisdom to add. Sometimes they grew bored because the interviews were so long and tedious. More often than not, they would go into the Comandante en Jefe's kitchen beside his office for some rich Cuban coffee and talk among themselves. So much still needed to be done, and there was no one more aware of that fact than José Martí. The Apostle realized that the Cuban people would need to make many more sacrifices to achieve true independence.

The Plaza of the Revolution was an enormous place that could hold over a million people. From the start Fidel Castro developed a direct dialogue with his people, especially the peasants. Just as when he was young, Fidel had an uncanny ability to communicate complex ideas to uneducated simple people. Over a million peasants would arrive in Havana just to hear him talk about the future of the revolution. Residents of Havana would welcome the peasants into their homes with great delight. Then everyone would go to the Plaza to hear the Comandante en Jefe speak about the needs of the revolution.

The first thing that he explained was that each Cuban would have to produce more than he or she consumed. This was a basic premise upon which national independence rested. Therefore, the workforce should expect to work long hours and have very few consumer items. Fidel wanted to do away with consumerism. He did, however, assure his people that they would have an improved, well balanced diet of meat, fish or fowl and a great variety of vegetables along with plenty of milk, eggs and coffee. The decision was to invest the most resources in new social programs like the great cooperatives in the countryside. The veterans were delighted with these pronouncements. In his writings José Martí had always stressed the need to produce more than was consumed. As far as he was concerned, Fidel was right on the mark so far in the ideas he expressed, particularly when it came to production and consumption. He was glad Fidel was following his precepts.

The relationship of Cuba with the United States was difficult since the embargo was established in the decade of the sixties. The embargo obligated Cuba to look to other countries for its commerce. The most convenient places to go were the socialist countries of Europe. Fidel tried to maintain a distance from any new commercial dependence. However, economic difficulties made it that much more necessary to approach the Soviet Bloc in 1972. Next Fidel Castro made a momentous announcement. He told his people that Cuba was soon to become a member of the Council of Mutual Economic Assistance (COMECON), the trade organization of the Soviet Bloc. The Soviet Union had guaranteed to buy all the sugar that Cuba could produce at inflated prices while selling Cuba much needed petroleum at below market prices.

Fidel explained to his people that it was a wonderful arrangement. If Cuba produced enough sugar, it could buy consumer items and industrial goods through credit and pay virtually nothing. The crowds cheered. Don Quixote noticed that José Martí had a worried look on his face. José Martí was quick to explain that this was just another form of dependence. If Cuba had to continue to be a one crop economy and produce mainly sugar, it would never develop a diversified agriculture or industrial base. José Martí mused to the knight and the veterans that Fidel had no choice as a result of the vicious American embargo. The Americans were at fault. Also the blockade would force Cuba to build a huge army to protect itself from the Gigante del Norte. The Apostle went on to explain that this would prohibit the development of both agriculture and industry. Don Quixote and the veterans were concerned. The idea of joining the Soviet Union and other socialist societies had seemed like a good one to them at first. But now they too had their doubts.

According to Cede Hamete Benengeli, the Comandante en Jefe went about explaining a very important principle, one which in his mind would make or break the revolution. He explained to the people the concept of the New Chivalric Man. Che Guevara first articulated this notion and Fidel was quick to pick up on the idea. The New Chivalric Man would be dedicated to the principle of producing more than he consumed. He would value sacrifice, hard work and the conviction that the whole of society was more important than any one individual. He would not be motivated by material incentives but rather his sacrifice and hard work would be based on a new moral framework. The veterans pricked up their ears. José Martí did not believe that moral incentives were enough. He saw that the revolution found itself in very difficult circumstances

Economic and social development demanded resources that were very scarce. Cuba was also affected by the embargo and the illegal terrorist acts against Cuba by the Yankees. The decision of the directorate of the revolution, principally Fidel and Che, had opted for the only solution that seemed possible. They asked the people for more sacrifice and harder work as well as reduced items of consumption. The main necessities were provided by the government including housing, food, education and healthcare. This seemed to be the only way to develop the island. It was also a necessary condition to maintain the independence of Cuba.

José Martí observed with curiosity how the revolution had used his own idealism to strengthen the valor of the people. Don Quixote, on the other hand, was wildly enthusiastic about the idea of the New Chivalric Man. The man who understood the values of sacrifice and hard work had understood the essence of chivalry. The knight stipulated that the values of chivalry had taken the revolution a long way. He was ecstatic at the thought that the common man could ascribe so wholeheartedly to the sacrifice inherent in chivalric values. José Martí stood by listening very intently to all the knight had to say. He was very impressed by the idealism that motivated Don Quixote. However, given his historical and political experience, he was worried about the affect this kind of politics would have on Cuba in the long run.

Next from the podium of the Plaza of the Revolution, the Comandante en Jefe explained that Cuba needed to diversify its agriculture. Cuba needed to produce more kinds of fruits and vegetables, both for internal consumption and for export. Why Cuba could become a veritable truck garden for the socialist countries. He also concluded that state farms, cooperatives and private farmers had to produce more milk, eggs and meat for local consumption. Cubans would have an improved diet with many more calories at each meal. The crowds cheered and the ghosts were delighted since one of their main pleasures in life was eating.

Next Fidel announced that Che Guevara was to become the new Minister of Industry. Fidel said that Cuban industry would have to grow and expand to produce many more consumer items. New factories would be opened to produce domestic clothing, furniture, refrigerators, stoves, soap, toothpaste, razors and all kinds of durable goods. José Martí was all for this idea. The Apostle told the veterans that to be independent Cuba would have to develop its own industry for internal consumption as well as for export. Don Quixote who knew nothing of industrialization kept quiet and had no comment. The veterans were very supportive of Fidel's ideas.

For the next month, Fidel drove around the countryside all over Cuba to see to the expansion and diversification of agriculture. Don Quixote rode along with him in the front seat, with the veterans crowded in the back as usual. They went from one state farm and cooperative to another and one cattle station to the next, checking on produce and the status of the animals. Don Quixote thought these large estates looked like estates described in books of chivalry. Fidel had read a great deal of late on genetics and animal husbandry. He got it into his head that he wanted to import Holstein steers from Canada to breed with local cows for the purpose of producing more milk. He was also concerned about how to increase the poultry population and egg production. Don Quixote and the veterans were in agreement but also somewhat amused at how the Comandante en Jefe got involved in all aspects of agricultural production. Fidel always questioned the workers about how to up the production of chickens and cows that gave more milk. Don Quixote had never heard of a Caballero Andante who involved himself so much in farm production. He thought back on all the novels of chivalry he had read, and could think of no examples of knights who bothered with questions of produce.

José Martí and the veterans were concerned that Fidel was micro-managing the economy. They thought this would eventually have to change. Fidel also talked to the workers about expanding the kind and amount of fruits and vegetables produced on the island. Not long afterwards, Fidel decided that the Isle of Pines should be renamed the Isle of Youth. There, new citrus trees would be planted by the thousands to produce all kinds of citrus like grapefruit, oranges, lemons and limes. These fruits would be for internal consumption but a large number would be reserved for export to places like the Soviet Union. There the climate did not permit the growth of such fruits and vegetables. Don Quixote and the veterans were delighted and thought this was a very good idea. Thousands of young Cuban students and people from other parts of the globe would go to the Isle of Youth to study and work in agriculture. José Martí was ecstatic that the revolution had decided to adopt his idea of combining work and study as part of the educational process.

The veterans were eager to get back to their room at the Habana Libre. They had been gone the better part of a month. They often slept on makeshift cots when visiting cooperatives or individual farms. Máximo Gómez and Calixto García looked forward to trimming their mustaches and beards in front of the mirror in the bathroom. Don Quixote cared not one wit where he slept since he loved the Cuban countryside so. Fidel felt the same way. However, duty called so he had to return to the Palace of the Revolution.

Once back in Havana, Fidel picked up his old custom of never sleeping in the same place twice. The Yankees had made many attempts on his life so he needed to move around a lot. Fidel Castro now focused on the problems of industrialization he had discussed with the people at the Plaza of the Revolution. He met with the new Minister of Industry, Che Guevara. They'd have talks lasting into the wee hours of the morning of how to diversify Cuba's industry and how to increase production. Both men agreed that industry had to become more efficient. As with agriculture, both men agreed that the New Chivalric Man would provide the key to both diversification and increased production. Don Quixote was highly enthusiastic about the role of the New Chivalric Man.

Plans were made to open new factories for a clothing industry in Cuba. Also Fidel wanted Che to increase the output of nickel, rum, tobacco, hemp and canned goods. The planning and control of such activities would remain with the office of the Comandante en Jefe. Fidel did buy several Holstein bulls from Canada. His prize bull artificially inseminated over two thousand cows. The bull then he dropped dead from the effort. Don Quixote and the veterans felt sorry for the bull but saw the humor in the situation. The Apostle was concerned that Fidel was going too fast and that he was skipping steps. Don Quixote disagreed and thought everything Fidel did was just marvelous. The veterans agreed with José Martí and added that Fidel was too impatient. The veterans and the knight then discussed the fact that there were so many attempts were made on his life that the Comandante en Jefe perhaps thought he did not have that much time left. He wanted to do everything quickly while he was still alive.

Meanwhile, Che talked to the workers about the New Chivalric Man.

Che told them of the delights of working for the good of chivalry rather than for material gain. The workers listened to his every word. There was an intense discussion about the importance of moral incentives and their relation to material incentives. Che vehemently defended moral incentives. Fidel supported Che's vision while other leaders of the revolution warned of the importance of not forgetting material incentives. The Comandante en Jefe remained ambivalent for a long time. Then reluctantly he introduced material incentives such as higher wages or gifts such as stoves and refrigerators. He even offered trips abroad to the Socialist Bloc. José Martí was sure the situation would improve. Production went up in the factories and fields. People were generally happier and there were more consumer items in the stores.

Some time later, it became clear that both moral and material incentives were important. One should not hold sway over the other. Fidel went on the stipulate to his comrades and Che that revolutions are complex processes accompanied by a large dose of idealism. He said sometimes it takes years to respond to their many challenges. José Martí listened carefully to these discussions and referred them to his own political experience. At moments he wanted to contribute his ideas to the discussion. However, his condition as a phantom prohibited him from doing so.

Fidel had studied hard at La Salle, Colegio de Dolores and Belen. Yet he envisioned a different kind of life for Cuba's youth. Studying all the time was too one-sided. He concluded that to lead a balanced life, people had to be both active and contemplative. Fidel decreed that all school children over twelve would study but also work in factories or fields. At first they were sent out into the countryside to work beside the peasants on the big cooperative farms. This practice turned out to work very well. The children were much happier and better balanced. Then Che introduced the concept of 'voluntary work.' Those who had extra time after their normal jobs or those who did not work or study would be asked to work voluntarily in factories or on cooperative farms. This practice also turned out to be a big success. Many people found extra time after work to contribute and now felt more a part of the revolution. The practice lent a sense of cohesion to the population. José Martí and the veterans were delighted, as was Don Quixote. The knight announced that in the chivalric world all people worked voluntarily and had no need for money or material gain, especially in a society when education, healthcare and housing were free. José Martí liked what he heard from the knight, as did the veterans.

For the next few days, Fidel took off in his jeep with the phantoms to travel the countryside. He went to the cattle stations and there learned of a cow who gave more milk than any cow in Cuba. Fidel was delighted as were the ghosts. Fidel put his arms around the animal and declared that she was the most revolutionary cow in the country. The phantoms all broke out laughing. José Martí often said Fidel Castro was more like Don Quixote than Don Quixote. Fidel Castro was so happy to see production had improved and that there was a greater diversification of fruits and vegetables. He knew that this would bear well on the lives of his people. Then he went about visiting many factories in Cuba. First he went to the old Bacardi rum factory which had improved its output by fifty percent. The ghosts were delighted and each of them had a drink of rum to celebrate the progress being made. Then they went to a cigar factory and smoked the latest Cuban cigars made for export. Fidel was also very pleased and smoked a newly hand-rolled cigar. He and the phantoms drove on to hemp factories, clothing factories, stove and refrigerator factories and other factories which made personal items like razors, soap and deodorant. The Comandante en Jefe reluctantly admitted that the material incentives now offered by the government were working well. In all factories there was an increase in production. The new economic relations with the Soviet Union were very important for sustaining this period of growth.

Fidel Castro decried the fact that things weren't moving along faster. He was well satisfied for the moment with the increases in production in both factory and field. He returned to his offices in the Palace of the Revolution. The phantoms now decided to move from the Habana Libre to Fidel Castro's old room on the top floor of the old pension in old Havana. There they had more privacy and could look out on the sea.

Next Fidel Castro turned his attention to increasing sugar production on the island. He constructed a series of new sugar mills. He modernized the old mills like the one which formerly belonged to the United Fruit Company. Once these new mills were in place, sugar production soared to new heights but still did not reach the specifications desired by the Comandante en Jefe. So in 1968, it occurred to Fidel to have a ten million ton harvest in 1970. The entire population would have to be mobilized for this effort to succeed. The previous year, the sugar harvest had yielded only five million tons. Fidel called his people to the Plaza of the Revolution. He explained to them that if Cuba could reach the goal of ten million tons, the island would be independent at last. It would no longer have to depend on any other nation. The people were ecstatic and danced in the plaza. The phantoms were also in a very good mood and continued to celebrate throughout the night. Antonio Maceo and Calixto

García had too much rum so Don Quixote and the other two veterans had to help them back to their room in the pension. They were all excited at the prospect of cutting sugarcane with their swords alongside the Cuban peasants.

It took several months for the campaign for ten million tons of sugar to get underway. People came from all over the globe to help the Cubans, even from the United States. The workers were organized into brigades and went out into the fields each morning at sun up to start cutting cane. They cut cane well after sundown until there was no more light. Foreigners and Cubans alike lived side by side in makeshift housing in the fields. The effort went on for months. For a while it seemed that the Cubans would reach their goal of ten million tons. Then some untimely rains came which slowed down the workers. A hurricane swept through the country destroying a sizeable part of the sugar crop. Things went from bad to worse. In the end, all their efforts added up to only eight and a half million tons. It was the biggest crop in the history of the island but less than the commitment of ten million tons. However, this was a vast improvement over the crops of the preceding years.

Fidel Castro worked in the fields beside the peasants cutting cane. He now returned to his offices in the Palace of the Revolution. The phantoms went with him. Fidel had never felt so despondent or disillusioned. His hopes for economic independence went up in smoke. The ghosts noticed that the Comandante en Jefe took the loss very personally. For him the question was a matter of honor. For once he had failed and it proved devastating to him. He moped about his offices for days at a time, not knowing how to proceed. He was disappointed in the people even though they had made an all-out effort. The moral incentives had not worked along with the material incentives. Fidel again could not understand why moral incentives alone had failed to motivate his people.

José Martí, on the other hand, had a hard time understanding the Comandante en Jefe's disillusionment. For the life of him he could not understand Fidel Castro's attitude toward the event. Eight and a half million tons was nothing to scoff at. In fact, it was a great improvement over previous years. José Martí again concluded that the Comandante en Jefe was more like Don Quixote than Don Quixote. All veterans laughed. Don Quixote, however, was not the least bit amused.

Don Quixote took the eight and a half million tons to be one of the Comandante's greatest exploits in this belated history. He was jumping for joy at the thought that the Cuban people had banned together to carry out such a feat. For Don Quixote the eight million tons was one of the greatest collective accomplishments in the history of chivalry. José Martí and the veterans agreed completely.

It was about that time that Fidel decided to take a trip to the Soviet Union. The phantoms boarded the plane with him just as they had when he went into exile. José Martí shared Fidel Castro's preoccupation about the need for more integration with the Soviet economy. At the same time, Cuba had to maintain its political independence. Don Quixote seemed not to share in their worries. The knight was convinced that good giants always watch out for knights. When Fidel landed in Moscow, he was greeted by Khrushchev the Prime Minister of the Soviet Union. Fidel gave him a big bear hug and the cameras snapped photos. These pictures were seen all around the globe. Don Quixote was ecstatic as were the veterans.

Fidel Castro toured both factories and giant cooperative farms throughout the land. He was duly impressed. The Soviets had always used material incentives to motivate their people. Both the factories and the cooperatives were highly productive and efficient. The workers in both factory and field were enamored of the Comandante en Jefe. Back in Moscow Fidel and the ghosts were treated to a marvelous symphony. When they emerged from the symphony however, it was snowing hard. Fidel had seen snow before in New York, as had the veterans. Don Quixote gathered his suit of armor around him to try and keep warm. The veterans laughed at the knight but were also cold. They all held on to each other until they reached their hotel. There each phantom, along with Fidel, had several glasses of vodka to try and keep warm. Meanwhile Fidel, José Martí and Don Quixote sat up and had a pleasant chat with Prime Minister Khrushchev. He was a merry old man and seemed to enjoy the company of Fidel Castro enormously.

They stayed there into the early hours of the morning, talking and planning the future of the revolution. To his surprise, the Soviet leader presented Fidel with a beautifully bound copy of The History of Don Quixote in Russian. Don Quixote and the veterans were very impressed by Khrushchev's understanding of Fidel Castro. Don Quixote had no idea his history was translated into other languages and he was thrilled. In the end, Khrushchev extended large credits to Cuba so they could buy durable goods on the open market. The next afternoon, Fidel boarded his plane satisfied that he had achieved his goals on the trip to Moscow. José Martí was concerned about the complexities of the close relation with the Soviet Union. Meanwhile Don Quixote thought that everything Fidel did or said was absolutely perfect. Fidel Castro could do no wrong in the knight's mind. The Apostle and the veterans had a more complex vision of these latest decisions. Don Quixote was so incensed at this point he almost drew his sword. The knight then thought better of taking out his weapon. It wounded the knight whenever he heard the veterans doubt or question his protégé.

When the plane landed in Havana, Fidel and the phantoms were met by Raúl Castro and his closest comrades. There was bad news to be had. The Yankee imperialists had sent their henchmen, the Cuban exiles, to bomb sugar mills, schools and hospitals all over the island. Raúl Castro had mobilized the army to defend the people and had caught the most of the culprits who were now languishing in prison. Fidel felt his heart sink. When would these incursions end? What price had to be paid to end Yankee imperialism? On the way back to the Palace of the Revolution Fidel contemplated these questions but unfortunately had no answers. Meanwhile, according to Cide Hamete Benengeli, the knights of old, including Amadis and Esplandian, continued to patrol the beaches lining the island on the lookout for traitors. They caught many of them trying to land on the beaches in small catamarans and turned them over to the army. According to Cide Hamete, when Fidel Castro and the phantoms learned about these developments they were delighted. The patrols of the knights had worked. There were many fewer incursions on the island after this.

The next week the Comandante en Jefe gave a long speech at the Plaza of the Revolution. This time he spoke against sectarianism as an evil to be avoided at all costs. It made no sense in a society where everyone was equal for women or blacks to single themselves out and voice their displeasure. Don Quixote and the ghosts couldn't agree more. It was then that Fidel Castro announced the very sad fact that Che Guevara was leaving the island. No one knew exactly where the exceptional guerilla was going except they had the idea that it was somewhere in Latin America. Che would fight another war to liberate yet another people from oppression. Fidel was very sad and upset when he made this announcement. Tears came to his eyes when he read a goodbye letter written by Che to the Cuban people. In the letter Che praised the Comandante en Jefe for his magnificent guerilla war in the Sierra Maestra. He also said that he intended to carry forward guerilla warfare in another place where the people sought freedom from oppression. He was very sad to be leaving Cuba. He felt that his destiny lay elsewhere. Don Quixote and the veterans were all very upset at this news. They adored Che and realized that he was one of the principal proponents of chivalry on the island. It was with great sorrow that they listened to his letter where Che renounced his Cuban citizenship. The phantoms believed that Che should always be a Cuban citizen even if he were absent. Fidel Castro thought the same thing. The people standing in the Plaza, especially the campesinos, were very sad at the thought of Che leaving them.

Cide Hamete Benengeli tells us that soon after this the phantoms decided to return to Hacienda of the Spirits. They were tired of all the activity in Havana and wanted a rest. As soon as they arrived, Doña Lina had a marvelous meal of pork, Moors and Christians and yucca awaiting them with a delicious flan for dessert. Ramon Castro came inside at dusk after working all day on the perfect circle of sugarcane. He was tired and hungry so he wolfed down his dinner and then was off to bed.

Meanwhile the veterans went to the library awaiting them in the attic. José Martí was the first to grab Cide Hamete Benengeli's history of the

Caballero from Biran off the antique desk. He perused through the pages until he came to the part where Fidel spoke in the Plaza of the Revolution the first time. The veterans and Don Quixote gathered in a reading circle at his feet. Then the Apostle read about Fidel Castro's concept of the New Chivalric Man. Don Quixote was overjoyed at the concept. The knight felt it was in keeping with the demands of chivalry for sacrifice and selflessness. José Martí proceeded to read Cide Hamete Benengeli's description of their travels around the island to the many cooperatives. He read about the bull that inseminated two hundred cows and then dropped dead. Don Quixote and the veterans couldn't help but break into raucous laughter at the thought of this bull. Then José Martí dwelled on the description of the offices of the Comandante en Jefe in the Palace of the Revolution. The old Moor focused on the books in Fidel Castro's new library. Many books were gifted to him by visiting journalists. Cide Hamete did not lose sight of the fact that Fidel had a complete collection of Amadis and his son Esplandian. He also noted that Fidel Castro had an entire bookshelf devoted to different renditions of Don Quixote's history, including editions in many languages.

Next the Apostle read about their trip to the Soviet Union. He also touched on the new economic agreements that had been reached by Castro and Khrushchev. Again José Martí had his doubts about such agreements, but for the time being could do nothing. Then the veterans fell asleep and the Apostle lit the oil lamp next to the overstuffed easy chair and began reviewing his own writings. Having read them all, the phantom sat back in the comfortable overstuffed easy chair and pondered the fact that he and Fidel Castro seemed to differ on so many issues. It wasn't like that before when Fidel and his comrades were up in the Sierra Maestra. Nor was he in disagreement with the Comandante en Jefe when he was planning the agrarian reforms, the literacy campaign, new schools, hospitals and housing for the people of Cuba. The Apostle sat there and thought about the need to combine centralization and decentralization techniques. For the phantom central planning must be compatible with autonomy at the municipal level. The Apostle had written in his former life that the municipal level is the salt of democracy. On the other hand, for José Martí the role of the state in protecting social and economic development was crucial. He concluded that maintaining small private and cooperative businesses was also important. Eventually the Apostle fell asleep and started to dream about life up in the Sierra Maestra. He remembered their long treks up to Pico Turquino with the knights of old following by their side protecting them as they went along.

The next morning Don Quixote and the veterans awoke early and went downstairs to the kitchen. Doña Lina Castro had left a pot of hot coffee on the stove with four cups on the table Angel Castro had made. The ghosts helped themselves to a cup of coffee. Then Máximo Gómez went into the parlor and found the old deck of cards. The veterans sat down and started a card game among themselves. José Martí and Don Quixote were not interested in such things. Instead they went outside on the porch and greeted Carlos Manuel de Céspedes and Ignacio Agramonte who were still blowing perfectly round rings of white smoke into the cold crisp morning air. They proceeded down the stairs and went to the bakery where each received a hot bun for breakfast. Then they went to the smithies and saw a horse get new shoes. They went on to the lands now belonging to the Haitian peasants. There they were delighted to see newly constructed small houses in a circle all painted white. They went into one of these little houses and saw that the Haitians now had plenty of good food like eggs, meat and milk. Then the knight and the Apostle wandered over to Local School #15 and to their delight and surprise found all the Haitian children reciting their A, B, Cs. This was a source of great contentment to the Apostle as he was a firm believer in education for the peasants. Now they were all well clothed in their uniforms and concentrated on the lesson at hand because they were all well fed.

Eventually Don Quixote and José Martí made their way back to the house on stilts built by Angel Castro to the best specifications of a childhood spent in Galicia. The Apostle headed back up the spiral staircase to the library of his own invention. There he settled back in his easy chair and started to read the classical philosophers. He read Plato with great affection and came to his theory of ideas. He put the book aside for a moment and wondered if ideas affected phantoms differently from mortals. He asked himself if ideas had an afterlife or was it the afterlife of an idea that counted.

Then he picked up a copy of Hegel and again asked if the dialectics of history applied to phantoms. He had no answers but loved posing these impossible philosophical questions. The Apostle looked over at the corner of the attic and saw Don Quixote in a wicker chair reading romances of chivalry. By now he was into the third volume of Amadis de Gaula. Never was Don Quixote quite as happy as when he was reading romances of chivalry. José Martí went downstairs as the afternoon was getting late. The Apostle helped himself to a glass of rum and joined the veterans on the porch. There they all toasted the Comandante en Jefe and raised their glasses over that perfectly crafted circle of sugarcane. They were so glad that Fidel Castro had decided to leave it in the family. Then they came inside for another wonderful meal of pork, Moors and Christians and yucca, with another beautiful flan prepared by Doña Lina. Don Quixote stretched on the divan in the parlor and soon fell asleep. Strangely enough he dreamt of patrolling the beaches of Cuba on the lookout for traitors along with the knights of old. When he awoke he felt disappointed that he had not joined these knights of old on the shores of the island.

Meanwhile, José Martí went back to the library and sat down at the antique desk in the middle of the room. He pushed aside The Caballero from Biran and started to review his own writings. The Apostle took a break for a while and thought about the development of the revolution. Then he went over to the overstuffed easy chair and fell asleep. He awakened and went outside where he found Carlos Manuel de Céspedes and Ignacio Agramonte still blowing rings of white smoke into the cold night air. He walked down the stairs and out to where the Haitians had their circle of white huts. He was delighted to see that they had lights. This was unheard of before the revolution and certainly something to be proud of as an achievement. Fidel had made sure that all the new housing for the poor peasants throughout Cuba had electric power and running water.

José Martí decided it was better to dwell on these more pleasant aspects of the revolution. The ghost wandered down to the Biran River and watched the waters pass him by as he contemplated the more numinous aspects of his existence as a phantom. Finally he made his way to the Bay of Nipes. It was a particularly warm night so he decided to go for a swim. He jumped into the warm waters of the Caribbean and right away a large shark passed him. Then the ghost slowly made his way back to the house on stilts where everyone was starting to stir. The veterans got up from the table where they had played cards all night. Don Quixote got up from the long wicker divan in the parlor and joined them. Then they headed for the pot of coffee on the stove.

The phantoms stayed on Hacienda of the Spirits the better part of a month before heading back to Havana. They wandered around the hacienda and even went up to the Sierra Crystal to visit with the Guajiros. A young Guajira girl was bathing in the pool under the waterfall not far from the village. The phantoms stopped to see her. She was absolutely beautiful and reminded them of the Guajira that captivated Fidel Castro in his youth. Then they continued to follow the paths of the Guajiros all the way to the top of the Sierra Crystal, just as Fidel Castro had done. Don Quixote as usual felt that they had returned to the magical lands described in romances of chivalry and that they were about to have another fantastic adventure.

Once back in Havana, the phantoms met with the new knights in the conference room designated for that purpose. Fidel led the discussion. He wanted to know about the progress of the literacy campaign. Che was delighted to report that Cuba was almost a hundred percent literate now. All the old knights suddenly appeared behind the new knights around the round table. They all raised their swords and smiled as a sign that they were delighted with the results of the literacy campaign. So were José Martí and Don Quixote. Don Quixote stipulated that the revolution had taken chivalry much further than in his own era. All the knights of old agreed and there was great celebration and joy in the room.

Now new plans were being made to buy much needed farm equipment from the Soviets. Also Fidel Castro had decided at the very beginning that Che Guevara should head the central bank. Then the discussion moved to literature and the arts. The comrades decided to build a new film institute. Cuba could make films about Cuban history as well as critique the revolution. There would be a renewed Cuban ballet. The ballet had always been strong in Cuba but now more funding was available. The ballet would go abroad to demonstrate just how far the revolution had come in the arts.

The comrades decided to establish a state-owned publishing house. The name of the house would be 'Casa de las Américas.' Fidel and Che decided that the first book to be published would be the History of Don Quixote. Don Quixote was thrilled. Now all the Cuban people would have the chance to read about his exploits. Next the histories of the great knights of old would be published. Amadis de Gaula would be the first knight of old to have his history published by Casa de las Américas. The knight smiled and lifted his sword in the air to indicate his approval. Then they would publish the tale of the first Spanish knight ever to have his history recorded, Caballero Zifar. These would be followed by the adventures and exploits of Esplandian, and finally Tirant lo Blanc. Don Quixote jumped up off his seat. He was ecstatic at the thought that the people of Cuba would now be able to read about the famous knights of old. Chivalry would be brought that much more alive. The old knights present were also delighted, especially Amadis who said that his history had not been published in centuries. There would also be a new association of writers who would get support from the government. The 26th of July Movement was disposed to support creativity on all levels.

It was then that the Yankees started a defamation campaign against the Comandante en Jefe and the revolution. They placed articles in newspapers all over the globe to defame the image of Fidel and to tarnish the image of the revolution. Again Don Quixote and the knights of old thought that the evil Giant to the North was worse than any of their enemies in the past. In a sense their attempts to defame the revolution were an indication that the example set by the 26th of July Movement was in all aspects stellar. Fidel Castro was not so worried about the Yankees and what lies they invented about him. However, he was concerned that an inaccurate portrayal of the revolution be put forth to the world. The Comandante en Jefe did all he could to counteract the vicious attacks by placing articles in newspapers all over Europe and Latin America. He also encouraged people from all over the globe to visit the island and see the revolution for themselves. His plan of action worked as the revolution became more popular worldwide. Intellectuals from Europe, Latin America, and even the United States came to see the new agrarian reforms, the new educational system and the new healthcare system as well as the advances in publishing and the arts. These intellectuals praised the Comandante en Jefe for his ingenuity and creativity.

The Cuban people carried on with the work of building new hospitals and schools. Despite all their attempts to complete the work of the revolution, Operation Mongoose under the guidance of the CIA continued to work. There were more terrorist activities than ever before directed towards the Cuban population. Cuban exile paramilitary groups financed by the CIA continued to arrive at night in small boats to burn sugarcane fields and bomb sugar refineries, schools and hospitals. According to Cide Hamete Benengeli, Amadis, Esplandian, Caballero Zifar, Palmerin and Tirant lo Blanc started to patrol the beaches all around Cuba as a means of stopping these acts of terror. The old Moor tells us that their efforts paid off as the invasions and terrorists acts were not as frequent as they had been. Don Quixote heard about the military action of the knights of old on the beaches of Cuba. The knight was sad that he had not participated. José Martí and the veterans heard the news almost immediately. The phantoms were less doubtful than before about the knights of olds' involvement with the revolution. Now these phantoms were willing to accept that the relationship between mortal and ghost was ambiguous. Don Quixote considered this attitude to be a vast improvement in their thinking. He also felt that now they were more in tune with Cide Hamete Benengeli and his history of the Caballero de Biran than they used to be.

# Chapter Fourteen

The phantoms made their way back to Havana and went to their room in the Habana Libre. There each veteran spent time in front of the mirror trimming his mustache and beard. Don Quixote followed suit despite his displeasure. Then the phantoms went to the offices of the Comandante en Jefe in the Palace of the Revolution. There they found Fidel Castro giving a long-winded interview to some foreign journalists. As usual he talked for hours about the advances of chivalry. He also spoke of the Yankees' latest incursion in the island and that fact that they had bombed sugar mills, schools and hospitals. The foreign journalists were horrified but not surprised. Some of them were Americans and very ashamed that their country had engaged in such violent, illegal terrorist activities. They asked Fidel Castro when these attacks would stop. He answered by stipulating that the Yankees would never give up despite their promises to the contrary. He felt that they would continue with the violence to try and destroy the revolution. The journalists once again were taken aback and all of them condemned these acts.

After the departure of the journalists, Fidel Castro left the Palace of the Revolution and went to spend the night at the home of Celia Sánchez. The phantoms returned to the pension in Old Havana. By the time they arrived it was early morning so they went back to the Habana Libre for their morning cup of rich black Cuban coffee. They concluded that all problems were exacerbated by the cruel embargo which didn't even allow for food and medicine. The factories and farm equipment lacked spare parts. This was a big problem and even caused some factories to close. The spare parts from the Soviet Union did not match the machines in Cuba, which had mostly been made by the Yankees.

That morning the phantoms noticed a large group of Soviet technicians seated at a large round table in the dining room. They had been sent by Khrushchev to help out the Cubans in terms of running more efficient factories and farms. They were for the most part jovial happy people who were only too glad to help the Cuban people. Their technical knowledge would prove invaluable to helping open factories that had closed down for lack of technical know-how and spare parts. These brilliant technicians knew how to construct new parts for the machines in the factories and fields and were a tremendous asset to the island. Soon factories were running again. The tractors were running again and plowing the fields for the planting of fruits and vegetables.

The Comandante en Jefe was very pleased with the results of this new technological help from the Soviet Union. The Russians were a generous and expansive people. At night they would frequent the bars in Havana, drinking rum and making merry with the local women. Often the ghosts would join them in the bars and have and glass of rum in the bargain.

Once again the following week, Fidel Castro took his jeep loaded up with the phantoms and headed out to the countryside. It was during the time of the harvest. He passed fields of sugarcane blowing in the winds of history. There he saw the local peasants cutting the cane. Cide Hamete Benengeli tells us that many knights of old, including the Caballero Zifar, Amadis and Tirant lo Blanc were cutting cane with their swords. When they arrived at the cooperative farms, there were women with brightly colored scarves wrapped around their heads to protect them from the sun. Don Quixote told the veterans that these beautifully manicured fields had to be out of a book of chivalry. The old knight had read many descriptions of the lands tilled by peasants guarded by Caballeros Andantes. They were harvesting fruits and vegetables and preparing them to go to market in cities like Santiago de Cuba, Santa Clara and Havana.

Don Quixote found a horse and rode out into the fields. He of course was invisible, but admired the hard-working women from afar. Finally Don Quixote had to return to Fidel Castro and the jeep which was awaiting him. Then off they went to another cooperative not far down the road. There they slept and Fidel Castro was up at dawn to observe his favorite cow give milk in the morning. As much as they could milk her, the cow just kept on giving. The phantoms and the Comandante were amazed at the output of this unique animal. As Fidel Castro went from cooperative to cooperative he never left off telling the peasants of the value of hard work. He also explained to them in language that they could understand the value of sacrifice. Only through producing more than they consumed could Cuba become an independent nation. The peasants listened to him attentively, hanging on to his every word.

Once back in Havana, Fidel Castro and the phantoms went straight to his offices in the Palace of the Revolution. According to Cide Hamete Benengeli, when he was alone Fidel reminisced about his recent trip to the countryside. He was delighted that the peasants were producing more than they were consuming. This was great news for the revolution as it meant that for the first time Cuba was on its way to real national independence. The phantoms couldn't have agreed more with the Comandante en Jefe. They too were delighted that the common peasant was now motivated by moral incentives rather than material incentives alone. Everyone agreed that this represented a giant step forward for the revolution. At this time, according to Cide Hamete Benengeli, a terrible event was about to take place, one which would be remembered for a long time by the entire Cuban population.

Several hundred Cubans tried to break into the Peruvian embassy by breaking down its iron gate. Most of them broke through, but a Cuban soldier was killed in the process. They wanted asylum in Peru as a bridge to the United States. More and more people came. Another group on the opposite side of the street shouted names like 'traitors' 'gusanos' (worms) and 'lumpen'. Fidel Castro and the ghosts rushed to the site. It was a terrible situation and one that had to be resolved quickly. It was obvious that it was impractical for all these people to go to Peru. There was no way to get there. It was simply too far away. Fidel went back to the Palace of the Revolution with the ghosts. There he had to make the very painful decision of letting these people go. With a heavy heart he contacted the American interest section in Havana and spoke to representatives there. He told them that they could have the boats of the Cuban exiles come and fetch these individuals who were so dissatisfied with chivalry.

The representatives of the United States Government agreed and began calling the Department of State in Washington, D.C. The Cuban exiles in Miami were notified that they should mobilize their boats and come to the port called Mariel. There, for the next three weeks Cubans from all walks of life, including peasants and factory workers, boarded the boats of their relatives and friends from Miami. It was indeed a sad event for the Caballero Nino and the phantoms. Why people would want to desert the perfect chivalric society in the making went beyond the understanding of Don Quixote and the rest of the phantoms. José Martí was particularly upset and felt that the Yankees had had a lot to do with this sad state of affairs. Fidel could not figure out the disenchantment with the revolution on the part of so many people. Both phantom and mortal were broken hearted. Yet, as they overheard Fidel talking with Raúl Castro, the phantoms felt better. He said that most of these individuals were loafers and vagrants who sponged off the state. They didn't work and only consumed. Raúl concluded that Cuba would be better off without them.

The phantoms agreed with him, all except Don Quixote who had tears streaming down his face as he watched the people defect to the lands of the Gigante del Norte. Don Quixote could not figure out why these people would desert a country built on the values of chivalry. The knight was at this point extremely disillusioned and disappointed. When the veterans tried to cheer him up it was a useless enterprise. The knight continued to weep into the evening. When he learned that over one hundred thousand Cubans had defected, he started to weep all over again. The veterans could do nothing but help the knight back to the pension. When his comrades tried to get him to eat dinner, he wouldn't touch his food. Finally they got him into bed. There the knight dreamt of his former life and all the people who had tried to stop him from bringing back the era of chivalry, like the Duke and the Duchess. He awoke in a cold sweat and called to José Martí in the next bed to bring him a glass of water.

Back in the Palace of the Revolution, Raúl and Fidel Castro continued talking about the current situation. Their other comrades joined them. It was then that the Comandante en Jefe decided to empty the jails of those criminals who wanted to go to the United States. Looking at the last criminals leave from the port of Mariel, Fidel Castro received a call from the Cuban interest section. President Carter had decided to end the exodus of Cubans to Miami. He had closed the port of Miami and instructed the Coast Guard to stop all further boats returning from Cuba. Fidel was delighted that he had emptied the jails just in time. But in his heart of hearts he was devastated to see so many Cubans betray such a hard fought battle to bring back the era of chivalry. Why they had betrayed the revolution was beyond his understanding. The Comandante en Jefe brooded for the next several weeks before he regained his sense of balance. Then it was on to other things. He had a long trip planned to several African nations and then on to a number of socialist countries including Guinea, Algeria, Bulgaria, Romania, Hungary and East Germany.

Before boarding the plane, the Comandante en Jefe left the government in the hands of Raúl Castro, a very capable leader who was in charge of the armed forces. He remembered the last time he had traveled abroad. The Yankees had taken advantage of the situation by sending mercenaries to bomb sugar mills, hospitals and schools. He didn't want the same thing to happen again. Raúl Castro listened intently and said that he would be ever vigilant of such activities. This time the mercenaries would not succeed in promoting violence throughout the island. Fidel felt much relieved as he boarded the plane for Africa. The ghosts joined him as they always did wherever he went. There were many reporters from throughout the globe on the trip who were eager to question Fidel about his upcoming visits. They also wanted to know about his personal safety. These reporters wanted to know about the security of the whole island. Fidel responded that Cuba was in good hands with Raúl Castro. As far as his own wellbeing and safety, Fidel asserted that he had the best security apparatus in the world protecting him. So far they had done a magnificent job. There were at this point over six hundred attempts on his life. When they heard this number, the journalists traveling with the Comandante en Jefe could not believe what they were hearing.

When the plane landed in Guinea-Bissau the president of the country awaited Fidel Castro. There was a military display made up of highly decorated Guinean soldiers in dress uniform. Fidel was impressed, as were the ghosts. After a wonderful local dinner with a display of dancing, Fidel and his party went to bed. Over the next week, they visited both factories and the large cooperatives in the countryside. It was wonderful to see how motivated the people were to work and sacrifice for the Guinean Revolution, which was not unlike the Cuban Revolution. They had come to power through guerilla warfare just as Cuba's revolutionaries had. The cooperatives were full of cows that gave milk, chickens that laid a plethora of eggs and gardens of local peasants that were replete with fruits and vegetables. Fidel was delighted to see such progress in what was a very poor country only a few years previously. Guinea-Bissau for Fidel was living proof that chivalry was the answer to social justice and national independence. Upon leaving, the head of state of Guinea-Bissau gave Fidel Castro a copy of Don Quixote in the local language. Don Quixote was again amazed that his history was being translated into so many languages. Fidel was honored by the gift. He was somewhat amused that people identified him with Don Quixote throughout the world. Popular opinion at this point was that Fidel Castro was a carbon copy of Don Quixote. In fact his similarities to the knight were the topic of conversation of the tongues of all Cubans.

Then Fidel Castro was on to Algeria. Here was another country that had recently undergone a chivalric revolution with guerilla fighters getting the upper hand. Fidel and his party were again met at the airport by the president of the country. There was again a full military display of highly decorated troops from the war.

Fidel and the ghosts were welcomed into a luxurious hotel with fountains everywhere. Water bubbled out of the fountains and the sounds were soothing to the phantoms. That evening there was a sumptuous banquet serving all the local delicacies. Then for the next week, Fidel toured the factories and cooperative farms in the countryside. The countryside of Algeria was beautiful this time of year. Lush green palm trees gave way to rolling green hills covered with colorful wild flowers. The factory workers were full of energy and enthusiasm as were the peasants in the local cooperatives. All in all it was a wonderful visit and one which Fidel would not easily forget. Again before he left the head of state gifted Fidel Castro a beautifully bound copy of Don Quixote in the local language. José Martí and the veterans couldn't be happier at the thought that the world was beginning to identify Fidel Castro with Don Quixote.

Then it was on to Bulgaria for the same kind of visit. Fidel saw factories going full swing and cooperatives producing a plethora of fruits and vegetables. Bulgaria, he concluded, was truly a remarkable country. With Romania, Hungary and East Germany it was the same. Peasants in the fields turned out to greet him. Fidel spoke briefly when they stopped at the large cooperative farms as well as the factories. Each head of state presented Fidel Castro magnificently bound copies of the History of Don Quixote in the local language. In Bulgaria when they saw Fidel Castro, the people immediately identified him with Don Quixote. Finally there was a stop in Moscow where Fidel met with the new Prime Minister Brezhnev. Khrushchev had died recently and Brezhnev was elected to take his place. There Fidel worked out more economic aid for Cuba with no strings attached. This pleased the Apostle enormously as he had long held the belief that foreign aid without strings was the best possible solution to the problems of development. Then the entourage headed back to Cuba.

Upon returning to the Palace of the Revolution, Fidel was greeted by Raúl Castro who reported that everything on the island was calm and peaceful. There were no further attempts at sabotage and no factories were burned nor buildings bombed. Cide Hamete Benengeli was quick to assert in his History of the Caballero from Biran that Cuban exiles had tried to invade the island. They tried to bomb hospitals and schools and burn fields of sugarcane. They had been stopped by the great knights of old who battled fiercely to end their quest for violence. The phantoms couldn't have been more delighted with this news.

Not long after his trip abroad, Fidel Castro was hit by all kinds of accusations that he was trying to export a chivalric revolution in Latin America. Fidel responded that he believed each nation had the right to autonomy and national independence. But the Yankees continued to wage a defamation campaign against Fidel stipulating that he had sent guerrillas to both Colombia and Venezuela. These two nations had their own guerrillas and didn't need Cuban forces. The defamation campaign continued for the next several years. The Yankees accused the Caballero Nino of being a dictator with a heavy hand over his people. Upon hearing these accusations, Don Quixote and the veterans were visibly upset. José Martí was quick to point out that although Fidel commanded every aspect of the economy from his offices in the Palace of the Revolution, he always maintained a direct dialogue with his people. He answered their concerns and questions faithfully.

Meanwhile the Comandante en Jefe had received the news that Che and his band of guerilla soldiers had been killed while fermenting a revolution in Bolivia. Fidel called his people to the Plaza of the Revolution and broke the sad news of Che's death. The people were heartbroken and wept openly in the Plaza. Fidel and the ghosts returned to his offices and there Fidel wept uncontrollably for the longest time. Che had been his loyal companion since the earliest times in Mexico. Che was the first comrade Fidel Castro chose to tell of his secret desire to carry out Don Quixote's mission to resurrect chivalry. Fidel thought that it was Che's recklessness that got him killed. Bolivia was not ripe for a chivalric revolution. Then Fidel learned that it was the Central Intelligence Agency of the United States in conjunction with local authorities who killed Che. This made Fidel that much more upset, as it did the ghosts. Don Quixote wept uncontrollably as did the veterans. They all had a great love and respect for Che and José Martí and the veterans wanted him buried in Cuba with a proper state funeral.

A short time after the death of Che Guevara, Salvador Allende, the newly elected president of Chile, invited Fidel Castro to visit his nation. Fidel decided to go and the ghosts of course boarded the plane with him. There were many journalists onboard who wanted to know if Fidel thought it was possible to achieve socialism through parliamentary means. Fidel thought yes, it was possible. However, Allende would have to keep control of his army. This was very important. When Fidel and the phantoms landed in Santiago, they were met with great pomp and circumstance. The army marched by in full regalia and they were immediately taken to a luxurious hotel in downtown Santiago. Then Allende held a special state dinner in Fidel Castro's honor. The phantoms were in attendance as well. Don Quixote and the ghosts found Salvador Allende to be a wonderful, expansive, generous man. He wanted them to see all of Chile. Fidel spoke in the stadium in Santiago and addressed the Chilean people. He told them that Cuba considered Chile to be the closest of allies. He assured the Chilean people that the island would stand by them through thick and thin. The Chilean people cheered and the ghosts were delighted. Then Fidel went north to the enormous copper mines in the desert and spoke to the miners. The miners wanted to know what motivated the Cuban people to work so hard for chivalry. Fidel answered that all their sacrifice and hard work was based on a moral commitment to the values of the revolution and the values of chivalry. The miners were delighted to meet the famous Comandante en Jefe in person.

Then Fidel flew back to Conception where he again gave a speech on the solidarity between Cuba and Chile. As Fidel learned later on, a Cuban exile mercenary had a long range rifle pointed at Fidel Castro's head. He planned to kill Fidel while he was giving his speech. For some unknown reason, the assassin changed his mind at the last minute and Fidel was saved once more from sudden death. Salvador Allende wanted to take Fidel down toward Antarctica and Tierra del Fuego. Fidel and the ghosts were very excited about this part of the trip. None of them had ever seen this part of the world. They traveled on a Chilean navel vessel and stood out in the cold to observe the landscape. The saw great icebergs that had broke off from the mainland and were floating aimlessly about the southern waters of the Pacific Ocean. Fidel and the ghosts stood in awe of what they saw before them. Then on the way back they stopped at Puerto Montt, the southernmost city in the world. When they arrived back in Santiago, Salvador Allende took them to his palace offices and showed them his enormous library. The ghosts found the library indeed impressive. It had many of the same books that were in Fidel's library such as the great philosophers and poets. Then Fidel gifted the Chilean president the complete works of José Martí, recently published by Casa de las Américas. José Martí was delighted and felt gratified that he was remembered so often by the Comandante en Jefe of the revolution. Fidel wished Allende well and reminded him to keep control of the army. Upon leaving, Salvador Allende gave Fidel a very valuable and very old first edition of the History of Don Quixote. Fidel Castro was deeply touched by this act of friendship and vowed to return to Chile soon. Then phantoms and mortal alike boarded the plane back to Havana.

From 1975 to 1986 there was a greater institutionalization of the economy and also greater support from the Soviet Union. There was great economic growth. It was also a period of great influence from the Soviet Union in an ideological sense. During this time, Fidel played a relatively minor role in the economy. Then a few years later, he declared a Rectification Period. Following many of the precepts of Che, Fidel took direct control of the economy once more. He opted for a more decentralized economy. Fidel changed the law and again there were markets in Havana where peasants from the cooperatives and small farms brought their produce. There was, for a change, all kinds of fresh fruits and vegetables. There was also plenty of meat, fish and fowl. The people were eating well in those days.

Some months after liberalizing the economy, Fidel Castro made an announcement that was to shake the phantoms to the core. He called his people to the Plaza of the Revolution. He then announced that Cuba was sending twenty thousand troops to Angola to fight the South Africans. It was a just cause and in keeping with the international character of the revolution. Don Quixote jumped for joy and was delighted. He thought this would be another great exploit for Fidel and one that surely would be recorded by Cide Hamete Benengeli. José Martí and the veterans thought that going to Angola was within keeping of the international character of chivalry and they were very supportive. Fidel Castro had not consulted the Soviet Union when making this decision.

The war lasted thirteen years and there were many ups and downs. Cide Hamete Benengeli tells us that the knights of old joined the Cubans in fighting this most grand of guerrilla wars. Some were killed but immediately came back to life as was their habit and custom. In the end the Cubans and the revolutionary forces in Angola prevailed against the South Africans, but not before they had sent over one hundred and fifty thousand troops into battle. Two thousand became ghosts before their time and were honored as heroes by the Cuban Government. Cuba also sent thousands of doctors, engineers and teachers to help the people advance.

The exploits of the Comandante in Angola would go down as among the greatest in the history of chivalry according to Don Quixote. The fact that the exploits in Angola were such a success warmed the hearts of the Cuban people. They were now keenly aware of the international nature of the revolution. As such, when Fidel Castro decided to send advisors to Nicaragua to help the Sandinista, the people of Cuba were very supportive. Fidel also sent hundreds of doctors, engineers and teachers to

Nicaragua. He wanted to help the people advance towards the goal of independence. The Yankees got wind of this adventure and were furious. The CIA sent mercenaries to try and destroy the Nicaraguan and Cuban forces. They killed doctors, engineers and teachers but did not succeed in destroying the revolution. The Gigante del Norte warned Cuba to stay out of Latin America and not to export chivalry. Fidel did not care and continued sending advisors and economic aid to the Central American nation. José Martí admired Fidel Castro's idealism.

Not long after the war in Nicaragua, Fidel Castro was elected the President of the non-aligned countries of Africa, Asia and Latin America. This was a great honor and Don Quixote and the veterans could not have been prouder of him. Fidel took his new position seriously and started to study statistics. He wanted to prove that the developing non-aligned nations could not possibly pay their external debt. The International Monetary Fund had lent these nations billions of dollars with very few restrictions. But the interest grew over time and these poor nations just got poorer trying to pay their external debt.

Not longer after this, Fidel Castro visited the United Nations in New York. The ghosts went along as usual. There the Comandante en Jefe delivered a long speech on the reasons why the poorest nations in the world could not pay their debts. He used a plethora of statistics to prove his point. His ideas were very well received by the poorer countries, but not by the developed countries who wanted their debt paid back in full.

Fidel and the phantoms stayed in Harlem and Fidel spoke to hundreds of people gathered in a local church. He reiterated what he had said in the United Nations and declared solidarity between the Cuban people and the

American people. He said his argument was never with the American people, who were good and generous at heart. His objection was with the government of the United States. Most of all, the Comandante en Jefe had problems with the CIA who continued to make illegal terrorist incursions onto the island. Their hope was that they could kill the revolution through violence propagated against the Cuban people.

When Fidel Castro returned to his offices in the Palace of the Revolution, there were a plethora of journalists awaiting an interview. The news of Fidel's declaration that the Third World should not pay its debt had reached them. Fidel again defended his point of view on the debt and said that developed nations like the United States, France, Germany and Italy should forgive the debt of the poor and struggling nations. José Martí, Don Quixote and the veterans thought Fidel was right on the mark. These poor nations would never repay their external debt even if they worked themselves to the ground. Don Quixote and the veterans were touched by Fidel Castro's idealism as well as the strength of his convictions. They hoped that in the future the poor nations would be liberated from their burden. The interviews finished in the early hours of the morning and the phantoms returned to their room in the pension in old Havana.

# *Chapter Fifteen*

Cide Hamete Benengeli tells us that Fidel Castro was in his offices in the Palace of the Revolution when he received word that the Soviet Union had collapsed. Don Quixote and the veterans were horrified. Don Quixote could not understand how a good giant could desert a chivalric society in need of help. Now Cuba would have to sell sugar on the open market. There would no longer be guaranteed prices as there would be an end to trade with COMECON. Selling on the open market was risky at best because there was no longer a guaranteed buyer. The fall of the Soviet Union dealt a terrible blow to the revolution. José Martí told Don Quixote and the veterans that he had predicted this all along. Cuba had depended way too much on the Soviet Union and now the chickens had come home to roost.

In the Plaza of the Revolution, Fidel announced the beginning of the 'Special Chivalric Period,' much like a period during wartime. How would Cuba survive was a question on the minds of all Cubans both in the factories and fields. Fidel spoke to his people in a gentle, low tone of voice. He said that Cuba was in for some hard times. Certainly food and other consumer items would be rationed and there would be food shortages throughout the island. Cuba had a deficit of more than one hundred and ninety-nine million dollars and an external debt of almost four billion dollars. The people were horrified when they heard this news.

José Martí and the veterans were not surprised. José Martí said that all the borrowing from the Soviet Union had led to this situation, a situation that was becoming more intolerable by the moment. Fidel had to ask his people to work harder and sacrifice even more. The people were willing but did not know how they could sacrifice more than they already had. In the coming months, there were absolutely no consumer items in the markets. So Fidel Castro opened the infamous dollar stores where Cubans with dollars could go to by durable goods and food. Gorbachev had introduced the concept of perestroika, a relaxing of central control, along with the introduction of glasnost, or openness.. Fidel Castro rejected these ideas, although some time later he decided to accept some of these measures due to the fact that the Cuban economy shrank by forty percent in one year. The peasants brought meat, eggs, poultry, fruits and vegetables from the state farms to market in the cities to sell at reasonable prices.

In the beginning, most Cubans could afford to go to these markets to buy food. But the demand became so great that the prices increased. The goods were no longer accessible to most of the population. It was a very sad state of affairs when the Comandante en Jefe announced on television that there would be a further rationing of food. This was terrible news and the ghosts were very upset. People started to look thinner and thinner on the streets of Havana. There was no longer joy in their eyes. Don Quixote and the veterans shrank a great deal.

Fidel Castro then did something unprecedented. He knew that the one saving grace for Cuba was the tourism industry. People flocked from all over the globe to Cuban beaches which were among the best in the world. It was decided that the government should go into business with private industry from abroad for the purpose of constructing many new tourist hotels and resorts throughout the island. Businessmen from

France, Germany, England, Canada and Italy started flocking to Cuba. Before long there were grandiose hotels springing up on Varadero Beach and other keys off the coast of Oriente Province such as Cayo Coco and Cayo Guillermo along with Cayo Largo in the south. Tourists flocked to the island by the millions from Europe, Latin America and particularly Canada. The Cuban economy improved but people still did not have enough to consume at the beginning of the 1990s. The calorie intake went down by a third and Cubans started to develop some diseases related to malnutrition. The people grew even thinner and so did the ghosts. Don Quixote rattled around inside his armor. José Martí and the veterans shrank from an insufficient diet and low calorie intake.

One thing that José Martí and the veterans could not understand was the fact that tourists had plenty of food. There was plenty of meat, eggs, poultry, fish and milk in the lavish buffets of the luxury hotels on the beaches. Together with the dollar stores, Cuba was divided into two Cubas. There were those with dollars who could afford to go to the beach and to buy goods in the dollar stores. Then there were the majority of Cubans who could do neither. This seemed like a very bad policy indeed to José Martí. He reluctantly admitted that it was a necessity for the moment in order to guarantee the basics of healthcare, food, housing and education. If Cuba was to ever find its way out of the present situation, they needed tourists and the dollars that they brought with them.

The Special Chivalric Period demanded even more sacrifice from the people if such a thing were possible. All the people were mobilized into special workforces to build luxury hotels for the tourists. Ironically enough, tourism was the last great hope of the revolution. Martí told the veterans and Don Quixote that he hated to admit it but that he had been right all along. He again declared how much he hated the Yankees for pushing Cuba into the arms of the Soviet Union.

Gorbachev came to visit Cuba and brought along the ideas of perestroika and glasnost. He discussed various matters in Fidel Castro's offices in the Palace of the Revolution. However, the two leaders did not reach any major agreements. Fidel Castro was suspicious of perestroika and glasnost. He felt that these ideas represented a weakening of chivalry and accounted for the downfall of the Soviet Union. He voiced his objections and doubts openly to the Soviet Prime Minister. José Martí told Don Quixote and the veterans that he agreed with Gorbachev. Cuba should have more competition and market mechanisms. However, he did not agree with tearing down the revolution through unlimited criticism.

After the Prime Minister left Cuba, Fidel Castro and the ghosts once more hopped in his jeep and headed for the Cuban countryside. There they found a sad state of affairs. There were only a few bulls left in Cuba to artificially inseminate the cows. There were fewer chickens. Most had died because of poor feed. There were no more imported fertilizers from the Soviet Union. Therefore the fields had a poor output of fruits and vegetables with many dying on the vine due to poor fertilizers. Tractors lay idle in the fields because there was a shortage of petroleum and no more spare parts. Now boys were pulling the plows slowly and painfully through the fields which rendered practically no harvest for several years. Things on the island were growing more desperate by the moment. Fidel Castro for once had no idea how to remedy the situation.

Back in his offices in the Palace of the Revolution, he started to study books on agronomy again. However, without fertilizers and other proper feed for the animals, there was no way out. Then Fidel and the phantoms visited the factories throughout the island. They were just as disappointed as when they visited the state farms and cooperatives in the countryside. Most factories had shut down for lack of oil. The shortage of petroleum was ruining the economy as people could no longer drive cars and had to take Chinese bicycles to work. The factories were in a state of disarray because there was a shortage of petroleum and no spare parts. Machinery broke down often. So for the first time since the revolution, people had no common items like soap, toothpaste and toilet paper. Of course there was no rum or tobacco. Fidel even had to forego his usual Cuban cigars.

The country was in dire straights for several years as the economy shrunk by over forty percent in the first year of the Special Chivalric Period. To add insult to injury, there were great blackouts in the cities when there was no electrical power available. The lack of petroleum showed its ugly head everywhere. What little electricity there was available had to be reserved for the army and tourist hotels. The rationing cards gave less and less food to the Cuban people. There was one chicken and one pound of rice, sugar and coffee a month.

José Martí and the rest of the phantoms headed back to Hacienda of the Spirits. There, up in the library, the Apostle wanted to think about the current situation. He was all for allowing small businesses and introducing some market incentives. Fidel Castro, however, was unbending on this point. Cuba needed small businesses desperately to supply the much needed consumer items absent from the shelves in stores. Also Fidel was trying to export everything to get dollars. The Apostle had his doubts on this matter. Yes exporting some goods was not a bad idea. However, Cubans couldn't even get a pound of fresh fish because the catch was being sent abroad. José Martí said the problem with Fidel Castro was that his iron will was both strength and a weakness. The fact that he was unwilling to change was wreaking havoc on the Cuban people.

José Martí sat there in the overstuffed easy chair with the veterans on the floor around him. Don Quixote was on the divan. Reluctantly the knight had to agree with the Apostle on his characterization of the Caballero de Biran.

To entertain themselves the ghosts returned to reading Cide Hamete Benengeli's great tome. José Martí picked it up and started to read about the Special Chivalric Period. He read about how the peasants had to use boys to plow the fields in the government cooperatives. He read about the fields that produced neither fruits nor vegetables. Cide Hamete talked about how the chicken population was falling and the egg output was failing. He focused on how the Cuban people had little or nothing to eat. He talked about how people were exchanging their Chinese bicycles for slaughtered pigs peasants brought them from the countryside. He discussed the desperation of the Comandante en Jefe. He focused on how Fidel Castro wanted to do something to alleviate the situation but he could not see a way to solve any of the problems.

Yet the Comandante en Jefe of the revolution had to admit that this was the first time Cuba was truly independent. Independence, he said, was a great accomplishment. The new society followed the precepts of chivalry to the letter. Yet his people were still suffering enormously, mainly due to the blockade imposed now by the Gigante del Norte. It was a heartless and brutal campaign against chivalry. Don Quixote pointed out the miracle of being able to sustain chivalry while being continually bombarded by terrorist attacks.

Don Quixote was very sad that things were going so badly with the revolution. The veterans were also critical of what they called the two Cubas. There was one Cuba for those who had dollars and could buy food and other durable goods at the dollar stores. There was then another Cuba for people without dollars who had no recourse except to do without food and other consumer items. Cide Hamete commented on the latest events in Cuba by stipulating that things would get better. The phantoms of Hacienda of the Spirits doubted the old Moor. They stayed on the hacienda instead of going back to Havana because they could always get a square meal from Doña Lina Castro. Luckily, the hacienda was productive. The circle of sugarcane had a high yield that year. There were plenty of fruits and vegetables in the garden tended by Doña Lina. The Haitians and Cuban peasants working the land continued to eat well and send their children to school. Thank God for that declared the ghosts as they dug into another sumptuous meal prepared by Lina Castro.

Finally there was a great fuss astir as the ghosts learned that Cuba had a new friend in the region who could supply much needed petroleum. Hugo Chávez was just elected president of Venezuela. He had become a very close friend and admirer of Fidel Castro. The assistance each country offered the other was a two way street. Venezuela had always been a powerful country and was able to export all kinds of durable goods to Cuba. But most of all it was the petroleum that the Comandante en Jefe coveted the most. With petroleum the factories could start running again and the tractors could start plowing the fields more efficiently. Cuba could obtain the right fertilizers for planting and the right grains to feed the animals. This was a great step forward.

With petroleum the sugar mills could run again and start producing sugar for export. It looked like the economy was on the upswing and the ghosts were delighted. Eventually they made their way back to Havana and the offices of the Comandante en Jefe. They found him in a very good mood. He was entertaining some foreign journalists and explaining the windfall of petroleum from Venezuela. It was a gift from the Gods, he explained to the journalists, who were all hanging on his every word. The ghosts couldn't have been more delighted. Fidel told the foreign journalists that he planned to send hundreds of doctors to Venezuela along with teachers and engineers. This was the least he could do when Hugh Chávez had come to his rescue in his hour of need. The ghosts were absolutely delighted with this new turn of events. Then Fidel went on to explain that the tourism industry was a great success. Tourists by the hundreds of thousands flocked to the island every year now. They brought sorely needed dollars with them. The journalists took down his every word.

Fidel had great hopes for the tourist trade and wanted to expand it greatly. The idea was for the state to go into business with Italian, French and German industries to build even more elegant hotels. Don Quixote was ecstatic as he thought of the economy being on the up swing. He desperately wanted to believe that everything his protégé did was absolutely the right thing. The veterans were still critical. Next Fidel explained to his foreign visitors that Cuba's industries would open again because of petroleum. Now the machinery could run smoothly and production would increase tenfold. The veterans were delighted with this state of affairs. Fidel also told his visitors that agriculture was improving due to new enriched fertilizers and special feed for the farm animals. People would have more poultry because more chickens were surviving. They would also have more eggs and milk. The cows in the fields were much healthier as they were grazing on rich grasses produced by the new fertilizers. All in all things were looking up for the first time in five years. Not that the Special Chivalric Period was over. People would have to continue to sacrifice more and work harder in factories and agriculture to grow and flourish. But at least there was hope. For the first time in its history Cuba was completely independent. Fidel Castro spoke to his people from the Plaza of the Revolution. The general population was jubilant at the good news.

After the foreign journalists had all left, Fidel decided to spend some time on Hacienda of the Spirits. The phantoms all hopped into his jeep. As he drove through the Cuban countryside, he was delighted to see tractors plowing the fields. There was a large array of fruits and vegetables growing. He saw contented cows in the pastures grazing on the new grasses which flourished because of the new rich fertilizers. Finally he reached Hacienda of the Spirits and Ramon opened the gate for him. He greeted his brother with a big bear hug. Doña Lina Castro had passed away. Then he went inside and had a glass of rum from the liquor cabinet in the parlor. He and the ghosts went outside and toasted Hugo Chávez who was such a generous economic partner. Then they went inside for a sumptuous dinner of pork, Moors and Christians and yucca with a beautiful flan the cook had made especially for this occasion.

It was then that the Comandante headed up to the library. The ghosts were already there and it was if he sensed their presence. He stood still awhile, just staring around him while the ghosts stared back at him. Then he grabbed a copy of Amadis off the shelves and started to read about the exploits and adventures of his favorite knight. He sat there reading for several hours until he fell asleep. Then he fell to dreaming about his youth on the hacienda. How happy he was in those days playing with the Haitian children. He remembered going down to the Biran River and swimming with his small comrades. He remembered also going up into the Sierra Crystal to find the village of the Guajiros. He thought back on the Guajira girl in the pool beside the waterfall and how she would always run away from him into the dense green jungle. His thoughts turned to the Bay of Nipes where he swam alongside the sharks. Then the Comandante en Jefe awoke and felt good. He looked out on the moonlight covering the Sierra Crystal and thanked his Maker for giving him such a wonderful childhood.

The phantoms were all awake and were delighted that Fidel felt so good again. Fidel slept in the overstuffed easy chair until morning. Once awake, he went down the spiral staircase to the kitchen below where he found the old Spanish cook making a pot of coffee. He drank a cup and then headed outside to the local bakery where he took a hot bun for breakfast. Then he went to the smithies to see a horse get some new shoes. From there he went to the barn where he picked out Angel Castro's enormous black stallion and started towards the Sierra Crystal. He passed the circle of tiny white houses where the Haitians lived and was happy to see them doing so well. He went out into the fields and saw the Haitian women with their brightly colored scarves to protect them from the hot sun. Then he headed for the upper reaches of the Sierra Crystal and finally arrived at the Guajiro village high up in the Sierra. It took him several hours to reach the place. He stopped for some rice and beans as well as water at the Guajiro village. Then as he used to do as a youth, the Comandante en Jefe headed up towards the top of the Sierra Crystal alone.

According to Cide Hamete Benengeli, as Fidel headed deep into the forest he was greeted by all the great knights of old. First there was Amadis on his beautiful white stallion. Then there was Esplandian on his big black horse followed by the Caballero Zifar, the Knight of the Moon, the Knight of the Mirrors, the Knight of Iron and finally Tirant lo Blanc. Fidel made his way up to the very top of the Sierra Crystal. When he started to descend the knights of old followed closely behind in single file. Then slowly but surely they fell by the wayside. First the Caballero Zifar, then the Knight of the Moon and then the Knight of the Mirrors disappeared into the forest beside the path Fidel Castro followed down the mountain. About halfway to the Guajiro village, Esplandian went off to one side into the forest, then Tirant lo Blanc and finally Amadis disappeared. When he looked behind him, the only knight to follow him out of the forest into the clearing where the Guajiro village was located was the Caballero del Hierro. Then he too simply disappeared.

Fidel then made his way down the mountain, crossing the Biran River as he went on his big black stallion. When he reached the perfect circle of sugarcane, to his surprise he saw Angel Castro and the Haitians working the land as in old times. Then he put the horse back in the barn and headed for the house. The ghost of Lina Castro was preparing dinner and looked up at her son as he passed her by. He took a right down the long hall with the many bedrooms and started to ascend the spiral staircase to the library. He pushed open the large wooden door and looked around him. His eyes lighted on a large green book with gold lettering bearing the title, The Caballero de Biran. The phantoms dropped what they were doing and stared at Fidel in amazement. Fidel picked up the book and lo and behold, to the surprise of the ghosts, the letters were visible to him.

The phantoms could not believe their eyes. This was the first time that the book was visible to a mortal. José Martí concluded that the Comandante en Jefe had the reading powers of the phantoms. Fidel slowly sat down in the big overstuffed easy chair and started to read the book. First he read the descriptions of his childhood and was surprised but delighted to learn about Don Quixote and the veterans who were so devoted to him as a child. He continued to read about his magical childhood. He read about how Don Quixote introduced him to books of chivalry. He then read the descriptions of spending the better part of his youth reading the histories of the great knights of old. He concluded that his idyllic youth was indeed privileged beyond what he had previously thought.

He then read the descriptions of his life with the Hibberts in Santiago and how lonely and desperate he felt away from the hacienda. He read about the ghosts forming a circle around him in the rundown house of the disillusioned school teachers. He put the book down unable to believe what he read. It was all so fantastic and magical. His whole life he had been surrounded by some of the most famous phantoms in Cuba along with the invincible Don Quixote. Now after reading The Caballero de Biran, he was absolutely certain that the ghosts were with him in the library. It was a logical conclusion because he had just learned that they had accompanied him all his life. What a marvelous feeling it was indeed to have such devoted companions.

The Comandante en Jefe read on. He read about La Salle school and the Padre Jesuita. Cide Hamete Benengeli had written a beautiful description of their relationship. He focused on how the old Jesuit shared the exploits of Don Quixote with him. Fidel Castro put the book down a second as tears came to his eyes. He was remembering the first time he set eyes on The History of Don Quixote as well as the impact of the book on his life. He remembered how the old padre first read the book out loud to him before he read it on his own. There was something marvelous about having a book read out loud. Fidel Castro concluded that there would never be another Padre Jesuita.

The Comandante en Jefe went on to read about Colegio de Dolores and the Explorers. He read how he went up into the foothills of the Sierra Maestra with his tiny comrades in tow. He was the leader of the group and was always planning all kinds of magical adventures for them. In retrospect Fidel Castro could see these early experiences climbing mountains as the foundation to his later successes in the Sierra Maestra.

Throughout all this time in schools in Santiago reading Don Quixote nonstop, Fidel Castro was enthralled and delighted about the prospect of fulfilling Don Quixote's lost dream. He could see that it would not be easy but he would try his hardest. Then it was on to Belen College where he had learned so much about giving oral arguments and formulating all kinds of discourse. The training he received from the Jesuits had held him in such good stead during his time as leader of the revolution. He remembered the excellent humanistic training he had received from the Jesuits despite their rightist tendencies. The Comandante en Jefe was particularly touched at how the old Moor had included his love affair with Socrates. The old Greek had influenced him in any number of ways.

He then went on to read Cide Hamete Benengeli's descriptions of his university years. The old Moor focused on the dangers confronting Fidel during that time. His life was up for grabs for most of that period. Fidel put the book down for a moment and thought about those dangerous times. Then he went back to reading the book which up to now was only visible to the ghosts. He read with such rapidity that soon he was reading about Moncada and the adventures he had there. He read about his time in prison and how he formed a school so that his comrades would be prepared for the future. Fidel was constantly amazed that the ghosts accompanied him everywhere he went from the time he was little and how they always had his best interests at heart. They were even there fighting in Moncada. What a fantastic event, chivalric to the core.

How wonderful he exclaimed out loud for the ghosts to hear that they were with him when he faced solitary confinement. How wonderful he thought when they were with him in exile in Mexico. How fantastic an exploit when they followed him on the Granma back to Cuba and then on up into the Sierra Maestra. How fantastic it was that they protected him and his comrades when they were hiding in the cane fields from Batista's henchmen. How marvelous it was that they accompanied him wherever he went up in the Sierra Maestra. They were even with him on the incredibly long marches up to Pico Turquino.

How wonderful it was for the knights of old to join him on these long marches up the Sierra Maestra to prepare his comrades for battle. How marvelous it was to see the veterans and Don Quixote share the labors of the battle against Batista. Cide Hamete Benengeli's descriptions of the knights of old in the battle against the dictator were fantastic. Fidel reveled in the thought that these knights went up against his enemies.

Fidel loved the old Moors description of the knights of old following him down the mountain single file all the way to Havana. The Comandante en Jefe laughed when he read about how Don Quixote stepped into the pictures taken by Herbert Matthews and into the picture of the paloma landing on his shoulders. He loved the description of the knights of old around the large round table in the conference room on the top floor of the Habana Libre. He loved the picture of Amadis, Esplandian, Palmerin and Tirant lo Blanc raising their swords in the air in agreement with the planning of the revolution. He reveled in the thought that this was the first history where all the knights of old and Don Quixote appeared together in a brotherhood forged in battle. The Comandante en Jefe thought it was so wonderful that he asked man and ghost alike for a moment of silence for the dead.

He loved the descriptions of Don Quixote and the veterans accompanying him wherever he went in his jeep in the Cuban countryside. He was particularly delighted with Don Quixote by his side for an entire lifetime. Who would have thought? He loved the knight and José Martí in equal measure.

Fidel put the book down for a while and thought about the wisdom and intelligence of José Martí during his second lifetime. The ghosts looked on in amazement as Fidel read on in The Caballero de Biran. They were amazed that the book was visible to him in the first place. This was an incredible fact and as far as the phantoms were concerned simply an indication that he had powers beyond most mortals. Fidel Castro came to the place where José Martí tells Don Quixote and the veterans that he had read all the books ever written about Fidel Castro and remained convinced that The Caballero de Biran was the only true history ever

355

written about the Comandante en Jefe.

Then Fidel came upon the final meditation in the book by Cide Hamete Benengeli. The old Moor pointed out to the reader that this was the first time all the greatest knights of old had appeared in the same history. He also stipulated that the spirit of chivalry was strong in Cuba and that these knights all came back from the dead simultaneously to fight the battles needed to bring about revolution and resurrect chivalry. The old Moorish historian mused about the fact that Fidel Castro was more like Don Quixote than Don Quixote. Once he got something into his head, nothing could stop him.

The knights of old tried to promote justice for the peasants along with shelter and education. They fought battles to end the abuses of the kings. The knights who were immortalized were those that actually achieved some of these aims. Although most of these knights fell short in historical terms, they never forgot their ideals. Thinking further, Cide Hamete concluded that the Knight from Biran achieved more in terms of bringing back the era of chivalry than any of these knights. The old Moor realized that with Fidel Castro he did not have to invent episodes to please the reader. This knight had so many incredible adventures beyond those of most knights of old that he, the author, did not need to invent exploits but rather simply tell the truth. He bemoaned the fact that he had to leave out so many of Fidel Castro's exploits in order to create a history with a beginning, middle and end. He went on to stipulate that the achievements of the revolution were completely compatible with chivalry.

Then the old Moor made some reflections to the reader concerning the fact that the Comandante en Jefe had the worst enemy ever recorded in a book of chivalry. To his knowledge, having read practically every book of chivalry ever printed in Spanish or Portuguese, no knight had ever fought a giant as vicious and spiteful as the Giant to the North. The old Moor deliberated this point for some time. The truth was that the Comandante en Jefe's enemies were afraid of his stellar example and that others would follow suit. The Giant to the North could not risk letting its population see Don Quixote in motion. They did everything they could to dispel the fact that Fidel Castro was the reincarnation of Don Quixote. This information was simply too dangerous to unleash to the general populace. Nonetheless, despite all their efforts, the image of Fidel Castro transformed into Don Quixote got through to the people inside the Gigante del Norte.

He thought of the fact that over a fifty plus year period, there were over six hundred attempts on Fidel Castro's life. Most of these attempts were planned by wealthy Cuban exiles and the CIA. He lived with the constant threat of assassination even before he came to power. Yet he thrived under these conditions more than any other knight so he could achieve the long lost dreams of Don Quixote, Amadis and Tirant lo Blanc. As long as he could remember, he lived every moment as if it might be his last. He did so with grace and determination in the way of Socrates. All the knights of old were proud that he had followed in their footsteps.

The old Moor was certain that when the Comandante en Jefe did pass on, he would go the way of the phantoms. Fidel Castro would join José Martí, the veterans and Don Quixote and live out a second lifetime in their company. Like the phantoms of Hacienda of the Spirits, he too would be affecting the lives of mortals. The future social and economic realities of Cuba would once again come under his influence.

The old Moor stressed again towards the end of his meditation that no knight of old, with the exception of Don Quixote, had ever faced such a vicious defamation campaign as that heralded by the Yankees to impugn his honor. He reflected on the fact that in the times of the old knights and Don Quixote the mechanisms of mass global communication were not as nearly sophisticated as they were in the twentieth century. There were hundreds of false and licentious histories published to defame Fidel Castro and the revolution. Having reviewed them all, the old Moorish historian finally concluded that The Caballero de Biran was the only true history written about Fidel Castro, with all other falling short. He concluded his meditation by saying that his history about Fidel Castro would be read by future generations because it so effectively counteracted all those lying books propagated by the Gigante del Norte. He added that he truly believed that the Caballero de Biran's history would turn out to be as popular or more popular than the History of Don Quixote. Coming to the end of his miraculous meditation, the old Moor concluded that he was born five hundred years ago to write The History of Don Quixote. He then thought that he was reborn a ghost to write The Caballero de Biran. He decided the second was a sequel to the first and concluded that the two histories would be read as one.

After reading and rereading Cide Hamete Benengeli's fabulous meditation, Fidel reached the phantom chapter that was not visible to the ghosts. The letters suddenly surfaced on the pages. He read the chapter and then fell asleep and dreamed about it. In essence, the chapter told him that one day soon another great leader would be born in Cuba to take his place. He would have to pass through all the same experiences and have many of the same adventures. However, before he was through, he would take Cuba that much further. He would bring the ideals of chivalry alive in ways Fidel Castro never could. He was bemused by what he had read. He also thought that it was a good thing that another knight would come along to bring back the era of chivalry in ways he never could.

In coming to the end of his tale, he told the reader that Fidel Castro had indeed carried out the mission Don Quixote left unfinished, the resurrection of chivalry. When Don Quixote and the knights of old tried to bring chivalry back to the world, they failed. The Caballero de Biran was the only knight who actually turned fiction into history. The old Moor had enjoyed writing The Caballero de Biran as much as he had enjoyed writing the History of Don Quixote. He called Fidel Castro the most famous and accomplished knight in chivalry. He had taken chivalry much further than the knights of old or Don Quixote could ever imagine.

After reading the musings of Cide Hamete Benengeli, Fidel Castro sat back in the overstuffed easy chair and pondered the words of Cide Hamete in this amazing and magical history. At first he was simply overwhelmed with disbelief. Then slowly doubt gave way to the realization that on some subliminal level he had always been aware of the presence of the phantoms around him. He remembered back on certain moments of his life where he sensed the presence of the ghosts, including moments that had escaped Cide Hamete Benengeli. He reflected on how at moments he sensed José Martí in the room. He always carried Don Quixote close to him in his heart. He loved them both with equal passion and conviction. Fidel Castro was sure that this was the only completely truthful history ever written about him. He knew it would be read by thousands of people over centuries. The phantoms of

Hacienda of the Spirits stood in amazement as Fidel Castro finished the book on his life. Don Quixote thought that it must have been more satisfying to write The Caballero de Biran than his own history. In The Caballero de Biran, Don Quixote and the veterans had had a chance to see chivalry restored to the world. They had even had the opportunity to fight in decisive battles in order to make chivalry a living reality.

Finally Fidel got up from the overstuffed easy chair and walked down the spiral staircase. He then walked out on the porch and looked in the direction of Manuel de Céspedes and Ignancio Agramonte. He was glad to know they were there.

The moon was high in the sky so he made his way down to the Bay of Nipes. It was a warm night with a warm breeze. The Comandante en Jefe took off his clothes and went in the warm water for a swim. Then he returned to the white sand beach and lay down staring at the moon as it illuminated the graceful Caribbean Sea. He thought about all he had read in The Caballero de Biran. He was certain of the presence of the ghosts and knew they were right by his side. He looked at the stars above him and felt like a child again. He had come full circle and was prepared for anything, even death. The Comandante fell asleep on the beach and lay there until the sun came up, surrounded by the phantoms of Hacienda of the Spirits.

## THE END

www.ingramcontent.com/pod-product-compliance
Lightning Source LLC
Chambersburg PA
CBHW030635260626
47157CB00007B/2336